Ungrateful Dead

The Rock & Roll Murders: A Rennie Stride Mystery

Ungrateful Dead

Murder at the Fillmore

Patricia Morrison

Lizard Queen Press

This book is a work of fiction. Although certain real locations, events and public figures are mentioned, all other names, characters, places and events described in the book are the product of the author's imagination or are used fictitiously. Any resemblance to actual events, places or persons (living or dead) is purely coincidental.

UNGRATEFUL DEAD: Murder at the Fillmore
© 2007 by Patricia Kennealy Morrison. All rights reserved. No part of this book may be reproduced in any form whatsoever or by any electronic or mechanical means, including information and retrieval systems, without permission in writing from the publisher, except in the case of brief quotations embodied in reviews. For further information, contact: Lizard Queen Press, 151 1st Avenue, Rm. 120, New York, NY 10003.

pkmorrison.livejournal.com
myspace.com/hermajestythelizardqueen

Author photo by Linda Bright

Jacket artwork and design by Andrew Przybyszewski
Book interior designed by the author
Book produced by Bianca Arvin

"Knight of Ghosts and Shadows" © 2004 by Patricia Morrison for Lizard Queen Music

ISBN: 978-0-6151-6262-1
Printed in the United States of America
November 2007

Acknowledgments

We Fought For Rock 'n' Roll

My thanks to the people who were there for it, in all or in part, with me and for me and even against me, for good or for ill, for love or for hate, for the music and the words, for valor on the field and squalor in the tents, notably among them:

Vince Aletti; Bob Altshuler; Ian Anderson; Signe Toly Anderson; Sam Andrew; Joan Baez; Marty Balin; Ginger Baker; Lester Bangs; Frank Barsalona; Jeff Beck; Karin Berg; Sid Bernstein; Eric Blackstead; Vaughn Bode; John Bonham; David Bowie; Kathleen Brady; Stefan and Linda Bright; Kurt Brokaw; Jack Bruce; Sandy Bull; Jack Casady; Robert Christgau; John Cipollina; Eric Clapton; Kip Cohen; Lee Coppola; Mike Corbett; Pat Costello; Michele Cottler; Janice Coughlan; Thomas Courtenay-Clack; Bobbi Cowan; David Crosby; Roger Daltrey; Monika Dannemann; Clive Davis; Jim Dawson; Bob Defrin; Sandy Denny; John Densmore; Miss Pamela Des Barres; Susan P. Donoghue; Donovan; Alan Douglas; Ian Dove; Spencer Dryden; Bob Dylan; Sara Lowndes Dylan; Henry Edwards; John Entwistle; Ahmet and Nesuhi Ertegun; Jim Farber; Mimi and Richard Fariña; Danny Fields; Ronnie Finkelstein; Diane (Annie) Fisher; Pete Fornatale; Jim Fouratt; Myra Friedman; Gina Gangi; Jerry Garcia; Arthur Garfunkel; Genie the Tailor; Mike Gershman;

Ralph J. Gleason; Danny Goldberg; Richard Goldstein; Bill Graham; Richard Grant; Ren Grevatt; Albert Grossman; Elin Guskind; Pamela Hannay; Cynthia Heimel; Herb Helman; Dave Herman; Jimi Hendrix; David Hinckley; Chris Hodenfield; Jan Hodenfield; Janis Ian; Ron Jacobs; Elton John; Bob Johnson; Pete Johnson; Brian Jones; John Paul Jones; Janis Joplin; Michael Kamen; Paul Kantner; Murray the K Kaufman; Jorma Kaukonen; Lenny Kaye; Soozin Kazick; Rick Kemp; Regina Kennely; Peter Knight; Al Kooper; Jay Kotcher; Eddie Kramer; Harvey Kubernik; Jon Landau; Bill Laudner; Alvin Lee; John Lennon and Yoko Ono; Phil Lesh; Wendi Lombardi; Gary Lucas; Bruce Lundvall; Michael Lydon; Greil Marcus; Dave Marsh; Linda Eastman and Paul McCartney; Country Joe McDonald; Jim/Roger McGuinn; Ron "Pigpen" McKernan; Jacqui McShee; R. Meltzer; Bill "Rosko" Mercer; Anne-Marie Micklo; Carol Miller; Doreen and Tom Monaster; Stan Monteiro; Keith Moon; Scott Muni; Dan O'Neill; James Osterberg (Iggy Stooge/Pop); Mo Ostin; Jimmy Page; Sandy Pearlman; Harvey Perr; Michelle Phillips; Robert Plant; Alice Polesky; Maddy Prior; Bonnie Raitt; Phil Ramone; Keith Richards; Pauline Rivelli; Laura Roberts; Bob Rolontz; George Romonchuk; Lillian Roxon; Raeanne Rubenstein; Jay Ruby; Buffy Sainte-Marie; Janice Scott; John Sebastian; Noreen Shanfelter; Dennis F. Shaw; Paul Simon; John Sinclair; Patrick Sky; Darby Slick; Grace Slick; Jerry Slick; Bill Smith; Patti Smith and Fred "Sonic" Smith; Skip Spence; Alison Steele (the Nightbird); Stephen Stills; Dave Swarbrick; Bernie Taupin; Derek Taylor; James Taylor; Bill Thompson; Richard Thompson; J.R.R. Tolkien; Terry Towne; Pete Townshend; Twiggy; Robin Tyner; Ian and Sylvia Tyson; Elmer Valentine; Sal Valentino; Frankie Valli; Eric Van Lustbader; Dave and Terri Van Ronk; Billie Wallington; Bob Weir; Paul Williams; Stu Woods; Kim Yarborough; John Zacherle; Frank and Gail Zappa...

and to all the others, then as now, who can only wish they'd been there for it. I wish you could have been there too.

And to the places — for the music, the sleepovers, the food and drink, the clothes, the books, the illegal substances, the triumphs and disasters...

1841 Broadway; A&M Records and Studios; Abbey Road Studios; Abracadabra; Academy of Music; Albert Hotel; Alice Pollock; Allan Block Leather; Alley Cat; Altamont Speedway; Anderson Theater; Annabelinda; Annacat; Atlantic Records; Avalon Ballroom; Avery Fisher Hall; Barney's Beanery; Beacon Theater; Bel-Air Hotel; Ben Frank's; The Berkeley Barb; Betsey, Bunky & Nini; Biba; Biblo & Tannen; Bido Lito's; The Bitter End; Black Rock (CBS Building); Brentano's Books; Bridge Theater; Brown's Hotel; The Burton Hotel; Café Au Go-Go; Café Bizarre; Café Figaro; Café Le Metro; Café Reggio; Café Wha?; Calendula by Paul Mayersohn; Capezio on Macdougal Street and at 1855 Broadway; Capitol Theatre; Carnegie Hall; Carousel Ballroom; Chateau Marmont; Chelsea Cobbler; Chelsea Hotel; Cherokee Books; Chumley's; Circus Magazine; Claremont Hotel; Club 17; Columbia Records and Studios; Cosmo's Factory; Crawdaddy! Magazine; Creem Magazine; The Crystal; Dakota Transit; Different Drummer; Duke's Coffee Shop; The Dugout; The East Village Other; Ebinger's Bakery; EKO; Electric Circus; Electric Ladyland Studio; Elektra Records; Epic Records; EYE Magazine; Felt Forum; Fillmore Auditorium; Fillmore East; Fillmore West; Folklore Center; Gaslight; Gem Spa; Gerde's Folk City; Gifford-Wallace; Gina Fratini; Gorham Hotel; Gramercy Park Hotel; Grand Hotel; Granny Takes A Trip; Grunt Records; Harpur College; Harriet Love; Harrods; Henry Hudson Hotel;

Holly Harp; Hotel Hana Maui; Jazz & Pop Magazine; Jeff Banks; Jenny Waterbags; Jim and Andy's Bar; Kenny's Castaways; Kiehl's Pharmacy; Knobkerry; Landmark Hotel; Lanza's; Limbo; Lion's Head; Little Venice; Lookmasters Guild; Love Saves the Day; London Fog; The Los Angeles Free Press; Madison Square Garden; Madora/George Michael of Madison Avenue; Manny's Music; Matt Umanov Guitars; Max Nass; Max's Kansas City; McCabe's Guitar Shop; Metropolitan Opera House; Naked Grape; Navarro Hotel; New York State Pavilion; Night Owl; Nobody's; Old World Restaurant; Ondine's; Orchidia; Ossie Clark; Pancho's Pit; Paraphernalia; Paterson Silks; Peacock Café; Philharmonic Hall; Philippe's; Pink's; Piraeus My Love; Plaza Hotel; Possible 20; Premier Talent; Propinquity; Quorum; Rags (magazine); Ratner's; RCA Records and Studios; The Record Plant; Ridge Antique Furs; Ritz Hotel (London); Rock Magazine; Rogers Cowan & Brenner; The Roundhouse; The Royal Albert Hall; St. Bonaventure University; St. Marks Leather; Salvation; The San Francisco Oracle; San Lorenzo; The Scene; The Second Avenue Deli; Serendipity 3; Sharkey's; The Shed House; Shelly's Manne-hole; Shrine Auditorium; Sign of the Dove; Sing Wu; Slugs; The Spectrum; The Stitching Horse; Strand Books; Studio B; Sunset Marquis Hotel; Sunset Sound Recorders; Sylvain's; Tales of Hoffman; Tamala Design; Tanglewood; Thee Experience; Themis; Town Hall; Trader Vic's; Tropicana Motel; Troubadour; Trude Heller's; Ungano's; Upsurge; Veselka; Village Gate; Village Theater; Village Vanguard; The Village Voice; Whisky A Go-Go; Wally Heider Studios; Wartoke Unltd.; White Horse Tavern; Wine & Apples; Winterland; WNEW-FM; Wo Hop; Woodstock Festival of Music & Art...

and anyplace or anyone else I might have forgotten.

Much love and many thanks to the Usual Suspects:

New York Division: Michael Rosenthal, Grace Adair, Christopher Schelling.
Austin Division: Susan, Mic and Patricia Kaczmarczik.
Florida Division: Fernand Amandi.
L.A. Division: James Allen Davis, Kathleen Quinlan, Bruce Abbott, Lisa Derrick, Steve Hochman. (If you think someone's missing, see page 11…)

The Hawaiian Connection:
Mahalo nui to Laird Hamilton and Gabrielle Reece,
for the fitness inspiration .
Mahalo nui loa to Barbara Beardsley and Andy Morrison,
for the friendship and the orchids.

The House of the Wolf:
Catherine, Shannon, Jonathan and Stephanie Kennely.

Thanks to Prince Andrew Przybyszewski for the incredibly cool cover artwork and design. (And to Their Royal Highnesses Diana and Emma.)

Thanks to Bianca Arvin, who did the Lulu thing and made this book both groovy and real.

Thanks to friend and fellow author Scott MacMillan and the SFPD (Park Station, Haight-Ashbury) for police information and advice.

Thanks to my friend, colleague and fellow rockchick Ellen Sander, who if anyone is the real-life Rennie Stride, she is.

Extra-special thanks to David Walley, with great affection and equally great exasperation. He'd have very much enjoyed this, I think…

And of course to my Jim…

For Mary Susan Herczog,
who bossed me around

Knight of Ghosts and Shadows
(adapted from traditional nursery rhymes)

With a host of furious fancies
whereof I am commander
With a burning spear and a sword of air
through the wilderness I wander
With a knight of ghosts and shadows
I summoned am to tourney
Ten leagues beyond the wild world's end
I think it is no journey

For to trip with Tom o' Bedlam
ten thousand miles I'd travel
Mad Maud she goes on painted toes
to save her boots from gravel
Still I sing bonny lads, bonny wee lads,
lads and birds so bonny
For they all sing fair and they live by the air
and they beg both drink and money

Tom, Tom, the piper's son,
came to town to have some fun
The only tune that he could play
was "Over the Hills and Far Away"
The only song that ever he knew
Was "Little Miss Muffet Loves Little Boy Blue"
(Over the hills and a long way off
the wind is blowing my topknot off)

Boys and girls come out to play,
the moon is shining bright as day
Out of the houses and into the street
Down the road both swift and fleet
Come with a will and come with a call
Come with me if you come at all
(Across the hills and a long way from here
the wind is blowing both far and near)

[bridge]

A fire-eyed girl with hair of night
stands with her back turned towards the light
Before her, her shadow runs away
turns around and starts to play
The brighter the light, the darker the shadow
streams and billows over the meadow

Tom, Tom, the piper's lad,
stayed in town and went to the bad
Ale and whisky and riotous life
Tom could never find him a wife
Too many pills and too much pain
Came Tom never home again
(Down the valleys and into the town
the wind is blowing my cloak around)

Girls and boys go home to sleep,
the sun is shining dark and deep
Into the houses and up to your beds
Down on the pillow you lay your heads
Under the fences and over the wall
Go with a smile or go not at all
(Up on the hills at the break of day
the wind is blowing the sky away)

Over the hills and valleys
A long and lonely road
The leaves are green upon the trees
The time has come to go
Beyond the enchanted mountains
A wild and weary way
The leaves are falling from the trees
The time has gone to stay

–Turk Wayland, Lionheart

"They told us, 'Here's what you *ought* to be doing. You ought to be marrying a lawyer and getting two cars and da-da-da-da.' ... What our parents had told us was just wonderful didn't sound awfully exciting. It may have been secure but it sounded really boring. The Sixties was simply a bunch of well-educated kids going, I *don't* think so, I don't, I don't, I don't *think* so!"

— *Grace Slick*

Prologue

Tam Linn, lead singer of the rock group Deadly Lampshade, has a beautiful rich husky tenor voice, for which he writes songs that show it off to best advantage – a practice which is not always, or even often, to the best advantage of the rest of his band.

He also has a gift for gorgeously singable melody lines that make great hooks for hit singles – but only if he sings them. He is an inventive guitar player – but only in the service of his own songs. Even in this time and place of amazing hair – Haight-Ashbury, San Francisco, 1966 – he has some of the best: thick, straight, shoulder-length; and he isn't above tossing it around like a Civil War whore to pull in chicks.

He is well aware of all of this, and aware also that it doesn't exactly endear him to a whole lot of people. Especially not to the people that know him best and have to work with him most closely. And he doesn't particularly care.

But it hardly seems to matter. Under their British manager's tutelage and Tam's selfish though effective leadership, within a year the Lampshade have evolved from a sloppy Oakland bar band to a hard-playing, brilliantly creative, psychedelic outfit. But in the process of becoming stars, they have lost — some say cynically tossed overboard — much of the political and spiritual consciousness that had been their original stock in trade.

Well, when it comes right down to it, they're not the only Bay Area rock group to have done the same in the service of their music, steering clear of at least the most overtly political stuff — though nobody is entirely apolitical, in the sense that politics doesn't deeply affect their music and their persona, their way of being in the world.

Because you can't be, not in this time and place; it isn't possible to think and feel and stand apart. Politics is part of the scene, part of what makes the music move and live and thrive — it was so from the first, and it will be so until the last.

Likewise the drugs. Nothing nasty, or not that often anyway, not till later. In the beginning it's just pot and acid and mescaline and psilocybin; speed is the worst of it. The reign of terror that heroin and powder cocaine will bring about is still a few years off: if they are used — and they are, even now — they are used in secret, and junkies and speed freaks and cokeheads are looked down on in the social milieu. Musicians, of course, have their own rules...

Whether the drugs make the music or the music makes the drugs is one of those headachey questions like Can God create a rock so big he can't lift it, or if a really bad band plays suckily in a forest with nobody there to hear them do they still make a sound, and if they do is that sound still sucky or is it just a sound.

Though on further reflection maybe it is the drugs that make questions like that.

But Tam is by far the most enthusiastic substance fan among the Lampshade's personnel: he can blow a kilo of grass in days, a gram of coke in a few whale-sized snorts, a whole blotterful of acid, thousands and thousands of mikes of Owsley's finest, in a week.

And that's only what people actually see him do: there are tales of much harder stuff, and even not-so-veiled whispers of him *dealing that harder stuff on a professional scale, not just those amiable transactions among friends that are like asking someone to pick up a quart of milk for you at the grocery store next time they go to buy milk for themselves. But no one knows for sure.*

Strangely enough, the drugs don't affect Tam's creative work in the slightest, which almost seems to be missing the point. His output is brilliant, and his voice is amazing, and even drugs can't improve much on that — or, if you take the other view, can't hurt it much either.

But one point nobody misses about Tam is that he has aggravated, annoyed, incensed, infuriated and enraged pretty much everyone he has ever come into contact with. The only reason most people put up with him at all is because he's so freakin' talented, and of course he's a rock star, and also of course he's so very very cute. Apart from that, though, Tam Linn, born Tommy Linetti, is a terminal pain in the behind.

So when he is found pretty darn terminal indeed backstage in the Fillmore Auditorium dressing room one spring afternoon, stuffed into one of his own band's road cases a couple of hours before the Lamps are to headline there, not even his own band is particularly sorry about it. Shocked, yes; irritated, yes; pissed off that even in death he's managed to find a way to inconvenience them and screw them over once again, yes yes yes.

But grief-stricken? No. You couldn't say that about them. You couldn't say that at all.

Chapter One

San Francisco, March 1966

IF IT WAS STILL TRUE—if it ever had *been* true, however universally it may have been acknowledged—that a single man in possession of a good fortune must be in want of a wife, then how very sad and sorry it was that things apparently hadn't changed all that much since dear Jane Austen's day.

And, Rennie Stride now legally Lacing bitterly reflected, with the resolve not unmixed with fury that flooded her anew every time she thought about it, men like that got the wives that they damn well deserved. Not to mention the wives that damn well deserved them. Though she did have a soft spot for Mr. and Mrs. Fitzwilliam Darcy. It was just that, God willing and the creek don't rise, she herself—not to mention her husband of barely a year, who didn't have much if any choice in the matter—wasn't going to be one of their number a whole lot longer. If indeed she ever *had* been one of their number, at least more than technically.

This spring afternoon, Rennie was headed toward the Golden Gate Bridge, in the wine-red Corvette that had been a wedding gift from that very same husband, and then north into hilly, rustic Marin County, to an encounter that would spell, she had good reasons for hoping, the beginning of her professional success.

Needless to say, this had *not* been the way she'd planned it. Not much more than a year ago, she'd still been Rennie Stride, still back home in her beloved native city of New York, a year ahead of schedule on her journalism degree at Columbia; and Stephen Lacing, six years her senior and cute as a bug, had just finished some refresher courses at that august institution's law school.

Predictably, they'd met at the Cloisters one afternoon in the fall of 1964, in the magical presence of the Unicorn Tapestries, and after some rather coy and utterly corny jesting about unicorns and maidens—lines that the tapestries, having heard a million times before, must have been rolling their embroidered eyes at—he'd taken her out for hot chocolate. After a decent five months of steady dating, he had proposed and she had accepted, because in the spring of 1965 that was what a well-brought-up young man and a virginal younger woman were supposed to do, unicorns to the contrary notwithstanding.

The one wild and romantic thing they did manage to do was elope. Other college girls and boys ran off to Fort Lauderdale on semester break and got blind drunk for a sunny seaside week; Stephen and Rennie ran off to Maryland and got married on a snowy morning. She was twenty years old, and he had just turned twenty-six, her first serious boyfriend, the first guy who'd ever asked her to marry him; they'd never slept together until their wedding night, so she wasn't even pregnant. Nobody could figure it out. Including her. Their families and friends didn't know about it until it was done. It just seemed to be the thing to do.

Then, a month later, he'd zapped the move on her—a literal move. He was a top-flight corporate lawyer and executive and partner in a San Francisco import firm only marginally less old than his family, and, indeed, owned by his family. These days, LacingCo was less an import firm than a giant huge multinational conglomerate that had been founded by the Lacings back in Gold Rush times, and Stephen had never planned on anything but going back to work for the family firm in their longtime hometown, as he'd done for the past five years. He'd never bothered to mention this to Rennie—just took it for granted that since she'd signed on as his wife, she'd be happy to toss her Cornell journalism degree over the windmill and drop out of Columbia grad school and come to *his* town to live, since he wouldn't be staying in hers. Oh, and by the way, she wouldn't be working once she got there, either; Lacing ladies simply didn't.

Rennie, who'd been eagerly looking forward not only to a real newspaper job but to Manhattan living—since leaving the parental nest, she'd only ever lived in a college dorm, and briefly with four roommates in a huge and rackety Upper West Side flat—had concealed her disappointment and rage, and obediently started packing. The relocation was the least of it: San Francisco was a gorgeous city, she might well have wanted to move there one day herself. She just didn't happen to believe that a forced march to the West Coast was the best way to start off their marriage, and she'd been genuinely angry with Stephen's unilateral decision. Still, there were newspapers in San Francisco, good ones too; as for that working thing—which was to say that *not* working thing— well, they'd discuss that when she got there.

But she'd still had an uneasy feeling about what she'd gotten herself into—Stephen, marriage, San Francisco, his unbelievably wealthy and socially prominent family, the whole trip. Which was the chief reason they'd eloped in the first place, why they hadn't gone in for the big society wedding that she had above all things dreaded. She had felt an elopement would be the best way to start off, just them, and Stephen, eager to put his ring on her finger as fast as he could get it there, had convinced himself his family would understand. How very, very wrong they both had been.

For the Lacing family, of which Stephen was the youngest son, were the Lacings of Pacific Heights and Belvedere and the Napa Valley and several other prime real-estate locations; and the Stride family, of which Rennie was the middle daughter, were the Strides of the Bronx, New York. Well, okay, Riverdale. Down the block from where the Kennedys had lived. *Those* Kennedys. But still.

So here she was, on a jingle-jangle morning, married for just over a year at the ridiculous age of just under twenty-two, how had *that* happened, to someone whose fortune was so far beyond "good" it wasn't even funny. In fact, Rennie reflected, downshifting as she approached the last gas station before the bridge, Stephen could buy himself a whole harem of wives were he so inclined, and still have plenty left over for toe bells.

She laughed at the idea, and the mustached young attendant filling up the 'Vette's tank grinned right back at her—pretty chick, long-haired and curvy, legs up to there under that miniskirt, nice sunny day, groovy car, why not? Still smiling, Rennie paid him for the fill-up, waved bye-bye and sped off toward the bridge approach. No, Stephen was far too strait-laced for even a harem *fantasy*, let alone a real harem; that was part of the problem. God knew, she had tried.

Crossing the soaring red-gold span, radio blasting the Byrds, who were even now assuring her that they're not sleepy and there ain't no place they're goin' to, Rennie couldn't help throwing a quick glance over her right shoulder, and was, as always, surprised that she didn't turn instantly to a pillar of salt. Yes, there it was, a blot upon the glory of the landscape. Hell House. Her private name for the Lacing family's spectacular town mansion.

Of course, the famous real true name of it, the one that appeared in all the guidebooks and led tourists there to gawk outside its wrought-iron gates and formal gardens, was Hall Place. Kings and queens and presidents had guested there; Mark Twain had scribbled a bit at leisure in its vast library; Oscar Wilde had epigrammed his way all over its blue drawing room; after the 1906 earthquake the divine Sarah Bernhardt had spent a few days under its roof (and also, or so it was rumored, a few nights under its master).

Plainly visible from the bridge, it squatted there like a big malevolent albino toad, in all its white warty mid-Victorian splendor, sheltering Lacings now as it had done for more than a hundred years, on a rise in Pacific Heights right up against the green of the Presidio, commanding one of the most staggering views of all in a town chock-full of them.

But she'd never really *lived* at Hell House, had she. In the eyes of the mansion's reigning empress, Rennie had merely been a lodger, wife of its junior heir though she was, and not a very welcome lodger at that; so she couldn't by any stretch call it *her* house, much less "home." She hadn't been able to from the first, and now she never would, thinking now, as she had when she first laid eyes on it, and indeed evermore after, *Oh holy Mother of God, what* have *I done…*

She had known from the day she'd set foot in San Francisco last year, fresh off the plane from New York, all her defenses like a naked saber in her hand, that she had made a huge, tremendous, howling kicking scratching screaming biting bug-eyed mistake. Stephen and his older brother Eric had met her at the airport, a reassuringly loving welcome, but when they'd reached Hall Place and she'd gotten out of the chauffeured limo—and not a hired one either, her first uneasy taste of how the Lacing family did things on their own turf—and taken one look at the vast Victorian pile looming above her through the fog, as enormous and pallid and scary-looking as Moby-Dick himself, she'd had all she could do to keep from dashing into the street, flinging up her arm and shouting "Taxi! Manhattan, and step on it!"

Too late. The jaws had gaped, and Rennie Pequod was engulfed. But the true Whiteness of the Whale had been waiting for her within, sitting behind the tea table in the exquisite morning room—in the utterly terrifying person and persona of her new mother-in-law, Marjorie Elaine Beldenbrook van Leeuwen "Call Me Motherdear" Lacing—and as soon as their glances met, with the click of crossing harpoons, they both knew it was away all boats.

True to her own private predictions as well as her mother-in-law's aggrievedly public ones, Rennie hadn't lasted long as a young San Francisco society bride, though she had a feeling she'd probably lasted a hell of a lot longer than Motherdear's cynical estimate. It had taken a while—for Stephen's sake, Rennie had tried heroically for months—but by autumn the whole uneasy trip had blown open like the San Andreas Fault on a tear.

Not only had Rennie refused to assume any of her Marjorie-mandated duties as the newest Lacing recruit, not to mention refusing to begin dutiful and immediate production of the next heirs in the direct male line, but, going up against that terrifying woman's express, and coldly expressed, wishes—"Women of this family, *ladies* of this family, do not work outside the home" was the party line, obviously hammered into Stephen at an early age, or maybe he really believed it, she just didn't know anymore—she had taken her j-school training in one hand and every ounce of courage she possessed in the other, and she had gone out to look for a job.

What she wanted to do more than anything was write for a newspaper; that was why she had pushed herself through school as fast and as hard as she had, graduating from Cornell in three headlong years. But it wasn't just that: she had discovered a consuming desire to write about the music she had come to love—the amazing new rock that had begun in London and was now cross-pollinating itself right there in San Francisco, up the hill from Hell House in the big old houses and tiny new clubs of the Haight-Ashbury district.

It was nothing less than the soundtrack of our lives, Rennie thought now, as the Byrds gave way, out in the middle of the bridge, to the Rolling Stones seeing a red door and wanting to paint it black. You could chart your days by the music: what was playing on the stereo or the car radio or at the dance, when you got stoned, got drunk, fell in love with somebody, went to bed with them, fought with them, made up with them, broke up with them, cried your eyes out, found somebody else, partied, studied, graduated. The first two notes of any song, any song at all, could trigger a flood of memory associations good or bad, from the weather to what you'd been wearing the night you heard it, and anything as important and powerful and all-encompassing as that deserved, no, *demanded*, to be written about.

For a while she hadn't seen how she might achieve her desire. Rock music and the phenomenon soon to be known as rock journalism were both just starting up bigtime, true, but there were very, very few women involved. Guys all over the place, all of them long-haired, most of them decorative and well-educated. But not many of them enlightened. And hardly any chicks at all.

Except, of course, in the usual only acceptable position for chicks: supine. Terrific. Nobody would let her write, or be a lead guitarist, or a producer, or an a&r exec at a record company, but if she wanted a career as a groupie, no problem. All she had to do was show up and put out—turn off her brain, open her legs and shut her mouth. Or open her mouth, depending. Yeah, the job opportunities *there* were endless, all right. Anything else, she would have to fight like hell for. And, make no mistake, she would.

Yet if there are gods who rule such matters, they must have heard Rennie's angry, passionate prayers and deemed her worthy, for it hadn't been long at all before she'd landed a little tiny job as a record and club reviewer for a weekly Bay Area paper. Not what she liked most, or even what she was best at, but it got her going, and not so incidentally proved that she really could write.

And could *really* write. Bylined as Rennie Stride, to claim her own and also to appease Motherdear by not dragging the sacred Lacing name into it, she'd very quickly multiplied the little reviewing job into several stringer gigs at a few of the new underground newspapers, the fancifully named and typographically outrageous rags that were popping up like magic mushrooms coast to coast, west to east and on across the Pond: the Oracle, the Freep, the Phalarope, the Barb, the East Village Other, the Phoenix, the Gilded Lily, Queen Anne's Fan.

It wasn't the steadiest employment, but it was solid and it paid. Enough. Well, a little. More importantly, it got her name out there to the people who cared about the same things she did. Rennie was learning as she went: learning about her subject and her craft and herself, getting better all the time. Strangely, for quite a while many of her readers thought she was a guy: duped by the non-gender-specific first name, they'd assumed, from the strength and passion and anger and singularly opinionated un-chickness of the writing, that this Rennie person was testicular.

Which, actually, she was. Balls to spare. Just not the anatomical kind.

And then, magnificently, The Job, as she reverentially

thought of it, had come into her life just before Christmas, a new star rising over her own little manger. As always, Santa had known what was best. Apparently he'd thought her letter to the North Pole was a real winner, for he brought her what she'd wanted most and could best use.

The gates of Olympus had swung open: a fourth-rung music reviewing slot at the San Francisco Clarion. Her old Cornell journalism professor, an unlikely Santa's helper, had pulled a few strings and called in a few favors, and had done her the biggest solid imaginable, getting her a real job at a real newspaper; her own track record, modest though it yet was, did the rest.

Noting the rising rock tide that was beginning to lift all journalistic boats from London to L.A., and noting likewise the hated archrival Chronicle's commitment to this crazy new music, the Clarion had decided that, in addition to the three men it already had on staff as entertainment reporters, it needed someone to report solely about rock and roll.

And, they figured, since no other newspaper in town had even *dreamed* of hiring a woman music columnist—it was standard procedure, and perfectly legal, for employers to designate jobs M or F in help-wanted ads, and wasn't it odd how all the M jobs were cool and promotable and all the F jobs required typing and paid half as much—maybe all those female rock fans out there would buy a bunch more copies of the Clarion every day with which to do their relating if they had a female rock reporter they could relate to.

So the gods of rocknroll, who are trickster gods at best but gods all the same, had decreed that Rennie Stride should be that one, and in so decreeing they laid down the pattern for more lives than just hers. Other editors at other newspapers would have been satisfied with someone who looked hip and foxy and could spell correctly and would piffle on about how cute and sexy the musicians were, since everybody knew that that was all that women really wanted to hear about.

But the Clarion thought otherwise; and though with this particular hire they certainly got hip and foxy and orthographically impeccable, what they had also gotten, though they didn't know it yet, was Santa's gift that year to them as well. And for many years thereafter.

The night before she was to report for her first day on the new job, Rennie had lain awake in bed, almost ill with excitement. Oblivious to Stephen asleep beside her, she had stared blindly at the patterns of moonlight and tree branches on the ceiling, the sheets drawn clear up to her chin. Would it be okay? Would she be able to do it? True, it was what she had been so expensively trained for, but maybe she wasn't any good after all. Maybe rock wasn't the thing to write about, even. Maybe Marjorie was right.

She shifted on the pillows, willing herself to get at least a few hours' sleep before she had to get up and face the future that was waiting for her downtown at the Clarion building. No, *she* was right, and she was *good*, and it *was* the thing, and she would prove it. Mrs. Stephen Lacing wasn't ever going to happen, and Rennie Lacing had never really existed, but Rennie Stride was off and running. Don't look back.

She'd settled down right away. Sure, she was far from the heart of Olympus, but at least she had a seat at the gods' table. This particular Olympus chanced to be ruled by a mighty and benevolent Zeus: the great Garrett Larkin, the Clarion's senior editor, good friend and worthy rival of the Chronicle's legendary music critic Ralph J. Gleason. Like Rennie, Garrett was a Cornell j-grad, and the co-founder of a righteous new venture called Spare Chaynge, first and most successful of the funky new rock publications now being born.

As the most junior of junior music staffers, Rennie didn't often get to interact on such exalted levels, of course. But even spear-carriers on Olympus can occasionally hang with the gods, upon the gods' errands...

This assignment today, for instance, the one that was taking her across the bridge and into uncharted territory. Rennie's immediate editor, Burke Kinney, old enough to be her father and a journalist of the eyeshade-and-shirtsleeves school, a man whose musical tastes ran to operetta and whose pop-music education had ended with Perry Como, had thought an interview with a young, on-the-rise local girl singer might be something local people would want to read about, and as soon as Rennie had heard that the assignment was up for grabs and the other writers weren't interested, she'd begun lobbying for it to be her very own.

Since every story so far done on the San Francisco sound, as it was already being called — not that there had yet been all that many stories — had featured crystal-voiced Grace Slick, who as homegrown Palo Alto talent had the inside edge with her band the Great Society — a wild-haired ex-folksinger from Texas called Janis Joplin had not yet blasted her way into the town's startled attention — Rennie had thought the piece should deal with somebody completely new.

And even though she had yet to do her first interview in a professional capacity, and no one, herself included, knew if she even could, if she was capable of anything beyond the little reviews and snippets that were the only things she'd so far been allowed to write, Rennie had argued long and hard with Burke Kinney over this, harder and more eloquently than she'd ever argued over anything in her life. Because this was different: this wasn't about punctuation or writing voice or how to properly construct an inverted-pyramid news story, the way all the journalism books and classes taught you. This was about people: her, him, the readers, the already chosen subject. And Rennie wanted it more than she'd ever wanted anything in her life, and she laid both want and reasons on him in no uncertain terms.

And though he could have smacked her down anytime at all, for any reason or no reason except that he was the editor and she was not, for some reason Burke had leaned back and listened to what she had to say, and even more to what she didn't say, and in the end he had given her the assignment.

Well, as he'd really put it: "You're a nobody, she's a nobody, what have I got to lose? But listen to me, Strider" — and here he'd leaned forward, suddenly serious, wire-rimmed gaze fixed on hers — "I have a feeling that neither of you is going to be a nobody for long. And I want to see that in this piece. I pay attention to those feelings when I get them, and if it pans out the way I think it will, I want all three of us to never forget I'm the one who said so first. Now go talk to her, and don't make any of us sorry I gave you this. Especially don't make *me* sorry."

She'd thanked him at least six times before he cut her off and waved her out. Outside his door, she'd collapsed against the wall in mingled relief and horror — horror that she'd dared, relief that he hadn't shoved the paper spike right through her forehead and out the other side — and begun to breathe again.

'Strider'...when he calls me that, I know I'm okay...

Then it all blazed up into something very different, something that felt for a moment almost religious, a medieval mystic's ecstatic freak-out with God. She had done it. She had gotten what she wanted. This was going to happen.

As she'd told Burke, she already knew who her subject was going to be. A few weeks ago, someone at one of the clubs had turned her on to a young folk-rocker from Marin County, who was moving on to harder and edgier sounds, and Rennie had not only already phoned to set things up, she'd made sure she'd heard her a few times with her band.

Karma Mirror, the group was called: four guys and this one girl playing absolutely mind-blowing music, all of which they wrote themselves but she wrote most of it, and most of the best of it — melding rock with folk in a killer blend that no one else had ever tried before, maybe hadn't even imagined. All topped by a contralto voice that could hit a note like a baseball, swinging not just for the rock fences but all the way out to the parking lot of the music next door.

Someone Rennie's exact own age. Someone called Prax McKenna.

Rennie suddenly slung the car off the road at the famous scenic overlook just north of the bridge, parked slantwise and got out, leaning on the open door, letting the sudden rush have its way with her. This was it. She felt it, she *knew* it. Her first serious assignment, and as Burke had implied, if she did it right it could get her some serious attention from people who mattered. Not to mention a better class of things to report on. And as for this Prax chick—what the hell kind of a name was "Prax", she must remember to ask—it might get her some serious attention too. And, maybe, a better class of places to play in.

She crossed her arms and clasped her shoulders, hugging herself against the floods of cold fresh sea-tinged air, long gold-brown hair flying, staring unseeing at the glorious view. She could do this. This was just talking to people, and people had always seemed happy to talk to her. As her idolized journalism mentor had told her, it wasn't enough to ask good questions, though from that all else proceeded. It was even more necessary to "hear good answer", as he'd put it, to give careful and attentive listening to the responses, and then to play off them—*that* was the way to make people tell you things they might never in a million years have told you otherwise.

And then you went to work: you built the story like a writer and you felt the story like a reader and you reported the story like a witness under oath and you edited the story like a hanging judge. Because that was your job, that was what you did. And now she was going to get to do it for real.

After a few minutes Rennie slid back in behind the wheel. But she didn't start the car just yet. Then, with a deep breath, and a feeling of fate rolling down the pike to meet her, she turned the key and hit the gas, and pointed the Corvette's red nose toward Sausalito, just beyond the Marin headlands — the charmingly funky, impossibly pretty little bay town tucked into the hills, a few miles to the north. Just goin' up around the bend.

Chapter Two

THERE IT WAS, a small white vine-covered house, clinging to a hill overlooking the town and the bay—Rennie's destination, and, perhaps, her destiny as well. She turned off the street and pulled onto the parking apron next to not the predictable psychedelically painted hippie van or Beetle bug but a classic Morgan roadster in British racing green, obviously old but just as obviously lovingly cared for. Which majorly pleased her, and was her first real clue as to the nature of the person she'd come to talk to. Someone with a sense of style, at the very least. But as both Rennie and the world were about to learn, Prax McKenna always went her own road.

She opened the door to Rennie's knock, and they both said forever afterwards that they'd recognized each other at once, as if they'd known each other before. That separated-at-birth thing, that must-have-known-you-in-a-past-life thing, that kindred-spirit Anne of Green Gables thing: they were both of the race that knows Joseph.

"Hi, you must be Rennie." Prax extended a hand—strong, small, three or four silver rings adorning—and Rennie took it. "Come on through, we can talk out here."

Following her hostess inside, Rennie immediately started taking copious mental notes on everything she saw, smelled, touched, tasted, heard or vibed. "Out here" turned out to be a glassed-in, ivy-trellised sun porch, in sore need of both paint and repair. But once you looked out over the sparkling bay you forgot all about that, as completely as the tenant had. Slinging herself into a brightly colored Mayan hammock, Prax cordially gestured Rennie to dispose herself on a white wicker sofa. Showtime!

Prax McKenna, born the same year as Rennie, late August as opposed to late March, was of middling height and slight build, with eyes of an incredible blue-green shade and wavy blond hair down past her shoulder blades. She was smart and funny, smiling rarely but laughing often, and she suffered fools not only not gladly but not at all. And she had never been shy of saying so—and, now, of singing so. Which, in these new-born times of peace and free love, baby, had already earned her a local reputation as one pret-ty scary white chick—especially among the guys. A little hesitantly, Rennie mentioned that as an icebreaker, and when both of them stopped laughing they were off to the races.

Rennie's j-school training sessions had taught her that you got interviews started by asking harmless usual things to set up a baseline reading for your bullshit detector, priming the pump for the hardball to come: where did you grow up, how did you get into whatever it is that you're into, what kind of musical schooling if any did you have, who were your big influences. But looking at the clever, pretty, amusedly alert face across the porch, Rennie suddenly put away her tricks.

"This is my first real interview," she said honestly, giving herself up for scorned. But astonishingly, a great big warm smile crept across Prax's face.

"How far out is that, mine too!"

Rennie managed to get most of her formula questions answered early on. Prax was a Northern California girl: native San Franciscan, child of academic-bohemian parents, grew up in Mill Valley with sacred Mount Tamalpais as her backyard. Got into music early on, thanks to those same parents: flute, viola, piano and voice lessons as a kid. For musical influences she claimed pretty much everything she'd ever heard, which had the effect of making her sound like nothing anyone *else* had ever heard.

Which was to Rennie's way of thinking the mark of the true artist: you take it all in, the art that is everybody else's, all times and places and voices, and when it comes back out again it is only, purely, unmistakably and forever your own.

After half an hour's talk, progressively easier and funnier, Prax got up to roll a few joints and make them some tea. She beckoned Rennie to follow her inside, and Rennie took advantage of the opportunity to look curiously around.

The décor was not very different from the way she was furnishing her own newly acquired place on the heights of the Haight: big soft floor cushions, bead curtains in doorways, lace curtains at windows, Maxfield Parrish prints and psychedelic posters of local bands, a round claw-footed oak table, a brass bed in, of all places, the living room.

Well, okay, *that* was different. But mostly because in the one bedroom that the little house boasted, music had triumphed over sleep—had in fact beat the living crap out of it. The room was stuffed solid with guitars both electric and acoustic, a violin or two, a huge and beautifully carved floor harp, recorders, flutes, chimes, exotic foreign instruments like marimbas and ouds. Notes for lyrics and tunes and other bits of paper covered the carpet like musical snow; there was a small electric organ against one wall, an impressive sound system and an impressive quantity and variety of records to play on it. Not to mention some strange-looking electronic devices and a beat-up Victorian upright piano cased in carved rosewood. A musician's room, for sure—the workplace of a working artist.

And all at once Rennie felt her insides buckle and ache, with the sudden overwhelming awareness of how very much she had wanted and needed to find a friend. For months after she'd arrived in San Francisco, Stephen had been the only friend she had—the only person she even knew, really. Eric, bless him, had happily taken her on as a younger sister, but he had a rough path of his own to walk—that of eldest son, and gay closeted eldest son at that, as Stephen had confided in her shortly after their marriage—and he couldn't always be around to make things easy or right for Rennie.

The few young women of her own age that she had managed to meet had all been snipped from the same industrial-weight society sheet iron as her mother-in-law. No surprise there: they'd been carefully vetted by Motherdear as suitable company for her son's new and clearly impossible wife, and they were all little Marjorie Lacings in training. They would have sold their tiny souls to be married to Stephen, and bitterly envied and resented Rennie because she hadn't sold a thing and yet had landed him anyway, and they couldn't understand why this parvenu New York ingrate wasn't worshipping at Motherdear's size five, stiletto-encased feet. So, since they looked upon Marjorie as their mentor and queen and Rennie could only behold her in her true form as a soul-sucking she-demon from the bottom-most pits of Hell, the potential for friendship was cut way down right there.

But here was someone who thought as Rennie thought, liked what Rennie liked...

"I've seen threads like that before," said Prax suddenly, breaking into her guest's reverie as she came in from the kitchen with the joints and the tea tray. She was eyeing Rennie's fox-trimmed red pythonskin maxicoat, where it lay across a Mission rocker. "I bought a little vest that looks just like it, only in green, from that boutique on Haight Street, the one with the tropical fish tanks in the window—I love it, I wear it onstage all the time. Shirtless and bra-less, of course."

"Mine," murmured Rennie shyly, with a touch of unreasonable pride that this utterly cool person had actually bought something she had made, and not only that but wore it onstage, to make music in. "I mean, I made it. The vest. The coat, too. I sew a lot of my own clothes, and also I make some to sell, just to get a little extra bread. That shop takes a lot of them on consignment."

"Far out! How did that get started?"

"Once I started working as a rock writer, I needed a whole different wardrobe. My evil mother-in-law pitched a fit, but I gave all my lady suits and tea dresses and gloves and hats to the Goodwill, bought myself a sewing machine and hit the flea markets and fabric remnant stores."

Rennie didn't mention that she'd also taken a little speed from time to time to keep her going, though Prax wouldn't have given a hoot. She'd always liked to sew; it was a nice creative outlet when writing failed or faltered, or a different kind of outlet, so she'd started making what felt good and looked great: pantsuits crafted from lace tablecloths, paisley Mao jackets and bellbottoms to match, crocheted see-through dresses, skirts whose hems either barely reached the top of her thighs or else frothed around her ankles, pirate-wench dresses with laceup bodices slit to her navel, coats patchworked from brocade curtains and edged in fur, pouchy suede bags with beaded fringe that touched the floor.

"I'm married, but separated," she went on to explain, seeing the curiosity and interest on Prax's mobile face. "I won't take any money from my husband, so I can't afford to buy the things I like—when I first moved out on him, I could just about pay the rent and feed myself and keep the lights on. But I dearly coveted all these rich-hippie clothes I saw around, so if I wanted to have them, I had to make them. I've always been pretty good at designing and sewing and knitting and crocheting and stuff, if I do say so myself, and as I made all these things for me, I got *so* good that my brother-in-law suggested I start selling some. So I did."

"Clever girl," said Prax, smiling, and as if she were rewarding such cleverness, she passed over to Rennie a pottery cup of tea with one hand and a fat, beautifully rolled joint with the other. "Clever brother-in-law, too. See, I got a cool vest out of his idea. Be sure to thank him for me. And not rip-off priced either, so thank *you*."

Rennie accepted the joint with more conviction than confidence. She'd smoked pot before; in her last year at Cornell she'd roomed with an impossibly sophisticated Bostonian who looked as if the tea her rebel ancestors had tossed into the harbor had flowed in her veins ever since. Though they would have been pretty surprised, to say the least, to see their descendant doing her own rebelling over a very different kind of tea. Or maybe not.

But though Rennie had enjoyed her few mild episodes of grass-induced spacey silliness, she disliked smoking, and pot wasn't something she sought out. If it was around, fine. If not, that was fine too. Still, since coming to San Francisco, she'd ventured into buying a bit for herself every now and then: ten dollars would score a lid, a plastic bag like a little pillow, stuffed plump with a short ounce of beautifully cleaned grass, no sticks or seeds, greenly fragrant and fine as beach sand, that would last her for weeks. She'd turned Stephen on to it a couple of times, to the noticeable improvement of their sex life, but he was too straight-arrow to really let go and get into it.

She was unsure ever after if it had been the tea or the, well, tea, but all of a sudden Rennie found herself chain-eating chocolate cookies and babbling away, telling Prax things she had never told anyone in her life. It was as if the magnetic field that ruled the occasion had mysteriously reversed itself, and now Prax was interviewing *her*.

"Everything went downhill, fast," Rennie heard herself saying. "Down every hill in San Francisco and straight into the bay. I didn't see much of Stephen, I fought with him when I did, and that made him stay away even more. The in-laws immediately started sniffing around for a grandchild by the only son of the name who might ever produce one for them, not that they even *know* their other son is as gay as a treeful of parrots, but I told them I was on the pill and not coming off it for anyone, and then before they could recover from their swoons I ran out to get a prescription."

Prax inhaled deeply on her joint, spoke around the held-in toke. "Oh wow."

"You may well say so. It was a big fat stupid old mistake, marrying Stephen." Rennie couldn't imagine why she was telling all this incredibly personal stuff to this girl she'd only just met—well, she could, really—but she kept right on telling her. "I thought I loved him. I *do* love him. I'm just not *in* love with him. I never was. I married him because—well, because he was the first guy who asked me and the first guy I ever slept with. Only guy. And not until we were lawfully married, so how uptight was that? I guess I never really saw how—how stiff he is. And not where it counts. No, not that, we never had a problem in bed, but I've never been to bed with anyone else so I wouldn't know if we did, would I. But stiff in the sense of standing up to things. He never takes my side against them, and he never protects me; I don't think he ever even learned how to protect himself. I don't want to hurt him: he's the kindest, sweetest, nicest man you could imagine, he's *too* nice. But nice isn't enough. And I just don't want to be married to it anymore."

"And you don't have to be. No woman does, not these days. That's all changing now, and we're part of it."

Rennie had pulled in her horns again like a little stoned snail, suddenly shy and embarrassed at having cleaned house so extensively in a stranger's presence, not to mention bogarting the joint as well as the conversation. *This is supposed to be an interview, not group therapy...*

"I guess... But what about you?"

"Me? Oh, nobody special. I just broke up with my girlfriend of over a year, and I haven't been looking to meet anybody new just yet."

"Girlfriend?" This was news to Rennie, and perhaps to everyone else as well.

Prax ran a hand through her hair, not embarrassed she'd made the disclosure, or sorry for it, but a little uncertain, as if she'd given away something she'd maybe really wanted to keep.

"Sure. Before that it was a boyfriend, and it could go either way next time. I love boys, I truly do, but occasionally I get romantic with someone who happens to be a chick. Occasionally I even fall in love with one." She glanced up, smiling a little nervously. "Does that freak you out?'

"Why would it freak me?" Rennie's voice held a touch of bitterness, or maybe envy. "My brother-in-law is gay and I absolutely adore him, not least because on almost every count he understands me better than my husband does. Maybe I should have married *him*. Or you."

Prax laughed. "It's just sex, honey. Free your ass and your mind will follow. Other way round with drugs. But it all gets you to the same place."

"So it seems. So it, you know, seems." Emboldened, Rennie reached for the pot and papers, and began industriously, and unsuccessfully, rolling a joint of her own. Prax watched for a while, a smile widening on her face.

"Don't tell me, nobody ever taught you how! Gimme. Now watch and learn, my young apprentice. And while you are being instructed, tell me how the hell you managed to get the hell out of Hell House, 'cause you sure wouldn't be sitting here talking to me if you hadn't."

Rennie watched as bidden, and learned much. "Sheer self-preservation. I didn't want to go insane, so to keep myself from axe-murdering every single Lacing where they slept, including or perhaps beginning with my husband, I started exploring, and pretty soon I found the Haight."

"People like us always do. Or someplace like it. In L.A., it's Venice; in New York, the East Village; King's Road in London. For us, it's home."

Prax being a child of Marin County, when it came time for her to fly the parental nest she hadn't gone far at all. Nor had she needed to: she'd high-tailed it across the Golden Gate like a forty-niner in reverse, making a beeline for the old Haight district, now called Haight-Ashbury, or even Hashbury by the vulgar press—for obvious reasons. Once an elegant nineteenth-century *quartier* with huge townhouses belonging to scions of great families like the sugar-baron Spreckelses, then downhilling into an Irish and German middle-class district, and further down into a college-student habitat, the Haight was still run-down and shabby, and more than a bit dangerous.

But its wonderful old houses bordering Golden Gate and Buena Vista Parks had survived the great earthquake and fire of 1906, and now they were being invaded and rejuvenated by colorful hordes of migrant gypsy ants. Ants who had somehow learned to create the most vibrant and wonderful music and art and poetry and style imaginable, and who were not shy of using chemical or organic means to enhance both creation and experiencing.

"It saved my life, or at least my sanity, finding the Haight... Oh, I forgot to ask—what the hell kind of name is Prax, anyway?" inquired Rennie, in that straight-out dolphin-smile way which only pot allows.

"Here, you roll some more, now you know how...there ya go! Well, it's Praxedes, actually. Mary Praxedes Susannah. St. Praxedes was one of those early Christian virgin-martyr chicks who never even existed but were invented to make good sticks for the Church to beat women with. Anyway, this alleged Prax allegedly vowed she'd rather die a horrible death for her imaginary boyfriend Jesus than marry this pagan dude and be forced to submit to his probably pretty darn groovy pagan lusts. So her noble Roman parents took her at her word, and who could blame them. Talk about tough love! *My* parents just thought it was a cool name."

"Your parents sound like a hell of a lot more fun than the original Prax's parents. Or than my parents-in-law, for that matter."

"Well, I want to hear all about it. Spill."

So Rennie did.

"I realize you already have a mother, Rennie dear," Marjorie Lacing had said, pouring tea from a silver pot that first fateful morning at Hell House, "and I do *so* long to one day perhaps meet her, and of course your father too, since obviously we didn't have a chance to meet before the, ah, wedding. So calling *me* Mother would be rather silly. But perhaps you could manage to call me Mother Lacing, or Motherdear, as my two darling sons-in-law do. If 'Marjorie' makes you too uncomfortable, that is."

Rennie had thought then, and had been proven correct a million times since, that "Marjorie"—let alone "Mother Lacing", and no way in HELL "Motherdear"—was going to make her a damn sight more than just uncomfortable, but she'd numbly acquiesced, seeing Stephen nodding and smiling encouragingly at her from the facing sofa, as if he were praising a half-housebroken puppy who'd just successfully used the paper for the first time, oh there's a *goooood* girl...

"That's settled, then." Marjorie—ice-blond, sharp-featured, talon-fingered, gaunt as a heron, simultaneously the chic-est and most frightening thing Rennie had ever seen—

had flashed a brief scary smile and waved a fleshless, diamonded claw. "And the General is, of course, just that. He couldn't get away from the office to welcome you home, but he'll be here for dinner. Which is at eight for eight-thirty, by the way; we gather in the rose drawing-room for drinks before we go in, and we do dress. Of course you take lemon in your tea, dear?"

Too cowed to say no, she really preferred milk and sugar, Rennie had choked down the lemoned tea and suffered through twenty minutes of being verbally poked, prodded and pinned down like a butterfly on a board. Dismissed at last, she had gone upstairs to her new rooms, escorted by her brother-in-law Eric. Stephen had been asked to stay behind with his mother for a cozy private chat, though the invitation had sounded a bit more ominous in Rennie's ear, as if he was being made to stay after school and clean the erasers for unspecified offenses, and Rennie thought she had a pretty good idea of what those offenses might be...

"You call your father 'General'?" she'd muttered as they climbed the grand sweeping staircase to the upper regions, still reeling from blood loss to Ahab's harpoons across the tea table.

"No, of course not, he'd hate that. We call him 'General, *sir!*' "

Eric Lacing — six years older than Stephen and a couple of inches taller, with his brother's middling-brown hair and his elder sister's hazel eyes — had looked sideways at her, and they'd both burst out laughing. Then, walking down the silk-walled, spacious, art-lined hallway, they'd come to a set of double doors that gave entry to Stephen's suite of rooms, now hers as well. She'd looked at him, trying desperately to find something, anything, to say, anything to delay the inevitable moment when she would have to go into that room all by herself and shut the door behind her.

But Eric had seen her trouble, and he'd leaned forward,

given her a quick kiss on the cheek.

"I'm so very glad you've come to join us; Stephen needed someone like you. I, of course, can only do so much. See you at dinner?"

And so Rennie Stride newly Lacing had crossed her own first married-woman threshold all alone.

"Yow!" said Prax, when Rennie had finished. "Well, take comfort in the fact that she'll get hers sooner or later. Karmically speaking, that is. Maybe if she got hers in any other sense she'd be a bit easier to deal with."

Rennie tried vainly to erase the nasty mental picture. "Karmically? You mean like the 'karma' in Karma Mirror? Buddhist karma? What does that mean, why did you name the band that?"

Prax pushed herself off with her foot, so that she swung back and forth in the hammock, and took another deep drag off Rennie's newly rolled joint.

"You know how karma works, right? What goes around comes around, what you put out you get back?"

"Sort of. You're a Buddhist, then?"

"Not really—but it's not just Buddhist. Lots of world spiritualities believe in something like that. Well, people are karma's hands, the instruments of karma; we all have to do the work of sending the changes back to whoever needs to learn the karmic lesson."

"So—"

"So sometimes your job is to hold up a big old mirror, to reflect the karma back on those who sent it out. Good karma or bad doesn't matter, we learn from both. The return is the thing that matters. And it changes your own karma, too, when you do that—that's the trip. And that's the karma mirror."

She pushed off again in the hammock, smiling at Rennie as she swung from side to side.

"And speaking of karma… I see how marriage got you out here and how raised consciousness is now cutting you loose. But how in the name of little stone ponies did you get hooked up with the music scene?"

"It was just something I loved and wanted to write about. I knew some musicians back home, when I was at college in upstate New York and then later in the city, and I got into the club scene there when I was at Columbia. And then when I got out here, I was lucky enough to get in at a few underground papers and now the Clarion. But first contact — now that was my sister's college roommate's doing, Sharon Pollan. She and my oldest sister, Dana, met at Finch, this posh Manhattan finishing-school college, graduated a few years ago. Anyway, Sharon moved back here to live after Finch, and when I first came here myself, I was so lonely and homesick and, and, and *forlorn*, yes that's the word, that my sister took pity on me and insisted I look up Sharon. She's the one who really got me started…but it's kind of a long story…"

Prax passed the current joint. "Time is infinite — both stretchable and condensable. Especially when you're stoned. So let's have it, and, to quote dear Oscar Wilde, pray make it improbable."

Rennie hadn't been looking for sympathy when she'd told Prax how lonely she'd been. Just stating the facts. Stephen worked all day, and often well into the night, and she'd found herself at Mother Lacing's baleful beck and call if she stayed home. And you could only do so much wandering around the streets of San Francisco before you got either tired, hungry or developed scary world-class leg muscles from all the hills — which were picturesque as all get-out, sure, but not if you'd been clawing your way over them for three hours straight.

Finally, back in October, at her sister's urging, she'd phoned Sharon Pollan, and Sharon had suggested she check out someplace called the Longshoremen's Hall, down in

North Beach, a huge cement-block union hiring hall that looked like a bombproof bunker. There had been big antiwar demonstrations all day long over in Berkeley and Oakland, with peace marchers and Hell's Angels all in the mix, and there was going to be a rock concert at the hall that very night. Rennie might enjoy herself, might even meet some people.

Sharon obviously had a gift for understatement. The event to which she had so off-handedly consigned Rennie that damp October night in 1965 hadn't been just a concert: it had been a commune called the Family Dog's idea of a rock and roll party, a post-demonstration "Tribute to Dr. Strange", with bands performing who were named exotic things like Jefferson Airplane and the Great Society and the Charlatans, and people like Allan Ginsberg wandering benevolently amongst the crowd.

And as Rennie said now to Prax, "I never saw anything like it."

Nobody had. The place had been filled with people in her own age bracket, five years older or younger, most of whom were deeply under the influence of unlawful substances and all of whom were clad in the most amazing outfits. Not costumes—these were people's actual clothes that they wore in their actual lives; you could tell by the way they *lived* in the clothes, the way they looked and moved in them. They dressed like Victorian viscounts, like French buccaneers, like Jane Austen, like Eleanor of Aquitaine, like Robin Hood or Geronimo or Daniel Boone or various combinations thereof. The only commonality was hair—long, longer, longest. And the only other commonality was stoned, stoneder, stonedest—dozens and dozens, scores upon scores, hundreds upon hundreds of the happily, deeply, deliberately mindfucked.

And seeing them, Rennie had felt that for the first time since she'd left New York, maybe for the first time ever, she was among kin and peers. *These are my people! I am one of you! I have escaped from prison and evil queens and psychic jailers, and found my way home at last!* And for their part, they couldn't have been happier to see her, and they welcomed her to their midst as if by birthright, the lost lamb back safe in the fold.

Rennie didn't know it at the time, of course—no one could have—but she had been present at the third creation. Dylan had gone electric at Newport back in July, setting the table for everybody else; and the Beatles had already moved on, under the influences of those very same unlawful substances, from "I wanna hold your hand" to "I once had a girl, or should I say, she once had me." Now it was San Francisco's turn to open the door.

These were the concerts that launched it all for not only the San Francisco scene but for the new rock as a rising power in the land. The week after the Dr. Strange event, the Family Dog presented a New York band named the Lovin' Spoonful; and in December, in a mostly black neighborhood, the trifecta was completed with the opening of the Fillmore Auditorium, owned and run by an energetic, abrasive, potty-mouthed promoter born Wolfgang Grajonca, a New York transplant now self-rechristened Bill Graham. Shabby and borderline dangerous had turned hip and chic: Rennie had gone up red-carpeted stairs, past a barrel full of apples, to find herself in an Edwardian-era ballroom amongst others of her kind, and had rejoiced.

Arguably, San Francisco rock, lifting off out of the gravity well of 50's pop and early 60's folk, the booster stages of the communes and the club scene behind it, achieved escape velocity right there, powered by some of the baby monsters soon to grow into psychedelic colossi that bestrode the world, or at least the rock universe, the rockerverse— Jefferson Airplane, Quicksilver Messenger Service, Big Brother and the Holding Company, the Great Society, the Warlocks who had just changed their name, practically onstage in mid-chord, to the Grateful Dead. A creation midwifed by this Bill Graham cat and by tall, quiet Texan Chet Helms, who'd managed to get the Family Dog together enough to start up another rock temple, this one called the Avalon Ballroom.

But all that came later. That first night, in the cavernous echoing octagonal cement hall of the longshoremen — who surely would have puzzled plenty at what was going on there, and just what did any family's dog have to do with it, anyway — Rennie had found herself a place right in front of the speaker stacks, elbows on the stage, to listen to Jefferson Airplane, and the bone conduction of the bass notes shook her ribcage like brontosaur footsteps and the long ringing guitar lines took off the top of her head, as she just gave herself over to the music.

On the stage loomed a backdrop poster of an eagle — American Imperial, not Roman Imperial — an eagle that grasped a sheaf of dollars in one taloned claw and a sheaf of bombs in the other. The dollar claw said Freedom and the bomb claw said Peace and above the eagle's head was a streamer that said Bad Taste, though it seemed to Rennie that that was pretty naive and simplistic and there was quite a lot more to be said, even if no one here felt like listening to the message. But the music *demanded* listening.

This Airplane, now. Quite something. It had been their bassist and lead guitarist, Jack Casady and Jorma Kaukonen, who'd just given Rennie such a musical rush, and their two singers were amazing — a cute guy called Marty Balin and a chick named Signe Anderson. The other groups that night, not so much. One particular assemblage, shambling onstage for only their second public performance ever, had been announced as the Great Society: more cute long-haired boys with guitars, though most of their music wasn't in the same weight class as the Airplane's. Not that most people cared one way or the other.

But it was a beautiful brunette in a miniskirt and

purple tights, standing to one side behind a microphone, who had been the focus of all eyes, and when she started to sing about a white rabbit and asking Alice and one pill that made you larger and one pill that made you small, in a voice that coiled like smoke above a wall of sound, you could hear the clang of ears and minds alike opening wide all over the hall. And Rennie had been transported.

She'd heard amazing music before, of course, everybody her age had—she still recalled the first time that she, a diehard folkie, had heard the Beatles on the jukebox in a campus rathskeller, she'd been so taken she'd forgotten to finish her cheeseburger, had just run out and bought up every record she could find, you could tell they were important and wonderful and different—but this was even more different. Something somehow life-changing. Something that was going to change *her* life, almost certainly beyond all expectation or recognition. Like falling in love. And hearing, listening, drinking it all in, Rennie thought that was just fine with her. That night, *she'd* achieved escape velocity too.

"That Grace," said Prax at the end of the story, laughing. "She turns more people on to rock and roll than she does to dope. Well, maybe it's about even. She won't be with the Great Society long, though; she's too good, and they're nice guys but just musicianly ordinary—even though the drummer's her husband, Jerry Slick, and the guitarist is her brother-in-law Darby Slick, who happens to have a big giant crush on her, and they'll both flip out when she splits. Which she will, soon now, I think, and she'll take a couple of their songs with her when she does. She's going to be a big, big star. Just not with them. But that's quite a dramatic little rock baptism you had."

Rennie nodded happily. "The very next day I went out looking for a job writing about music, and a week later I landed a little tiny reviewing gig for the Noe Valley Weekly and a couple of local free papers across the bay. And then at Christmas the Clarion thing came along. My in-laws are still pissed off and embarrassed that I've got an actual job, that my name is in the papers in weensy little print twice a week. They're lucky I don't use theirs. I think even my husband, though he says he's proud and he supports me in it, wishes I'd stop. But I won't. Not ever. Not for anybody."

"But you did get out of their house."

"You bet! Sharon—the one I was just talking about—lives over on Buena Vista West, couple blocks up from Haight Street across the street from the park. I needed to find somewhere I could afford to live—I support myself, I'm only a Lacing by name, not by checkbook, I don't take a penny from them. Out of spite as much as out of pride, in case you're thinking how noble and independent and liberated-woman of me it is. No. I'm just royally pissed off, and I'd starve to death out of pure orneriness sooner than take their blood money. Anyway, the idea was to move into the Haight, so I could be as close to the scene as possible. I figured since Sharon lived there, she might know a place, or hear about one."

"And she did?"

"The whole top floor—six big old Victorian rooms—of her own big old Victorian house. She'd inherited the place from an aunt and hadn't done damn-all except clear out the rubbish. The house was built for some flour magnate's daughter, back in the 1860s—her family would have known the Lacings of the time, so that's either pleasing symmetry or creepy coincidence, depending on how you look at it. And Jack London wrote part of 'Call of the Wild' there, and Mark Twain stayed there a while, he worked on San Francisco newspapers, just like me, and Bret Harte lived there too—not all at the same time, of course."

"That should mean a lot to a writer."

"To live where Bret and Jack and Sam hung their hats and paced the floor and swore at the blank page just as I so often do myself, on my own of course far humbler level? I'll say! But Sharon was up-front honest; it did need a lot of work to make it livable, and she wasn't sure she was ready to take on a tenant. Still...six rooms, view of Golden Gate Park and the actual Golden Gate out the back, window-seated turrets, Buena Vista Park for a front yard? No-brainer."

"How'd you convince her?

Rennie grinned. "All at once, as if from a great distance, I heard myself saying I'm a very *quiet* person even though I hang out in rock clubs, or maybe *because* I hang out in rock clubs, and I'd never have big noisy parties because I don't have any friends to invite to them, and I hardly drink at all, only a bit of wine, and I only smoke a *little* grass every now and then, never *never* cigarettes, and I'm a very *clean* person, and I'd find a way to afford the rent if I had to deal pot or dance topless or moonlight as governess for Mr. Rochester."

"That would persuade *me*, all right," said Prax judiciously. "Though maybe not most landlords."

"Well, it persuaded her. She just laughed, and said she'd phone me in a couple of weeks one way or the other, and she did—cutting me a great deal on the rent if I fixed the place up a bit—and I moved out of Hell House and into the Haight."

"And the rest is history. Or soon will be." Prax leaned back and started another joint going, then uncovered a plate of sandwiches and opened another box of chocolate cookies. "Soooo—what do we want to talk about next?"

Much later that day, Rennie drove back across the bridge, brain buzzing from the pot, mind ringing from the talk, Donovan's crystalline "Tangerine Puppet" dancing on the radio, courtesy of the local free-form FM station—another new thing, freedom from Top-40 tyranny. And she went not home to the Haight but straight to the Clarion, to the little desk in a corner of an alcove that they'd given her almost as an afterthought.

Great day in the morning, I am going to DO this...okay, now, Ren-Ren, time to rockandroll...

And sitting down at her ancient stand-up Royal typewriter, she began to let the afternoon just past stream direct from her brain down through her fingers and onto the page. Mirroring karma, all the way, every single word.

Chapter Three

"WE JUST SIGNED ON with this new manager," said Prax to Rennie one day on the phone a month after their interview. She was trying to sound ever so blasé, but Rennie knew that inside she was jumping up and down and squealing like Piglet—'A manager, a *manager*, we have a freakin' MANAGER!'

"English guy," she continued. "Has a lovely accent. Well, they all do, don't they, even the bus drivers. Gives me such an inferiority complex. He's smart and he's educated, too. As a person, total sleazebucket. But he can make the record companies eat out of his slimy limey hand."

Rennie smiled into the phone. "Which is what you guys want. And need."

"Which of *course* is what we want. All the bands do. A *real* manager, not just some doped-up surfing buddy you drag in to help out. And, yeah, need too. Well, I say 'signed', it's really just an oral agreement. But it's all because of your story, Strider, I can't thank you enough...."

"You don't have to thank me at all. It worked out

pretty well for me too, you know. Of course, you realize how lucky you are to have such a magnificent writer and all-around splendid human being as your best friend..."

"Oh, I do, I do. In fact, I'll embroider it on a sampler and hang it above my piano. Or send it to your mother-in-law, just so she can see what she's missing. But, right, karma in action? Didn't I tell you that's how it works? That's why we're Karma Mirror. Anyway, his name is Jasper Goring—do you know him?"

"I know *of* him. Roaring Goring, the English bands call him. He's insidious, rude, nasty, obnoxious, British—you know, this just might work. I think his other big local band is Deadly Lampshade."

"Yes, he told me," said Prax, shyly thrilled at that 'other', though too embarrassed at her own vanity to let Rennie know. "He's a real agent-manager, did I say that? He's got his own management firm, with a bunch more clients mostly in L.A. and London and New York. But a few here too, like the Lamps and that gasbag Fortinbras De Angelis."

"What, that creepy ancient guy from the bikini hootenanny movies?"

"He just *looks* ancient—it's the scary hair and that truly frightening perpetual tan. He's really only thirty or so, he started singing professionally before his voice even broke. All those falsetto doo-wop ditties, back when we were grade-school milk monitors just beginning to hear about Elvis."

"Bo Diddley, actually. Though I do recall this dim but sweet girl, name of Maureen, thirteen years old and still in the fifth grade—where I was nine, just by way of comparison—telling our teacher that she planned on marrying Elvis 'Prestley', as she called him. Hey, thirteen years old, betcha El woulda gone for her, too. But Bo...I remember we had a little sock hop in the school cafeteria a year or two later, and I heard this amazing music, this beat that sounded like, well, you know what it sounded like. Anyway, I plucked up the nerve to ask this eighth-grade greaser girl named Vera-Ellen Rinaldi who *that* was. I'd never heard anything like it."

"Who had?"

"Right? And Vera-Ellen Rinaldi stood there in her skin-tight pink angora greaser sweater and her skin-tight kick-pleated greaser skirt and looked at me in my sweet little plaid dress and saddle shoes as if I was lower than a bug and said, 'Bo Diddley-o, kid!' I told Bo the story when I met him two weeks ago; he was thrilled, the dirty old man. Oh, and I was *hall* monitor, not milk monitor. I had supreme authority to enforce traffic rules, and I used my powers only on the side of Good. I even had a badge. I wore it on my Girl Scout uniform, which I wasn't supposed to do. But I loved it so."

"*You* were a *Girl Scout*?"

"I was only in it for that cool little knife they let you carry on your belt."

"Of course, silly me, why else... Listen, must split, we're all supposed to be working out parts and charts at that rehearsal house on Masonic. But meet me tonight at Morton's Fork for dinner? Bring Stephen, if you like. I'll buy."

"Stephen wouldn't enjoy himself; the Fork is too— unusual for him. But damn straight you're buying. You're the rock star here."

"Yes," said Prax, wonderingly, as if she'd only just realized it and was surprised and pleased. "Yes, by God, I am."

The story about Prax—warm, funny, sympathetic—had been, despite Rennie's fears and uncertainties, a resounding success. It did more for Karma Mirror than any number of little coffeehouse gigs, resulting in third- and second-on-the-bill bookings to major acts in the ballrooms, even a few top-lines in some of the hipper small clubs, and it did more for Rennie Stride than any number of little reviews, soon resulting in a promotion to minor features, and a better desk, and more interviews, and more significant ones. Burke, her editor, was well pleased with how she was coming along; from time to time he even told her so, and that was worth more than everything, more even than the occasional treasured words of praise from the great Garrett Larkin himself.

But most of all, the story made Prax and Rennie friends, or at least it set them on the road to friendship and gave them a big hard push. Rennie wasn't disposed to hurry it: she was too grateful that fate had found her someone to be her friend at all; and Prax also seemed content to let the friendship strike its own pace. So they hung out together, and with other hopefuls of their own age and sensibility; and Morton's Fork was one of the places they hung most.

It was a famous Sausalito institution: a huge old psychedelically painted wooden barge permanently tied up to the main pier, with add-ons and bump-outs and built-ins that always seemed ready to topple right into the bay, diners and all. The Fork served, if that was the word, food that was delicious out of all proportion to both its incredibly low cost and its haphazard arrival at table. Prax had introduced her to the place early on, and they both went there as often as they could.

Now Rennie sat there waiting for Prax, in a corner of the outside row of tables that overlooked the bay and the lighted city skyline beyond. *I'm a New York girl forever, but I must admit, this is mighty nice...*

"And I owe it all to Stephen," she confessed to Prax over dinner.

They'd chosen the restaurant partly because they liked it and partly because their friend Tansy Belladonna, née Concetta Annamaria Cavolina, newly arrived in San Francisco and even more newly self-rechristened, another struggling singer-songwriter like Prax, was doing a waitress turn there that week, and Rennie and Prax believed in supporting fellow artists. Though Tansy, one of life's originals, didn't make it easy: waiting tables was obviously not her destiny, and all whom she attended in that capacity wished devoutly that her rock dream would come true as soon as possible and take her far, far from the food service industry, forever and ever, amen.

She was indeed a friend of theirs, though not quite to the same depth or extent that Prax and Rennie were now friends. She lived in a riotous crash pad house over on Fell Street, full of musicians and anybody else who needed a place to get off the streets for a night, or a month—every time you walked past, you could hear the most incredible music floating out, little knots of people standing on the sidewalk, blissfully listening.

They'd met Tansy in some club, and she'd latched onto them in her vague, casual sort of manner—a drifty rock dandelion puff who nevertheless possessed the charged push of an oncoming storm front and the clinging power of a tidepool limpet. Weary sometimes of the push and cling, they occasionally wished she'd just drift away again, or at least find someone else to cling to.

But they felt sorry for her, and they really did love her and care about her even when she was exasperating them beyond belief. For all Tansy's annoying little ways, she never messed with their heads and she never brought them down. And for all their stone cool hippie-chickness, Prax and Rennie were kind and loyal and good-hearted, and they always left Tansy bigger tips than they could really afford, on the correct and sound principle that it really *does* come around and who knew what was ahead for any of them so they should take care of one another how and as and when they could.

Prax raised her brows. "Owe Stephen? You think? How do you figure? How does that make you feel?"

Rennie stabbed her fork into a huge shrimp dripping teriyaki sauce, bit it in half, spoke around the mouthful.

"Not sure. I guess some guilty, since he married me and brought me out here and all, and now I don't want to be married to him anymore."

"And yet you still are."

"Yeah, but that's only because there's no real reason to get divorced. Look at Grace Slick—she's been married to Jerry for years but that doesn't stop *her* from doing whatever, or whoever, she wants. Still, she uses his name, and I don't use Stephen's... But the way things are with us now, the Lacings don't get any more bent out of shape than they already are, or would be with a divorce. It doesn't matter to me, but if it makes life easier for Stephen then I'll do whatever I can. I don't accept their payoffs, not even hush money to keep me quiet about the bodies buried in the back garden—I'm kidding, at least I hope I'm kidding—so I don't feel obligated to tug my forelock. It's not as if I'm selling my soul for a mess of pottage."

"Or teriyaki." Prax focused on the middle distance and straightened a little in her seat, as if she'd seen someone approaching their table over Rennie's shoulder, which in fact she had. "I, ah, have a bit of a confession to make. I didn't want to tell you in case you begged off coming tonight, but someone's joining us."

"That's uncommon devious of you, Mary Praxedes. Who? When? And where?"

"Me," said a cultured British voice. "And here. Now."

Rennie looked up. Jasper Goring stood there, smiling like a shark. A shark with a carefully cut moptop hairstyle and an Oxbridge accent, a shark that did its clothes shopping on Carnaby Street: high-cut lapels and striped shirt, stovepipe pants, little Mod boots on little English feet.

Rennie regarded him with an expression of entirely suspended judgment. "And *why*?"

Jasper chuckled and sat down in the corner by the window. "Rennie, Rennie! So young, so new, already so suspicious... Why, to talk to you about Prax, of course, and perhaps a little about the Lamps. I promise it won't hurt. I hear *such* good things about you, Garrett Larkin really likes what you're doing, when I was talking to him just last week he said..."

"And that was how I—"

...discovered the Northwest Passage and the all-water route to the Far East. Invented chocolate, baseball and the Second Law of Thermodynamics. Found the Holy Grail. Lost the Ark of the Covenant...

Rennie pulled herself up with a sharp jerk on her mental reins. She could go on like that all night. It was more fun making stuff up than listening to Jasper's blimp-sized Best of Britain ego, claiming he'd sired all four Beatles. Or whatever the hell he was blithering on about; she'd tuned her brain radio over to white noise ten minutes ago.

With a start, she noticed they were both looking at her: Jasper narrowly, Prax all but rolling her eyes.

"I'm sorry, did I say that out loud?"

Prax kicked her, not gently, under the table. "Jas was wanting to know if you'd come to the Fillmore and write something to follow up on our interview, if he can talk Bill Graham into giving us the opening slot there the week after next for the Lampshade."

"Surely, sure-ly. I only have space for just a wee scrappet, though, not 'The Lord of the Rings'. I don't *get* much space, you know: I am but fourth in the Clarion's line of rock succession, not heir apparent to the Larkin throne."

"Well, not just *yet* you're not," said Jasper, doing his best Uriah Heep impersonation—the smarmy suck-up Dickens character, not the newly formed English band. "And a scrappet would be lovely. A crumb, a snip, a mere morsel— whatever you can do, I'm grateful. But speaking of Lampshade, don't you think Tam has the most incredible voice? That nice folky tenor, so amazing for a lead singer—"

Rennie smiled evilly. "Tommy Linetti, you mean, who presumes to call himself Tam Linn, presumptuously taking in vain the name of one of the best ballads that ever lived? But, yes, I do think so. Though I think Marty Balin's nice folky tenor is a hundred times better, and Marty may have founded the Airplane, but they're damn lucky to have him amongst them. Plus he writes great songs. And he's a total cutie. Let's hope they can hang onto him for years and years."

They shop-talked for another half-hour, over wine and dessert: about Prax and Karma Mirror, about Deadly Lampshade, about Jefferson Airplane and the Grateful Dead and Quicksilver Messenger Service and the Charlatans and the other Bay Area bands. And about Sunny Silver, a fiery chart-topping singer from Greenwich Village via London and Toronto; and Owen Danes, a New Yorker who led a just-out-of-the-box group down in L.A., Stoneburner; and Ned Raven, whose outfit Bluesnroyals was beginning to tear up England and give the Stones bad dreams; and another Britband as yet known only to the hippest American fans, a band called Lionheart, with an absolutely amazing lead guitarist who went by the unlikely name of Turk.

Plus other new groups and clubs and places to play. Jasper never once missed a chance to flatter Rennie, and Rennie never once let down her guard.

"Why were you so bitchy to him?" Prax demanded as soon as Jasper, bidding them goodnight at last, drew away out of earshot. "He's just trying to get some press for us and the Lamps."

"Well, you'll get press from me any time you need it and anyplace I can work it in, you know that—but because of *you*, not because of him, and I hope he knows that. I adore the Lamps, but Tam is such a little prick—"

"Actually—"

"Don't wanna know! But nobody likes him, not even

his own band."

Rennie was silent a moment, then erupted again. "And what the hell was Jasper thinking, trying to pimp that lame-o Fortinbras De Angelis off on me? As if I'd ever give him any more ink than a squid... Even dear Mr. Larkin can't stand him, and he's the nicest, most polite guy in the world. Garrett, not Fortinbras. Did you see him—Fortinbras, not Garrett—in the other rag"—by which Rennie meant the august San Francisco Chronicle, the Clarion's detested rival—"just last week, shooting his mouth off, all down on the scene? Bunch of pathetic druggies and sluts, he said. Unmusical illiterates dressed up like little kids freaking out in their mommies' ragbags, he said. Untrained voices that could curdle milk at a hundred yards and people playing their instruments with their elbows, he said."

Prax nodded. "I read it. Blew my mind. He said absolutely *horrible* stuff about the Dead and the Airplane and the Chrome Panther and Quicksilver and the Better Mousetrap, and that was just for starters. I tell you, I was glad our band is too insignificant to attract his attention. Nasty jealous spiteful little bastard. I wish somebody would curdle *him*. Permanently."

Their waitress friend—"Hi, I'm Tansy Belladonna, I'm your waitress tonight, want to hear my demo record?"—came over during a lull in the dining traffic and poured them both wine, though they had been refilling their own glasses all along, and they paused to chat.

Frankly, Rennie was more than a little surprised that Tansy hadn't been hovering round all night, seeing as an actual rock and roll manager had been sitting there both accessible and helpless.

But when taxed with it, Tansy unexpectedly, and charmingly, disarmed them both. "Well, you *know*, I didn't want to bogart Prax's time with Jasper, and something just as groovy is going to happen for me too, very soon now. The I

Ching and the fairyfolk and my dead Cherokee great-grandmother all *promised*, I know I can trust *them*—and once Mercury is out of retrograde and Jupiter goes direct again it should all be cool, don't you think?"

Rennie nodded noncommittally, taking care not to look at Prax or both of them would lose it; but for that staggeringly uncharacteristic, and rather sweet, discretion she resolved to leave Tansy an extra-large tip.

When Tansy was called away again by the demands, if that was the word, of her professional duties, Prax looked after her, shook her head, grinning, and returned to the topic.

"Yeah, but about Fortinbras...nobody wants to hear his kind of music anymore, and he can't make the kind of music they do want to hear. He's just scared."

"With good reason! Who wants to listen to him warbling teen-angel ballads when they can listen to Jerry Garcia or Sunny Silver? No wonder Jasper can't get him a contract. He's just jealous 'cause all you cool bands have record deals and he isn't."

Prax looked down and fiddled with her wineglass. "Well, *we* don't, you know. Have a record deal."

"Matter of time. Someone will snap you up, I promise, if I have to write something about you every single damn day until they get so screamingly bored of hearing about you that they sign you on just to buy my silence."

Prax smiled. "That would be nice."

Rennie smiled back, but she was also staring balefully after the long-vanished Jasper, as if he'd left some kind of visible fetid trace on the air, a psychic oil slick.

"I don't like that little ratbag, and I don't trust him either. He'd better not screw you over, Praxie, or I swear I'll cut him into little pieces and feed him to the geese."

Prax was laughing now, though she was also looking at Rennie admiringly, and perhaps a little nervously.

"And yet you still claim the Lacings haven't had any

influence on you whatsoever? Man! And people say *I'm* a scary white chick!"

But as she staggered back with Prax to the house on the hill, and flopped into the porch hammock she was crashing in that night because she was way too stoned to drive all the way from Sausalito home to the Haight, Rennie could not shake a feeling that had gripped her as she'd watched Jasper Goring walk away: the feeling that Prax had dealt herself in for more than she'd bargained for.

She gazed muzzily over the sparkling lights below in the town and reflecting dancing on the water, and, across the bay, the silent white and gold blaze like a billion candles that was San Francisco at night.

What was it they said about dining with the devil? Something about long-handled spoons. Yes, that was it. And they weren't talking about coke spoons, either.

Chapter Four

RENNIE INCHED THE CORVETTE along Central Avenue above Waller Street, looking for a parking place. When she found one around the corner on Buena Vista Avenue West, her very own block, almost in front of her very own building, she pulled in, then just sat looking at the place she had called home for the past six months. When she'd first heard about it, she hadn't thought it would be quite so—spectacular. Yet there it was, in all its glory.

As she'd mentioned to Prax, her sister Dana's old roommate Sharon Pollan owned the house, actually *owned* it: perhaps the finest Victorian dwelling on this very fine Victorian block, one of the steeper streets that even the citadel of steepness which is San Francisco can boast. Facing Buena Vista Park, two blocks from the heart of the Haight, the three-story-plus-high-basement Queen Anne house was one of those tall Easter-egg-colored minimansions charmingly called painted ladies, with all the Victorian bells and whistles: turrets and bays, carved caryatids, bow windows framed in fretted tracery like the stern cabin of a Spanish galleon. In short, the kind of massively enviable housing that Rennie and everybody else who ever set their ten little piggies down in San Francisco lusted madly for as soon as they laid eyes on.

Stephen was already there, a few places up on the park side of the street, sitting waiting for her in his banker-gray Mercedes, and now he got out and waved. She ran across to him and kissed him briefly, then, suddenly turned on, pulled his head back to hers for a longer one. He was looking particularly good today, in fact quite hunkish, in a charcoal wool Irish fisherman's sweater over a long-sleeved shirt, wheat cords; his brown hair, which had been creeping downward toward his collar of late, was rather sexily disheveled, in a totally manly way, and tortoiseshell reading glasses framing his blue-gray eyes completed the look.

The very picture of a young, handsome, successful corporate lawyer out on a sunny afternoon with his young, pretty, adoring wife, people would think to see them. Yes, and how very wrong they would be to think it...

"I can't believe this is the first time you've been here to see the apartment since it's been finished."

"Wasn't invited," Stephen pointed out mildly, as they went up the curving turret stairs to the top floor. "Once the painting was done with, you didn't want anyone coming over until you had all the furniture in. Anyway, it's your birthday today — you know I'd never miss that."

"So much of it's thanks to you anyway — the furniture, the wedding presents. I wanted you to see it all fixed up. And to give you something nice to eat. Oh, and supper too, of course."

"I left your birthday cake in the car," he said quickly, as they entered the apartment, pretending he hadn't heard, though he'd gone suspiciously pink around the ears under the newly lengthening hair, and Rennie grinned. She went into the kitchen to start on dinner, while Stephen peered out the downhill windows at the Haight spread out below and the green Panhandle beyond and Golden Gate Park itself stretching out to the west.

"This neighborhood's changed so much. I remember it used to be all Irish and German, then it was a student quarter for San Francisco State and USF."

"It still is. There's a lot of the old community left, they're outtasight, and students too. But new people now. People like me."

Rennie heard him pottering around, checking everything out. She was glad to see him so relaxed; they had had a strained final few months before she'd quit Hell House, and some rocky times immediately after. It was a lot easier now: from the minute the front door of the Lacing mansion had boomed shut behind her, Rennie'd felt as if she could breathe again.

She wasn't destitute; contrary to what Marjorie had hopefully predicted, she wouldn't starve shivering and homeless in the dark. She had a bit of money saved from jobs and gifts, and her rock-seamstress sideline helped cover the bare places; her parents had given her something when she left New York, and Stephen had cut her way more than her share — if not all, as she suspected — of the wedding cash. And then she'd gotten the Clarion job. So she was doing okay, more than well enough to buy food and drugs and books, and fabric to make clothes, and to pay the rent and light and phone bills. Music came free — the chief perk of being a rock writer. But there wasn't a whole lot left to spend on frivolous things like, oh, home furnishings.

"It all looks great, honey," Stephen called from the book room. It did, too: when she'd first moved in, sleeping on a mattress on the floor, Rennie had started by refinishing the oak window frames and cabinets; Sharon had hired professionals to sand and seal the beautiful old oak-plank floors, as her gift to her first tenant. After that, Rennie had rolled up her sleeves and relaid the original bathroom tiles and nailed up bookshelves and put window seats into all the windows.

Then she and her merry crew — people she'd met at the paper and in the music scene, happily working for a payoff of good pot, excellent beef stew, killer chocolate-chip cookies and hot sex (that last would be just Stephen, not the others — the floor mattress had gotten a number of workouts, maybe latex paint was an undiscovered aphrodisiac, or it could have just been how cute Rennie looked in cutoffs and paint smudges and a work shirt knotted up to show a bare midriff) — had painted the rooms Chinese red and forest green and old gold and eggplant purple.

Once the walls were dry, she had hung colorful, gorgeously lettered posters, so ornately calligraphed that you couldn't even *read* them unless you were stoned. Posters advertising the new bands playing all over the Bay Area — Grateful Dead, Big Brother and the Holding Company, Screaming Prawns, Country Joe and the Fish, Jefferson Airplane, Hovering Boudoir, Moby Grape, Theodolite, Deadly Lampshade, Quicksilver Messenger Service, even Prax's band Karma Mirror.

Stephen had contributed furniture liberated from the well-stuffed Lacing attics, but he'd been careful not to be over-generous and scare her or make her feel like a charity case, so most of Rennie's freshly acquired household goods came from lucky street finds or the second-hand shops in her new neighborhood. Now he was checking out the bedroom; good thing she'd tidied up and changed the sheets. A handsome old Salvation-Army-bought brass bed held pride of place, topped with a vintage fur bedspread she'd splurged on with the proceeds of a timely article, forty dollars, and the crocheted afghan throws she'd had in her college dorm room — affagans, as her Italian grandmother, who had made them, called them — lying across the foot.

Out in the living room, there was a perfectly

serviceable Victorian sofa that somebody around the corner had unbelievably tossed out, and two wicker peacock chairs from the Goodwill. She'd also found on the street a black Parsons table that worked great in the kitchen and a file cabinet she'd put in the guest room. Again in the living room, a pair of huge overstuffed expensive leather armchairs (a housewarming gift from Eric, and Rennie had burst into tears when he brought them over) flanked the original brown-tiled and marble-manteled fireplace, and her old college trunk with a piano shawl over it served as sideboard to hold the stereo. In the small dining room stood an antique cherrywood set, one of Stephen's guilt gifts, with the wedding-present silver and china and crystal sparkling in the hutch. The whole place was further spruced up by faux-Persian carpets and some second-hand stained-glass lamps and lots and lots of pillows.

Now Rennie, in the kitchen fixing dinner—her best quick menu, steak and mushrooms, hand-cut home fries, tomato salad—smiled to see him so comfortable. She'd finished everything up just in time. Only last night, she'd sat on the bare shining oak floor, in the moonless midnight ticking down to her twenty-second birthday, a glass of good wine in her hand and a lone slice of suicide-by-chocolate cake on a plate, a lighted white candle in a pottery cup in front of her next to a vase of purple lilacs and "Scheherazade" on the turntable, and looked around her with utter and complete satisfaction, not feeling sorry for herself one bit.

In these six chambers, she was not just home, she was *at* home: living room, bedroom, guest room-bookroom-writing room, dining room, windowed kitchen and tiled Victorian bath—it was all good, and if maybe it wasn't anything like what she had expected when she came west a year ago, it was hers and nobody else's, and that made every difference.

"Make a wish, Rennie," she'd whispered, to anyone or anything who might hear, and on the stroke of twelve from a nearby church bell tower had leaned forward to blow out the single candle. "Happy days."

So now her first official guest prowled around the high-ceilinged airy rooms, approving what she'd done, remarking on how well things went with other things, suggesting she move this here or that there, putting a stack of LPs on the turntable—Stones, Beatles, Lionheart, Dylan, Budgies; then, remembering, ran down to his car and came back with a huge cake box, courtesy of the Hell House cooks.

In the months since Rennie had fled Hell House, she and Stephen had evolved into a comfortable pattern, seeing each other a couple of times a week; in fact, they probably saw more of each other now that they no longer lived together than they had when they did. And got along far better, too. Usually he would take her out to dinner, or they'd stay in and she'd cook him one of the seven things she *could* cook: roast chicken, roast beef, roast duck, steak, spaghetti and meatballs and pork chops with sauce made from scratch from her Grandma Vinnie's recipe, beef stew, a whole stuffed roast turkey and fixings for really special.

Usually, too, they spent the night together; they were used to each other, and sex if not on the earth-moving level was at least a pleasant no-brainer. Though Rennie had in the course of her job met a couple of musicians she found herself speculatively eyeing, and though she knew Stephen's office had a new and gorgeously red-headed law assistant recently graduated from Stanford, neither of them had as yet acted on their theoretical sexual freedom. But that could change.

"Make a wish," she said later; dinner was long over and they'd moved on to the entertainment portion of the evening, which took place in the wide brass bed, with TV to follow. "I made a wish for me, now you make one for you. And because it's my birthday, yours will have to come true, too, 'cause I say so."

Shifting on the pillows, Stephen resettled her in his arms. Though he knew even as it came out of his mouth that he was making a mistake, before he could help himself he said, "I wish you would come back to me."

Now why didn't I see that coming? Or did I, and was I just asking for it?

"You told the wish," she said at last. "Now it won't come true."

She stirred next to him. If only he weren't so damn nice — but he was, and a lot more besides. Perversely, she was irritated.

"I do give you some credit, you know, Stephen. You did try sometimes to pull the family jackboot off your wife's throat, or at least ease the pressure. But not often enough, and maybe you never really wanted it off altogether — maybe you still think I should be obeying my wedded lord and master and toeing the clan line. But, birthday wish or no, we're not getting back together, and if you still think that, I suggest you get over it. Or if you can't, then please just keep it to yourself. I'm not coming back and I'm not going to be guilted into it."

Now that was manifestly unfair, and both of them knew it. He had never once pressured her, though every now and again she would catch him looking at her with a terrible patient longing. But neither had there been any talk of divorce, so perhaps on some level Stephen could be forgiven for continuing to hope. They never discussed it, nor could it be said they even thought much about it, but if they had, the thinking would have gone something like: Why bother rocking a boat that's already lying at the bottom of the sea? Neither of them had the tiniest wish to get married again any time soon, maybe not ever, and in the meantime at least it was good for sex and taxes.

But Stephen chose to keep his silence now, and Rennie felt like a bitch on wheels, as she always did when he outclassed her, and after a few tense moments she got up and went to the kitchen to clear away the dinner rubble. After a while he came to help, and by the time the dishes were dried and put away they'd worked their way back into a birthday mood.

After Stephen left the next afternoon—though not before Rennie had fixed a special penance-for-bitchery brunch of hash made with leftover steak and potatoes and topped with poached eggs, and had given him some equally special atonement sex and kissed him all the way down the turret stairs—she found a tiny exquisite watercolor sketch of the backyard lilac bushes on the inside window ledge where she was accustomed to find her mail, tied with a silver ribbon round its silver-painted wood frame.

Sharon's birthday present...how cool! Rennie took it inside, propped it up on the kitchen table to look at it with delight, then cut two big, thick slices of leftover buttercream-iced raspberry-jam-and-whipped-cream-filled chocolate-and-vanilla sponge birthday cake, wrapped them in napkins and went downstairs again to visit her landlady.

While she waited for Sharon to finish up with a therapy client—shrinkery never sleeps—she amused herself by remembering the first time they'd met in San Francisco. She'd only spoken to her that once on the phone, when Sharon had advised her to go to the Longshoremen's Hall and had thus started everything off, but Rennie recalled her from visits to the Strides' Riverdale house, when her sister Dana would bring out-of-town holiday orphans home from college for decent mom-cooked meals: a blurred recollection of someone short, brunette, wickedly funny.

That first time, Rennie'd come to Buena Vista to look at the flat, and the young woman who'd opened the oak and stained-glass-paneled door, though clearly Sharon, still short and just as funny, had been very different from the memories Rennie had of her. Her blond hair was down to her waist, she was wearing an old gold-braid-heavy drum major's jacket buttoned askew over a bare torso and flowing black-satin pleated palazzo pants, and intricate henna tattoos adorned her wrists and ankles and curled over her left shoulder from behind.

By vocation Sharon was a Jungian therapist, and as such had bags of good counsel in store, though after half an hour's talk that first day she had refused to take Rennie on as a client, saying dryly that in her professional judgment Rennie wasn't the Lacing who needed help. But that wasn't all she was. Having studied art at Finch, she'd put both talent and training to good use: she moonlighted as a portrait painter, much in demand by not only society matrons but the new nobility now on the rise—the personnel of rock bands, just coming into fame and money and success. Not rich-rich, not the way bands would be in the future; but well off enough to think a portrait affordable and aesthetic enough to think one desirable.

And she'd soon developed quite the reputation: so far she'd painted the descendants of any number of illustrious San Francisco families, as well as most of the Dead and Airplane, the prettier half of Quicksilver, several British music gods who'd come to town specifically to have Sharon commit them to canvas, acid king/sound genius/millionaire Augustus Owsley Stanley III, who'd insisted on being depicted as a Venetian doge in velvet robes, and why not, and even Dr. Timothy Leary, who'd forthrightly requested she paint him while tripping naked. The subject, not the painter. Well, as it turned out on further inquiry, the painter too. It had been an interesting experience, though perhaps not an artistic triumph, as Sharon, laughing, had recounted.

"I'm confused," she said now, coming in from the back parlor where the therapy happened and greeting the birthday girl with a hug and kiss, waving away Rennie's stammering thanks for the little painting. "I seem to recall you telling me you left your husband and moved out of his house. Now I know you live in *this* house, since I get rent checks from you, so you obviously moved, but who was that I saw going upstairs with you yesterday and coming downstairs with you half an hour ago? Sure looked like a husband, and he didn't look so left to me."

"The husband should never have been the husband in the first place—I should have just slept with him, not married him. So now that's what we do. He was just here to give me my birthday present, lookit!"

Rennie held out a wrist encircled by a delicate Art Deco white-gold bracelet set with pearls and small but excellent diamonds.

"Very nice. I'll keep any shrinkly observations on bracelets as symbolic shackles to myself, shall I? Yes, I believe I will... Oh, while we're discussing your marital kin, I keep forgetting: you know that mother-in-law of yours, emaciated blond she-weasel?"

"I do know her."

"She asked me to do a portrait of her. I turned her down flat. I've painted tons of San Francisco society bitches, as you know, but I didn't like her vibe. And not just in loyalty to you—that woman is toxic."

"You were very wise to decline; you'd have been picking her poison blowgun darts out of your ass for a week. Do you believe, she's still on my case about my job and why I'm not staying home spawning little Lacelets and going to Junior League teas and transforming myself into a carbon copy of her. Give it up, Motherdear!"

" 'Motherdear'," said Sharon, shaking her head but laughing. "Infreakingcredible."

While her hostess was making tea, Rennie wandered around as she always did, looking at all the beautiful things there were to look at. Sharon's triplex was as much an eye-opener as Sharon herself. She had decorated it in eclectic fashion, making herself a warm, comfortable, elegant refuge: a carved-oak partners' desk, a ruby-glass vase filled with white lilacs, a modern steel and velvet sofa, William Morris tapestries hanging above Swedish-modern rya rugs — everything chosen for harmony and counterpoint, and all ruled by a painter's masterly eye and sure taste. It was very different from Prax's funky place in Sausalito and from her own pad upstairs — more complexly elegant, more grownup. But it had the same feel: a sense of women doing what they wanted to do, in the way they wanted to do it.

The way I want to do it...the way I hope I can do it...

"Finch! That white-glove hellhole!"

They were out on the second-floor back porch that overlooked a small but beautifully jungly back garden; Rennie had given Sharon an account of her birthday celebration, and mentioned her earlier quick mental jaywalk down memory lane, and Sharon's hoot of laughter was probably heard across the bay in Oakland.

"The only, I say the *only*, decent things about it were that it was on the island of Manhattan and it had some decent art courses. And of course your darling sister Dana and our other classmate Grace."

"Grace?"

Sharon cut herself another chunk of birthday cake. "You never met her back in New York, I don't think. She didn't go in much for meeting people. Insecure, though you wouldn't say so to look at her; she covers up with sarcasm and a bit of an alcohol and drug problem, said the all-knowing therapist. Grace Wing."

"Chinese?"

"Norwegian. Originally Vinge, pronounced Veen-ya but Americanized to rhyme with 'stingy' — and actually *meaning* 'wing'. The family went for the straight translation, obviously. She was from Palo Alto, and she came right back here after we graduated. Nice family, strange girl. If you haven't met her yet, I'll introduce you."

"What does she do?"

"Oh, she modeled for a while right out of college, got married—like you, like me, though I got unmarried pretty quick and looks to me like you will too, in spite of agreeable birthday boffings. Grace gets around, as they say, but she's still married. Though not seriously, obviously. Her husband was literally the boy next door. I hear her brother-in-law has a crazy mad crush on her and they've indulged themselves in at least one bonk session that I know about, so that makes for a nice fraught family situation, especially considering the three of them have a rock band together. Very classical-Greek, don't you think, Orestes and Electra should be showing up any minute now...I could do a lot with them, professionally speaking. The Slicks, not the House of Atreus. Well, them too. If they'd only had therapists, the Trojan War might never have happened... But, like you, being a decorative society wife was definitely not what Grace had in mind. I'm surprised you haven't run into her so far, you writing about music and all."

The niggling association that had been politely tapping on Rennie's memory lobe finally hauled off and used its fist.

"Wait a minute, you can't mean *Grace Slick*? She went to school with you two? Dana never said... I mean, I've seen her with her band. Darby and Jerry's band. The Great Society. I've even written about her. Never met her, though."

"I thought I mentioned her, when I sent you to that thing last fall? Huh. Must have been too stoned. Listen, why don't we go down to the Fillmore tonight? The Great Society's on the bill. You can meet her. You're a rock writer for a newspaper, she'll be thrilled. Come down early and we'll go out to eat; I'll buy you a birthday dinner."

The show was amazing, but being introduced by Sharon to her former Finch classmate, backstage after the show, was even more so. Rennie was conscious of a penetrating, smileless though amused regard from huge violet eyes under smooth, deep, coal-colored bangs; clever — some might have said snotty, Rennie would have too but she was very much enjoying it — conversation in a Northern California drawl; an honest-sounding invitation to come back anytime. She was surprised by the smallness and thinness, how a voice like that could come out of a frame that looked as if there wasn't room enough for lungs at all.

"Oh yes," Rennie breathed fervently to herself, feeling like Scarlett O'Hara saying she'd never be hungry again. "You just *bet* I'll come back...because, I swear to God, I'm here to stay."

Then, a week later, as Jasper Goring had promised, Prax McKenna and Karma Mirror went to play the Fillmore, third on the bill to the headlining Deadly Lampshade and a founding bluesman by the name of B. B. King in the pocket slot, which meant the Karms would be the opening act, first to take the stage. And Prax had been over the moon about it.

And that afternoon was when Tam Linn, né Tommy Linetti, was found in a deserted Fillmore dressing room, stuffing his drummer's trunk.

Chapter Five

"I KEEP TELLING YOU," said Prax wearily, on the point of either tears or tantrum or possibly both, "I went to scrounge some guitar strings from him, 'cause I broke two of mine at the sound check and then I broke the spares too. I was nervous and I overtuned, and there wasn't time to go out and buy more. Tam plays the same kind of guitar I do, I figured he'd have some extra ones I could borrow. I wasn't going to *steal* them. I would have given them back, or paid for them. It's the first time I ever played here, I didn't know who to ask or where to go. I didn't even see him at first."

"Who *did* you see?" asked the detective. "Backstage?"

"Just people. Nobody who stood out. There's always a lot of people backstage before a show. The Fillmore stage crew. The cats who do the lights and the light show. Roadies for the bands, mine included. Plus friends of the bands, you know. Groupies and people just here to — wish us well."

"People with drugs?"

"Maybe. Probably. Bill Graham doesn't like drugs himself, but he doesn't stop musicians from doing them backstage. Or even onstage. Or the audience either. But you can't bust him for that—"

"Miss McKenna," her inquisitor said, not unkindly, but making damn sure she heard the exasperation in his tone, "I assure you we have bigger things to think about tonight than a few pothead musicians toking up. So when did you first see him, then? The victim."

Prax hesitated, and the official police pen abruptly stopped scribbling. *'The victim'...he means Tam...how very strange...*

"Not him himself. I saw the—blood," she said reluctantly. "It had trickled out of the road case, you could see it on the floor."

"Out of the what?"

"The road case, the anvil case—the big trunk that you put things in to take on the road. Amps and drums and stuff. Anyway, I thought it couldn't possibly be what I thought it was, what it looked like. When I went to check, just to be sure, I saw that the trunk lid wasn't latched and when I touched it it swung open, like a book, and he just—fell out. Well, his right arm did. Not the rest of him. He was in there pretty tight."

"He'd been stuffed in the trunk?"

"You know he was, it's—he's—just like he is over there."

Prax didn't look, but jerked her chin Tam-wards, over to where the double-sided case, big enough to take a full-grown man if he was well folded up, stood with rubber-gloved police technicians surrounding it. Thank God its open side faced away from her.

"He was sitting there in the case, his knees right up to his chin. He was wearing that fringed jacket he always wore on stage, and his face was turned away from me. But I knew it was him. I could tell by the hair. I couldn't see where the blood was coming from, except that the side of the jacket was all wet and dark. So I screamed for help."

"What time was this?"

"I don't know, I don't wear a watch. Maybe six? We had come early for the sound check. B.B. and the Lamps had to do theirs too, and we wanted to get it over with and then go out for something to eat, not have to rush. But Bill Graham doesn't let bands leave once they're here, so we ate first and then came over."

"And you were alone in the dressing room?"

"Yes. Well, except for him. Tam. Dead Tam."

"When was the last time you saw him alive, then?"

Prax unfocused her gaze, trying to remember. "I guess—when we all got here. He was just sitting, watching the house crew and his own roadies unloading Deadly Lampshade's equipment."

"He wasn't unloading equipment himself?"

She snorted with laughter before she could help herself. "*Tam*? He never lifts a finger. He doesn't bother with checks; he even has other people tune his guitar for him. What sort of musician is that?"

"I'm sure I don't know," said the detective cheerfully, and Prax felt a little better. *Maybe this won't be so bad, it's almost over, how many more questions can he ask...*

"How many crew were around, Miss McKenna, and how many band members?"

"Well, my band has two roadies, Tank and Idaho, and a sound guy, Ziggy, but we all help with the equipment; there are five musicians, counting me. Six in the Lampshade, plus three roadies, a sound guy and a light guy; and I think B.B. King has eight cats in his group. He used the Fillmore crew to set up, he didn't have any roadies that I noticed, though I'm sure he does."

"So you and the other band, the Lampshade, you have your own help and you didn't use the house crew at all."

"No, no, the Fillmore crew is great, they do most of the

work. I just meant that with the house crew around, our guys didn't have to bust their hump like they usually do."

"And they all were where?"

"Onstage. Setting up. Like I said. When I came backstage to ask Tam for the guitar strings, I didn't see anybody."

"But you had seen him earlier. Not just sitting lazily onstage. Here?"

Prax's voice had gone wary and reluctant. " — Yes."

"Well, what? Did you have a fight with him?"

"Not exactly."

"Miss McKenna — "

"Oh, okay, you're going to find out anyway... He tried to hit on me."

"You mean he made a pass at you. A physical pass?"

"It wasn't the first time." Despairingly: "And since someone's bound to tell you about it sooner or later, I might as well tell you myself. Yes, we did have a, a *thing* once, Tam and me. It didn't go anywhere, a couple of weeks was all. But that doesn't give him the right to feel me up every chance he gets."

"It certainly doesn't. What did you do?"

"Same thing I always do when he tries that crap with me. Told him to go screw himself."

"And something else?"

" — I slapped his face. Really hard. But that's all. I *swear*. It was only because he was, you know, groping me — *seriously* groping me, please don't make me get into anatomical specifics — and he wouldn't stop until I hit him."

"What did he do when you hit him?"

"Rubbed his cheek and laughed. Then he left the room. I didn't see him again until — "

"That's fine, take your time." The voice was professionally neutral, and Prax shivered. "When you came back later looking for the guitar strings, and you saw him, if you didn't touch him how did you know he was dead?"

"Well, there was all the *blood*, wasn't there? Kind of a tip-off? And he wasn't moving or anything, and I thought that if he was actually *alive* he probably wouldn't have let anybody stuff him in there like that."

The unspoken "You fucking moron" hung between them in the breeze, and the detective, no doubt hearing it telepathically, looked all at once a bit more human.

"No. Of course not. I'm sorry to make you go through this."

"Am I a suspect?" asked Prax after a pause.

"Everyone who was in the Fillmore tonight will be questioned, Miss McKenna. And probably plenty more who weren't."

"Should I call my manager? Or a lawyer?"

"If you want to. Nothing stopping."

"Do I *need* a lawyer?"

"You tell me."

As the discoverer of the body, Prax was being dealt with much like Columbus when he came back to Spain full of big fat whoppers about a whole New World: people weren't exactly disbelieving her, but neither were they buying her story entirely. Or maybe that was just how it seemed to her. Other cops were talking now to the rest of Karma Mirror and to B. B. and his musicians and to the Lampshade and the Fillmore crew, but no one was saying very much, and they all looked every bit as freaked out as she felt. And anyway, nobody else had been around when she walked in and found Tam dead, so she was on her own.

The detective saw Bill Graham enter the room, and excused himself to go question him. Or, more likely, be screamed at by him. Prax found to her chagrin that she was on the verge of tears again, and couldn't decide, to her shame, whether she wanted the detective to see this and feel sorry for her, or whether she'd rather he didn't see it and think how cool she was. Either way, she was still alone, and she didn't know where she stood or what to do or whom to trust.

Maybe I should call Rennie, she's the only person I know who might be able to help. Jasper wasn't home or at the office, no one even knows I'm in trouble...would they let me make one more phone call, since I couldn't reach Jas? Or is that one-call deal only if you've been busted? Which I don't think I have yet? Or have I?

The moment was interrupted by forensic technicians getting down to work, by morgue attendants coming in to remove Tam and the road case together, and then, like some kind of miracle, by a hippie dea ex machina: Rennie entering in a great swift rush of air and energy, her red snakeskin coat flying behind her like a Valkyrie's cloak, intent only on getting to Prax. Before her approach, people leaped aside in terror; in her wake, Stephen came bobbing helplessly, a dinghy behind a destroyer.

"Not another word, Praxie, here's your lawyer, shut up at once, do you hear me?"

"He had such a great voice," Prax heard herself saying somewhere far away, into one of those sudden silences, and everyone within earshot turned to stare at her, so out of it had she sounded. And looked: all glazed and dazed.

"Yeah, well, the first time I ever met him he was being a total jackass," said Rennie brutally, hoping to shock Prax back to normal, heedless of scandalized looks from the eavesdroppers clearly thinking Who *is* this chick, hasn't she ever heard of speaking no ill of the dead?

Apparently Rennie had not, or if she had, she didn't particularly care. "It was a photo shoot for the Clarion—Garrett Larkin had written the story himself. Tam couldn't be bothered fixing his own goddamn hair. *Good* hair, I must say. Thick and straight. Like goat hair. He just tossed his head, flicked me a leather headband like I was Mammy dressing Scarlett for the barbecue, and said, 'Do it for me, babe.' "

"What did you do?" asked Prax, diverted; she had had such a rush of relief and gratitude at seeing Rennie that for the moment she'd forgotten what was going on around her.

"What I *should* have done was loop the thing around his throat and strangle him right there... Just kidding, officers! No, I took that headband and tied it so tight I hope he got a migraine. Anyway, I think he dyes the lovely mane. Dyed it. Died it. Oh, dear."

"I've been doing that myself. That detective hasn't helped— What? No, the kinda cute one over there arguing with Bill. I think they think I did it. But I only found him, you know."

"I do know. It's going to be fine."

Prax belatedly noticed the other person standing patiently behind Rennie. "Stephen! What are you doing here? Well, what are *both* of you doing here? I was going to call you, Rennie, I couldn't get hold of Jasper, but I just—I didn't—"

"It's okay," said Rennie, with a swift glance at Stephen. "It's okay. I was coming anyway, to do that little piece Jasper asked for, remember? But Stephen phoned to say you were in trouble, and we both came straight here. I drove, he cabbed. We just met up outside."

"Then, thank you, Stephen—but how did you know?"

Stephen smiled at her—encouragingly, he hoped. He liked Prax, a lot, but she scared him even more than Rennie now did.

"I got a call from—oh, there he is. "

Rennie followed his eyeline. "Him? That's the detective who's been hassling Prax. I'd call him the pig detective if I were a Berkeley girl. Which, thank you God and Cornell and Columbia, I am not... *He* called you?"

Across the room, the detective's eyes widened and warmed as he noticed them; he left Bill Graham, with whom he had been talking, or rather, by whom he had been being profanely shouted at, and came over to them at once.

"Marcus! Glad to see you!"

They *know* each other? Rennie stared as the two shared

a manly bear hug. The detective stood about Stephen's height, just shy of six feet, with a great build and gray eyes and caramel-colored hair, on the longish side for a cop, sort of 1964 Beatles. He was even cuter than Stephen, and he looked vaguely familiar.

"Hi there, cousin. And of course you're Rennie."

Cousin? COUSIN?

"Of course, if you say so—and you are...?" asked Rennie politely, if a touch tartly.

My cousin-in-law, I presume...

"Marcus Dorner. Detective Inspector Marcus Lacing Dorner, SFPD," he added, in case she hadn't yet gotten it.

"Marcus is my second cousin on my father's side," said Stephen. "I didn't get a chance to tell you before you hung up and ran out of the house. He called me because he knew I knew Prax."

Marcus nodded, smiling. "And I also knew, because everybody in the family does, that cousin Stephen's wife is the Rennie Stride who writes for the Clarion. We've met before, at one or two family events, but you won't remember. I've read your stuff."

"Thank you, glad you like it."

"I only said I *read* it," said Marcus, amused. "But yes, I do like what I've read, very much. You've got a nice sharp style."

"And speaking of sharp—"

"Right, right. So it was you who found the body, Prax?" asked Stephen.

But Marcus intervened, all cop again. "Are you really acting as her lawyer, Stephen? I'll have to ask you all to come down to the Hall of Justice, then. Just to talk."

"Prax?" asked Stephen, looking with concern at her bent blond head. "Do you want me to—I'm a corporate lawyer, I don't have much experience in this sort of thing, but just for now—"

"That's right, just for now," snapped Rennie. "Now is all we need. All right, then, let's split."

But as it promised turned out, Prax could leave after all, as long as she to show up the next day for fingerprinting and further questioning, and to sign her statement. Bill Graham had canceled the evening's show — though not without further profane and heated protest, and nobody *ever* got more heated or more profane than Bill Graham, especially with cops in his face. But Marcus had been firmer than Bill was furious, and besides, he was the law — so there was no reason for anyone to stick around.

Rennie wouldn't allow Prax to drive back to Sausalito in her shell-shocked state, but took her home to Buena Vista to crash in the guest room's old maple bed, and Stephen followed them, happily driving Prax's Morgan. After Prax had dropped half a Valium and was tucked up under Rennie's grandma's affagans, Rennie sat with Stephen in her own bedroom down the hall, curled up on the bed, quietly talking.

Stephen cast about for a safe subject, settled for the safest one he could think of.

"Prax seems to be holding up well — how's she doing otherwise?"

"Oh, I think, okay? Yes, okay. Well, you saw."

"And how are *you* doing?"

Rennie shook herself mentally; she was more rattled than she had cared to admit. Rough tough journalist chick goes all sissy at the sight of a dead body…well, in fairness, it was the first one she'd ever seen, let alone the first murdered one, and also someone she knew.

"Oh, I'm okay too. But about Praxie, I know she's pleased with Jasper, he's Karma Mirror's new manager — and I wonder where the hell *he* was tonight, he's the Lampshade's manager too, he really should have been there… She's been seeing that Mill Valley guitarmaker guy I told you about, and she met a chick last week at the Anarchists' Bookshop, they were supposed to go out tonight after the show. Does that bother you?" she added, as she saw his face change just a little, then change back again.

"Me? Why should it bother me? I have a gay brother, remember?" As Rennie lifted inquiring eyebrows: "All right, then, it's just that I've wondered, once in a while, sometimes, if —"

"If Prax and I are — ?"

"Well. Yes. Are you?"

Rennie laughed. "Sorry to disappoint you! No, not in the least. We're friends. That's all. Or were you hoping that's the *real* reason I didn't want to go on being your wife? Maybe I just haven't met Miss Right yet," she added wickedly. "No... Anyway, Prax likes boys mostly. And I like boys only. Which is neither here nor there."

"Of course. Sorry. Would you like me to stay with you tonight?" he asked after a while, carefully. It always seemed to be an emotional minefield around her these days, he never knew how she'd respond to anything—and all he really wanted was to be with her and them both to be happy. Was that too much to ask? Apparently so, at least most of the time... "I'd be happy to sleep over. Just sleep. So you won't be alone. Or would you rather be?"

"Actually, I think I'd like the company," said Rennie slowly. "I think I'd like it a lot."

Stephen saw that she was trembling. He held out his arms, and she crept into them, and they sat like that on the bed until she fell asleep.

Chapter Six

NEXT DAY STEPHEN LEFT EARLY for his offices at LacingCo International, downtown in the financial district— feeling much better and very grateful, Prax had driven herself off to the Hall of Justice after breakfast, and then home to Sausalito—and later rescued Rennie, in a depressed and clingy state, from the Clarion, whisking her out to his car and carrying her off. They drove around for hours, aimlessly, through Pacific Heights and the Marina and the Mission and North Beach and all the other old San Francisco neighborhoods, then up Twin Peaks and down again, heading west past Golden Gate Park, through the Avenues and out to the ocean, along the Great Highway and over the bridge into Marin, beyond Muir Woods to the empty expanses of Stinson Beach. Where they sat companionably, mostly silent, staring out at the cold gray waves.

Heading back to town, Rennie remembered the first time they'd driven around like this. It had been the afternoon of the day she'd arrived in San Francisco, all girded up to face her new life. Her mother-in-law had knocked the sword out of her hand in five minutes; hence her shaken state. But Stephen had swept her off then as he did now.

On the way back, he had turned aside unexpectedly just before the bridge, driving up the hill and parking in one of the little scenic lay-bys, where he'd made her close her eyes, then led her out of the car, turned her around and told her to look.

"Oh my God, it isn't TRUE!"

She was looking at San Francisco at sunset: the rose and gold and amethyst light flooding in from over her shoulder and falling on the white city—the majestic hills and towering clouds behind, the great bridge flaming above steel-colored water, a sense of unseen oceanic immensity away to westward and the weight of equally endless land to the east. One of the most beautiful things she had ever seen in her life, or ever would... Stephen had put his arms around her from behind, and she'd raised a hand to touch his face and had softly said no more than 'Thank you.'

"Thank you," she said now, smiling faintly, never taking her eyes off the view, as they sat parked in the same lay-by. But today it was foggy and spring-drizzly, and the city was ghost ruins seen intermittently through the flying wisps of mist, so they stayed in the warm dry car.

On the radio, the Kinks were singing over a terrific backbeat about how you and me we're free, we do as we please, yeah, from maw-ning till the end of the day. Yeah, if only, Britboys. Rennie reached over and turned it off. A little too apposite, as rock and roll so often had a habit of being.

Stephen shifted behind the wheel. "Thank me for what?"

"For everything." She leaned over against him. "Remember when we came up here, that first day? Remember what you said?"

" 'It's early days'," he said, quoting himself, " 'and everything's new. Once you get used to it, it'll be so good. I love you, you know.' "

"And I said, 'I do know'. And I do, and I remember. But it isn't what we thought it was, or would be. *We're* not."

"No... But apart from that, why are you so upset?"

Rennie moved away a little. "Don't know. I'm just — weirded out. I think, I say I think, it's something about Tam's murder."

"Of course it is. Why *wouldn't* you be upset? Someone you know, however casually, killed in this horrible awful way, your best friend finds the body — that's enough to put anybody off."

"No, I don't know, it seems like something more."

He turned to look at her. "Oh, surely you don't think Prax — "

"Oh, God, no! No, I don't think that for a second. But I have a strange feeling, like it's not over, the other shoe hasn't dropped, the feeling you get before a thunderstorm hits. All edgy and — bad."

After a silence, Stephen glanced at her again. "So I'm thinking this would probably not be the best time to talk about us?"

Rennie laughed, a little ruefully. "I'm not sure there'll ever be a better. Or a worse. What did you want to talk about? You know I'm not coming back. I told you that on our anniversary in February, and also on my birthday. I know it's not what you want to hear. But I mean it."

"So you keep saying."

Snappishness suddenly flared up like a smoldering bonfire. "And yet you keep on not believing me when I say it, how insulting is that — as if I don't really mean what I say, or know what I want. It's not that I don't love you. I do. But I've never been *in* love with you. I thought I was, but I wasn't. And I'm not. And that might be good enough for most people, but I'm sorry, it's not good enough for me. And it's not good enough for you either. You deserve so much better."

"Why don't you let me be the judge of that?"

"Because you're too good and you put up with too much. You should be with someone who completely adores you, Stephen, you are so worth being adored. There's nobody else, I promise. I'm not even *looking* for anybody else. Except for me. I'm looking for me. And I'm not going to find her with you. I should never have married you; more to the point, you should never have married me."

"I love you," he said simply. "I wanted to be married to you. That seemed like reason enough. I still want that." Long, long silence. When it didn't appear as if Rennie was ever going to speak again, he asked gently, "Are you okay?"

"No," said Rennie after another long pause, and the city had vanished in the mists again before she spoke. "No, I'm not okay. I'm not okay at all. But I will be. I have to."

When she'd complained of how weirded out she felt, Rennie hadn't just been speaking of the immediate personal effect of the murder. The screaming headlines, with their smug declarations of something rotten in the land of peace&love, were pretty hard to take for pretty much everyone in the hippie and music scenes, especially for a community that so prided itself on caring and nonviolence. And for an artist, especially, to be murdered in such a particularly brutal way, in one of the shrines of the music that was the engine driving the movement—well, that was almost beyond comprehension.

In the line of duty, Rennie went out into her homeplace neighborhood, into the head shops and the bookstores and the little boutiques, the bakeries and the butcher shops and the greengrocers, the benevolent storefronts of helpful organizations like the Diggers and the psychedelic anarchist lairs, asking around, testing the collective psychic temperature. Nobody was at flashpoint over the media sneers and jeers; that wasn't how it was done. But running through the community was a brass thread of shock and fear, metallic, so sharp she could taste it, like blood in her mouth.

Of course, some people were only too happy to capitalize on the bad feeling, even stir it up worse. That faded Philly doo-wopper, Fortinbras De Angelis, was all over the papers and TV and radio shows, leading the brigade of easy deriders taking shots at the hippie community for Tam's murder. Oh, it's not all flowers in your long unwashed hair, is it, he jeered; it's just surface stuff, that peace and love crap — it's all about drugs and money when you get right down, just like it is for everybody else. Even though as yet there was not the slightest evidence that drugs or money had played any part at all.

But then — and this was what had fired Rennie up to fury — Fortinbras started personally slagging Prax, dropping nasty innuendoes, making her out to be the prime suspect and guilty as sin on one hand, and maybe innocent but not above using this as publicity to further her career on the other.

Rennie wasn't able to do much to refute him, at least not in the Clarion. But the underground papers she also wrote for allowed her freer rein and greater latitude, the freer and greater the better, in fact, and she nailed him to the wall every chance she got, like some mangy varmint a farmer had caught raiding the hen-house and had staked out as an example to any other varmints that might be thinking of following his lead. Burke remonstrated mildly and, if truth be told, amusedly, but he had no control over how she felt or how she expressed herself in her other publications — not when other rock writers were expressing themselves in Garrett Larkin's new magazine Spare Chaynge to much the same effect — so there were no repercussions.

Or so she thought.

"Why the hell is he doing this to me?"

Prax scowled angrily at her manager, and slammed the

offending newspaper to the floor. She had dutifully gone down to the Hall of Justice to get fingerprinted and give a further statement to Marcus Dorner, and had reported to Rennie that he had been polite, respectful and even gentle in his questioning.

But that was not the case all around the town. There had been yet another rock-phobic piece in yet another San Francisco paper, in which yet again Fortinbras De Angelis had trashed Prax McKenna, and Prax had summoned Jasper Goring to her house to demand an explanation.

"You may be his manager, Jas, but you're my manager too, and I swear if you don't shut him up, or at least get us together to talk face to face — we'll end up either kissing each other or killing each other but at least we'll have gotten everything out in the open — I'm walking out on our agreement and taking the rest of the band with me. I'm fed up with this. And since a verbal contract isn't worth the paper it's written on..."

Jasper Goring sighed. "Technically it is, Prax darling, but I know what you mean, and I understand, I truly do. And you are right, you are so very right. Fort is *hugely* out of line, but —"

"But nothing." That was Rennie, from her observation post in the hammock on Prax's porch, where they all were sitting in the Sausalito sunset, watching the lights blink on over in Tiburon and Belvedere. "He has no business saying stuff like that about Prax. And Tam was your client too. So, Jasper, you make him stop. Right now."

"Strider, light of my life, I would be pleased to obey. But it isn't all that simple."

"Then *make* it simple." Rennie sat up and swung her feet to the floor, fixing Jasper with a cold stare. "Talk to him, tell him it's bad form to bad-mouth a fellow client. Maybe he won't stop for Prax's sake, or for the truth's sake or the community's sake, but he might stop for his own self-interested sake. I don't have a lot of power at my paper, but I work for people who do. People who control what gets written about whom. And who better to shove that in Fort's face than his own damn manager? And *don't* call me Strider," she added, slinging herself back into the hammock. "Very few people are allowed to call me that, and you are not one of them."

"As you wish, Rennie, of course. As to the rest, you do make valid points, both of you. No promises, mind. But maybe I can come up with something."

The something Jasper Goring came up with a few days later was a peace dinner: just him and Prax and Fortinbras, all together to work things out, one big happy Jasper artistic family.

"I suggested they all come over to my place," said Prax to Rennie when they ran into each other in the Matrix, where Rennie had come to check out Tansy Belladonna's new act. Tansy was thrilled to bits to see them both, and had burbled away brook-like for twenty minutes before she'd had to go backstage and get ready for the gig.

The Matrix was the hottest rock music club in San Francisco, though it was true that once groups had made it even a little bit big in the ballroom scene they didn't often come back. It had been purpose-built out of an old pizza parlor by Marty Balin, founder of Jefferson Airplane, pounding nails and painting walls with the help of his bandmate Paul Kantner, to serve as a Haight homebase for the band. The Airplane had made their debut on the Matrix stage last September, but they didn't turn up there themselves much anymore, now that they were beginning to pop.

The club wasn't much: a cramped cupboard that could hold maybe sixty people if they were well stuffed in, never paid more than a hundred bucks a night, the sound loft right above the toilets. Even so, among new and aspiring Bay Area music outfits, it was considered quite the score to get a chance to play here.

How much more so to be opening, as Tansy was, for the Airplane itself, who were playing one of their infrequent gigs here tonight—they were already proving to be Rennie's absolute favorite group, both musically and personally. Plus it meant that Tansy's waitressing days might soon be coming to an end, and Rennie and Prax were happy to do whatever they could to speed that happy event, if only to spare the San Francisco dining public from Tansy's further attentions.

"What did they say?"

Prax shrugged. "Too far. Precious Foot-in-ass won't drive to Marin. Six goddamn miles to Sausalito! I *ask* you! Maybe it's true what they say about vampires and running water. Or is that leeches? Anyway, he wants to have it here in town, the lazy pig, somewhere private and central, so Jasper thought maybe a hotel room, where if people hear us screaming it won't be such a big deal."

"No, no, that's stupid, not to mention non-conducive to what you want to accomplish—hotels have such a downer vibe. Listen, why don't you borrow my place for the evening, have them over to dinner?"

Prax stared at her. "Are you serious? Oh Rennie, that would be *perfect...*"

"Not at all. Hey, I'll even cook. Then I'll get the heck out and you can have your little lovefest. But no throwing things. I like all my stuff too much."

"Yeah, but making you cook and then turfing you out of your own house, that's not very nice."

"Well, I'll join you for dinner first. Otherwise, not a problem. Jasper just signed a new L.A. band, the Honest Mollusk, can that be possible, yes I suppose it can, and he suggested that I should go and catch their second set some night at—continuing the weirdly zoological motif—the Silver Lizard. I can go to the club, come back and kick Fort and

Jasper out—if you haven't already killed them both, that is—
and you can crash in the guest room if you don't feel like
driving home."

After Prax had thanked her several times more, and a
suitable menu had been hammered out, she shyly gave her
friend the big news she'd been saving.

"Did I tell you Jasper says I should consider leaving
Karma Mirror and cast my musical fate in with Deadly
Lampshade, as their new lead vocalist to replace Tam? He
said he'd suggested it to the Lamps, and they'd already been
considering it. Seriously. So, do *you* think that's a good idea?"

"No, I think that's a *great* idea. And not leaving all the
Karms, necessarily. You could take the best ones with you.
Dainis—the Lamps would sound great with a full-time
keyboardist. Bardo, of course: they should have gotten rid of
that squeaky cokehead bass player Neil Marten a long time
ago. And Bardo's way better. But clever old Jas, I'm very
impressed. You're a contralto—nice alto and tenor range,
some soprano notes—anything Tam could hit, you can, and
more. They wouldn't have to rework charts too much, just up
the keys a bit on a few songs. The Lamps are loud, but you've
got the sound production to carry over them. More than Tam
did."

Prax nodded eagerly. "And that Juha Vasso, what a
lead guitarist, right up there with Jorma and Jerry—he's got
exactly the right chops for my new stuff, can't wait to start
writing with him..." Her face clouded. "Oh, for what? I'll
probably be on Alcatraz by then."

"They don't put people on Alcatraz anymore I don't
think."

"San Quentin, then. That'll save time, isn't the gas
chamber right there?"

Rennie looked at her aghast. "That is *not* going to
happen, do you hear me? Marcus doesn't think you did it.
Nobody thinks you did it. You haven't been arrested or

anything, just questioned like everybody else who was there. Heck, they even dragged Bill Graham in, and I could believe *he* murdered Tam a lot easier than I could believe you did. In fact, now that I think of it—no, of course he didn't... But just because you happened to discover the body doesn't mean anything—you'll see, they'll find out who really killed Mrs. Linetti's incredibly annoying little boy, and then you will be back to being glorious again in the sight of all, without a stain on your character."

A gleam of amusement had crept over Prax's face. "At least not *that* stain."

The night of the peace dinner arrived. In honor of Jasper's Britness Rennie had cooked a lovely rare roast beef; Prax had done the veggies and brought flowers and dessert. Everything was perfect: Wedgwood dinner service on placemats of old tea-dyed lace, softly gleaming sterling, sparkling Waterford glasses—all of it wedding loot that Stephen had pressed on Rennie when she moved out. She still couldn't figure out if it was a consolation prize, a ransom payment or a bribe.

But wedlock had had its uses. "The *only* reason to get married, in my opinion," Rennie was saying to Prax as they finished setting the dining room table, "is to score china, crystal and silver for eight. Or maybe twelve. I'm talking breakfast *and* dinner china here—two different patterns, of course, as my dear Great-aunt Lillie taught me, and one may certainly use the breakfast dishes and dinner flatware to serve luncheon if one does not possess luncheon-size place settings, though it is considered a bit barbaric in some circles. And perhaps some small useful household appliances. Apart from that, no good reason to get married, no reason at all."

"And you could buy all that for yourself, even, if you really wanted it."

"Well, sure. But it's always nice to get given stuff."

When the guests arrived promptly at eight, as

expected, they were the perfect picture of affability. Rennie, prepared to hate and loathe on sight, found herself charmed by Fortinbras De Angelis ("Call me Tony, it's my real name, or Fort, whichever you like"), which she had *not* been expecting, and she could see that Prax too was disarmed. And he looked so much younger, which he really was, and the hair wasn't nearly as scary as it looked in his photographs, though the tan was quite a bit more so. But he flattered and flirted, and they all laughed, and Fort was full of bad little stories of his days as a young doo-wopper in Philadelphia and New Jersey, hanging out with Frankie Avalon and Fabian and Dick Clark, and Jasper too was on his best British behavior.

They were both voluble in their praise of Rennie's apartment: such groovy furniture! What beautiful woodwork! And the *view*! As if she'd somehow been responsible for that too, like a set dresser on a really big scale... Rennie thought of inviting Sharon up to join them, but recalled that her landlady was in Portland visiting her parents. So it was just them for dinner in an otherwise empty house.

And the dinner was a merry one. Everybody had seconds of everything, and Jasper had turned up bearing four bottles of a very nice Bordeaux. For about the twentieth time he apologized to Prax that he hadn't been at the Fillmore to help her and the Lamps the night of the murders, that he'd had a pressing family emergency, and Prax seemed happy to accept the excuse, Rennie not so much.

After dessert and a few joints and a glass or five of wine, Rennie took her departure, cautioning everyone to play nice in the sandbox while she was gone, no throwing toys or pulling hair. Jasper thanked her fulsomely for going to see his new group, and hoped she would enjoy them and write nice things about them, promising that they would talk if they happened to still be there when she returned, and that he and Fort would do all the washing-up and tidying.

"With our very own lilywhites, dear Rennie, so that

when you come home you don't have to lift one delicate digit to an instant's toil."

"Oh, you boys would do anything to get me out of here tonight, wouldn't you? What are you planning?" she said with a grin, opening the door to leave. She was unprepared for the look of sudden terror that flashed across Fortinbras's face. "Fort, I was kidding…"

His countenance had reset itself almost at once, and he laughed richly and professionally, the laugh of the born TV-show host.

" 'Course you were, babe. 'Course you were."

When Rennie had gone, Prax suggested they sit in the living room, where they could relax and talk with more ease. She was beginning to hope that something good could come of this. Fort wasn't nearly as much of a pig as she had thought, though there still remained that troublesome matter of the things he'd said about her and the music and the scene. But she was confident that if anyone could sort this out, Jasper could. He'd been such a good manager so far, and she was so grateful: he'd gotten Karma Mirror bookings they could never have gotten on their own, exposure to new audiences. In spite of what she'd threatened, she didn't want to leave him, and she desperately wanted him to hook her and Bardo and Dainis up with the Lampshades. Yes, this evening's good vibe could be a good thing for all of them.

And that vibe had been all-pervasive, so much so that when Rennie, in a good mood from a surprisingly pleasant performance by the Honest Mollusk, returned home to a candlelight-dim apartment at about two in the morning, and found Jasper and Fortinbras lying sprawled on the living room floor, she just grinned. If they were crashed there stoned, the evening must have gone with total grooviness. As for that wet dark stain on the carpet, well, spilled Bordeaux was a waste, but she needed to get the carpets cleaned anyway so no problem.

It was only when she noticed that the Scottish broadsword she'd found in a secondhand shop only last week, the one she'd thought would look really cool on the wall over the fireplace, was lying on the sofa, the same wet dark stain smeared all down its gleaming blade, that she turned on the ceiling light and stepped closer to see.

And wished to hell she hadn't.

Chapter Seven

EVEN RENNIE COULDN'T MANAGE to put a good brave face on this one.

The police had been duly summoned, and this time they had taken Prax away with them, in no uncertain terms. Rennie stood in the turret window, watching them go. *Well, at least they didn't handcuff her...*

But though they had been polite they had also been pretty darn emphatic that they would prefer to question Miss McKenna extensively, privately and well away from the murder scene. Nobody mentioned Tam, and how Prax had been around for that one as well, but then again nobody had to.

Rennie's first terrified reaction had been not police but Prax. She had gone tearing through the apartment to find her passed out on top of the guestroom bed, and had shaken her awake, with equal parts panic and relief.

"Prax, Praxie, oh Christ, thank God you're okay, what happened?"

Prax had looked up at her with dazed luminous eyes,

and Rennie saw that her pupils were so dilated that the blue-green irises were almost black.

What the hell is she on? They were all straight – well, except for the wine and a few joints – when I left the house...

They had gone back to the living room, Prax surprisingly unsteady on her feet for someone who'd only had some wine and a few joints, and no, it hadn't been just some horrible bad trip: there they were, Jasper and Fortinbras, strewn all over the floor like the end of "Hamlet." Prax had collapsed in a chair, Rennie'd phoned the police, and they'd shown up fast. No one she knew; she'd been half-hoping for Marcus Dorner. But they had instantly separated her and Prax like sheepdogs working a flock: Rennie was questioned in her own bedroom, Prax in the guestroom, while other cops worked to secure the living room, dining room and kitchen as crime scenes.

Prax gave her statement in a small, clear voice. Yes, they had been smoking pot—well she could hardly deny it, could she, with roaches and clips and spilled stash all over the coffee table. But she was vehement that that was *all*, just pot, nothing stronger. Anyway, she had gone into the bathroom to take some aspirin, a preventive measure for the grass-and-wine hangover she already felt revving its engines, and she didn't remember a thing after she had tipped out the aspirin tablets into her hand.

Which meant she had no idea how she'd ended up passed out on the guestroom bed, she had no idea who could have killed Fort and Jasper, she had no idea how long it had been before Rennie came home. Actually, when she was in the bathroom, she said, she'd thought the guys were leaving: Jasper had said something earlier about splitting, and she distinctly recalled hearing the door open and close. Then nothing, not until Rennie had shaken her awake and led her out to the living room to see the two bodies on the blood-sodden carpet.

After giving her own account, which wasn't much since she hadn't been there for the operative moments, Rennie had sat huddled in a corner of her bedroom as far out of sightline of the living room as she could get. Running through her head on an endless tape loop were her off-hand words to Prax, when she'd made the offer of the apartment for the peace dinner: "I can go to the club, come back and kick Fort and Jasper out—if you haven't already killed them both, that is." But she'd been *kidding*. And she certainly wasn't about to mention that little jest to the fuzz. Prax probably didn't even remember that Rennie'd said it, given that she couldn't remember anything else.

As soon as they had recovered from the initial shock and the cops were on the way over, Rennie had of course called Stephen, and he of course came straight there, arriving just as Prax was leaving with the police. The bodies remained where they were lying, so he couldn't avoid seeing them as he came in, and though he'd known what he'd see there, he looked even more shocked to see it than Rennie had. But he hadn't come alone: thinking ahead, the way he'd been trained, he'd brought with him King Bryant, not a Lacing family counselor but a Lacing family friend, a defense attorney well known in California and even national trial circles, impeccably clad for court even at four in the morning.

"King Bryant?" she said aside to Stephen. "You're joking, surely? It sounds like a big fat old-time cigar-smoking Louisiana redneck politician."

"For God's sake, don't tell *him* that!"

But Rennie did anyway, and was rewarded with a kissed hand and a roar of laughter. Kingston Bryant was a tall, distinguished man of seventy, with white hair and a neat white beard; being introduced to him, Rennie was reminded of a suave frontier lawyer, come west from Boston or Baltimore or New York to ply his trade, with plenty of Eastern Seaboard airs and graces to make it go down smoothly but

also with all the tricks of a gypsy horse coper at his disposal —
or, failing that, a gunman's cold-eyed stare.

And, no doubt, an aim to match...

"I've been hearing all sorts of things about *you*, young
madam," he said, still smiling, still holding her hand. "Pretty
little troublemaker from New York, not wanting to stay
married to a nice boy like our Stephen. Well, we'll just have to
see about that."

And Rennie was too numb and sad, too beaten down
and blasted by events, too dumbly grateful for his presence, to
take the offense she would normally have taken.

They sat in Rennie's bedroom, as the one place in the
apartment least involved and thus the least likely to contain
clues they could mess up, while the body positions were
outlined in tape, and then at last Jasper and Fortinbras were
loaded onto stretchers to be removed to the morgue. The
forensics team had already begun its work, and the sword
and the wine bottles and the remnants of dinner and even the
contents of the kitchen trash can and bathroom wastebasket
were being carefully packed to be carted away to the lab.
Rennie and Stephen would have to be fingerprinted, for
purposes of elimination — Prax being already on file — and
anyone else who'd been in the apartment recently would also
have to get done.

Rennie stared down at her hands, still unable to get
behind all this, to believe it was really happening, and
Stephen put a tentative arm around her shoulders, relieved
when it wasn't shrugged off.

Legal representation was a given. "King will be your
lawyer if you need one," he said, in a tone that brooked no
objection, and he got none. "And if it's Prax who needs one
instead, or in addition, then he'll be *her* lawyer, and she's not
to worry about the legal bills, either. I'll take care of it."

"You don't have to do that for me," said Rennie almost
inaudibly.

"Don't I? Well then, let's just say I have to do it for *me*."

By the time Marcus showed up, like someone in a Brecht play, Rennie and Stephen and King had been allowed to relocate to the kitchen. As Marcus sat down across from her, Rennie could tell by his expression how very serious the situation was, and she implored him tragically and mutely.

"Oh, God, don't look at me like that, Rennie. We had no choice. She was present at two murder scenes, we had to bring her in."

"You can't question her without her lawyer there, Stephen, tell him they can't ask her anything until King is with her..."

"It's okay," he said soothingly. "Marcus and his little friends know how it's done. Don't you, cuz?"

Marcus gave him a level look. "Yes, we do. Don't worry, Rennie, she'll be fine."

"Was it really necessary, to drag her away like that?"

"It's procedure. It's murder. There were drugs."

"Are you charging Mrs. Lacing, Inspector Dorner?" That was the deep, urbane voice of Kingston Bryant, and Marcus looked over at him with a singular lack of enthusiasm. "Though, as you know her, are indeed even related to her by marriage, should this really be your case at all?"

"Oh, hello, King, did Stephen rope you in on this one? Well, since you ask, I reported the relationship to my superiors, and they don't have an immediate problem with it as long as other detectives"—he waved a hand at his two companions, who had come up behind him—"are around for the major moments. They felt that as I had been at the Fillmore murder scene, I should continue with—well, anyway. Detective Wilmot, Detective Hasegawa," he added by way of introduction, and everyone politely nodded at everyone else. "And yes, we can certainly charge Rennie with possession, if nothing worse."

"Prove it's her marijuana," King Bryant said at once. "Her fingerprints on it? No? Well, then."

Marcus looked annoyed. "This *is* her apartment? Yes? Well, then. But a bit of grass should be the least of anyone's worries right now."

"Including yours?" Rennie asked.

He sighed. "Including ours... Rennie, I know you laid it all out for the uniforms, but, please, if you could go over it again for us? If that's all right with you, of course, counselor?"

King Bryant grinned and gave a shrug, most of which was in his remarkable eyebrows rather than his shoulders. So Rennie recounted it all once more: the peace dinner, how it had come about in the first place, her leaving to cover the club date, her arrival home to a quiet apartment lighted by a single candle and blood on the floor and bodies everywhere.

Marcus and the two other detectives had pulled kitchen chairs around and were taking furious notes.

"And the sword hung where, Mrs. Lacing?" asked Hasegawa.

Rennie waved vaguely at the living-room fireplace visible through the kitchen archway, glad they were far enough away that she couldn't see the horrific spatter pattern of blood droplets on the walls and furniture and the huge wet splotch on the carpet.

In the movies it looks so clean and neat when you kill people with swords, who knew it would be so — messy...

"Over the mantel. I just bought it last week, I thought it would look nice there. I *like* swords," she added into the silence, suddenly defensive. "Why shouldn't I have one if I want? There's nothing wrong with that. I just never thought about it slitting someone's — you know, throat."

"It wasn't a question of slitting their throats," said Marcus, running a hand through his hair. "According to the medics, they were practically decapitated..." He saw Rennie flinch, and was instantly sorry. "You bought the sword last week, you say? Where?"

"Some little antique shop—Page Street? Fell? I could find it again. What difference does it make where I bought it? Oh, wait, I know, it's just routine."

"And so it is. You didn't sharpen it?"

"No. In fact, the shop owner warned me it was really sharp, and I was going to take it to the hardware store and have it dulled. A little, anyway. I thought a sort of sharp sword might be a useful thing to have arou—" She broke off, then continued with visible firmness. "To have around in case I ever needed to defend myself. Against burglars or—something."

After a moment, Stephen asked, "Is there much more of this, Marcus? She's exhausted."

Rennie looked up, bristling at his tone, which had only been one of protective concern, and said a bit more sharply than she had meant to, "I'm fine. I was tired before, but I'm better now. Marcus, what happens next?"

"The apartment will be sealed, and you'll have to move out for a couple of days while the forensic team is working," he said apologetically. "Don't worry, the place will be totally safe. Oh, and I'll send someone to talk to your landlady—Sharon, is it?—when she comes back from Portland, let her know what's going on, why her lovely old house is full of cops. We'll need her prints, anyway. And didn't you say Eric had been here? His as well. In the meantime, you could stay in a hotel, or with friends."

"She'll come home with me," said Stephen coldly. "We have plenty of room, as you know."

"I'll go back to *your* home with you," replied Rennie, more coldly still. "*This* is my home, as *you* know."

Or at least you damn well should know, by this late date...

But Stephen was quite right: it was coming up on noon and she'd been up for thirty hours straight, and she wouldn't admit it but she was overtired and on the verge of tears and worried sick about Prax. But she was grateful both for the legal muscle and for Stephen's arm around her, and didn't want to shake either off.

"Rennie. *Dear.*" Marjorie Lacing, resplendent in a lace-trimmed silk dressing gown, offered a frigid cheek to be kissed.

Holy Mother of God, am I to be spared NOTHING? Rennie duly complied, brushing her lips over the apparently enameled surface. *Man, the Khumbu Icefall in December is warmer than that...you'd need an ice axe and a team of Sherpas to crack through...*

"How completely distressing for you, dear, I won't even insist you join me here for lunch, though of course I'd love company. Stephen darling, take her straight upstairs. You were so right to call ahead and let me know you were bringing her home. Make sure she gets some sleep. Take those cashmere blankets out of the chest for her, they'll be nice and comforting, and I'll send Lucy up with a tray in case she'd like something to eat. Toast and tea and an omelet, perhaps. No, I'll speak to Cook, something really nice."

Hey! Standing right here, *you know...* Rennie shook her head, half-laughing, half-appalled, as she went upstairs with Stephen, her suitcase borne before them by one of the house servants like the Ark of the Covenant before the Hebrew hosts. Things sure didn't change much at Hell House, did they...

The police had let her pack some clothes and whatever else she needed. King Bryant had parted company with them long ago, heading down to the Hall of Justice to attend Prax for questioning; they would hear later how that had gone.

"Nothing like being talked about in the third person...hello, I *am* in the room! But she never thought I was there even when I was here. By the way, where am I sleeping? I've always fancied kipping in the Chinese suite. Cashmere blankets sound good too, I could sleep for a week."

He glanced at her, astonished. "Where are you sleeping? You're sleeping with me, of course. In our rooms." As Rennie stopped dead on the curving staircase, balking like a wary little goat: "Look, just come with me for now, we can sort it out later."

She resumed trudging upwards. "Oh, I do so think this is such a very, very bad idea."

"We slept together three nights ago!" he said in an undertone. "What's the damn difference?"

Pas devant les domestiques...but there isn't anything goes on around this house that the domestiques haven't heard first...

"Yes, we did sleep together that night, you are so right, and two nights before that and a week before that, and a fine time was had by all," agreed Rennie in a much louder voice.

Stephen sighed. "Then why is it all of a sudden such a problem?"

"Uh, because it's *here*? Anything that happens in Hell House, oops, sorry, that just slipped out, is ten times more fraught with significance in your mother's eyes than everything that happens anywhere else. If we sleep together here, she'll think we're back together. And we're not."

They had reached the familiar doors of their formerly shared apartments, where Stephen had dwelled in lonely splendor since Rennie's departure. Stephen nodded to the impassive houseman, who was doing a great imitation of a block of wood with no ears.

"Mrs. Stephen will be staying with me, Carlos," he said, and Carlos murmured "Very good, sir," and opened the doors and took Rennie's bag inside. She followed, looking around. It was still the same exquisite suite she had first lived in: Chippendale splendor in the sitting room, silk-draped half-tester bed in the bedroom, bow-windowed dining alcove with its eastward view over the gardens, table set for lunch.

'Mrs. Stephen'...I never even got my own damn name in

this dump... And suddenly Rennie was swamped with memories that came in like a tide in the Bay of Fundy, so hard and high and fast that her knees almost gave way. *There were good times, just the two of us, even wonderful times — but there weren't that many, and what there had been hadn't been nearly enough, or the right kind. At least not here...*

She glanced over at Stephen and saw him looking at her with all his dear honest soul in his eyes, and she wanted to weep. What was her problem? Ninety-nine women out of a hundred would kill to be in her funky little backwards-facing witch-heeled hippie shoes. A year and a half ago, *she* would have killed to be in her shoes, to be lucky enough to marry this handsome, charming, kind guy who absolutely adored her, whom no woman in her right mind would kick out of bed even though he wasn't the most passionate or inventive lover in the world, through whom she was so rich as to never have to work again for several lifetimes.

Sure, he had a pill of a mother and a martinet of a father, but they wouldn't live forever, and then, apart from Eric's share of control and co-rulership, and the payoffs to the sisters and their spouses, the empire would all be Stephen's and hers: the houses, the businesses, the vineyards, the estates, the ranches, the planes, the yachts, the whole perfect global realm of unmitigated perfect Lacingness. All belonging to them and their perfect Lacing children, which of course she as perfect Lacing wife and mother would perfectly produce for her perfect Lacing husband in their perfect Lacing marriage and send off to perfect boarding schools and prep schools and colleges: two boys and two girls — tall Robert, brilliant Sara, dear little twins Edmund and Emma.

What was so wrong with that incredibly enviable picture? Marriage and kids: it was only what she had grown up vaguely expecting would be hers, some distant day in the future, what others expected of her and for her and had at every step urged her to choose. She liked kids, certainly wanted to have her own eventually: it was what most women on the planet did, and she had it better than pretty much all of them. Yet Rennie had chosen to fight it: society, his family and hers, her youthful expectations—she had made other choices, her own choices, and she asked no more than to be able to keep on making them. Okay, some of them had been wrong. But they were still hers. Why did everybody keep wanting to chain her, limit her, hold her back—Stephen included?

All she had to do to make their lives that pinnacle of unexamined perfection was to do what she had already done: say yes to a very nice man. What the hell was the matter with her? But the answer came at once, and as he looked at her Stephen saw that answer come, and knew in that instant that he had lost her: other women might kill to be in her shoes, but she would not kill herself, her self, to be in her shoes. And he saw too that she had never really been his to lose. Only hers.

Prax phoned Rennie at Hell House on leaving the Hall of Justice later that afternoon. She sounded surprisingly cheerful, and Rennie woke up from an unrefreshing nap to talk to her and devour lunch at the same time. On arrival, she'd dropped two Valiums, and though they'd had no effect at first, by now she was feeling as if someone had clobbered her with a telephone pole, or at least with a telephone.

"Talk to me. How'd you know I was here? What happened? How did it go?"

"My, so many questions, you must be a reporter or something... Well, for starters, Mr. Bryant told me you were at Stephen's, that the fuzz had turfed you out while they did their thing. I didn't mean to wake you, but I wanted to let you know how it went. You can come and stay here with me in Sausalito if you'd rather."

"Oh, thanks for the offer, but I'm settled in. It's just for a few days. Until the cops are done and the place is cleaned up. And Stephen has been great. Totally brickish, as—"

She caught her breath, heard Prax's sudden stillness through the phone. *As Jasper used to say...* But neither of them addressed it, and after a moment Rennie soldiered on.

"Well, even Hell House is survivable short-term. At least the food is good—seafood crêpes for lunch, I'm scarfing them even as we speak, hope you don't mind—and I don't have to pick up after myself. Though I do have to endure Motherdear's little anvils dropping clangingly on my head, like the gentle goddamn rain that falleth from heaven: 'Rennie dear, you and Stephen! So lovely to see you back together at home again, so contented. Can we expect some happy news anytime soon?' Even the General is making occasional harrumphing paterfamilias-type noises, concerned for the future of his DNA. See, I *knew* that would happen if I stayed here. Just because we're sleeping together..."

"The fiends! Still, they can't make you drop a blue-eyed heir for them if you don't want to. But what about work?"

"Burke and Garrett told me to take some time off. In fact, they ordered me to, and I obey. But don't sidetrack me like that, what about *you*? Was it all right? We haven't heard from King yet. At least *I* haven't, but I've been asleep."

"I think, yes, I do think it went okay. King was *amazing*—I can't thank Stephen enough, for getting him to help me."

"Write a song for him. For Stephen, I mean. He'd think that was so cool."

"There's a thought... Anyway, the cops took me down to the Hall of Justice, and went over the time frame, when everything had happened, as best I could remember—what I heard and saw, what we did after you left for the club, what we talked about. You know, I really wine think Jas or Fort slipped some kind of downer in my, because I was stoned, but I wasn't *that* stoned, and I honestly don't remember any more than what I said up front, what I told you."

"Oh, Praxie, are you *sure?*"

"I'm sure for now, and that's the best I can say. Maybe something will pop up later. In the meantime, I'm going to go take a nice hot bath and do some yoga and listen to some music and smoke about ten joints and try not to—oh God, Strider, I'm so, *so* sorry this had to happen in your pad. If I'd made them come to Sausalito, the way I wanted in the first place—"

"Not to worry. I'm just glad that you're all right. If it's not too crass to say so at this time, we'll find you another manager. Dare I say it, a better manager. You'll be fine. Trouble done with."

Wrong again. Soooo very, very wrong. Trouble just beginning. Trouble not even begun.

"What is it, Lucy?"

"Oh, Mrs. Stephen, Mr. Marcus is here, and he says he needs to speak with you and Mr. Stephen right away. You're to come down to join them in the blue drawing room, please."

It was three days after the murders. Rennie had been reading, curled up in a chair by the sitting-room window, when Lucy, the head upstairs housemaid, came in to make her announcement. Now, telling Lucy to tell them she would be down directly, she dashed into the bedroom to change her hiphugger elephant bells and poor-boy top for a respectable Mary Quant dotted-swiss minidress she found hanging at the back of the closet.

Oh, that's where that dress got to, I guess I left a few things here, Stephen really should have brought them over, and I can't deal with it now but what does it mean that he didn't? Or is he into cross-dressing now? Must remember to ask him later...

Buttoning the dress, she slipped her bare feet into red suede clogs and clattered downstairs to the drawing room. Stephen was already there, sitting on a chintz-covered sofa by the white marble fireplace in front of which Oscar Wilde had once so amusingly held forth. He was talking quietly to Marcus, but when she entered, they both rose to their feet at once. She smiled a little nervously and gestured them to sit, herself taking the seat beside Stephen, facing Marcus, who sat on a matching sofa with the light-blue-silk-draped windows behind him, and blindly reaching for her husband's hand.

Oh God oh God oh God what could have happened that he has to come here to tell us in person? This is going to be so very very bad oh no oh please oh pleeeease...

"Marcus?"

He looked straight at her. "Prax McKenna has been arrested for double murder one. She was picked up this morning, and she's being held over for arraignment tomorrow. If she's denied release on bail, she'll be remanded right there. Taken directly to jail," he added, in case Rennie had missed it.

Rennie felt as if she had taken a step that wasn't there, a momentary dizzying whiteness blanking out her vision. Then:

"Are you people out of your *minds*? What did *you* have to do with this?"

"Me? Nothing. I wasn't even a participant. But they wouldn't have arrested her if they didn't feel they had a case."

"Oh please, *what* case? The pathetic excuse that she was in my apartment that night? So was I, you know. Are you going to slap the cuffs on me too? Maybe I killed them before I left the house, and drugged Prax to frame her for the job."

"Did you?"

"Are all cops as sarcasm-impaired as you are? Jesus Christ on a tricycle! No, of course I didn't, and neither did she."

Marcus gazed, as if for divine aid, at the marble sculpture of Apollo that stood upon the mantel.

"Well, though I shouldn't be telling you this, the lab reports say that the last wine bottle was loaded with barbiturates, injected through the cork and seal so the bottle appeared unopened—liquid Valium, they think—and her fingerprints were on the glasses, the bottle and the sword. And there was pot all over the place."

"I bet my prints were there as well. Seeing as they're, you know, *my* wineglasses and *my* sword and *I* put the wine in the fridge to chill. And the pot was mine too."

"Yes. We know."

But Rennie was undeterred. "You guys also know that Jasper brought the wine, and I daresay Prax poured it out herself once or twice. So she'd have to have, you know, touched it. If it was liquid Valium, that crap's a well-known amnesiac, so anyone who drank up would fade out and wouldn't remember anything. Hey, no surprise there, boys in blue, Prax doesn't! And in case you haven't heard, there's no such thing as reefer madness. Grass doesn't make you kill people. You'd be giggling too hard to swing a sword. Anyway," she added venomously, "shouldn't you be off the case? Because you *know* me?"

Rennie's voice had gotten progressively shriller and sharper. Marcus let it pass, and Rennie seeing sympathy on his face was flooded with fresh terror.

Oh God he wouldn't be looking at me like that if...

Marcus rose to leave, and, again, Stephen with him; manners, manners. "As I said, I told them all about it; several times, too. They don't seem to have the same problem with it that you do. But I just thought you might like to know about Prax, and to be there for the arraignment tomorrow morning."

He paused in the doorway. "Oh, and one more thing, a friendly reminder from your devoted copper-in-law: count yourself goddamn lucky you weren't busted for possession, Rennie Lacing. The Chrome Panther and some of Quicksilver and a bunch of other rockers were hauled in last night on considerably less than what you had lying around. Try to be more careful from now on, will you? Stephen, see if you can beat some sense into her. Use the whip if you have to."

In the stunned moment following his departure, like the silent aftermath of a monster earthquake that had leveled many structures, dust rising and random bricks still falling, Rennie and Stephen thoughtfully avoided looking at each other: Rennie because she didn't want him to see what was in her eyes, Stephen because he already knew and didn't want to see it.

"Well," said Rennie after a while, "we'll just *see* who uses the whip, shall we? Yes. I believe we shall."

Not to mention seeing who has the sense... But Stephen had the very great sense not to say that aloud.

Chapter Eight

IN THE CAR ON THE WAY DOWNTOWN to the Hall of Justice next morning, after an early and silent breakfast, Rennie fidgeted endlessly with the long fringe on her suede bag, knotting, plaiting, unplaiting. Stopping for a light, Stephen reached over and gently stilled her fingers from their nervous plucking, and she shot him a grateful glance. She'd had a restless, mostly sleepless, night, and he'd been awake right along with her.

"I know, I know," she said, and let one hand rest briefly on his. "But I'm just so scared for her." She gave the fringe a final irritated scruffle and punched the bag once and was still. "Why does it have to be so goddamn early in the morning? I only acknowledge one eight o'clock a day and this isn't it."

"You can have a nap when we get h—back from court. It shouldn't take too long, these things never do."

"Yes, well, that's *your* story."

Both of them were well aware she hadn't solicited reassurance that it would be all right, that Prax would soon be out on bail: Rennie hadn't wanted to ask, and Stephen didn't want to answer.

The light changed, and Stephen eased the gray Mercedes into the choked and snarling traffic on Van Ness.

"What does Prax remember? I know you told me, but tell me again. Maybe we missed something, something we could tell King to try to use."

Rennie, who'd been fidgeting with the fringe again, now began nervously crimping pieces of her lap-length hair instead.

"She doesn't remember anything new. We went over and over it. But, okay: I went out to the club. They all sat around the living room with joints and the last two bottles of wine, only two 'cause we drank two at dinner, and maybe somebody dropped a pill on her, but she can't say for sure. If the wine was doctored the way the cops claim, she didn't notice. Unless it was done before they got to my place, but all four bottles were sealed when Jasper put them in the kitchen. I saw them. And Jasper wouldn't spike something he was going to be drinking himself. Besides, Prax says she didn't taste anything odd in the wine."

"What does she say the mood was? The whole idea was to make nice, wasn't it? Fortinbras was supposed to apologize for slamming her in print?"

"That was the idea. They had a good talk, and peace seemed to reign at last in the Vale of Song. Fortinbras admitted he'd shot off his big fat Philly boy mouth and talked out of his ass, and he promised Jasper and Prax he'd make it all right. Prax graciously accepted his apology. Of course, we have only her word for this."

"I'd take Prax's word."

She flashed him a grateful smile. "Anyway, then they all drank some more wine and rolled some more joints. She went into the bathroom to get some Excedrin, because wine and pot always give her a splitting headache unless she takes two Excedrins first, and that's the last thing she remembers."

"And —?"

"Hasn't the faintest idea how she ended up in the guest room. She didn't even know Jasper and Fort were still in the apartment until I woke her up and showed her. Because she says she heard them leave."

"Leave."

"She swears she heard the door open and close, and assumed they had split, though she was surprised they didn't bother to say goodbye. Then since she could still hear someone in the living room, she thought maybe one of them had just gone down to his car to get something. And that's where she blacked out. She says," added Rennie, reluctantly if scrupulously.

"Someone else came in and killed them?"

"You *think*? No sign of forced entry. No other fingerprints. The only prints were theirs — the three of them. And presumably the cops found mine, yours, Eric's and Sharon's. I haven't had any other company.."

Stephen stared straight ahead at the rear end of the car in front, spoke to the question she would never have asked him.

"I'm having our money man Brooks from the office meet us there, to make any necessary arrangements for bail. King should be with her by now. Don't worry about it. And Prax is not to worry about it either."

"I don't want to be beholden to your parents for anything."

"You're not beholden to them. You're not beholden to me, either. It's our money. Yours and mine. Even if you refuse to touch it. It's still yours. Legally. Always has been. What better to spend some of it on than helping your best friend?"

Rennie sighed. "Thank you, anyway." She paused for a deep breath, then hurried on before she lost her nerve. "I hate to sound so — so *calculating*, but... If there are strings attached — well, I understand quid pro quo. Reciprocity, if you want to call it a nicer name. And that's fine, really it is. Whatever you want. We go on as we are, and I'll sleep with you whenever you want me and I'll join you for major Lacing occasions. If that's being your whore, I don't care. Won't be the first time in your family, I hear. But if you're doing this to get me to be your wife again, it's not going to happen. I won't move back to Hell House and I won't stop writing. That's too high a price. Even to help Prax."

He stepped viciously on the accelerator as the traffic melted away ahead of them, and the car surged powerfully forward.

"Who said anything about strings? And you are *not* a whore. It's not about that. It's not to get you back." Though he knew it absolutely was, and so did she. "But maybe it *is* to please you, to make you happy. So how about, as you say, we just go on as we've been doing? Is status quo — not status quo ante — enough of a quid pro quo for you?"

She leaned over to kiss him lightly. "I love it when you talk dirty in Latin... You are definitely a lawyer. But you're also definitely too good to live."

His heart leaped, and he kissed her back, a little harder, before the light changed.

"Thanks, but maybe we shouldn't be throwing metaphors like that around just now. You know, considering."

Rush hour and the sheer volume of people sleeting through the Hall of Justice delayed them enough to end up timing out perfectly. As they hurried into a half-empty courtroom, Prax's arraignment was just about to get under way.

At the defense table, the about-to-be-accused, looking tired and drawn after her night in custody, gave Rennie and Stephen a tiny upwards nod of head and lift of brow when she saw them, the two small motions combining to give the effect not of a smile, more like an Oh God there you are at last and oh God am I ever glad you're here. Standing beside her, King Bryant, looking more imposing than ever in a charcoal-gray suit and sedate striped tie, nodded ceremoniously.

They took seats behind the railing, right behind the defense table, next to Eric, whom Rennie hadn't known would be there and whom she greeted with joy, and an icily impeccable individual who could only be money-man-Brooks-from-the-office. When Rennie and Stephen had settled themselves, Brooks spoke quickly and quietly to Stephen, with just the right mix of deference and competence and familiarity, and, on introduction, shook hands with Rennie most correctly.

It was over as quickly as Stephen had predicted. Mary Praxedes Susannah McKenna, twenty-one years of age, resident of Sausalito, was charged with the first-degree murders of Jasper Edward Goring, forty-two years of age, British national residing in San Francisco, and of Franco Anthony De Angelis, professionally known as Fortinbras, thirty years of age, also a resident of San Francisco; plus various small counts of drug use and unlawful possession.

Prax, speaking in a clear firm voice, entered her own pleas of not guilty. King Bryant, looming like a one-man mountain range, argued in an avalanche of eloquence for dismissal, then for a reduced charge of manslaughter, but his motions were both denied. As was his request for bail.

When the gavel came down—so hard that Rennie flinched as if it had whacked her personally—they sat frozen as a dazed Prax was led away. Then Rennie, every bit as stunned and white-faced as her friend, leaped to her feet so violently and flung herself against the railing so suddenly that the bailiffs' hands flew to their weapons. Stephen drew her back, nodding to the scowling officers. But she wrenched away from him to shout after Prax as she disappeared into the jaws of detention.

"We'll get you out, Praxie, I promise! It'll be okay!"

"It will *not* be okay, if you don't shut up right now," her husband muttered savagely. "You'll be in the cell right next to hers for contempt of court." Brooks again murmured something in Stephen's ear. "And apparently there's a bunch of reporters outside the courthouse waiting for us."

"Some of whom are no doubt from my own place of employment." Rennie's green eyes were blazing like an angry cat's. "Stephen, they put her in JAIL—"

"I know. We'll get her out. We'll ask for a new bail hearing in a couple of weeks."

"A couple of *weeks*? She'll never—"

"Yes, she will. We'll have more information, we can ask them to reconsider. Let's go now."

But at the back of the courtroom, a man stepped up to them as they left. "Miss Stride? Rennie Stride?"

Rennie checked, surprised, and glanced at him, automatically giving him the reporter's once-over. Nobody she knew. Older than they were, early forties probably. Nice clothes. Good hair. Vaguely hip-looking. Odd vibe.

Stephen put an arm around her. "Mrs. Lacing."

Rennie shrugged herself away from him. "Yes? I'm Rennie Stride…"

He put out a well-kept hand, which she automatically shook, and with the other hand extended two cards, one business, one personal, which Stephen equally automatically intercepted.

"Randyll Miller. Dill Miller, I should say. Jasper Goring's partner? From Los Angeles. I know there's not much I can do, but… When I heard that Miss McKenna had been arrested and was being arraigned this morning, I came straight here. Is there someplace we can talk?"

Stephen moved in again on Rennie's left, a lot more assertively this time. "Mr. Miller. How nice to meet you. I'm Stephen Lacing, Rennie's husband. We'd be very glad to talk to you. But not here."

Having successfully eluded the reporters, Stephen, Brooks, Randyll Miller and King Bryant stood outside talking for some time, while Rennie sat in the back seat of the Mercedes with Eric, keeping a weather eye out for any of her marauding press colleagues and an appraising gaze on Dill Miller.

How was it that she and Praxie hadn't known about this dude before? Weird. She knew vaguely that Jasper had had agent partners in L.A. and London and New York, but none of his San Francisco clients had ever met or mentioned Miller. And to the best of her recollection, Jasper never had, either.

Certainly Prax hadn't. And Rennie would have to find out a lot more about him before she felt comfortable letting him into their war councils. Or was letting him in the best way to find out? It had been hard enough dealing with Prax's parents, persuading them not to fly back from Vermont, where they were giving seminars at Middlebury College. In any case, Prax was being well taken care of, and that was all that mattered.

"I know this is totally horrible for you," said Eric after a while, putting a comforting arm around her, and she startled a little, still absorbed by her speculations, then managed a shaky laugh.

"It's not about me for once. Yes, yes, that's right, you actually heard me say that. But we'll get her out, and she won't ever, *ever* be going back there. King will get her off, but long before it comes to that Marcus will solve the case, and if he doesn't then I will solve it myself. Hey, I'm a big-time journalist, remember? You just *bet* I'll work it out, Brenda Starr Reporter's got nothing on me..."

Eric smiled, and gave her a squeeze, and they sat on in silence. Outside on the sidewalk, Dill Miller had shaken hands all round, with every appearance of cordiality, and was walking swiftly away down the street. Rennie made a mental note to call him later. But now her glance went to Stephen: she stared at him through the window and was all at once seismically rocked by a feeling that seemed composed of equal parts lust, doubt and resentment.

Nothing in particular set it off, except that his hair was a lot longer than she'd ever seen it; he'd been letting it grow lately, and he'd loosened his tie and opened his collar, which always turned her on. He looked soooo fine—just weary and distracted and rumpled enough to give his usual good looks an incredibly sexy edge.

Why do men always look their best when they're a little tired and a little stubbly and a little preoccupied?

"Why can't I give him what he wants?" she said irritably.

Eric looked quizzical. "I'm confused. You *do* sleep with him on a regular basis, to the satisfaction of all concerned?"

"Oh, that. Sure, why not, we both enjoy it. No, I meant why can't I just be married to him like a normal wife? Like the normal wife, come to think of it, he thought he was getting. He's such a nice guy. A dear, sweet man whom I absolutely do not deserve. It would make him so happy."

"I think we all know the answer to that," said Eric gently. "And I think Stephen knows it better even than you do."

Chapter Nine

WHEN TAM LINN WAS MURDERED, Fortinbras De Angelis had gloated publicly about there being not as much freaking smile-on-your-brother-everybody-get-together-and-love-one-anotherness in Hippieland as its denizens liked to think.

Now Fort was dead too, of course—which may or may not have proved his point. But it left more of a mystery than ever for those who lived in Hippieland and for those whose business it was to solve such matters, and also for those whose job it was to report on them.

"It doesn't have to be someone from the scene, you know, let alone Prax," Rennie said the next day to her editor, Burke, who was putting together an in-depth story on the shocking events in the Haight—a report from which Rennie was barred. "Fort came from some very rough neighborhoods in Philly and Jersey and Brooklyn, for God's sake, not some bible-thumping Alabama crossroads or sweet little Iowa corn town. I'm sure he had plenty of enemies from the bad old days. And probably Jasper did too."

"I'm sure you're right," said Burke placidly. "And I'm

not saying I think Prax is guilty. That's not the point. The point is, those guys were murdered in your house. That makes you part of the story. You knew them both—you cooked dinner for them, for Pete's sake—and you'd met the first victim, and you're friends with the prime and so far only suspect, who's now in jail. These are all excellent and compelling reasons why you have to back off. And, you have to admit, evidence implicating another suspect isn't thick on the ground."

Rennie brooded a bit about that. Then: "But I can still come back and write? It's okay if I write about other stuff? Even other rock stuff?"

She was more than a little uncertain as to her own status in the midst of this. She'd taken a week off at Burke's order, and now she was very glad to be back at work. Even so, she was deeply worried. It was one thing to be Joanie-on-the-spot with news beats, but it was quite another to be the breaking news yourself; and she wasn't sure what the paper's official position might be on low-ranking staffers getting their names in print in a non-byline context.

But Burke had heard the subtext, and gave her a reassuring smile.

"It's okay, Strider. I've talked to Garry and he's talked to the managing editor. You won't be allowed to write about the murders—or the trial, if it comes to that; that's to protect you as well as the Clarion. But you're also not to worry about your job. In fact, you can take some more paid leave if you want—I know it must have been horrible for you, coming home and finding that. I'd be flipped out too. If you'd rather work to keep your mind off it—which is what I'd do if I were in your shoes—you can have anything I can rustle up for you, until it all gets sorted out." He grinned up at her. "Just promise me you won't make a habit of this. You're supposed to report the news, not make it. So no more dead bodies, okay?"

Rennie smiled back, deeply relieved. "That's exactly what my husband said."

If she didn't promise, she couldn't break the promise; and Burke never noticed that she didn't. As things turned out, she couldn't have kept it anyway.

The first thing she did that afternoon was go to visit Prax in jail. It was every bit as bad as she thought it would be: the drab visiting room, the forced searches, the horrible atmosphere, the other prisoners. Prax, when she came in dressed in prison fatigues, looked ghastly: tired, terrified, trying to hide it for Rennie's sake. Rennie stayed for the maximum allowable time, only leaving when King showed up to talk to his client, and promising to come every day.

Walking out into the street, she felt like a traitor, like someone who'd left their kid or their dog in the middle of the freeway and driven heartlessly away. Why should Prax be in jail and not her? It had been her sword, her apartment, her dinner party. But Rennie knew that was so bogus, that the best and only thing she could do for Prax now was to be free to check things out, so that the real guilt could be fixed where it belonged.

She decided to take Burke up on both his offers, combining a bit of leave with a lot of work, and thanked him and his bosses for their consideration. But though she couldn't write about what were being blared all over the country as the Fillmore Murders — although being as only one of them had actually taken place *at* the Fillmore, "the Haight Murders" would be more descriptively correct, if less sensational — nonetheless she had vowed to clear Prax's name. And now that Prax was in jail for the foreseeable future, the mission was not just to clear her name but get her sprung. So Rennie headed home to begin.

She'd been free to return to her apartment for some time now, as the crime scene had been closed, but she was still ensconced in Lacingland. Despite Marjorie's interference, she and Stephen were content and comfortable together. The realization that the marriage was over, paradoxically, made things better between them than they had ever been, at least since that unreal, brain-chemical-unbalanced, altered state of romance's first blush. So Rennie had happily shared the marital bed and her husband's arms, and they had spent long hours talking, and she had brought a sunnier aspect to the family dinner table than ever she had when she had been forced to dine there every night. It had been disgracefully easy to slip back into coddled-and-cosseted mode, and before she knew it, almost two weeks had gone by since the murders.

So this was the first time she'd set foot in her own home since the morning after. She hadn't even gone to check the damage, terrified of facing the place alone, of what horrific vibe she might find there, of what she would have to do to fix it. She had even feared she might not be able to get past it, might have to give up and move. But when she turned the key and entered, she saw that Stephen had gotten there first.

The whole place had been cleaned, as Marcus had promised. But it had also been completely repainted in soft cream tones, flooding the rooms with that particular San Francisco light. The floorboards had been sanded and refinished where the blood had pooled, and invisibly restored where the force of the sword strokes had gouged out splinters. Genuine antique Persian carpets, replacing the tatty faux ones, lay on the gleaming oak, and two new damask sofas flanked the fireplace. Even her posters had been carefully and beautifully framed. Once the apartment had been unsealed as a crime scene, several work crews must have beavered away around the clock at Stephen's orders. Amazing what unlimited thoughtfulness and even more unlimited money could do.

Rennie, standing there staring, inhaling the smell of new paint and floor varnish and furniture polish, was grateful, relieved, staggered and furious all at once.

He does things because he says he loves me, and I know he does, but he doesn't think ahead to what I'd like, what I'd be comfortable with, he just assumes his wishes and sensibilities are the right ones — and that anything's okay because he's still my husband and I'm still his wife. And then he goes and does something like this — just so I wouldn't have to deal with it myself... The new paint does look nicer, I must admit — and just think of all the coats it must have taken to cover the purple and dark red and green — and I didn't have to lift a finger... See, see, that's *the way to the Dark Side — lie back, be adored, be taken care of....MUST. NOT. GIVE. IN...*

She was there that afternoon with a purpose. She'd brought company, company that she'd wanted to entertain on her own turf. Up until a couple of months ago, Berry Rosenbaum, a young lawyer friend of both hers and Stephen's from New York, had been employed at an old-line law firm in Los Angeles. Thanks to her brilliant research work on a case a colleague of his had going, King Bryant himself had scouted her for his own offices, and had been so pleased with what he found that he had actively lured her away to work for him.

As in every other profession and workplace, lawyers who happened to be female were still a novelty, and subject to sexist evaluation. King, an old-school Romantic but no fool either, hadn't hired Berry because of her glass-blond hair and big dark eyes — what had seduced him was that gold Phi Beta Kappa key she wore on a thin gold chain around her neck, and her top-of-the-Ivy-League class ranking, and her law review editorship. Though being a tall, brown-eyed blonde sure didn't hurt. And for her part, Berry had been thrilled at the chance to work with the man many called the most brilliant defense and civil liberties lawyer to practice in California for fifty years, and who'd immediately assigned her to help him on Prax's defense.

Now she followed Rennie inside, having taken her time

coming up the turret staircase, alternately looking at the posters and trinkets and tchotchkes on the walls and ledges and the ever-amazing view through the lancet windows. Sitting down on one of the new sofas, Berry gazed around at all the velvet and brocade, Rennie's grandma's purple and white Staffordshire china, the silver tea service on the low, piano-shawl-draped coffee table, and started to laugh.

"For a hippie rock chick, you live amazingly like a nineteenth-century English gentlewoman—are you aware of the titanic irony of that? And it has nothing to do with the Lacing family; it's just your way."

Rennie laughed too. "And for a Manhattan lawyer girl, you're looking very California these days—tall, tan, teeth…"

"Weird how it takes you over, once you're out here, isn't it? It's like being a pod person."

They talked for a while, Rennie detailing why she'd been so floored when they'd walked in just now, what Stephen had had done here all unbeknownst to her, and Berry was suitably amazed and touched.

"If I may say so, Ren, I'm not surprised at what I see."

"Why do I get the feeling you're not talking about my décor anymore?"

"Listen, I adore you and Stephen, you know I do, but you also know I never thought you two were meant for each other. That's why I was so surprised when I heard you'd eloped. I thought you'd just fall into bed together and it would be very nice for you both and that would be that. Sweet lovely girl, cute adorable boy—a pleasant way to get rid of one's virginity, a few good solid starter bonks with suitable guys afterwards. No muss, no fuss, no guilt, no strings."

"That would be *my* virginity, of course," observed Rennie acidly. "I'm sure the Lacings set Stephen up with a clean, gorgeous, above all discreet high-class call girl for his eighteenth birthday, to relieve him of his according to the no doubt long-standing family custom for Lacing males. After all, the original matriarch was a very successful hooker and madam. Founded their fortunes."

"Yes, so I've heard, great story… As for Stephen, he probably never even knew the girl was a pro."

"I've never dared ask. But nothing about that family could ever surprise me… And it was very nice being deflowered by Stephen, even quite lawfully. But where were *you* then, counselor, to counsel us out of ill-advised matrimony?"

Berry shrugged, getting up to stroll around the room, checking everything out, much as Stephen himself had done, not so many days before.

"Even lawyers can't stop their friends from making crap decisions. You'll both survive. You'll both find the people you're supposed to be with. It's just not each other."

"I know," said Rennie after a long moment. "I think I always knew. And I wish I could *wish* it was different. But I can't even do *that* for him… Do you know, Stephen is paying personally for Prax's defense? Because she can't afford it. He's doing it for me. To make me happy. He was all set to put up her bail, too. From his own money, not family money. Well, he says it's our money, but I consider it his, not mine. I've never touched a penny of it."

"Now, see, that makes all my instincts sit up and itch, not just the legal ones. And it is too your money, by marital law, every bit as much as it's his, and I've told you before that there is absolutely no reason on earth why you should be starving in a garret and not using some of it to make yourself comfortable. But I don't think he's doing it just to make you happy."

Rennie shook her head. "No. There's a claim being staked here. And *that's* why I don't take the money. He comes from an old Gold Rush family; he knows how far I'm prepared to allow further, uh, prospecting rights in the main lode. And the only thing he asks—he didn't spell it out, though we both know that's what he's asking—is that there be no claim jumping by other miners. Or if there is, that he not have to know about it: see a sign posted at the, um, mine entrance, say, or hear about it by chance at the assay office. But enough with the coy metallurgical metaphors... I told him I was never coming back no matter what he did, whether he did it for Prax or for me or for the endangered California sea lions, and he said he could live with things the way they are. The status quo, as he says, not the status quo ante. He comes from an old China-trader family; he knows when the haggling is done. And, as we've already mentioned, he comes from an old hooker family, so he knows all about whores. And I guess now so do I."

"Besides," she added, "I'm not starving, and though I *am* living in a garret it's a rather nice garret. I'm doing rather well, actually. I just got a promotion at the Clarion, and I've picked up a few more stringer gigs. I do not need help from the Lacings."

Berry snorted. "As you say. So then, why don't you tell me about this friend Prax and her troubles. King has already filled me in on the legal stuff. Now I need to hear everything else."

Two nights later, Rennie assembled the ad hoc McKenna defense team for a dinner party at Hell House, in the yellow dining room, its French doors overlooking the Presidio. Just the A-team: herself, Stephen, Eric and Berry. Prax was of course not in attendance, but Randyll Miller was. Rennie had wanted some face time with him in the presence of her most trusted intimates, to hopefully get a handle on what Jasper's partner was like, and some insight into what his intentions were Prax-wise.

And she wanted to know all this stuff *now*, before things got too unbearably complicated. Miller had stayed on in San Francisco after Prax's arraignment, helping take care of Jasper's and Fortinbras's funeral details once the bodies were released for burial—Rennie had not felt able to attend the services, though Stephen went, representing her—and also trying to cope with the business upheaval. So she hadn't seen him except for that once, at the courthouse, though she'd spoken to him a few times on the phone. In any case, he'd accepted immediately when she phoned to ask him to dinner, sounding very pleased to be included. On the other hand, King Bryant had not been invited, not out of any dark exclusionist policy but simply because this was a dinner for friends, meant as much to raise spirits as to plot strategy.

Dinner had been left in the hands of the kitchen staff, and as usual it was superb: crab newburg, fresh tomato bisque, poached salmon on a bed of spring greens, filet mignon, chocolate mousse in a box made of thin chocolate slabs and drenched in fresh raspberry sauce, all accompanied by vintage bottles from the Lacing wineries up in Napa.

The well-oiled diners didn't let serious conversation too much hinder an hour's steady, pleasant going, but by the dessert and sherry and coffee stage they pulled their heads out of the nosebag a bit, sat back and started to talk about the problem.

"There's no motive for Prax to have killed any of these people, right?" asked Berry Rosenbaum, taking charge and glancing round the table as at a witness box. Dill Miller, Eric, Rennie and Stephen all shook their heads solemnly, like a row of owls at a tennis match. "No, of course not. Tam did grope her, on the basis of prior congress, but you don't kill people you've bedded and dumped just for copping a feel."

"Much as she might have wanted to," remarked Stephen.

Berry laughed. "I'm hip! But the fact remains that she was at both murder scenes, and though every piece of evidence the police have turned up is purely circumstantial, sometimes circumstantial evidence can be very strong."

"'Such as when you find a trout in the milk'," murmured Rennie. As one they turned to stare at her, though Eric was laughing, and she grinned. "Sorry. Thoreau. Just popped out. Won't happen again."

"Dear Henry David is right on." Berry shook out her blond hair and declined an offer of more wine. "There's a strong smell of fish about this whole case. Okay, let's look at it. Prax discovers Tam's body at the Fillmore. Totally circumstantial. *Schools* of trout absolutely *swimming* in watered-down milk. There's not a shred of evidence to suggest that a five foot five, hundred-pound girl actually stabbed a man through the heart, a man who was heavier by sixty pounds and taller by five inches, dragged him across the floor and stuffed him into the equipment trunk, all without leaving any fingerprints and without getting a drop of blood on herself. And we know this how, class?"

Stephen raised his hand. "Because physically she couldn't have, and because she had on the same clothes from when she arrived at the Fillmore, and they weren't stained. Only the soles of her sandals were, where she'd stepped in the blood, and the footprints on the floor were consistent with that."

"Well, give that man some pie!" said Berry approvingly, and they all laughed.

"So that lets her off that hook," said Eric.

"Completely. But it was a non-starter anyway. Obviously that's what the D.A.'s office figured, and that's why she wasn't charged with Tam's murder, because they have no evidence that she did it and no reason to even think she did. But, as far as we know, neither do they have any evidence to indicate who *was* responsible. Which is the bad news."

"But Jasper and Fort."

"Ah. Now let's try to find some *good* news. What could

Prax's motives have been to kill Jasper and/or Fortinbras? Just Prax's; she's the only one we're concerned with."

"For Prax to kill Fort? Easy. He was jeopardizing her career," said Rennie. "He'd trashed her all over TV, radio, the papers and, for all I know, men's room walls. I might have killed him myself if somebody hadn't beat me to the punch."

"You don't want to let Detective Inspector Cousin Marcus hear you saying stuff like that," murmured Stephen, and she laughed. "But why would she kill Jasper?"

"Can't imagine," said Eric. "He had just taken her on as a client, and that was a very big deal, yes? Of course it was. So why make him dead?"

"No reasonable reason," said Stephen. "Maybe something personal?"

Rennie shook her head. "She'd never even met him until just before Tam's murder. Right after I did that story on her for the Clarion. There wasn't time for them to have had personal problems at all, let alone anything that could have made her want to kill him. She liked him and she needed him. Evenor all did."

"Did you know Jasper, Rennie?" asked Randyll Miller. He had conversed both amiably and amusingly all through dinner, but once the strategy session had gotten down, he'd seemed to Rennie's eye to withdraw a bit, and this was the first thing he'd said.

"Sure. Even before he called Prax asking if she could use representation. Everybody in music in the Bay Area knew him, or at least knew of him. He was a *manager*. All the bands want one, and he did very well for his groups. Look what he did for the Lampshade here, and for Prisca Quarters and the Holyboys and Flitcherwitch in England, and Toy Tyler and Megatherium in New York, and Owen Danes and Chris Sakerhawk in L. A. — for everyone he took on, really. But you were responsible for most of that too, Randyll."

All eyes went to Miller, and he smiled, a touch

nervously. As Rennie had by now found out, he was American-born, despite the Brit accent, and not far off Jasper's age — early forties, as she'd thought. Tonight he was wearing a beautiful Italian suit and tie, obviously chosen specifically to dine in the grandeurs of Hall Place, of which he'd equally obviously heard, and which he had praised effusively and informedly on arrival. A gold signet ring and, surprisingly though pleasingly, an antique gold pocket watch and chain went with the suit. Gray-flecked chestnut-brown hair in a neat chin-length cut looked far less incongruous on him than on most people over thirty who grew their hair longish.

Studying him openly, which she could tell made him all the more freaked and nervous, Rennie decided he looked like an Edwardian gentleman time-machined here against his will and trying to make his way as best he could. Maybe she was wrong to be suspicious of him...well, here was his chance to prove it, either way.

Still, there was something about him that felt not quite right: a stand-offishness, a need to distance himself, maybe. Or perhaps it was an ingratiating pre-emptive strike before the body was even cold — so to speak. Couple that with his out-front interest in securing Prax as a client — or was it just eagerness to do right by her and the band? Something about Jasper's death, too — was Miller too upset, not upset enough? She couldn't decide. If there *was* something heavy going on with him, though, she would find out...

"Dill, please," he said then, with a smile. "Randyll's my father — and grandfather. And I did handle the L.A. and New York acts you mention, and worked with Jasper on the rest. But I still can't think why anyone would want to kill him."

"And yet he's dead as dead can be."

"Yes...I don't understand it." He shook his head, and Rennie, watching him as a cat watches a promising hole in the baseboards, couldn't tell if he did or didn't.

"Something business-related, then?" asked Berry.

"We had hardly even started talking about Prax, business-wise," said Dill. "Jasper'd gotten Karma Mirror that one gig at the Fillmore, and a few club dates—the Blue Unicorn, the Coffee Gallery, Cocoa Chenille's, places like that—but nothing more, not yet."

"What were his plans for Prax's future?" asked Stephen. "Did he want her to stay with Karma Mirror for the long haul?"

Dill shook his head, seeming more confident on his own ground. "No—Prax had told Jasper a while back that she and the Karms were seriously talking about splitting up, and he approved. As did I. She's much, much better than most of them are, and she deserves a good backup band. Well, not backup so much, but a band that could make themselves stars behind her and make her a superstar. So we weren't looking to lock her up—sorry, sign her up—with a deal until we knew more about what she wanted to do. Jasper and I first thought of pushing her as a solo act, but we watched her a few times and she really does best out in front of a band she belongs to. After—well, after Tam, Jasper suggested that she should join Deadly Lampshade as their new lead vocalist. The Lamps themselves thought it was a great idea. They were our clients too, so it kept it all in the family. Though I did hear that one or two Karms weren't entirely happy about it."

"Interesting," said Eric. "A rock and roll coup d'état?"

Dill was warming to the topic, forgetting his earlier nervousness. "No coup. It just all worked out. Both bands were approached properly, it was all kosher. Prax talked to Juha Vasso and Chet Galvin and Jack Paris—the Lamps' lead guitarist, rhythm guitarist and drummer. Chet and Jack do vocals too, but Jack would like not to have to sing anymore, so anyone they take on, not just a lead singer, would have to help out with that. And since their bass player Neil Marten isn't that good and is getting flakier and more into drugs every day and they've been wanting to cut him loose, Prax would bring her own bass player, Bardo, with her; he's *unbelievably* talented, right up there with Casady and McCartney. Plus her keyboardist Dainis Hood—he and Bardo both do vocals. The Lamps have never had a dedicated keyboard player before, so they liked that a lot. Even if, as Prax says, it does feel rather like dead men's shoes—her taking over half Tam's band before his body's even cold."

Again with the unlovely and all too apposite metaphor. Rennie made a small impatient noise.

"That was just Praxie being defensive and self-deprecating, afraid the possibility isn't real and she'd protect herself by denying she really wants it so she's not disappointed when it doesn't happen. She does that way too much for a future rock star, I must speak to her about it—she's not a little girl claiming she doesn't want an ice cream cone in case the offer is bogus. But her joining the Lamps really does make a lot of sense," she added professionally.

She'd been listening to the new lineup in her head, enjoying the shop talk and pleased to hear that Dill knew his musicians, and now she ticked them off on her fingers.

"Praxie as lead singer, Dainis, Bardo and Chet on backup vocals—that'll sound outtasight. Chet can sing co-lead when it's called for; he and Bardo have great baritones, and Dainis has a nice tenor. Bardo on bass and Dainis on keyboards, very creative. Combine that with the Lamps' lead guitar—Juha is amazing—and Jack as drummer, if he stays on, though they can probably do better. That's a pretty front-line band. Way more experimental and progressive than the Lampshade, way more commercial and top-40 than the Karms. Sounds like a hit act to me."

"Still, not likely that Jasper killed Tam just to get Prax to go over to the Lamps," said Berry. "However lucrative a deal that might have been. There are easier ways."

"Or that Prax would kill Jasper and Fort because—" Eric paused. "Well, there's really *no* 'because', is there?"

Rennie shook her head. "Not that I can see. How does the rest of Prax's band feel about her leaving?"

"We haven't discussed it much, not specifically," said Dill, "but they've been wanting to move on to other bands or do studio work or solo projects. It's not a problem. Nobody's being dumped or abandoned. They'll all be taken care of. And Bardo and Dainis will go with Prax no matter where she ends up. The Lampshade will be lucky to get them, and they all know it."

He paused a moment. "I know what you're really asking, Rennie. And I can assure you that no one in either band is pissed off enough to frame Prax for murder because she put them out of a job. Because nobody *is* out of a job. Even Neil Marten, who's musically and personally the weakest of them all, has more session and fill-in ballroom work than he can handle, and *that* he's good at."

"So you're going to manage the group yourself now, Dill?" asked Eric, and Rennie blessed him silently for the naturalness of the one question she *really* wanted answered; but Eric had been carefully briefed, and besides, he was a pro. "How long were you and Goring partners?"

Dill set down his coffee cup and touched his napkin to his mouth before replying. "Only about twelve years. But I'd known him since we were both mere lads in short pants. Our families lived near each other in England, down in Surrey — our dads were in the diplomatic service. We went to different public schools, so we didn't see much of each other until we got to Cambridge. I wanted to study law, but I also was interested in the entertainment industry — my mother's a casting agent — and when Jas and I reconnected at Trinity that seemed the way to go. And that's how Goriller Unlimited got started."

" 'Goriller'?"

"M'hm. G-O-R-I-ng plus M-i-L-L-E-R. Silly, but it worked for us. Rennie earlier mentioned some of our rock clients — we also handle movie and stage actors, some classical musicians and opera singers. We've done rather well. I'm not going to lie to you, though: I want very much to keep Prax and the new band, but there's been a bunch of offers already. For all Jasper's personal acts, and for Prax specifically. Though I'm making no decisions just yet."

"Proving once more, as if it needed further proving, that there's no such thing as bad publicity. Right." Berry made some notes. "Okay... On what evidence was Prax arrested? Lab stuff, obviously, or they'd have taken her away the very first night."

"Her fingerprints were on a wine bottle that had been spiked with liquid Valium, according to Marcus," said Stephen.

"And?"

"Her prints were also on the wineglasses," said Eric.

"And?'

Rennie said before anyone else could, "Prax's prints — and mine — on the murder weapon; hilt, scabbard and blade. We're all over it; we played around with it when I bought it. Carefully, of course. So now it's covered with prints. You just can't get good help these days, nobody wants to clean swords. They'll do windows, but they won't do swords. But you'd have to know a lot about swords, you'd have to be good with them, to have employed that one the way the killer did. It's a broadsword, and there are only a few angles you can use it at in order to make the cuts that were made. You'd have to put some serious strength behind it to make it do what it did — it's not easy. In any sense."

"And I'm guessing Prax doesn't have sword experience?" asked Dill.

"She'd never even had one in her hand before," said Rennie. "But I have. I was captain of the fencing team at college, and I'm telling you whoever did this knew his way around a blade."

"Or her way," said Eric.

"Or hers," agreed Rennie after a while.

Berry made more notes. "Now, any more suggestions for Prax's motive? We really haven't come up with much."

"That's the thing," said Stephen. "Except for the marginal Fortinbras one, there really *isn't* much."

"So we're back to circumstantial. Prax discovered Tam's body, and Prax was there with the dead bodies of Jasper and Fort, and her fingerprints were in places we'd prefer them not to be, and there were drugs in the wine, and she was the only one left alive."

"What does King Bryant say?" asked Dill.

Berry rolled her eyes. "He's hoping very hard to find another suspect. But no one is leaping forward to oblige him."

"Cops?"

Stephen shrugged. "They can't say much, but Marcus did tell me—strictly against regulations, he's going to get into *so* much trouble one of these days—that he personally thinks it's a total frame-up. But he doesn't know who or why. And he can't prove it unless more information comes along."

"Like what?"

"Like who would benefit from framing Prax. Yeah, I know, the real murderer would. But how? And why would he choose Prax in the first place? All the detective stories say if you know how, you know who, but that doesn't seem to apply here. We do know how, but that's apparently all we know."

"Oh, they haven't got a clue, the damn fuzz," said Rennie scornfully. "And you know, Stephen, Marcus knew perfectly well you'd come running straight to us with that information... He even asked me, very privately, to keep my ears open, around the Haight and at the paper. Quite the Baker Street Irregular he wants me to be. He better be careful they don't bounce his little rosy detective ass right out to the curb, he's pushing the edge already."

While she spoke, Rennie had been intently deconstructing her dessert: disjointing the chocolate box and whacking the thin slabs into shards with her dessert knife, so that the mousse stood like a tiny hill in a raspberry lake filled with chocolate splinters, then leveling it with a bulldozer spoon. When she looked up to see why the table had gone so quiet, everyone was staring at her, and she laughed.

"What, you've never seen anyone treat chocolate mousse like that before? And now, having reduced it into submission, I devour it in peace." She suited action to words.

But all of them had gotten the message, and most of them were smiling.

Chapter Ten

ONE OF THE FEW NICE THINGS about being back at Hell House was that Rennie and Eric got to spend time together. Since moving out, she hadn't seen much of her brother-in-law: he had his own life, a life kept strictly compartmentalized and hidden from the family. Only Stephen and Marcus, and now Rennie and Prax, knew his secret, and it was safe with them: Stephen loved his brother unreservedly and would have supported him in anything, while Rennie had come to love him too, but was deeply angry that Eric's life had to be lived the way it was.

"It doesn't *seem* like six months since you've lived here," Eric was saying. They were sharing a teatime hour before they both went out with Stephen and the Lacing sisters and their husbands for dinner, to discuss an upcoming celebration in the General's honor. Prax's troubles were not forgotten, but, Rennie had to admit, it was nice to just sit and not have to deal with it for a while, and she didn't think that made her a heartless bitch, swilling tea and scarfing hot blueberry scones dripping with butter and jam while her best friend was rattling a tin gruel cup on the bars of her cell.

"No—either it seems like about six weeks, or else about a hundred years."

"With, alas, not the most auspicious of beginnings."

Rennie hooted. "To say the least! It's mostly a merciful blur to me now—those horrific little bunfights your mother held last year to introduce me to her cronies the society crones. They felt like state-fair livestock judgings—everyone she knows or is related to, all dropping by to vet the latest recruit, sex foremost in their nasty little minds."

"Sex? *Them*? That would be a first!"

"Breeding purposes only, I assure you. They kept giving me these quick furtive scans that never went above my chest or below my crotch—checking for swell, like surfers. And every last one of them wondering if the young bull, having obviously already mated the newly acquired heifer of dubious foreign bloodline, had gotten her in calf, hence the hasty elopement. And nobody approved of my not exactly built for childbearing breasts and hips."

"Dear God. This family has very few manners among them, but I do hope no one was so gauche as to actually say that."

"Well, at least they didn't say it where I could hear it. But you could see they were *thinking* it, and speculating as to whether a bastard prince had been narrowly averted by timely wedlock. Well, more fool they: no shotgun wedding, but no heir to the crown either."

" 'In *this* family, Rennie dear,' " said Eric, in a pitch-perfect imitation of his mother, " 'a woman has *far* too much to occupy her at home without working outside it. Not suitable, of course, a Lacing lady working at a common job, no, no, that will never do. You must think of your position and obligations, dear, and of course you never know when you'll be starting your first baby, you're not pregnant already, by any chance, are you?' "

Rennie stared at him drop-jawed. "That is *truly* frightening—how did you know she said that?'

Eric laughed and loaded up two more scones, passing the first to Rennie. "I didn't. But that's the female version, as I imagine it, of the rap my mother gave the sons-in-law when they joined the family firm—with heavy emphasis on their role as sires of the next generation, which I'm sure scared them sperm-less on the spot. You being the crown princess and matriarch-to-be, I imagine she came down on you especially ruggedly." He smiled, a little wistfully. "Well, you know *I* most likely won't be bringing a bride into this house any time soon, so it's up to Stephen to secure the direct male line. If not with you, then with someone else."

"Have you ever—" she asked, touched by the subtext.

"Talked to them about my boyfriends? Never. I've been with Trey for eight years, and we plan on spending the rest of our lives together, but our own parents don't even know we're gay. My father isn't imaginative enough to notice, much less comprehend, and my mother refuses to admit such things exist."

"But that's so sad…"

"Maybe. But it would devastate them if I told them," said Eric simply. "They would never accept it or understand it, and they would without a doubt say I was no longer their son. And maybe I'm not so fond of *them*, but I love this family and its name and its history, and I'm very proud of it, and I would never do anything to hurt it. Or to lose it. If that means staying in the closet, fine. If I were any *deeper* in the closet I'd be in Narnia. But it's okay. I'm not the only one by any means to make that choice, not even in our own circle. It's why I sometimes envy Prax."

"Praxie! But why?"

"Because social pressure is something she can make work for her. She can be with a man any time she wants. And she often is, from what you tell me; more often than she's with a girl. She can protect herself. It doesn't work that way for me." He grinned, and patted her hand. "But you never know—I may find myself some smart, funny, chic, well-educated, socially connected lesbian to marry. I've been with a few women, you know, and most gay girls have been with at least one guy. So we'd know the, so to speak, drill. We'd get together to make a kid or two and then never touch each other again. Close your eyes and think of Tuscany—or go the old tried-and-true turkey baster route. Wouldn't be a problem. After that, I'd have my boyfriend and she'd have her girlfriend: we'd get along fine and be terrific parents to fabulous children and stay happily married forever. It's not a totally terrible arrangement, you know; in fact, it goes on all the time."

"I didn't know. Somehow that's even sadder, and makes me even angrier. It's so unfair."

"That's because you're still so young. You still think unfairness is the worst sin in the calendar."

"I do think that. Isn't it?"

"No." But what was worse Eric didn't say.

"So you must completely hate me," said Rennie after a while, "since I fought every which way from Sunday to break free of the Lacing black hole. And I certainly didn't do what was expected of Lacing Bride."

"You weren't put on this earth to fulfill other people's expectations. You're *never* too young to learn *that*, and the quicker you do, the better off everyone will be."

"Even other people?"

"Especially other people."

Rennie sipped her tea—her favorite, the kitchen staff remembered things like that. *Well, after all, that's what they're paid to do, isn't it, cater to the whims of Lacings? 'Don't forget now, Mrs. Stephen likes that Harrods blend for her tea, and make sure you brew it with spring water, not tap'...*

"Not your parents, though, I'm thinking."

"No, perhaps not. But you know when I first knew I loved you—as a person and not just as my sister-in-law? That Painted Ladies tea party. You know the one I mean."

Rennie looked delighted and guilt-riddled and sheepish all at the same time. "I still can't believe I did that."

"Neither could I. That's when I decided I didn't just *like* you, I positively *adored* you."

She recalled it well. It was before she'd landed the Clarion job, when she had still been living at Hell House. She'd come home one afternoon from trying to sell her clothes creations in the Haight, tired and cranky, and had been waylaid by Marjorie, reminding her that daughter-in-law was required to attend mother-in-law publicly at a meeting of the society preservation group called the Painted Ladies, in, like, oh, ten minutes?

"And do try, dear, to at least *look* like a lady," she'd added, icy gaze sweeping distastefully over Rennie's streaming hair and velvet gypsy dress. The subtext clearly being, We know only too well that you can't actually *be* a lady, or even *act* like one, but we'll settle for *looking* like one, as third-best...

So Rennie had gone upstairs and wrathfully flung on a hot-pink Chanel suit, the only one she'd kept—hey, it was freakin' *Chanel!*—and her great-aunt's pearl choker and her absolutely blinding ten-carat solitaire pear-cut heirloom engagement ring, rammed a little velvet pillbox onto the smooth twist into which she'd pulled her masses of hair and skewered it there with a cameo hatpin. Low French heels with pale hose, and for the crowning insult, a pair of gloves. Hat incorrect indoors, gloves incorrect in the presence of food, but tough twinkies! If Motherdear wanted to play rough, at least Rennie would be armed with a gauntlet to fling in her face. There had been a surfeit of these occasions, and she had finally had it up to here. Maybe they both had.

With some satisfaction, she'd surveyed herself in the

big gilt mirror. *There! All I need is an armful of roses and some blood on the front of my skirt — Jackie at Dallas! Hey, maybe I can even do something about the blood, once I get downstairs in the same room with my dear mother-in-CLAW...*

As an afterthought, she'd grabbed something from her purse, and, tucking it into her little Chanel pocket, she had gone downstairs and swanned into the yellow drawing room, where she had been as demure and deferential as she could possibly have been. But all too soon her hands were sweating and her head was throbbing and her jaw ached from gritting her teeth and even her hair hurt, and she was bored to tears with the Ladies' idle yet venomous chitchat about bloodlines and fortunes and who was in pig to whom.

"If the old bats had actually ever *done* any preservation work," Rennie admitted now to Eric, "I probably wouldn't have done anything I did."

"Oh?" Eric was laughing. "So no antique Spode teacup would have met its sad end on the parquet?"

Rennie looked embarrassed. "I didn't do that on purpose. Not really. I was just angry and clumsy."

"Uh-huh...and the little extra sweetener you put into the tea?"

"Ah, that."

What Eric meant was the LSD she'd tossed into the solid-silver, jewel-encrusted antique Russian samovar full of Earl Grey — now *that* she *had* done on purpose. That was what she'd lifted from her purse before coming downstairs — not much, just a couple of tabs of Owsley's finest.

"Well, your mother asked for it, Eric."

She had, too. "Rennie, dear, why don't you pour out?" Marjorie'd said with poisonous sweetness, and Rennie had obliged. Be careful what you ask for: half an hour later some of San Francisco's most revered and pearl-swagged bosoms were heaving with happy sobs at how beautiful everything was, how much they loved everybody, their neighbor, the flowers, the chairs, the Russians, the dear black people, how they could hear color, see music, fall through their hands, have you ever really *looked* at your hand, how amazing *were* fingernails, really, how did your finger know when to stop being a finger on top and start being a nail, why didn't it do that on the bottom as well...

Marjorie hadn't known what had just happened, but she'd been certain that her evil depraved daughter-in-law was at the bottom of it, and she'd dragged Rennie into a corner over by the windows and hissed at her like a malignant goose.

"WHAT DID YOU DO TO THEM?"

Rennie hadn't favored her with an answer. She looked Marjorie square in the eye, then took off her shoes and gloves, unpinned her hat and let her hair cascade down. And then she'd marched barefoot out of the room. In the doorway, she'd turned to survey the mild lysergic chaos she'd left behind.

Yep, little dogies, I think my work in this here town is done... Blowing the smoke off two imaginary six-shooters, Rennie had moseyed on along, the psychedelic marshal who'd just cleaned up a very uptight Dodge.

"It was a bitchy thing to do," she confessed now to Eric, who had fallen over laughing. "I knew it even as I was doing it—it was mean and nasty and I never did anything like it in my life. But they're all so down on me, those snooty harpies, taking their cue from Motherdear. They never miss a chance to stick it to me for being a nobody and a foreigner and a charity case, at least in their eyes. The barefoot hippie goosegirl who inveigled the prince into marrying her. I was so sick and tired of their goddamn condescension, and so pissed off at your mother and the unending hoops she keeps putting me through, that I just thought I'd give them a tiny taste of *real* hippieness. I didn't mean to hurt anyone."

Eric was wiping away tears of mirth. "I hadn't heard the whole story before. You're a dangerous woman, Rennie

Stride... Well, anyway, nobody was freaked out beyond belief. No flashbacks. Nobody ran naked and screaming into the Presidio."

"It was just some orange sunshine. The stuff was so old it probably had lost most of its punch. I'd been carrying it around for weeks, in case I maybe wanted to try it — I haven't, in case you're wondering. It got way diluted in the tea, anyway. They got over it in a few hours, none the worse for wear. Though I did hear whispers that some of their husbands had a rather interesting time of it that night — actually, I was surprised no one called up to thank me."

"Electric Earl Grey for the Painted Ladies. What a trip."

"I felt I owed them something, your parents," she said abruptly. "No, not the acid... But that's why I tried so hard and stayed so long. And I did try, you know. I really did. Since I wasn't what they'd expected. Since they didn't want me in the first place."

"Stephen wanted you. He was the one who counted."

"Stephen wanted me... But we see now how wrong he was. Shoulda gone for the bony blond preppie princess your folks had already vetted for him. No wonder you all hated me."

"Sweetness, he was *not* wrong! And neither were you. You just weren't right. But the bony blond heiress wouldn't have been right either. And I didn't hate you for a *nanosecond*. I love you. I envy you. You did what I can't do. You got the hell out on your own terms. You didn't set out to hurt Stephen, but you weren't willing to let *us* hurt *you*." He leaned over and kissed her cheek. "That's brave and honorable and even caring, and maybe one day they'll see it. But I think what you're doing is tremendous, and I think you're doing a great job. It's hard being a pioneer."

"I'm not driving the plow that broke the plains here, you know," she said, a little embarrassed by his praise.

"Aren't you? Of course you are. More women are

going to be doing the same thing, very soon now. And I think, I hope, other people will follow; gay people especially. So maybe one day I *will* be able to tell my parents about my life, I *will* be able to sit down with the person I love at the Thanksgiving dinner table, like everybody else in this family."

Rennie hugged him hard. "You are a dear, dear man, and I hope you will, too. I never forgot what you did for me the day we met."

It had been at the airport: she was just out of the boarding tube off the plane from New York. Alone, as Stephen had preceded her by a week to get things ready for her. Exhausted after a bumpy and emotion-fraught flight, combative, defensive, she'd looked around at the sea of happy people happily meeting other happy people, how glad everyone was to see the ones they belonged to and who belonged to them, and she'd thought there was no one there for *her*, no one to greet her and hug her and take her home, and she had been about to cry.

Then she'd seen the hand-lettered sign held up over the heads of the crowd, like the ones limo drivers hold up for their passengers: *MRS. LACING I LOVE YOU!* And that had been Stephen, and of course it had been adorable. But right next to it, another, smaller sign, held just as high, read *ME TOO!* And Eric had been under it. And that *had* made her cry, as it did now.

"You are going to prosper and thrive and live a wonderful life," he said, seeing her tears. "I just wish you could do it as my darling sister-in-law."

"You know it's over for Stephen and me," she said, with devastating openness. "Well—the marriage is, anyway."

Eric nodded. "But not because you don't care about each other, because you do. I'm not sure if that makes it a little bit easier or a million times harder. And you and I and Stephen—we'll always be family. No matter what. No matter even my mother."

Chapter Eleven

WITH PRAX MCKENNA IN THE SLAMMER, even though that presumption of innocence thing as mandated by the great American legal system was allegedly in effect, her band was having an unexpectedly hard time finding work. Unexpected by them, that is; everyone else seemed sadly unsurprised. Rennie wasn't allowed to mention Prax or Karma Mirror in print just now, so even that small but steadily reliable publicity well had gone dry.

Bill Graham had been more than generous, slotting the band in at the Fillmore whenever he could, to fill up the programs and help out the Karms at the same time, and had asked other promoters around town to do the same if they had a free slot. So thanks largely to him, and to word of mouth, Karma Mirror was working at least semi-steadily.

"Everybody thinks we have job offers coming out our ears, that the murder publicity is good for us," Dainis Hood, Prax's keyboard player, lamented to Rennie. "Which is messed up enough right there. But it's just not true. And we're handling it all ourselves; that Miller cat, Jasper's partner, hasn't gotten in touch with us again, so the merger with the Lamps is stalled. But even without Tam, the Lamps are gigging more than we are, which means they're paying their rent and eating more regularly than we are. Plus we don't know what to do about Prax; should we start looking for another chick singer, should we wait. I don't want to keep singing lead, but I have to. If it weren't for the Silver Lizard making us the house band four nights a week, we'd be in big trouble."

"It won't last," said Rennie confidently. "The case will be solved, Prax will be cleared, and everybody will be pursuing you madly with record deals, promoters begging you to headline, throwing fistfuls of dollars at you, sending you chocolates and rubies, or rubies dipped in chocolate, kissing your toesies, all shall love you and despair..."

Dainis laughed in spite of himself; he'd always liked Rennie, and the more he got to know her, the more he could see why Prax was so fond of her, though he still couldn't understand why any chick as pretty as she was and with a rich society husband too would want to live and work the way she did.

"And you will make this happen how? I didn't know rock writers had superpowers."

"Oh, they don't. Just me. But don't tell anybody."

If the Karma Mirror had a bit more free time than they were either happy or comfortable with, Rennie had rather less. True to his word, Burke had loaded her up with stories and reviews, and she still had her underground columns to keep her busy and amused. And there was plenty going on.

Far from paralytically shutting down in the wake of the murders, following an understandably shocked moment and little bobbling check the music scene in the Bay Area went humming on just as before. There were more concerts and club gigs than Rennie could manage to cover; but the levels were already shaking out. You could see, even predict, which of the first-wave San Francisco bands were going to make it and which were going to be pushing up psychedelic daisies.

And of those on the uproll, which ones were going to be varsity superstars—Jefferson Airplane, Grateful Dead, Big Brother, the rather annoyingly named Creedence Clearwater Revival, hopefully the new band to be created from the Karms and the Lamps which had as yet no name at all, annoying or otherwise; which were going to be strong junior varsity—Country Joe and the Fish, Quicksilver Messenger Service, Steve Miller, Moby Grape; and which were already doomed to be footnotes to musical history—pretty much everybody else. And of course new bands were popping up every day, so there was really no rest for the poor hard-working rock reporter.

But apart from her duties, Rennie endlessly fretted over the stagnation into which the police investigation of the murders seemed to have fallen.

"Nothing's happening," she said crossly to Berry one day. "If the cops aren't going to come up with any suspects beyond Prax, then I'll just have to find a few myself. And since Burke is letting me try out other things for the moment, I might as well take advantage."

"But you're not supposed to be writing about Prax or the murders."

"Who says I'm going to *write* about them?"

She began by making friends with some of the Clarion's crime-beat reporters, who were suspiciously eager to oblige her interest and happy to answer her many questions. While she could no doubt have put it down to her feminine charms, and not denying that those might have played a tiny part—or that she was above using them, even—Rennie knew perfectly well that they were only being so helpful because they figured that she was connected, and if they were nice to her, she might give them a delicious inside tip on further developments. It was a completely cynical, thoroughly journalistic deal on both sides, and everyone concerned was quite rightly proud of themselves. To Rennie, it was more than worth it, though she couldn't speak for them.

Still, she learned a lot from listening to the older reporters, things about police procedure and the chain of evidence; and applying that to what she'd been able to glean about what the D.A.'s office had learned, she found herself, to her considerable surprise, much better comforted than before.

"I don't think they have much new, really, the cops," she told Stephen, one evening when he was over at her place for Wednesday spaghetti night. "But we do, and it's nasty. Well, it's good from our point of view; I just mean it's unpleasant. One of the crime beat guys at the Clarion, Ken Karper—fancies himself a street-fighting kind of heavy hombre, wants everybody to call him K—told me that a source told him that Jasper Goring had owed a boatload of money to various individuals, both shady and un-."

"How does that affect Prax and possibly getting her sprung on bail?"

"That part I don't know yet."

Stephen finished helping her set the table. "Goring might have been planning to use her as collateral." At Rennie's horrified look: "No, no, dear God, not like that! I mean her musical talent as a tangible asset, something he could sell. She's the star...or at least the future star. Pry her loose from the Karms and dump them, then negotiate her contract to a really big-time manager for a ton of money, give her relative peanuts on the deal and keep the real money for himself to pay off what he owed. She'd still be happy with the deal, because to her it would be tremendously more money than she'd ever made before and she'd never know he'd ripped her off."

Rennie looked at him admiringly. "Now *that's* thinking

like a shark! Right, and maybe he was planning on using the money to finance more—well, whatever it was that got him owing so much money in the first place. Hookers? The ponies? First editions of Edgar Allan Poe?"

"Whatever. But that only explains why he was so hot to sign her as a client. Not why he ended up semi-detached. What about the first murder victim?" asked Stephen after a while. Rennie had made the fresh tomato sauce from scratch, with thick fall-apart-tender pork chops and homemade meatballs and a ton of oregano and garlic and onion nicely browned in olive oil and a couple of handfuls of sugar, the way her Italian grandmother had taught her, and it was one of his absolute favorite things, so he had been giving his plate his full attention.

"Tam? What about him?"

"There seem to be remarkably few clues. Nobody saw anything. Well, nothing that they're admitting to. Nobody else was backstage when Prax found him. No motives have turned up. We don't even hear much about him anymore. It's almost as if everybody's forgotten him."

"Yes—it *is* kind of like that. But I don't know anything new either."

"So? Go dig something up. You're not a reporter for nothing, right?" He smiled at her raised brows and widened eyes. "I know, I don't remind you of that often enough. But what do you do better than any other writer in the scene?"

"Oh, stop, I'm blushing…"

"Well, that too, but no, I was thinking of how good you are at getting people to talk to you. They tell you things they wouldn't tell other people in a million years. I don't know how you get them to do it. But they do. Go ask Alice, as your friend Grace says. Or ask whomever. But by all means ask."

Rennie reached for the big tureen in the middle of the table. "For that you get another pork chop."

She'd been stupid not to think of it sooner. Tam had

been murdered for a reason, and in the shock of the subsequent murders and the aftermath of Prax's arrest and incarceration, as Stephen had just pointed out, she'd forgotten all about him. The cops, who certainly hadn't forgotten, might or might not be less focused on Tam than they were on Fort and Jasper, and were in any case inscrutable. If they knew, they weren't saying, at least not anywhere that Rennie could hear. But it had started with Tam for a reason, and it had progressed to Jasper and Fort for another reason. Maybe the same reason, maybe not. Though on the surface she couldn't see a connection, she had a deep-down feeling there was one. Tam had been the first, it could all be said to have begun right there; as to where it would end...well, that might prove to be an altogether different matter.

But Stephen was right. She *would* go and ask. And what she found when she did was alarming, and yet not entirely unexpected. And it might go a long, long way to explaining quite a lot.

"Heroin!" echoed Rennie. "Are you sure?"

Sitting on Rennie's sofa, side by side like two well-behaved children, Juha Vasso and Tansy Belladonna nodded. To find out why a musician had been murdered, Rennie had logically sought the aid of musicians, and since Prax was pretty well inaccessible just now, and Rennie didn't want to upset her anyway, she'd turned to Tansy.

Not without some major misgivings. Rennie and Prax both knew Tansy's shortcomings: she had the attention span of a flea on acid, and, they sometimes thought, the brains of one too. But Tansy knew people, and for once she had come through magnificently. Within three days she'd hit up every single one of her friends in every single Bay Area band, including Tam's fellow Lampshades. Who were, some of them anyway, only too eager to talk about Tam as they had apparently never talked about him before, even to the cops.

Especially to the cops. So Rennie had invited Juha, Chet and Tansy over to her apartment, and had made sure she had enough pot and drinks and munchies to cover them all day long.

And then she'd started asking questions.

"Why didn't you tell that to the police?" she asked now, not unreasonably.

Juha laughed, head flung back. "Would you? Did you?"

"I didn't know," Rennie pointed out. "But—well, no, maybe not. I can't say. But why didn't someone tell *me*? I never knew Tam was riding the horse. Or the horse was riding him, I guess."

"I thought you knew," said Tansy, wide-eyed. "Everybody did. Tam was a heroin glutton, just a little smack pig."

"We tried to keep it quiet," said Juha, rolling another joint from Rennie's stash. Lead guitarist for the Lampshade since their start at Berkeley two years back, he was considered by fans and peers alike to be one of the top axemen in San Francisco, right up there with Jorma Kaukonen of the Airplane and John Cipollina of Quicksilver and Jerry Garcia of the Dead. He looked the part: tall, intelligent, keen-eyed behind rimless glasses, scarecrow-thin, straight reddish-brown hair down to his shoulders, giving him a not unbecoming eighteenth-century look—Thomas Jefferson on peyote—and his clothes went right along with the trip.

"It's not the image that people want to see, or to project, of the San Francisco scene," he added, "and if word about Tommy's habit had gotten out it sure wouldn't have helped us land a record deal or a decent manager. As it was, we all had to swear to Jasper that we were straight as arrows and pure as the driven, so to speak, snow. And at least two of us were lying like rugs when we said so—one's dead, and the other...well, that's one of the reasons we're hoping to land

Bardo as our new bass player. But yeah, most of the musicians Tommy — we couldn't stand calling him 'Tam' — had ever played with were hip to it. I don't know how much you know about smack?"

With one bare foot, Rennie silently pushed the glass candy jar of cleaned grass closer to him on the coffee table. *You keep it coming, brother, and so will I...*

"Tell me."

"Well, you've probably heard it's not a warm and cuddly drug, it's not at all like acid or pot. Very different trip, very different dynamic. It could make you kill, maybe, but it would have to be cut with something really nasty and aggressive. As a rule you just nod out. But like Tanze says, Tommy was like a smack vacuum cleaner. Just hoovered it up. A whore for it; there was nothing and no one he wouldn't do to get it. He said he needed it to write his songs. And, as you know, he sure could write."

"Couldn't you stop him?"

Chet Galvin, the rhythm guitarist, two years out of Ireland and framed like a Renaissance portrait in one of the wicker peacock chairs, shook his head.

"You really don't know much about smack, do you. Or about Tommy."

"Apparently not."

"Rennie, he was so into it, nobody could have stopped him." Tansy's huge violet eyes widened even further, with something that looked like sorrow and sympathy tinged round the edges with guilt. "Everybody tried. Juha, Chet, Jack, even Jasper once he found out... But Tam wasn't going to stop until it killed him."

Chet got up, stretched lazily and perhaps a little longer than, strictly speaking, he had to, and went to sit in the window seat.

"I think we were all pretty damn surprised that in the end, it didn't. At least not directly."

Goodness, he's tall, and don't those buckskin pants fit well too, especially since he isn't wearing any underwear... Rennie looked after him a little longer than, strictly speaking, she had to, then registered his throwaway line, caught herself and turned back to Tansy and Juha.

" 'Not directly'? Then, indirectly?"

Chet laughed shortly. "You could say that."

"You think he was killed *because* of drugs? Dealing?"

"I surely do think that. It makes the only sense we can make out of it. But we haven't got any proof. He kept it all very quiet and very much away from us."

"Where did he get the bread to make the buys?"

"Now that's a very good question." Juha took a long toke on the active joint, passed it over to Rennie, who just puffed at it, the inhale equivalent of a quick peck on the cheek—she was working here, but she didn't want to seem inhospitable.

"We were doing well," Juha added, "but not that well. Not to support a jones that size, let alone front a dealership. We never could bust him on it ourselves, but we all thought— Chet and I did, anyway—that Tommy was dealing top-quality smack."

"Yeah, but everybody deals," said Rennie. "Just to get free stash for yourself—you buy a key of grass that people chip in for, then you divide it out and take a few extra cuts for your effort and risk. You deal the extra and you still have some to keep. I've done it myself, a bunch of times."

Okay, once, *to be strictly accurate...*

Juha smiled kindly at her. "No offense, but that's like a knitting club sending out for pizza compared to the sort of thing we're talking about here."

"Professional dealing? But who? Who was his source? He had to get it from somewhere. And did he deal it all himself, or did he have minions to delegate to?"

Over in the window seat, Chet shrugged. "We could

never manage to find out. Sometimes we'd hear him on the phone speaking good Spanish or bad Portuguese — we assumed he had a supplier in Mexico or maybe Hawaii."

"Didn't he come from back east?"

Tansy nodded. "Born in Philly. He grew up in Jersey City and Brooklyn."

Now that was interesting: the same geographic stratum that had oozed out Fortinbras De Angelis. Though there were millions of law-abiding citizens in New Jersey and Philadelphia and Brooklyn — Rennie'd been born there herself — there was also a definite organized-crime mulch as well. Be useful if she could learn whether Tam and Fort had more ground in common than just common ground. Maybe that guy Karper at the Clarion had some contacts to call...

"He dealt speed and coke, too," said Juha after a while, unenthusiastically. He'd made up his mind that if he was going to make a clean breast of it to Rennie, who had always been very good to his band in print, he might as well get on with it. Still, nothing said he had to be happy about it, ratting Tommy out like that, though the bastard deserved every bit of it. And what was he doing it *for*, anyway? Rennie was a stone fox, for sure, but she wasn't his type, so there wasn't even the pleasant possibility of some payback action later on; he liked them blonde, titless, short and stupid. But if it helped Prax...

"Grass, sure," he added, "really good and expensive grass. And acid. But mostly the harder stuff. More money."

"What quality?"

"Oh, killer pure, and the prices said so, but especially the smack. And I mean literally killer — I heard that at least six junkies OD'd out of one batch alone."

"Well, that's one way to clean the dog shit off the streets," said Rennie, and Juha glanced up, surprised.

No stupid blonde there. He'd liked Rennie from the first time they met, when she was covering East Bay clubs for that little weekly paper, before she got the Clarion gig, but he'd always thought her a bit too much the lady for some of the scenes. That remark just now, though—that hadn't been anything any lady would have said. That sounded like someone who worked for a newspaper.

"I thought people on smack generally died young and not very pretty?" she asked then.

Tansy shook her head. "Doesn't have to go down like that. There are old black jazz guys, blues cats, who've been on it for *years*. It's almost like vitamins for them. Vitamin H, they call it. They know just how much, and no more. But people our age, they don't want to know about limits, and sometimes the numbers add up."

Rennie nodded thoughtfully, knowing her friend spoke truth. By now she herself was totally familiar with the prevailing generational thinking that if a joint was good, a lid was better; one tab of acid might let you see God, but a whole blotterful, ten thousand mikes or more, well, that might let you *be* God.

We're all a bunch of spoiled baby-boom brats, really…what will we be like when we're fifty? Those of us who make it to fifty, anyway…

"How did you guys get along with him? Personally, I mean."

"We hated his guts," said Chet simply. "But that doesn't mean we killed him."

Rennie laughed. "Been known to happen."

"And not saying we never thought about it. I think Neil Marten, our little cokehead bass player, even worked up some scenario once, when he was stoned and bored, for getting rid of Tam. That Orient Express trip, where everybody on the train has a reason to send the evil bastard to hell and they all take a stab—literally—at punching his ticket. But we're all covered, alibi-wise. We either weren't there yet or we were onstage with the crew, setting up and getting ready for the sound check. Idaho—Prax's roadie—was the only one backstage, and the cops cleared him when some groupie swore she'd been giving him head in a closet during the operative timeframe."

Companionable silence as another joint was passed around. Rennie took advantage of the lull, a natural occurrence in stoned situations, to go out to the kitchen to fix some pogy bait, as her dad called it—not serious food, just sandwiches and cookies and something to wash it down—before the major munchie fit hit, reflecting as she worked on her own drug adventures, such as they had so far been.

Even in New York, the great head expansion of the late '60s had barely begun, though it was well on its way. She hadn't exactly leaped into the saddle to ride with the vanguard of the psychedelic crusaders, but she'd done some pot, a little speed, even some mescaline now and again—her contribution to the zeitgeist. When she'd come west, she'd seen the open and universal use of grass on the streets of the Haight; and in those earliest days, she had of course heard about something called "acid", had even wondered if it might be something she might one day want to try.

Her brother-in-law Eric, appealed to for counsel, had just laughed. "Women don't *need* acid, darling girl. They're so freaking far ahead of men in the expanded-consciousness sweepstakes—yes, even ahead of gay men, though not of course by as *much*, and not that I've tried it myself—that it's superfluous. Drop a tab on a chick and all you'll see is her dust." But heroin was something very, very different.

"When did Tam and Jasper get together?" she asked at length, after the pogy bait had been swallowed not just hook, line and sinker but rod and reel too, mere crumbs remaining. Juha and Chet had practically inhaled everything she'd made, and Rennie, who always felt vaguely maternal about anyone she fed, had gone back to the kitchen to assemble a second wave of fodder, which disappeared almost as fast. Chet had even accompanied her to help out, or perhaps to get a few extra bites to eat, which she'd taken pity on him and given him. Either they were really, *really* stoned or they didn't get fed very well at home by their old ladies, if they had any. "After you guys formed your band?"

"No," said Chet, polishing off the last sandwich and stretching out on the sofa. "They were already hooked up by the time Tommy came to join us. Jasper came with him, part of the deal. It was one of the things that made us decide we wanted Tommy around. Jas was a *real* manager, not like some of the others—you see all these bands who hire their college roommates or surfer buddies for the manager gig, and then they're all gobsmacked when they get ripped off because the guys are greedy thieves, or when they get screwed over because the guys are naïve and stupid."

Juha nodded. "Whatever else he was, Jasper knew his stuff. He had impressive credentials in England; well, you know the names. He also did one-off jobs for a few of the bands that are just now starting to hit big over there—Tenwynter, Lionheart, Dandiprat, Bluesnroyals. He even did some work for the Budgies, when they were still together, and for Gray and Prue after."

An awed and reverent silence touched them all for a moment. The Budgies. The five-man band out of Manchester that was the most famous, most successful, most influential, most creative, most superstarry band that had ever walked the face of the earth. Admired and aspired to by pretty much everyone. They'd been together since they were spotty little pre-teen Mancunian schoolboys, and even though they'd broken up a year ago, quite amicably, the aftershocks were still being felt, as the five giant stars of the fallen Budgie constellation began to pursue separate and successful new orbits. Of them all, Graham Sonnet, the godlike lead guitarist known to the world as Gray, would go on to the most humongous triumphs, along with his singer wife Prue Vye, as big a star in her own right as he in his.

"And you know this how?" asked Rennie, after they'd all duly reflected on the glory of Jasper's connections.

Chet smiled suddenly, and Rennie was struck yet again by how his whole aspect changed when he did so—something she'd first noticed when he was helping her out in the kitchen.

My, but he's cute...all that long shiny pretty hair... Irishman, too...just looove that accent...mind on the job, Strider!

"We checked him out before we committed to him," Chet informed her. "We're not entirely the flighty hippie cats we may, come to think of it, seem. We've noticed the trouble some of the Bay Area bands are already having with their managers—"

His hostess grinned. "Not mentioning any names Jefferson Airplane Matthew Katz who pronounces it 'Cates' how pretentious is that—"

"—and we didn't want to go that road ourselves. Jas had partners in New York, London and L.A. We never had dealings with the London or New York ones, but that Dill Miller dude, you've met him, he runs the L.A. office. We only met him the once, when he was up here after Jas died, and we liked what we saw, even though he seemed kind of—uptight in his management style. Not like old Jas. But we haven't heard from him since, and frankly, we're getting a little worried.."

Rennie filed the remarks on Dill Miller in her mental check-it-out compartment; Dainis Hood had said pretty much the same thing the other day, and she needed to look into it.

"Getting back to Tam?"

"He had a folk band for a few years in Berkeley," said Tansy. "Well, not really a band, just him on vocals and guitar, a chick singer and another cat on bass and sometimes accordion or violin. It played way better than it sounds. I forget their name."

"Maggie Dooley," said Juha, head resting on the back of the leather armchair he now inhabited.

Rennie burst out laughing. "No, really?"

"Why?" asked Tansy, eyes round and dark as blueberries.

"Oh, my Irish grandma calls us that. Me and my twenty-three first cousins on her side of the family. 'What's that little Maggie Dooley up to?' 'Heard from Maggie Dooley lately?' I'm sorry, you were saying?"

Tansy smiled at her angelically. "You're very nice, you know," she said with seeming irrelevance, and Rennie was promptly sucker-punched with guilt.

She loved Tansy, she really did, but she and Prax could only take her in small doses. Sometimes they thought she could detect this—usually after they'd been making fun of her behind her back and were feeling guilty and ashamed of themselves—though in that they were giving her *way* too much credit. But it was so easy, and so much mean fun, and really they couldn't entirely be blamed: Tansy and her airyfairy ways, Tansy in her floaty chiffon tatters that made her look like a refugee from an Arthur Rackham illustration, Tansy who babbled on so endlessly about Middle-earth and Narnia and the mountain-elves who lived in a palace underneath Mount Tamalpais and the tree-elves she'd seen in Muir Woods and the kitchen sprites who dwelled behind her stove that Rennie sometimes longed to bash her head in with a poker.

"Anyway," resumed Juha, "Tommy—*Tam*—had been a client of Jasper's for over two years and going nowhere as a folkie. Then all of a sudden Jasper seemed to take an extra interest in him—almost reinvented him and put him together with us. We'd just been this little funky outfit over in Oakland, and frankly, we never saw ourselves as much more. But Tommy had these great songs." He shrugged. "We just— you know, clicked."

Rennie did know. Setting Tommy Linetti up as Tam Linn to front this amazingly appealing bar band had been a stroke of genius, and if such musical matchmaking had truly been Jasper Goring's talent, then with superior stuff like Prax to work with he might well have become the premier rock manager of the age, eclipsing even the mighty Albert Grossman. But he was dead, though he had consigned to the world as his legacy the Deadly Lampshade and their phenomenal success: Tam's gift for singles lyrics and the Lamps' gift for catchy hooks and hummable arrangements had played perfectly off each other.

Not that the music was poppy bubblegum: far from it. The singles had scored, and airplay had driven sales of their one album, but the band had been too shaggy-dog to get it together to tour—just a handful of dates in L.A. and New York, though they were on the road more these days, mostly college and club gigs in the Northeast, a few in the upper Midwest, hip college towns like Ann Arbor and Madison. They'd managed to combine top-40 with the kind of thing the Beatles were doing now on albums: looser than the Airplane, tighter than the Dead, colorful as all get-out, they were exactly what they appeared to be—the quintessential hippie band that even straights could get into. Yes, Prax was going to work out very well with these guys, Rennie predicted quietly to herself. She could pick up on lyrics where Tam had left off, and together they would go farther and higher than either could have gone alone.

They were all stoned and happy together then for what seemed like about a week but was really half an hour, listening respectfully and only a little enviously to the new Stones album Rennie had put on the turntable. When Juha and Tansy at last stood up, a bit unsteadily, to take their leave, Chet stayed where he was in the window seat and waved a languid hand, and they waved back and nodded and left.

Rennie pretended not to notice, but that policy was hard to maintain, especially when Chet came over to the sofa, sat down beside her and started to kiss her. When she didn't bite his tongue off and flee screaming, he slid one hand up under her miniskirt with all the delicacy of a Doberman, the other hand pulling off her scoop-necked top, and his own embroidered denim workshirt and Rennie's skirt and lace bikini panties soon followed.

Rennie was really nervous—*I'm* naked! *I'm naked in front of a man, only the second man who's ever seen me naked in my life! And he's only the second man I've ever seen naked in mine!*—and more than a little shocked by her own undeniable, well, yes, lust *would* be the word, but she also realized she was more incredibly turned on than she'd ever been in her life. *No offense, Stephen...*

"How did you know I wanted you to stay and—do this?"

He seemed surprised at the question, even as he eased her off the couch and onto the big soft pillows on the floor.

"How did you know you wanted me to?"

Oh, I guess when I started noticing how you weren't wearing any underwear and wondering how much of a hassle buckskin pants would be to take off, that was my first big clue, and gosh, how easy was that, here you are out of them already...

She held him off a little, her hands against his bare chest as he lowered himself on top of her, gently nudging her thighs apart with one knee, and he looked down at her, smiling.

"What? This is going to be so good—"

"Well, yeah—but I've only ever done this with one guy."

His smile widened. "Not a problem. I've never done it with *any* guy."

Chapter Twelve

RENNIE WOKE UP THE NEXT MORNING to see Chet asleep in the bed next to her, the long hair on the pillow making him look like a slumbering Afghan hound. Once she was past her initial shock and flashback memory reconstruction — *oh, yeah, right, I did go to bed with him, didn't I, well, I guess I had to start somewhere with someone, just hadn't known it would be him* — she didn't know quite what to do. Though that certainly hadn't been the problem all night long; plus he'd explained, or demonstrated, anything that required it — amazing how quickly one could learn...

Certainly took the hoodoo off the living room floor, though. Making love with a cute guy on the same patch of floor where Fort and Jasper were murdered — whole change of vibe, and I don't think they mind, either...

Still, she felt a little weird, and shy, unsure of the etiquette of the morning after a one-night stand with a man you weren't in a relationship with. So she slipped quietly out of bed and into the bathroom and then out to the kitchen, so that by the time Chet woke up she had breakfast on the table.

He got the message; but he also got bacon and eggs and coffee and another quickie, which was only fair since Rennie was for reasons of her own still completely naked except for a wristful of silver bangles and her waist-length hair, and by the time he went downstairs to his car she had agreed to see him again that night.

"Well, I want to," she said to Prax when she went down to the jail for the usual daily visit, and Prax grinned at the defiance in her tone. "So, you heard it here first: I slept with another man, I *enjoyed* sleeping with another man—most educational, you have no idea, well, you probably do—and I'm planning on sleeping with him again tonight and enjoying it even more. So it's not a one-nighter. Even though I'd only met him a few times, and we weren't going out, and yet I balled him on the living room floor after everybody left and in bed all night long and again in the morning. And I'm going to ball him some more tonight. And other guys too, if I see any who want me and who I want back. Practice makes perfect, right? So what does that make me?"

"Normal and healthy, I'd say."

"Then why do I feel so guilty?"

"You're feeling guilty because you let somebody fuck you who's not your husband?"

"No, actually, I'm feeling guilty because I don't feel as guilty as I think I *should* feel that I let somebody fuck me who's not my husband. Somebody I'm not in love with, even. I broke my marriage vows. I *never* thought I'd do that."

Prax rolled her eyes, though she spoke with sympathy. "You didn't break anything. Your marriage was already broken—your marriage, not your feelings for Stephen. Big difference. Besides, you're not in love with Stephen either, and yet you let him fuck you all the time."

"That's different."

"Is it? Oh, I don't think it is, petal! You know, you're only as guilty as you feel, and you can feel as guilty as you want. Or not."

"So what shall I do?"

"Nothing. It's usually best. Sure, you can selfishly confess to Stephen and be all penitential and absolved, though I wouldn't advise it unless you really hate him and want to hurt him by stabbing him in the back with the Icepick of Confession, which I very much doubt is the case. Confession only makes the confessor feel better, not the confessee. Either way, it doesn't change anything that really matters... Did you find out anything useful, at least? I mean, apart from anything sex-related."

Rennie shrugged, glad for the change of topic. "Hard to say. Tam was majorly into smack, which apparently everyone in California knew but me. They thought he was dealing on the side. But so do lots of people."

Prax was silent a few moments. Even though she was in jail—*jail!*—it was so hard sometimes for her to remember that she had been arrested for double murder, that these inquiry sessions of Rennie's were all in aid of clearing her. She never spoke of how it was for her in there, and Rennie agonized almost hourly over whether or not she should ask, but now Prax told her just how it was. Quietly and calmly, almost as if she were reading aloud a dry newspaper account about someone else, which only made it all the more dreadful to hear.

"Oh, God... Sweetie, I know it's horrible and unreal," said Rennie, appalled and desperately sympathetic. "But I'm trying, King's trying, Berry's trying...if there's anything we can dig up anywhere that will help you, we'll find it, I swear. At least there's going to be a bail review hearing in a week or two, King managed to get that happening. Maybe by then we'll have something solid enough to get you out of here. God knows Marcus and his merry men don't seem to be turning up tons of information. Or if they are, they're not sharing."

"What about Fortinbras?" asked Prax after another lengthy silence. "And Jasper too, come to think of it? We know a bit more about Tam now, what he was into, what made him do what he did. And that's good. And thank you. But what do we know about *them*?"

Rennie stared at her. "What indeed."

She started the next wave of inquisition as soon as she was back in the Clarion offices on Monday. Tam may have been one thing, but Fortinbras was a different story—and yet there were odd similarities, as she found out once she really began to dig.

Pretty much played out four years ago, well before the rising psychedelic tide started lapping at the retreating beachheads of 50's rock and roll, the former Franco Anthony De Angelis had been taken on as a combination charity case/possible investment by Jasper Goring. And, just as he'd done with washed-up folkie Tommy Linetti, transforming him into Tam Linn, Jasper had magically reinvented Anthony too, reconstructing him into Fortinbras, the host of a popular hootenanny bandstand TV show, the star of a string of bikini movies, and—inevitably combining the two—the iconic presence in the bikini hootenanny movies that so annoyed Rennie.

Recently, though—even before Tam's murder—Fortinbras had started venomously speaking out against all things and people hippie and psychedelic as if they were the Devil's rubber duckies. He'd reserved especial venom for the rising San Francisco bands and artists, with the high point, or low point, being his public diatribes against Prax after Tam's murder.

Nobody knew why he had been so openly spiteful, unless it was out of pure hissing spitting jealousy that people like the Lamps and the Airplane and the Dead could fill clubs and get record deals and he couldn't. But his harangues did him no good, though they did raise the sympathy level for Prax, and only made people think him even more of a jackass than he in fact was.

And no matter how hard he tried, the best he could do was that grinning hootenanny host job and those godawful movies and the occasional second-guest-star gig on things like "Bonanza" or "Dragnet", invariably cast for bizarro name value—hey out there, TV audiences, dig this, it's Fortinbras pretending he's a gunfighter, or a gangster! But why had an ostensibly savvy manager like Jasper Goring taken him on if there really wasn't anything he could do for him? Or, if he *had* had plans, what might those plans have been? Now that both of them were dead, it didn't seem to matter much. But maybe it did.

It took a while, but Rennie ran the trail to earth like a particularly dedicated foxhound, and she found her quarry in a most unexpected quarter.

"And guess what?" she demanded triumphantly. Prax indicated her ignorance, and also her impatience with guesswork. "Somebody else with a big old drug problem! Only, a secret one this time…don't worry, I already told King all about it, he's on it. Tam didn't give a flying fuck who knew what he was doing, but Fort didn't want anybody to find out that he was a serious druggie. Coke, speed and, yes, you guessed it, smack. And we know now why he kept it quiet: it majorly ran against the squeaky-clean beach-blanket image, and therefore it might have cut off the movie work and the host jobs and the TV guest-star gigs."

"Well, that makes total sense. Soap company sponsors don't generally like to find out that their bought dogs of spokesman identity are into scag."

"Listen to this, though: I heard some delightful little tales about how Fort was mixed up with really rough types, borderline mob. One of the guys in Moby Grape told me that

Fort drove to the Oakland airport one day in a rented car with a trunk full of coke, and he flew to Miami and didn't come back for a month. He was so stoned when he left that not only did he forget the coke was in the trunk, he also forgot he'd left the car in the long-term parking lot. Unbelievable but true. So eventually the police towed the car and of course they found the coke. Jasper hushed it up and lied about the stash—oh, not Fort's, no way, had to have been put there by someone else, the car was there unattended for a whole month, who knows who got at it. Anyway, he kept Fort's name out of it, and in the end he made it go away and Fort got off."

"All of which would seem to suggest that maybe little Tony De Angelis from Philly and little Tommy Linetti from Jersey City didn't have the cleanest hands on their blocks."

Rennie nodded. "Or else the blocks they came from were dirtier than most. Though so far I can't make any hard and fast connections with any kind of mob stuff. But maybe the cops can. Because I bet none of this is news to them."

"Interesting. Well, that might explain why Fort was so down on hippies. We do drugs right out front, and he didn't dare. So naturally he would trash us any chance he got."

"Somehow I get the feeling that's only part of it." Rennie brooded a while. "I can't see the rest, not just yet. But I will."

She was pleased with the results of her sleuthing, though she didn't delude herself about the importance of it. Hey, if she could find this out, little Rennie Stride with her inexperience and her limited access and few connections, surely the cops, who did this sort of thing for a living, had been clued in ages ago.

But where had Jasper Goring figured into it? That was the question that had annoyed her almost from the first time he'd turned up as Prax's manager, slobbering over her that night at Morton's Fork. To be sure, Rennie'd done some checking on him too, and as Dill Miller had told them, Jasper had been the real goods. He'd come of a thoroughly respectable English squirearchy family who had been on houseguest terms with royalty since the days of Edward VII. Went to Haileybury, a good solid school, though hardly Eton, and to Cambridge after—Trinity, a fashionable, academically undemanding college.

And most astonishingly, considering the business he had been in and the company he had kept, he had never done any drugs at all, at least none that anyone could pin on him. Though he hadn't minded other people doing them. But nobody had ever seen or even heard of him indulging in so much as a single snootful of coke, let alone anything harder or nastier. Even in his university days, he'd never smoked pot; indeed, he'd seldom drunk anything but wine or beer, though in such Hooray-Henry quantities as was to be expected of a student of his social background.

So if not drugs, then what? On a sudden hunch, Rennie called Ken Karper again and pumped him for contacts, promising him the glory of the story, if there was one (he gladly accepted) and her firstborn child, if there should ever be one (he graciously declined), and after rootling around a bit in some unsavory areas of town on his say-so, brandishing his protective name like a flaming torch against the creatures of the night she found there, she finally came up with a not entirely unexpected answer.

"Gambling," she said triumphantly to Berry and King Bryant. "Our little Jas was so into gambling debt he probably wasn't going to get out from under until the turn of the millennium. The next millennium, not this one coming up. It's been going on for *years*. They called him Roaring Goring even back at Cambridge, that's where the nickname got started, and for good reason: he almost got tossed for setting up betting pools on the university sports teams. Then he got into horse racing, greyhound racing, football, card games, traffic conditions and weather forecasts and Prince Charles's future princess, for all I know—you name it, he bet on it. And he did really well, tons of money, but more recently he usually lost. Big-time."

"How did you find all this out?"

"Went to see some people he owed. Then I went to see his wife."

Well, ex-wife. She'd been very hard to winkle out, even with the long, sharp pin of Lacing connections that Rennie hadn't scrupled to employ. She'd covered her tracks extremely well, and Rennie wasn't surprised that the police hadn't gotten to her yet. She herself wouldn't have managed it, if Karper's contacts hadn't given her the tip—and, unbelievably, if Marjorie Lacing hadn't given her the entrée. Hard to believe Motherdear actually knew her. But she did.

The former Mrs. Jasper Goring was a gorgeous former model in her late thirties, called, in her professional capacity, Amira—half French, half Moroccan, almond-eyed, honey-skinned, sun-streaked hair. She'd divorced Jasper some years ago, and had married again almost at once—a very wealthy and much older City stockbroker called Markham, who did a lot of major business and socializing with the senior Lacings.

And it had taken all the might of the Lacing name to secure the audience in the first place. So much for trying to keep your personal life out of your work—but Marjorie had been overjoyed at Rennie's timid request, thinking that for once her son's wayward wife was showing signs of wanting to meet the right people. And never dreaming that it was all for what Marjorie could only decry as the most wrong of reasons. But she'd given Rennie the introduction gladly, and eagerly awaited what she thought would be suitable social developments. Some hope.

Jasper's ex's current husband owned a duplex apartment on the penthouse floor of a posh new high-rise building on Russian Hill, with views even more panoramic than those of Hell House. Rennie had been met at the elevator by a gloved concierge and personally escorted to the apartment door, where a maid took over, conveying "Madame Lacing" to a huge, glass-walled living room, where a slim figure in a caftan of pale orange silk had been standing at the windows, waiting for her in a poisonous blue Gauloise haze.

Marie-Laure bint Faid de Valtière Goring Markham had not been best pleased to be asked to discuss her former husband—though as she couldn't afford to offend Mrs. Stephen Lacing, and thus offend Marjorie Lacing, she had cooperated as far as she felt able.

Rennie, drinking sweet tea from a jeweled Moroccan glass, had heard a shrill French-accented voice telling her how highly Marie-Laure and her elderly supersuit spouse thought of the Lacings *mère et père* and valued their friendship and business partnership—well, sure, if it enabled them to live like this—and how the apparently unlamented "Zhaspair" indeed had had a major gambling problem, always running out of money to finance it.

"But you ask about Zhaspair, Madame Lacing," she'd said, with a smile every bit the glacial match of Motherdear's own. "We met in Marrakech fifteen years ago, when I was on a Vogue shoot. We fell rrrravishingly in love, of course. He was just getting started, and though I was so very much younger I supported us both for a while; I made quite good money, much more than he. Then his management company took off, and we were—content."

"When did he start gambling?"

Marie-Laure had taken her time replying. But it appeared that the serious gambling, under control for a while, had begun in earnest about six years ago, though the marriage had tottered on through all his many tearful heartfelt promises to do better, to change, to quit.

"He tried, truly he did try to stop. But always he slid back, even when I changed the checking account from joint to separate." She set down her glass on the inlaid mosaic table with a bit more force than necessary. "When I came home one day to an empty jewel case, and learned that he had taken all my diamonds to pawn so he could pay off his gambling debts — that was the last hay."

"Straw. The last straw."

She dismissed this with the actual French *Pfff* that Rennie had only ever seen in cartoons. "So I quite calmly walked out, redeemed my jewels with my own money and just as calmly divorced him, also with my own money. I married my present husband soon thereafter, and I have not seen Zhaspair since, nor do I wish to." She raised one perfect eyebrow. "May I ask why you require all this information?"

Swiftly Rennie had filled her in, and Marie-Laure visibly vibrated with Gallic indignation.

"I do not wish to be insulting, but if I had known this, Madame Lacing, I would never have agreed to see you. Surely you are not suggesting that I might possibly know anything about these frrrrightful murders, that I might have massacred my ex-husband *et ces autres pauvres*?"

Thinking that she'd never before heard "massacred" pronounced as a four-syllable word, Rennie had assured her she was no suspect on anyone's list, then thanked her and soothingly promised to remember her and the spouse to *la plus chère* Marjorie and *le grand Général*.

She'd departed still feeling that some big important pieces of the puzzle picture remained to be fitted in, and that someone had quite deliberately stuffed them down the back of the sofa. And then she took the information to the same place she'd brought all the rest.

"Okay — it is my firm contention that an outsider murdered

Jasper and Fort and knocked Prax out with the drugged wine, probably but not definitely the same person who murdered Tam. I think we are all agreed on that?"

Rennie looked questioningly at King Bryant and Berry Rosenbaum, who nodded, and she continued.

"So now it looks as if Tam, Jasper and Fort all had secret money issues that could be eased, at least, by drug dealing."

She outlined her discoveries of the past few weeks, and as she recounted her various conversations with her ever more varied sources, Berry and King began to look somber and elated at the same time, which was more of a trick than it might sound.

The three were having a small private strategy session at Rennie's place—a session to which Stephen had been asked. But to Rennie's surprise, and surprisingly keen dismay, he had begged off attending, citing the pressures of work and that he just couldn't take any more speculating, that he had no ideas and no clues and to keep on talking about it only made him crazy.

Well, okay. If that was how he really felt, Rennie wasn't about to push him; she owed him so much as it was. But deep down she had this dreadful sinking feeling that somehow Stephen knew she'd slept with another man and was avoiding her because he didn't want to see her faithless sluttish self right there brazenly in front of him; and even if he didn't know, she still felt guilty, for all her fine words to Prax. And shy of him, which was ridiculous. It wasn't as if she had a big scarlet A on her forehead, and she really only partly thought she deserved one—but now, in light of everything he had done to help, her trampery suddenly seemed especially heinous.

Here Stephen foots the legal bill—yeah, yeah, I know, I know, it's my money too—and his wife repays him by letting another man screw her brains out... She thrust it out of her mind.

Can't think of it now, won't *think of it...*

But as she had told King and Berry, there was still a long, long way to go before they got to the dark nasty bottom of this particular barrel, and at the moment it was nowhere in sight. True, she'd uncovered two very real motives, and though she doubted she was alone in mining this knowledge, she had wanted to go over it privately with legal minds; hence the strategy meet.

Besides, she needed to come to terms with all this on her own. In her year in San Francisco, her eight months in the Haight, Rennie had come to believe that there were far worse crimes and sins in the world than drug dealing. Oh, to be sure, she was only talking about things like pot and acid sold by and to aware and consenting adults — not playground perverts pushing smack on junior-high kids but responsible dealers who gave good count and stood up for what they sold. Owsley, the Bay Area Acid King, with his turn-on-the-world mission and gig as sound genius for the Grateful Dead, was merely the most visible of many such.

But he and his fellows were benevolent. According to what Juha Vasso had told her, there were people out there who weren't benign in the least — creatures to whom Owsley and his ilk were as the gently smiling dolphin to the hunting killer whale. People who would slaughter three inconvenient other people as easy as look at them, and not scruple to frame an innocent woman in the process. And there were still counties that hadn't yet been heard from...

"What did you find out about this Dill Miller cat?" asked Rennie, after silently brooding for a bit. "Jasper's L.A. partner? We had him over to dinner that one night, but we couldn't get a handle on him, and nobody's heard from him since. Have you turned up anything?"

King nodded. "As a matter of fact, I have. Prax asked me to speak to him on the band's behalf, since they don't have a lawyer of their own and he hadn't been returning their calls.

I was happy to help out; my brief isn't just for Prax's defense, you know—whatever I can do for her on any legal matters, and by extension the band as well. I talked to Miller yesterday for half an hour, and I must say I'm considerably relieved. He claims to have known nothing about any drug goings-on on anyone's part, and hates bad drugs and the bad people who push them. Though the fact that he denies it when it hasn't even been brought up by the police is enough to give one pause right there. Or at least to give *me* pause. But in my professional opinion, he's clean and straight."

"What did he say about continuing on in Jasper's little elfin footsteps? And why hasn't he been answering the Karms' phone calls? They're not having a very easy time of it, you know. He talks them up to a merger and gets them all happy and excited, then he leaves them hanging and half-starving while he sinks back into the tar pits of L.A. And we wonder why."

"Well, as to that, he said he went home after his couple of days up here, to work on the contracts, and instead he got sick as a dog. For the past three weeks he's been flat on his back in bed with a case of the flu that went into pneumonia and sent him to the hospital. He's only just gotten back home, and until yesterday his wife wouldn't let him talk to anyone but her and the doctor. He says. I suppose it can be checked easily enough, if you think it should be. He also says he still wants very much to act as manager to this wondrous new group to be assembled from the combined talents of Prax, Karma Mirror and the Deadly Lampshade, I do so love those names. I said I would of course have to review any contracts he came up with and also insist on a small living advance so his future clients could actually eat for the next few weeks, and he said fine by him."

"I see. Well, that's something."

King glanced shrewdly at her. "You do not seem to be entirely thrilled by this information. May I ask why not?"

"D'you think you're the only one who thinks around here?" Rennie softened the sharp words with a smile, then shook herself. "And of course anyone may *ask*... Oh, it's probably nothing, but I did a little checking of my own. With Jasper's secretary, who's been attempting to run the office here until the legalities get sorted out. And I found out that our Mr. Randyll Miller was in San Francisco recently. Twice. Just about the same time as the murders."

Rennie had been hoarding this little piece of information, and she was pleased to see the startled glances King and Berry shot each other; they clearly had not known, and were as instinctively alarmed about it as she had been.

"To be exact," she drawled, enjoying spinning it out, "the first unexplained visit was the week of Tam's murder. Then Dill was here again later on, into which time bracket the murders at my house come dead, as it were, center. I take it he never mentioned this in your conversation of yesterday? No, and he let us all believe he'd come here only *after* Jasper and Fort were killed. And maybe that's true, maybe he did. But why not tell us? And if he were up here already, it makes one wonder. If the cops do know about his two flying visits up from the Southland, maybe *they* just haven't gotten around to wondering either. Or at least not publicly. Hmm."

"Hmm indeed." King tapped his fingers on the arm of his chair. "As far as we know, they weren't aware of Miller's existence any sooner than we were. For some reason, his name didn't appear on the first list of people immediately questioned in connection, even though he's been Goring's business partner for years. If they didn't know about him right off the bat, obviously they wouldn't have known of his oddly timed jaunts. Though if you do, by now they do too. Still, lots and lots of people come to San Francisco every single day with pure hearts and good intentions, God bless them, why shouldn't he be among them?"

Berry favored them both with the brief expression that

is the facial equivalent of a scoff.

"But what would his motive have been? Killing Jasper and two famous clients — to achieve what?"

"Well, Miller told King he hates drugs and the people who use and traffic in drugs, yes?" asked Rennie. "If he's not lying about that, maybe he killed the three of them to make sure his stake in the management company stayed safe, and he would then inherit the whole thing from Jasper as surviving partner. Maybe he just wanted to keep the druggies and the crapshooter from screwing up his very lucrative livelihood. Plenty of murders have been done for less."

"What does Marcus say?" asked Berry.

Rennie rolled her eyes. "Hasn't exactly been what you might call forthcoming of late, at least not along the lines of suspectdom. But he did let on that his masters have just decided that Neil Marten — the untalented unreliable coke freak bass player the Lamps are planning on dumping so Prax's hugely talented and utterly reliable and non-druggie bass player Bardo can take his place — is not out of the running as a suspect."

"Was Marten even there? Backstage, I mean."

"Not that anyone's saying. The story is that he was out front overseeing the placement of his monitor and speaker stacks, highly visible to all and sundry, then, ever so mysteriously, no one could find him when it came time for the actual sound check. Bill Graham is notorious for not letting band members leave once they've checked in backstage for the performance, so this was pretty uncool. According to witnesses, the Lamps were furious, but they should have known better, as apparently Neil's pulled this vanishing act before. It's one of the reasons they want to dump him. Well, plus he's a sucky bassist, doesn't play well with others and does way too much blow."

"Who saw him out front?" asked King.

"Oh, Bill, half the Fillmore crew, B. B. King's drummer

and horn section..."

"Where did he go off to, then?"

Rennie shrugged. "Smoking a joint out in the side alley. He says. No witnesses, of course."

"And just what motive do we think Neil might have?" asked Berry, making notes.

"Kill Tam for, presumably, initiating the movement to fire him," said King at once. "Kill Jasper for floating the idea to Prax and the Lamps to get together and make a new band without him. Kill Fort—well, I don't know what that would accomplish; maybe it was just unfortunate proximity to someone who *was* wanted dead. But I don't see how any amount of murders could stop Marten being let go, if that's what the Lamps and Prax decide they want. It seems much too much of a stretch. I can't imagine why the cops like him for Tam."

"Ye-es," said Rennie thoughtfully. "And again it's only circumstantial: he was around, or carefully not around, during the operative times. I'll tell you what's been bothering me forever about the murders at my place, though. Method. Why would anyone use a damn *sword*? If you were the killer, why wouldn't you just load up all the wine bottles with lethal levels of downers and let overdose take its course? And why would you even decide to load up the wine bottles in the first place? Maybe the people you wanted to drink weren't drinking that night, so a waste of good drugs. Or bad. How would you get Jasper to bring an already dosed wine bottle to a dinner party and then drink from it himself? Since obviously you had no problem getting into and out of my apartment and you were clever enough to leave no tiresome physical evidence and nobody was around to hear any shots, why wouldn't you just blow everybody's brains out with a goddamn automatic? For that matter, why not kill Prax too, especially if you thought she might have heard something significant before she passed out?"

"Which she did," said Berry. "She heard the door open and close."

"So she says. But the cops don't believe her."

"They *say* they don't believe her," said King Bryant.

"They busted her for double murder!" snapped Rennie. "That sounds pretty believe-y to me!"

"And do you really think that nobody's ever been arrested purely in the hopes of the real killer getting overconfident and getting caught? All sorts of safeguards to the contrary notwithstanding, it happens more often than you'd think, or would like to think, my young friend."

"Well, it's way too trippy for me. Not to mention astoundingly illegal. I know I said I wanted to see more suspects to take the weight off Prax, but this is ridiculous." Rennie stared unseeing at the fireplace, where, in lieu of crackling flames, the hearth was filled with giant sprays of purple lilacs, supplied by Stephen from the Hall Place gardens. "You know, what's to rule out Jasper or Fort having killed Tam? Or both of them together having killed him. If we're going to get creative. But then who kills *them*? We're back to that."

"To your horror and distaste, there's more," said Berry, reluctantly but firmly, and glanced at King. "We only found out about it this afternoon, and haven't had a chance to go over it yet. Idaho, Prax's roadie—Todd Vance, his real name is?"

Rennie suddenly felt very cold and very tired. *Oh, I so don't want to hear this…*

"What about him? He's big and sweet and funny. He adores Prax. We all like him. He was getting head from some groupie backstage at the time in question, and she was as happy to alibi him as she apparently was to blow him. The cops checked it out."

"Maybe so," Berry conceded. "But his alibi has apparently decided she no longer feels like covering his ass—

so to speak. She now says there was *no* ever so romantic encounter. Which leaves Idaho alone backstage. For—you guessed it—more than enough time to kill an obnoxious druggie singer and stuff him into a road case."

After they'd gone, Rennie tucked herself into one of the window seats and stared out at the nighttime skyline, a view she never tired of. She was missing something here. They all were. True, they had some big motives now, which they didn't have before—drugs and gambling and money, it doesn't get much nastier than that.

But they still had no suspects but Prax. In spite of the new information, Idaho wasn't really likely. The other musicians, almost certainly not. Not Marten. Not even Dill Miller... Which left outsiders. There were, of course, plenty of barracudas cruising the murky waters of San Francisco rock and roll, right along with the schools of blameless sunfish and those smiling hippie dolphins. But where was the great white? The marauding orca? Who was the big nasty shark who would have benefited by offing the three little fishies? Not even the shadow of a hooked and purposeful fin slicing the waves—at least none that she could see.

She shifted on the velvet cushions. Enough with the piscine metaphors. It was of course entirely possible that Fort or Jasper or both of them together had killed Tam, as she'd suggested to King and Berry, and then someone else had killed the two of them to shut them up, or even just because. But however you played it, Fort and Jasper couldn't have killed each other, and logic would seem to require one killer for all victims. Occam's razor: the simplest solution is the solution most likely to be correct. As she had learned at school.

And the simplest solution was that Prax McKenna had killed Jasper and Fort, and maybe even Tam, and was lying through her teeth when she said she hadn't. Sometimes the trout in the milk turns out to be a shark. Or a Snark.

" 'For the Snark was a Boojum, you see...' "

Rennie shivered, and hugged her knees to her chest. Could that be possible? Could Prax actually have—no, she would never believe that. Never, never, never. True, she had known her only a short time, and didn't know much about her, but she did know *that* much. Not that Prax could never kill anyone—given sufficient reason, pretty much anybody except a Buddhist saint can kill—but that Prax had not killed Tam or Fort or Jasper. As strongly as she refused to believe that there ain't no cure for the summertime blues—oh please! There were several dozen cures at *least*!—THAT was how strongly she refused to believe in Prax's guilt. And she would prove her friend's innocence if she had to hunt Boojums until the cows came home.

When Rennie got to the cows, she stretched and straightened and pushed off the window seat, heading down the hall to bed.

"Well, if I have to shave my legs with Occam's razor," she said aloud to the universe, or whomever else might have been listening, "I sure could use some new blades. For preference, single-edged. See what you can do."

And sometimes, if you know exactly how to ask, the universe sits up and pays attention.

Chapter Thirteen

"GOT SOMETHING FOR YOU, STRIDER. Something nice."

Burke Kinney, on the phone, beckoned Rennie into his office as she went past on her way to her desk in the corner, speaking aside to her with his hand covering the mouthpiece. He finished his conversation while she stood politely in the doorway, then he waved her into a seat.

While she was waiting, she wondered what kind of job it might be that he had for her. Hopefully something non-rockish, to take her mind off the case; she'd been spinning blind ever since last night's revelations from King and Berry, and she was just about wiped out. From one suspect — Prax — to several, including two dead people. Terrific. Yes, something new would be a fine thing. Since Burke had put her to work on other assignments after the murders, she'd been doing sidebar color stories to news pieces and small interviews. Nothing major: nothing front-pagey or headliney — she was years away from that. But just enough to start to give her writing style some nice newsy polish, and she'd found she really liked it.

She was by no means weary of writing about rock, she never would be, that would always be the place she wanted her name to be made; but it was good to be able to get into other stuff, and Burke had been amazingly generous. Ever since a minor dressing-down and building-up he had given her a month ago, she'd been more on her journalistic toes than she'd ever been. So now, maybe...

Burke hung up the phone, grinned at her, made a few notes, and then leaned back in his creaky old chair and gave her his full attention.

"What do you know about redwoods?"

"Redwoods? Trees. Really big. Really old." She considered briefly. "Yep, that's it."

He laughed. "Well, go do some homework and find out some more. I want you to talk to Clovis Franjo."

"You say that name as if I should know it."

"And you've lived in San Francisco how long? Surely you've been occasionally inconvenienced by the traffic-stopping protests he and his merry band are always putting on. And your family, sorry, your husband's family, donates yearly and generously to his cause. He's a rabid, yes, that would be the word, rabid redwood protector. Heads up this group called the Warriors of Gaia."

"Oh, them. I hadn't realized such big strong trees needed mighty traffic-stopping warriors to protect them."

"Well, he and a lot of other wackos — sorry, environmentalists — think they do. There are a bunch of logging companies who'd like to get into virgin redwood forests and — "

"Devirginize them?"

Burke gave her a nervous grin, a little scandalized, not for the first time, at Rennie's flipness. Being of the old school, and more than a tad bit prudish, he wasn't quite used to, or indeed wholly comfortable with, such frank byplay with young ladies, especially young married ladies of good family who worked for him. But he tried to keep up.

"Ravish them would be more accurate. Wholesale harvesting, sweeping clear-cutting that will take a thousand years for the forests to recover from. Well, according to Clovis, anyway. Hey, he may be right, who knows. He's 'eccentric', apparently, so you'll have to talk first to someone called Foy Ballard, to see if you are spiritually and morally fit to speak to Clovis in person."

When Rennie got her breath back again after having her morals and spirituality impugned, even secondhand: "*Foy?*"

"Yeah—and get this, he's an ex-Hell's Angel who apparently was blinded by the pure green light of environmental correctness and had his eyes opened thereby."

"Not exactly the road to Damascus, but I guess it passes for conversion."

"I guess. It makes for a strange second-in-command, though; still, there it is, the whole damn outfit is weird. Anyway, nobody gets to talk to Clovis whom Foy hasn't vetted and approved first. Near as anyone can make out, he's a sort of combination bodyguard, high priest, private secretary and nanny."

"Terrific. So he interviews me to find out if I'm worthy of interviewing. And just what parameters does this Foy use to determine the merit of supplicants?"

Burke shrugged. "No one knows. Vibes. Astrological signs. Hair color. Taste in literature. How you feel about letting designated hitters taint the purity of baseball—which, by the way, if God cares about humanity at all he will never let happen. Just so you know, Foy's turned away saffron-robed representatives of the Dalai Lama for being insufficiently immaculate of purpose and has let Clovis eat lasagna in North Beach with Frank Sinatra."

"I see."

"Well, whatever it is, Strider, you just be damn sure

you make his cut. For publicity hounds dependent on public donations, the Warriors are strangely shy of formal interviews—you'd think they'd be media-slutting all over creation for any sort of attention for their propaganda, wouldn't you. But no, they're not, and I and quite a few others would like to know why. So this is something of a coup for us, to be asked. Could be an important piece. Ballard asked Garry for you specifically, said your Prax piece impressed both him and Franjo, so we thought we'd give you the shot. And the fact that you're a Lacing—I know, in name only—can't hurt. Names matter, and don't ever think they don't. So go, run, poke around, see what crawls out."

Before she had come to San Francisco to live, the only redwoods Rennie had ever known personally had been picnic furniture. To remedy this shocking deficiency, Stephen had several times taken her to Muir Woods, the amazing nature preserve just north of the Golden Gate Bridge. He'd pushed her along a few walks and mini-hikes—not too outdoorsy, nothing involving bugs or mud or trail mix, she was still a New York girl, her idea of back to nature was no air conditioning—and she had been every bit as awed and reverentially astonished as he had hoped.

She had fallen completely in love with the trees, and even more in love with the *idea* of the trees. These things had been here and vigorously alive when Rennie's ancestors had been cutting down Europe's oak forests to fuel the fires to make bronze spearheads, and they would be here and alive long after she was gone. Trippy, to say the least.

Now, two days later, on a misty moisty morning, she and Foy Ballard were walking side by side on a winding path deep in the heart of Muir Woods, Foy staring straight ahead, Rennie looking around her at the aisles of colossal trees stretching away on either hand into fog-fingered dimness: coast redwoods for the most part, with Douglas firs, big-leaf maples and tanbark oaks filling in the gaps.

She had dressed for the excursion: workshirt, jeans, embroidered sheepskin Afghan coat, Frye boots, hair in braids and head scarved with a colorful Ukrainian kerchief—and she was glad she had; the spring morning was cold, the sun not yet high enough to burn off the fog and break through to the forest floor, and it wouldn't warm things up much when it did.

Rennie shivered inside her jacket, rubbed her hands up into her sleeves to unfreeze her fingers. Except for the very occasional hiker clomping past, there wasn't a sound hitting their ears that wasn't entirely natural.

'This is the forest primeval, the murmuring pines and the hemlocks'....but redwoods don't murmur. I don't know what it is that they do, but it's deeper and louder and older than anything except the sea and the stars and the mountains...the song they sing the world...

She collected herself and cut her glance sideways at her companion. It was a good thing Burke had mentioned Foy's former affiliation, because otherwise Rennie would have bolted at the sight of the hulking creature approaching her where she'd waited as appointed, near the ranger station. As it was, she still had to control the urge for flight.

Foy Ballard was a huge, immensely strong, leathered-up motorcycle wrangler who walked with the rolling gait of a cowboy, and who had hair almost as long as her own. Though of course hers didn't have iron bars and feathers braided into it. Denoting his allegiance, Foy's black leather jacket had a god's-eye rather incongruously handpainted on the back, where once he would have sported Hell's Angels colors: in Earth-friendly tones of green and gold and blue and white, a stylized sequoia as the upright bar and a flaming sword for the crosspiece—the flag and symbol of the Warriors of Gaia.

As Rennie had introduced herself, wondering if the ex in "ex-Hell's Angel" was really as ex as Burke had claimed, Foy had taken her proffered hand with surprising gentleness and said how nice it was to meet her at last, he'd read a lot of her stuff in the East Village Other and the Berkeley Barb and the Gilded Lily, besides her Clarion pieces, she wrote really well, especially for a chick. But looking up into his small and piggish eyes, Rennie had seen things flickering there that she didn't find so nice and gentle at all, and wondered who else had seen those things, and what had happened to them...

They'd started talking at once, and they were still talking as they now came along the path, the conversation not so much about the great trees and their undeniable peril but any number of other far-ranging and unrelated topics, all comprising a checklist for approval that Foy was apparently reading off the back of his eyelids. Rennie had realized from the first that she was being manipulated by a master, at least judging by his choice of topic and unsuspected erudition, and she had decided to relax and go with the flow and just answer his questions as best she could, and hope she fit the profile.

So far they had discussed ecology, geology, the Grail motif in Arthurian legend, hamburgers vs. hot dogs, Beatles vs. Stones, cars vs. motorcycles vs. horses (very careful on that one, Rennie had been), faith, grace and the nature of trust, which was where they were at present.

"In the words of the revered guru Ralph J. Gleason, beads and buckskin can burn you as bad as a business suit."

Foy's buffalo-sized, buffalo-maned head nodded slowly and massively, the iron bars faintly chiming. "Wise. Very wise. What do *you* say?"

She never even hesitated. "It may walk like a head, and talk like a head, and dope like a head, but it can still be a dick."

Foy laughed thunderously, and the sound echoed off the redwoods. "Well put. But we don't need dope. And if we do, we have the drugs that Earth Mother made for us, pure natural highs like pot and peyote and shrooms. No need to mess around with that bad-fu stuff, coke and smack and speed. You gotta be righteous, gotta be down with the Mother and her loving works."

"I so agree... And I suppose the redwoods approve."

His eyes glinted. "They approve of more trips than we can imagine. They're sentient, you know — aware, self-conscious. They protect and defend those who look after them."

Ohhhhkay.... "You sound like my friend Tansy. She believes there are guardian spirits in the trees."

He looked narrowly at her. "And you don't?"

"Oh, I don't know. It sounds right, somehow. Yes, I do. Why should people and animals be the only ones who have souls?" She looked up at the giants that towered around her, surprised at her own answer, and the conviction with which she'd pronounced it. "If any trees had souls, it would be these. They've seen so much, been around through so much; how could they be alive for so long and not have picked up on something? And how offensive for puny humans to think they control them."

That must have been the big litmus-paper question, and Rennie must have passed the test — though it was only what she honestly felt, even if she'd never thought about it before, much less articulated it — and there must also have been some imperceptible signal like that whistle only dogs can hear, because all of a sudden Foy was backing away as if out of the presence of royalty, and this other guy, who had just stepped out of a hollow redwood trunk big enough to hide a Buick, not twenty feet away, was drifting toward her through the mist-dripping giant ferns.

As entrances go, not half bad, and possessed of a certain dryad drama that Tansy would have delighted in, though Rennie's benchmark for dramatic on-scene arrival would always be Omar Sharif riding his camel into the frame in "Lawrence of Arabia." But now she found herself shaking a limp white hand and looking into pale, silvery-blue eyes on a level four inches above her own.

"Clovis Franjo." Foy Ballard pronounced the name in such a reverential whisper that Rennie caught herself looking for a ring to kiss. She stopped just in time, though, and merely surveyed him.

So this was the self-appointed lord protector of the forests. Pity the trees couldn't have found themselves a worthier champion, or at the very least a more impressive one. Clovis Franjo, built more like a bamboo than a redwood, had seaweedy hair like dull brown kelp and a fluty, high-pitched voice that belied the words he spoke with it.

But those watery blue eyes held the unmistakable glow of the fanatic at work, and the grip he had on her arm as he steered her along the path was quite surprisingly strong. As he talked to her, or rather at her, Rennie realized that no matter the undeniable romance of his cause, Clovis Franjo was as charmless and humorless as they came.

She had already learned most fanatics were like that, be they of the hippie persuasion or straighter than straight. He didn't seem to pick up on her stance toward him, either, a stance so carefully and scrupulously neutral that it achieved negativity from the other side round—a stance that was an insult in itself, and which any right-thinking person would have noticed. But that was also par for the course with people like him. They just wanted you to hear them, pay attention to them. They didn't care what you had to say, what your opinion was. They only wanted to tell you theirs.

They turned down another path, walking slowly, Foy Ballard trailing ten paces behind them like some giant leather-clad duenna.

"Gaia is the Earth, the mother of us all, and we are her servants. Or should be. Look at these beings, her oldest and tallest children." Clovis waved his arms to encompass the forest depths, the redwoods standing like the aisle pillars of a cathedral, the lesser trees supporting them like flying buttresses. "How can you not wish to honor and help them? What sort of evil creature could wish to cut them down?"

"They are amazing."

"More than amazing, Miss Stride—Mrs. Lacing, I should say. These very trees were here before King Arthur, the oldest even before Jesus and Cleopatra and Alexander the Great, and they will still be here, or their offspring seedlings, when humans are gone and the world is ruled by rabbits and cockroaches and anything else that manages to survive the coming nuclear calamity."

"I didn't know you were such a pessimist," said Rennie, to goad him.

Clovis smiled deprecatingly. "I'm sorry to confess that even I sometimes lose hope, fighting the dark forces that are striving to turn forest shrines such as this into dead wasteland." He gestured around them again. "But you see what we're fighting for, we Aquarians, on the verge of the new astrological age. Standing here among the most ancient living things on the planet, the strongest and yet also the most defenseless, who could doubt the power of Gaia the Living Earth? We are merely Earth Mother's warriors, her sworn gladiators in an arena of greed."

Oh dear God, could you BE more pompous? If Earth Mother relies on people like you to help her out, I think maybe I'll start looking for a way off this rock...

"A fierce name for a group with such gentle, peaceful, dare I say hippie-like goals?"

"Sometimes one is forced to adopt the strategies and tactics of the enemy in order to achieve one's higher goals."

"And that doesn't make one the enemy oneself? 'We have met the enemy and he is us'? 'Live by the sword, die by the sword'? You even have a fighting blade in your logo."

Clovis turned to look at her. "A metaphorical sword only, I assure you. We would never harm another living thing in the course of our green crusade."

"And yet you stop traffic routinely in the heart of San Francisco—people could get hurt, ambulances could be delayed, all sorts of bad things could happen to people and it would be your doing."

Behind them, Foy rumbled to himself like a deeply troubled volcano; apparently he was within earshot, and not liking what his ears were telling him. But Clovis lifted a languid hand, and on the mere the mutters died away.

"We take precautions, of course, and to the best of our knowledge no one has ever suffered as a result of any of our demonstrations. As you would know, if you had taken the time and trouble to check out our safety plans and records; we offer approved media every cooperation and courtesy, should they choose to avail themselves."

Ouch... Rennie smiled, and returned serve at once. "I wish I could have. Only, the oddest thing, when I phoned your office to ask to do just that, I was told it was out of the question. But no doubt the person who told me was mistaken, and perhaps if I called again... Still," she added, countenance carefully blank, "I'm rather curious: my editor told me you don't give interviews to everybody who comes asking, that in fact you're quite selective about whom you talk to. And I was put through quite a set of paces just now by Mr. Ballard before I was deemed worthy of an audience with you. Considering you have a cause that needs all the publicity it can get, could you tell me why is that?"

"Ah, Mrs. Lacing—and as you know, your own family is one of our most faithful and generous yearly contributors—the Warriors of Gaia have learned through bitter experience that not all journalists are like you. Few are to be trusted, fewer still share the vision for the planet that would enable them to correctly portray us to the larger population. Small wonder that we choose carefully to whom we speak."

"Of course... Oh, which brings me to another small academic point, that of finances. You mentioned my family's, my husband's family's, contributions—surely more publicity and more coverage would bring in more donations such as ours? Can you run such an active and extensive organization on chance charity alone? Or do you have other sources of Aquarian-age financing? Something private, perhaps?"

Gotcha, you fish-eyed freak! Snap at me now and I might go running home to tell on you, turn off your charity I.V. from the family dole...

But Clovis only smiled again and refused the gambit. "I leave all such matters to my financial advisors. I concern myself only with my charges."

"Admirable," said Rennie piously, biting the insides of her cheeks to keep her face straight as he bowed to her for the compliment. *I will sew Burke Kinney's fingers together and string him up by his cuticles, he* knew *what it was going to be like...*

"Never think that Gaia is not aware of what we do for her—or to her. Aware and grateful, my trees are; they know how we Warriors work tirelessly for their good and well-being. They are our wards and dependents—our true Aquarian friends. And they return our devotion. The trees protect their own, my dear Mrs.—may I call you Rennie? My dear Rennie, then. I'm aware you know this but I'm going to say it anyway: they will not tolerate evil among them."

And his pale codfish eyes were staring straight at Rennie when he said it.

"When I am Queen of the Universe? You have no *idea* how in trouble you are going to be..."

Burke grinned and leaned back in his chair, putting his hands behind his head. "Back from Dingly Dell? What did Nature Boy have to say?"

Rennie sat down on Burke's couch, slung her bag and coat aside and started laughing.

"You are a bad, bad man...you know that, don't you?"

"So I've been told. But Franjo?"

"Oh, tons of stuff. You won't like it, though. Well, you will, but for all the wrong reasons. You didn't send me to do a comedy piece, I don't *think*..."

"No, but I might not mind if I get one. We can make that work too. Just go write it up the way it wants to come out, and then we'll see. Is he dangerous, do you suppose?"

"St. Michael and all angels, doesn't he wish! Clojo the Barbarian, Champion of the Trees... No, he's harmless. A pompous twit, but a harmless one. Tell you what, though: the one who really interested me was his henchman, the unlovely Ballard. "

Burke's eyes sparked. "Oh? And why was that?"

"Not sure. Maybe because he talked like an academic up before the tenure committee yet he looked, and vibed, like Bigfoot? It's these little things that most concern us. I have to tell you, he actually scared me, and if Clovis would just send Foy out to shake people down, oops, I meant solicit donations, the trees would never, ever, lack for pocket money. Also I think a quick review of police records may well be in order, Foy-wise. Maybe my annoying yet also impeccably official inspector detective cousin-in-law can help out. And I was thinking maybe we should try again for a peek at the account books of the Warriors of Gaia, if that's really its name. If we can get one. If there are any."

"You think they're 'doing business as'?"

"Well, I still find it odd that Clojo doesn't court publicity. Every other little wacko cause freak with a bee in his bonnet would eat glass for major coverage like the Clarion. And this dude has got not one bee buzzing around in the vast empty spaces between his ears but a whole freakin' hive. I have heard them humming his little honey-tree tune, oh yes, they are in there. Yet he not only discourages publicity, he makes his trollish minion inquisitionize would-be interviewers."

"Quite the dog and pony show, then."

"You bet. And no matter my enlightened earth-centric answers, care to have a tiny wager that I wouldn't have made his cut if my name hadn't been Lacing and he hadn't seen it every year on those big fat checks the family foundation shoves his way for charitable deductions' sake?"

"Mm. No, I don't think I'll take that bet." Burke stretched, stood up, smiled down at her. "Time to go home, I hear there's pot roast for dinner."

"Lucky you, then."

"Yes, I am. Walk out with me?"

Rennie shook her head. "No, I want to write up my notes, and grab a hunk of pizza, no pot roast waiting at home for *me* ... Then I have to go over to the Avalon Ballroom to see Quicksilver Messenger Service and the Mystery Trend and the Sea-green Incorruptibles."

"Dressed like that?"

"You don't dig it? I was going for that 'just rode in with Kipling down from the Khyber Pass' look. No, I have some concert threads here, I'll change later. The show doesn't start for another three hours, so that should time out just right."

"Okay, but that's a very long day for you. So I better not see your smiling face around here much before noon tomorrow. In fact, not before noon at all."

Pleased with the prospect of an unexpected morning's sleep-in, Rennie went off down the hall. She'd recently been promoted to the dignity of the last cubicle in a row of four by the windows: right before one dead-end wall and up against another, the little nook was almost as private as a real office. No door, of course, and just room enough for her desk, her chair and a visitor's chair, plus a file cabinet and small bookcase. But it had a precious window she could actually open, and a real view, and it was exalted far and above the open slice of alcove she'd inhabited before. She had been thrilled when Burke gave it to her, and had decorated it to her taste: rock posters, snapshots of her friends, some of the little boxes she liked to collect.

She had a lot to think about; but first she had to get her notes down before she forgot. That took about two hours, mostly because she couldn't resist writing just a little bit, and the writing in turn aided the memory process, so that then there were more notes and more writing. That done, she glanced through the day's messages while she changed — the other cubicle dwellers on her row had gone home long since, so she could strip off her Muir Woods gear in privacy and put on a velvet minidress and strappy low-heeled shoes at leisure.

Nothing from Stephen, which was worrying. And nothing from Prax. But Berry had called; her brother-in-law Eric; Chet Galvin, who wanted to see her tomorrow night, well, sure; Jerry Garcia, just to chat; Mimi Fariña, Joan Baez's sister, about some folkie benefit; the manager of Theodolite, about putting her on the list for a Fillmore gig; Chet again, how nice it felt to be wanted, and how, yes, hot it made her to hear his voice; some record company and radio station people. Too late now to return most of the calls, and in any case she'd probably see some of the callers at the Avalon. But she did want to talk to Berry and Stephen.

"They brought Idaho, Todd Vance as I should say, down to the Hall of Justice for more questioning about Tam's murder," said Berry upon hearing Rennie's voice. "What? No, the groupie he was with just can't seem to get her story straight, she's changed it at least twice. They're questioning her too. Separately, of course."

"Why is that, do you think? She seemed sure enough before. Someone buying her silence? Little bidding war going?"

Berry laughed shortly. "Who knows? We'd buy some alibis ourselves, if we thought we could get away with it. Just kidding! But maybe someone else can, or feels the need to."

Rennie hung up ten minutes later and tried to reach

Stephen at Hall Place, but the houseman Carlos, who answered the phone, told her that Mr. Stephen had retired early with a bit of a sore throat and was unable to take Mrs. Stephen's call, expressing regrets on both counts.

"No, no, Carlos, that's fine, don't bother him. Nothing important. I'll call in the morning, if he's up to talking."

After she hung up, she sat staring at the phone. She wasn't being paranoid. Was she? Stephen was *definitely* avoiding her, and it could only be because he knew she'd slept with someone else. Well—once they'd agreed to start seeing other people, someone had had to be first, right? It could have easily been Stephen; Rennie had always expected that it would be. But apparently not, and he was obviously angry and hurt. And how had he found out? And how guilty did she feel? Or maybe he really did just have a sore throat.

She came to with a start. Plenty of time to angst later; now it was time to go. She disliked the office when it was late and empty like this; it was easier to work, quieter, but the air was stuffy and she kept hearing odd noises just around the many corners. There were plenty of people still there, editors and writers staying late much as she had done, the night shift coming in; she didn't feel unsafe. But though she saw no one, she had the creepiest feeling she was being watched, or worse, followed—to the point where she cast repeated glances over her shoulder and walked more than usually fast when she headed for the elevators. No one troubled her; must have just been leftover freaky vibes from her day in the woods.

When she got to the ground floor, she signed out, exchanging pleasantries with the security guard, then for a moment or two she stood and stared at the lobby's famous marble fountain, out of which rose up amid the plashings a bronze statue of Mercury, messenger of the gods, lord of the realm of words.

Then, giving herself a shake, like a dog just in from the rain, she settled an embroidered Moroccan cloak on her shoulders and her fringed bag under her arm, and went out to get some pizza and after that a cab.

Coming out of the Avalon after Quicksilver's dynamite set, long after midnight, Rennie stopped on the rapidly emptying corner of Van Ness and Sutter to organize cab fare for the homeward trip, and never noticed when someone came lurching up beside her.

"Hey there, pretty little hippie chick, haven't *you* got legs that go down to the floor and up to your ears!"

Rennie looked up, saw a drunken short-haired straight in a suit that had seen better days, leering at her. Half stoned herself, or else she would have just laughed and walked away, instead she uttered a few clipped words recommending an anatomical impossibility. Suddenly she found herself pinned by the folds of her own cloak and thrown against the building wall, with this surprisingly strong inebriated pig, or maybe not so inebriated, wrestling her along it, trying to get his hand up her dress and drag her into the alley.

Oh, this is so not good, maybe this isn't even some random drunk, maybe this is the murderer, trying to make it look like just another street assault. And even if it is just another street assault, I could end up just as dead or raped or both...

Well, she wasn't helping herself just standing there blithering. She had gotten one elbow up and was raising her knee with intent when suddenly it was all taken out of her hands, literally: her assailant was lifted off his feet from behind and slammed against the wall himself. Rennie stared, blinked, stared again.

"*Marcus?*"

Marcus Dorner ignored her, flashed his shield, spoke to the drunk. "Police."

"Shit."

"Exactly."

"Not what it looks like, officer, this, this, this trosti—

prooshti—prostitute 'saulted me, 'costed me—"

"Guess again. I happen to be this lady's cousin, and I doubt she did anything of the sort. And even if she did, who am I gonna believe, her or you? So unless you're prepared to be arrested for assault, battery and attempted rape, take it down the street."

The drunk babbled on a bit, then drew himself up and produced a lordly tone as Marcus was turning to Rennie.

"I presume we're done here, officer. Though maybe you're not."

Marcus whirled so swiftly and violently that Rennie jumped. Grabbing the guy by the throat, he slammed his head against the overheated metal of the hood of his unmarked car and held his cheek there for precisely five seconds—long enough to be sure he got the message, long enough for him to scream from the burn—then released him with a little pat on the uninjured cheek.

"*Now* we're done."

"What are you doing here?" asked Rennie, deeply shaken, more than she would ever admit, especially to him, and more grateful than she had ever thought possible for police interference, as they both watched her brutish acquaintance flee lurchingly down Sutter Street. "Not that I'm not glad to see you—but how did you know?"

"Glad? I'm sure. As to how I knew, I called Burke Kinney and he told me you'd gone to the Avalon. I didn't like the idea of you alone down here so late, so I figured I'd pick you up. I just waited here for you to come out. Good thing I did." Marcus took her arm and pulled her around to the passenger side. "Come on, I'll drive you home."

"I can take a cab, look, there's one right over there." Obstinate to the last, even while her heart was still pounding from the violent little encounter. *God, just let him do the Galahad thing already, will you, you stupid stupid girl...suppose he hadn't been here...and he really didn't answer my question about what he* was *doing here, either…*

"I don't think so, green eyes. Get in."

"Oooh, police brutality, where's a reporter when you need one?" But she obediently got into the front seat, her legs all of a sudden rather wobbly, clutching the cloak around her so he didn't see her trembling.

Marcus laughed and shut the door. When he was seated behind the wheel, he didn't start the car at once, but looked over at her.

"Are you all right?"

"And by 'all right' you mean…?"

"He didn't hurt you? No—well, I mean all right in every sense. I know you've been asking questions all over town about things that don't concern you, and I must tell you I hate it, but I also understand it—you work for a newspaper, you're a reporter, that's your job. But as a detective, it's *my* job to solve this case. And I know you don't believe me, but I very much want to find Prax not guilty and see her out of jail, and any time you get in the way of that, you're only hurting her."

"Yes, but you haven't been burning up the track finding things out, have you?" said Rennie, with surprising venom given the circumstances. "And what if I come across something that actually helps clear her and gets her sprung?"

"You don't know what we've found. And we're under no obligation to tell your side until the D.A. says we have to. But if you do come up with something, Rennie, I beg you on my knees, bring it to me first, before you rush off like Nancy Drew, Girl Journalist Crimestopper. That's what I came to tell you. Promise me you'll at least do that. There could be a lot of trouble—and, yes, danger—if you don't."

He waited, but Rennie said nothing, and after a few moments he sighed and turned the key.

Pulling over to the park side of Buena Vista, Marcus started to get out to open the door for his passenger, but she was too quick, and with a murmured thank-you for her rescue, she was out of the car and running across the street toward her front door. He sat there until he saw the top-floor lights, dimly on behind the curtains, go brighter, and was sure that she was safely inside. Rennie didn't know it, but he stayed parked across the street, under the tall trees, for a long time.

If Rennie *had* known he was still there, though, she might have shouted for him out the front window, to come up and deal with what she was about to find inside. As she trudged heavily up the turret stairs, something was already frantically semaphoring to her from the depths of her instinctive danger-warning backbrain, but she was so tired and upset that it didn't register, not until she was a step or two from the top.

The door to her flat—which admittedly she seldom locked, the door at the foot of the turret stairs had always seemed to be security enough, though Stephen and Marcus both would pitch a fit if they knew how careless she was, and considering how things were going they'd be right—now stood ajar, letting a thin slice of light fall across the landing at the top of the stairs.

Rennie froze, her hand still reaching out to grasp the doorknob and her mind flooding with frantic thoughts—*Can I run downstairs to Sharon, can I get out into the street, maybe Marcus hasn't gone yet, can I sneak in and grab something to bash them with, how many* more *surprise attacks are there going to be in the course of one incredibly crappy evening?*

Then a voice came out of the shadows, and called her by her name.

Chapter Fourteen

"HELLO, RENNIE DEAR. You're home late tonight."

Marjorie Lacing sat there on the new sofa, legs decorously crossed at the ankle, pearls gleaming in the lamplight. When Rennie's heart finally slowed its fight-or-flight acceleration, for the second time in half an hour, she leaned back against the door and tried to master her rage.

And here I was thinking how difficult it must be to work yourself up to killing someone...not a problem! At the very least, some pummeling must occur...

"You septic bitch!" she snarled, still shaking with shock and alarm. In all the months of her marriage she had never once spoken to her mother-in-law like that, however much she had been tempted, and though it came now from the Planet of Pure Survival Instinct, and she heard herself saying it from a long way away, Rennie was nonetheless pleased to see Marjorie's head jerk as if she'd been slapped.

Hey, this is big fun...or it would be, if only my heart would stop pounding and I could breathe normally...

But she got right into the new groove, and decided she

would say some more bad stuff, and see how long it would take before Marjorie's head spun like a top and fell off and rolled all the way to Mexico.

Why did I ever think it would be hard, or a bad thing, to let her know how I really feel...

"What the hell are you doing here? And how the hell did you get in? Oh, wait, I remember now, rats can compress their little rodent skeletons to a mere half-inch thick, so they can get through the teensiest crack—even uncompressed, you're halfway there."

Marjorie had regained her composure. "I'm *so* sorry, dear, I didn't mean to frighten you—you're obviously still startled to find me here, or I'm sure you'd never speak to me like that."

Now, would I not! "I say again," Rennie repeated with iron control, "what are you doing here, and how did you get in?"

"Well, as to how I got in, I borrowed the keys you so thoughtfully gave Stephen; though he won't remember lending them, if you should happen to ask." Marjorie looked around. "I hadn't realized this was where you were living. I know this house very well from my work with the Painted Ladies; a most distinguished residence. You won't be aware of this, but the Kiefer family, who built it for their youngest daughter Livia when she married, were great friends with the Lacings of the time. This floor used to be their music loft. I understand that girl portrait painter who went to Finch lives downstairs."

Rennie, recovered, was coldly furious. "Sharon Pollan. The one who wouldn't paint you because she didn't like your toxic vibes. She *owns* this house, being actually *descended* from the Kiefers. But you won't be aware of that. Architecture aside—I ask for the third time, why are you here?"

Marjorie recrossed her ankles and looked her daughter-in-law straight in the eyes.

"I thought it was time you knew that I have had a private investigator following you ever since you moved out of my home."

Why am I not surprised... "Ah. Looking for dirt."

"And finding more than a molehill. I wonder what Stephen would do if he knew what his sweet young wife was up to. Or with whom. I'm sure I needn't name any names, you know their names as well as I do. Or perhaps you don't."

Now *that* was nasty. Rennie had slept with more men in the last month than she'd ever thought she'd sleep with in her whole life, but she certainly knew their *names*. There were only three, anyway; not all that hard to remember. There had been the three-nighter with Chet, and its pleasant sequels; and the two-nighter with Brian Jones when the Stones were in town, which could be a repeat should the occasion ever present; and the one-nighter with Bram Butler of Wentletrap, which was absolutely going to *stay* a one-nighter because of the whips and chains and laceup leather masks she'd noticed in his hotel room at the St. Francis.

But if Marjorie had thought to cow Rennie by her threat to tell Stephen, she was much mistaken.

"Call him up, ask him over," said Rennie coolly. "It's not the way I'd planned to tell him, but if you want to give him the news, hey, knock yourself out. Or, rather, in your idiom, be my guest. I'm not ashamed of anything I've done; just because I've slept with three, yes, three, men I'm not married to doesn't make me Satan's trollop. I left Stephen's bed and board—isn't that how the expression goes? Actually, I have a feeling he already knows that I've been with other guys, or at least he suspects. I'm sorry that he's hurt, but I didn't do it to hurt him. We agreed a long time ago to start seeing other people, and he's just as free as I am to do so."

"Excuse me, neither of you is free to do anything of the sort. You are a married woman. Married to my son. And he is married to you."

"Legally. That's all. We've been separated for months. I moved out, remember? If it's just a question of getting an official separation, I'll ask Stephen to put the paperwork in gear tomorrow. Will that make you happy?"

Marjorie's nose seemed to sharpen until you could have used it to cut cheese, her nostrils pinching shut to what Rennie, watching with interest, would have thought the point of self-asphyxiation. Amazing how you could turn both white and red at the same time...

"You little tramp, how dare you?" she hissed. "You may like to think you're your own woman, but I assure you, you are still very much a Lacing, or at least the wife of a Lacing, and by God you are going to *stay* the wife of a Lacing! You will do what I tell you, if you want to keep your good name intact in this town. Not to mention your job. I have influence you haven't even dreamed of."

"Do your worst, bitch."

Rennie looked at her mother-in-law with more contempt than she thought she could ever have felt for anyone. *I'm not afraid of you anymore, you mean old bag...*

Obviously, the situation had changed: this was definitely not going the way Marjorie had planned it, and now she returned Rennie's gaze with baffled rage and naked dislike.

"Do you really think you can manage on your own? I know from my detective that not only are you sleeping around, you're not having the easiest time financially. Stephen tells me you won't accept money from him, money you are entitled to as his wife; and according to our bank manager you've never used the joint checking account. Which is, forgive me, not noble but ridiculous. We could offer you so much if you came back to us and behaved as you should. We're prepared to forgive you and welcome you home, and even to let you continue to work. At a respectable publication, of course, and nothing to do with that dreadful music."

"I'm not for sale. What I do isn't for sale."

"You stupid girl, of course you're for sale! Everyone is, for the right price and to the right buyer. What did you think, that you could change the terms of the bargain as you please, to suit yourself? For whatever reasons, my son loves you: I hated it from the moment he told us, I can say that at last, but I accepted it for his sake. Accepted *you*. You made a binding contract with Stephen *and* with us; you signed off on the deal when he put that ring on your finger."

"On my finger. Not through my nose."

Marjorie never even heard her. "And you haven't lived up to your end of the contract. You came out here, a pathetic little nobody who was unbelievably lucky to marry into this family, and you took the honorable name of wife that Stephen gave you and you trampled it in the muck. Working on a newspaper was bad enough; but consorting with a murderess, and now getting involved with murder yourself—"

"You don't seem to mind that Marcus Dorner is involved with murder every day of his waking life."

Marjorie waved her claws in testy dismissal. "Marcus is a man; if he wishes to play policeman, he is free to do so. Also he is not of the direct line, not of the name; he is not a Lacing in the way that Stephen is, in the way that your children with Stephen will be."

She paused, and stared at Rennie with what seemed genuine perplexity. "What did we ever do to you that was so terrible, that you should do this to us, that you feel you must repay us so harshly? Do you truly enjoy hurting your husband? Are you that cruel? What has he ever done to you that wasn't done out of love?"

Rennie stared right back at her. That had almost sounded sincerely anguished, as if it had been an honest person's honest question. But Rennie knew from bitter experience that the pain, if pain it was, was not even faintly cognizant of the pain of others, but merely the expression of

Motherdear's displeasure at being done to as she did to everybody else.

She sic'd a private eye on me to find out if I was unfaithful! And yes, she was right, I was. Yet somehow she manages to make it be about her, how she's the one wronged. I can tell that she's jealous on some deep level, maybe she feels she never had the chances that I do, but that's so bogus. What's real is that she's totally protective of Stephen — she doesn't like me and she never will, because she didn't pick me out for him, but she was prepared to grudgingly coexist because Stephen wanted me and loved me...

"Stephen?" she said at length. "Nothing. Or Eric. The rest of you, everything and always. If you want to tell him, fine. Just be prepared for him to loathe you as much as I do."

Rennie stood away from the door; through all this, she hadn't once sat down.

"Good *night*, Marjorie. Keep the private eye on your payroll, by all means. I'll do my best to justify his salary. Oh, and if you ever, I repeat, *ever*, pull a stunt like this again, my hand to God there will be another sword murder here. Only there will be no mystery whatsoever about who committed that one, because I will be sitting waiting for the cops, sword in hand, with your headless bleeding body as my footstool. And once they hear what you were like, no jury in this world or any other will convict me. Are we clear on that? Yes? Good. Goodbye. Give Stephen my love. And the keys."

And slammed the door behind her unwelcome guest. *Dear GOD, that felt GREAT! Now that was something I could never have done last year! I guess Prax is right, I've learned quite a lot from the Borgias after all...*

She slid slowly down against the door all the way to the floor to sit huddled on the carpet, the way they always did in movies, limp in the backwash of adrenaline letdown, thinking of what Marjorie had offered. It would be so easy to accept, so simple. Nobody would blame her. She'd sooner be covered in honey and staked naked to an anthill than ever admit it to anyone, certainly not to Stephen, but on a few occasions since she'd moved out Rennie *had* found it hard to make ends meet. She wasn't extravagant: her Clarion salary was enough to manage on, and she had her underground newspaper gigs bringing in a little extra cash. But sometimes there were unforeseen expenses, and on those occasions, yeah, it had been difficult. That was why she still made clothes for that Haight Street boutique, though only Prax knew about it—and was under strict orders not to buy any.

She really knows where the weaknesses lie, that horrible, horrible woman, every chink in my armor... Oh, sure, Stephen would help out gladly any time she asked, it would be so easy to accept a dole from him. Or just claim her own; that unused checkbook in her desk did have both their names on it. But Rennie wouldn't do it. If she did, it would all have been for nothing. Still, if she went back to Stephen— Marjorie was only sixty-seven. It might be another twenty years before she died, or was at least sufficiently afflicted with age that interfering would be kept to a minimum; but Rennie herself would be in her early forties. She would not only be the ruling lioness of the Lacing pride, the queen matriarch, but still young enough to do whatever she wanted. Maybe...

No. Nononononooooo. That way lay not only madness but something like transgression, something like maybe even sin. She didn't love Stephen like that, to do that to him, and he so *deserved* to be loved like that.

And, for all her killer speech, now Rennie had a raging headache and was in a foul mood as well, the nice buzz she'd gotten from the Avalon show totally vanished. Yeah, a two-pronged offensive from a vicious attempted rapist and your evil mother-in-law would do that to you...

After a few minutes, she staggered stiffly to her feet, kicked off her shoes and tottered into the bathroom for some aspirin. Tossing them back with water, she grabbed a bottle of wine from the kitchen—best Lacing Napa Valley chardonnay, supplied by Stephen, but there was no help for that and

besides it was very superior swill—and went barefoot down
the stairs to Sharon's, where a light was still on in the studio.
When Sharon, paint brushes stuck in her loosely knotted hair
and paint smudges on her face, peered through the curtained
glass panels to see who the hell, Rennie smiled hopefully and
held up the wine bottle, and she heard Sharon chuckle as she
opened the door.

"Too late for wining? And, well, whining?"

"Never too late for either. I'm up till five painting,
these days."

Sharon swung back the door and Rennie came inside.
Looking around, she breathed in the sense of peace she
always found there: the perfect pools of light from stained-
glass lamps, the cool air that smelled of lemon oil, oil paints,
turpentine and incense. Sharon disappeared to grab a
corkscrew and glasses from the kitchen, then returned, and
they went through to the studio that occupied up the whole
first floor of the north turret, the studio of a working artist.

There was a canvas on the big standing easel, which
Sharon had apparently been addressing when Rennie
knocked. She went back to the easel and waved Rennie over
to a huge pile of pillows on a wide divan-style couch of
carved shesham wood, then put an album on the stereo.

"Sit. Talk. I'll keep on with this, if you don't mind. The
subject's an acquaintance of yours—that nice folksinger
Griffin Bolder, what a cutie. It's just studio stuff, pulling the
background into focus behind him. If I'd lived in Renaissance
Holland, I'd have had a stableful of handsome young
apprentices to do this sort of thing for me. And other things.
Alas, I do not live then and there, and so no cute adoring
youngbloods nor any studio help either. But I do need to
finish with the palette knife before the paint gets too dry to
work. Pour us some wine and talk to me."

Reclining on the deep soft cushions while Sharon
worked on the portrait of Griffin, Rennie, still plenty steamed,

recounted Marjorie's intrusion and take on what she thought Rennie's life should be.

"And you? What does Rennie Stride think?"

Before her visitor could answer, Sharon put her knife down, stepped back and studied the painting critically. Apparently satisfied, she moved to another easel and pulled a new, smaller canvas from a stack by the wall.

"Keep talking. I want to paint you very quickly, like a sketch in oils. Unbutton your dress, tits out, come on, all the buttons, down off the shoulder, pull the skirt to either side, I want you mostly naked, that's right, very pretty. Now stretch your left arm over the pillows, right arm arched over your head, more tit, right knee bent, skirt off your thighs a bit more, lean forward from the waist, head straight, chin down, eyes up, shake out your hair, point your toes, look at me. Perfect. Now don't move, just talk."

"God, you're bossy... But you asked what do I think?" said Rennie, aggrieved anew. "I think she's utterly and completely full of it. She wants to hang on through me to a past that's disappearing—hers and her kind's. An older woman I work with said the same thing, that I was just sowing wild oats and I wouldn't want this when I'm thirty-five and I'd be sorry then that I didn't stay with my nice rich adorable husband who would give me beautiful children and make me the society queen of San Francisco."

"And do you think that makes sense?"

"Of course it makes sense! What am I, an idiot? It just doesn't make sense for *me*. Marjorie wants to hang on to the past, this stupid woman at work wanted me to live out *her* past, a past that never even existed and that wasn't ever even really hers, how offensive is that... There would be starchy nannies for those adorable children and a big old price tag on everything else. In ten years I'd be hard as nails because that would be the only way I could cope. And Stephen himself— man, everybody thinks they know better than I do what I want, or what I'll be wanting a decade down the road."

"And you know what you'll want? Don't *move*..."

"Maybe not entirely," Rennie conceded. "But I know what I *don't* want, and I know it a hell of a lot better than they do. And if it means I'm alone for the rest of my life, then okay. I can ride that wave. I'm more afraid of being drowned in a pool I never wanted to swim in to begin with."

Sharon flashed a quick grin, kept on painting furiously. "Had yourself quite a day, didn't you? Listen, you don't have to listen to them. Any of them. You don't have to listen to me, either."

"Oh?" Rennie was laughing. "You think I haven't noticed what you've been doing, you clever little Jungian — distracting me with wine and painting and this really uncomfortable pig of a pose while you sneak in a spot of therapy... I talked to Clovis Franjo today, that Warriors of Gaia wacko I told you about. And then Marjorie, of course. Oh, and I almost got either raped or killed tonight, too, but Marcus rescued me. Want to hear?"

Sharon indicated that she very much wanted to hear about all these things, so Rennie talked while her friend painted, and slowly she realized how freaked she had truly been by the day's events, and by talking it out she worked herself back into a kind of shaky peace.

"So what do *you* have to say?" she asked at last.

Instead of answering, Sharon motioned her over. "Come and look."

And there on the canvas was her answer. Rennie stared at the little painting. It was amazing — in under an hour, Sharon had produced an oil sketch with the delicate sheen and thinness of a watercolor wash. There Rennie was, lolling all but naked and almost insolently seductive on the pillows, like one of Gainsborough's lusciously translucent beauties, skin gleaming, long light gold-brown hair tumbling.

But lolling and seduction were definitely not the vibe.

Instead, Sharon had caught her anger and refusal and mute intransigence, the infusing energy that blazed like a beacon from every line of her body, and had made it into a message and a challenge. Yet in the pose she had also found vulnerability and confidence, sensuality and hope — and in the face, a young girl with the outlines of the woman to come already visible, like the branches of a tree being clothed in a growth of spring leaves. A face that belonged to no one but its owner.

"Do I really look like that?" she asked presently, humbly. "Like — her?"

"You do now... I'll make a real portrait of you soon, though," said Sharon, staring critically at the canvas and touching up some brushstrokes. "I want to get you down on canvas before you change too much. While you're still Rennie. Before you become too much 'Rennie Stride'. And you will. And that's good, that's how it's supposed to happen. And then I'll paint her too."

"Can I buy this?" asked Rennie shyly. "Not for me. For Stephen. It's his Rennie, really, his girl. The one he actually married, not the one he thought he was marrying."

"You can have it. When it dries, not now. It might even do him some good. You haven't had dinner, I bet, have you? No, of course you haven't. Much too busy being assaulted by various creepy people. Me neither. Come on, let's go fix something to eat."

Out in the kitchen, Sharon sautéed two nice pieces of fresh haddock and had Rennie mix a bunch of greens. When they were seated at the table, fish and rice and salad on colorful Talavera plates in front of them, wineglasses full of chardonnay — Rennie hadn't realized how hungry she was, what a long hard day it had been, between Clovis and Foy and Marcus and almost being raped and a big dramatic scene with your mother-in-law the Queen of Hell, that kind of thing always brings on the famishment — they ate and drank in silence for a bit.

Then Sharon said quietly, "These are new waters for everybody. Full of currents and riptides, big scary rogue waves coming out of nowhere. We're all just beginning to learn how to swim in them. But you asked earlier what I had to say to you? I have only one thing to say, to that girl in the picture I just painted and to the person she's going to be in five and ten and fifty years."

"What's that?"

Sharon smiled, and poured out the last of the wine, equally, into the plain crystal glasses.

"Come on in, Rennie. I promise, the water's just fine."

Chapter Fifteen

As DAYS WENT BY and nothing further was discovered or divulged, the furor round Prax slowly began to die down, for which everyone who cared about her was profoundly thankful. Burke adjudged that it was safe to let his protégée Strider back to work on rock topics, though Prax was still firmly embargoed, and the godlike yet sympathetic Garrett Larkin concurred.

But the first two stories Rennie turned in seemed to be more phoned in than written up. Burke gave her one more pass, and then he called her into his office and lit into her.

"What the hell do you call this?"

Rennie looked at the much-scribbled-upon typescript. "My story on local guitarmakers."

He slapped down another on top of it. "And this?"

"Story on musician communes in the East Bay."

"And this?"

"Story on Moby Grape."

"Right. Stories. Technically correct. But they're *not* stories, that's the problem. They're random facts stitched together by a very nicely readable and undeniably smooth style, facts propped up to look like stories. It's good writing, Strider, but it's lazy journalism. You know and I know these little pieces aren't going to earn you a Pulitzer. But it doesn't matter. You have to engage every single story as if it would. I know you're upset, I know you're worried, I know you're distracted. That doesn't matter either. You have to write as if *nothing* matters but the story. Because nothing else does. And I know Russ" — her adored mentor at j-school — "taught you that, if he taught you nothing else, because that's what matters to him."

"I did my best with them."

"No, you didn't. You didn't even do what you *thought* was your best. I can hear it, I can see it. And so can you. This isn't just a thousand words about Moby Grape. It's your entire journalistic credibility. Whether you're writing a sidebar buried in the back of the book below the fold or the front-page headline story, you have to give it your full effort and attention and respect, either way, every single time. It deserves it, and so do your readers, and so do you. Otherwise, you're just a hack. There's no shame in hackdom — it's honest, respectable, professional journeyman work. But there's no glory in it either. The only shame is if you can do better and hackdom is what you settle for."

"I know. I'm sorry."

"I know you are. I'm sorry too."

"Have I done *anything* good lately?" Rennie was fighting to hold back tears: tears not so much of hurt but of embarrassment and anger with herself because she knew he was right. She was all set to throw everything into the air and run back to the welcoming embrace of Hell House, sink right into it and accept her fate and never be heard from again.

Marjorie was right, I'm no good, I'm useless, I'm pathetic, I might as well just go be the breeding machine they all want me to be, start up the baby assembly line, get Stephen standing at stud...at least maybe my kids will love me, they *won't think their mother is worthless and stupid...no, what am I talking about, they'll be* Lacings, *they'll despise me too...*

Burke smiled, though Rennie was looking down miserably at her hands and didn't see.

"Of course. That piece on Clovis Franjo and his little forest friends was goddamn brilliant. One of the funniest things I've read in a long, long time, though he'll never get it—which just makes it all the funnier."

"If it was so goddamn brilliant and funny, why hasn't it run?"

"Not because it wasn't good, I promise. The timeliness got overtaken by other stuff. But we'll use it. It's not a carton of milk, there's no sell-by date. It won't spoil by waiting, and if a redwood falls on him in the meantime because it thinks he's the moron he, come to think of it, is, you can always do a follow-up obit, interview the tree... It was good, Strider. In fact, it was better than good."

"That's nice to know." She still wouldn't look at him, still afraid she was going to burst into tears and shame them both forever; but the tight little voice she was using to control her hurt came across instead as pissy, because suddenly Burke leaned forward and swept the stories off the desk into the wastebasket, and at that her head came up, eyes startled wide but tearless.

"I'm only busting your chops over this because you *are* good. Because you *do* have talent. Because I think there *will* be a Pulitzer for you one day, and when there is I want to make damn sure my name gets mentioned in your acceptance speech as the guy who told you first. And, last but certainly not least, because I wouldn't waste a split-second of my time and energy on you if I didn't think you were worth the investment. End of lecture."

He pushed another piece of paper across the desk at her. "Right. Now I'm giving you this interview because all the others went so well. Because I know what Rennie Stride can do when she puts her mind and heart into it. Just try to make sure *this* girl doesn't end up accused of murder, too, okay? I don't think that's so much to ask, do you?" But he was smiling when he said it.

Rennie nobly resisted the impulse to look down at the name, and Burke laughed.

"It's okay, you can open the present now," he said, and grinned understandingly when he heard her gasp.

"Sunny Silver? *Sunny SILVER*? She's — she's — "

She sure was. Sunny Silver was giving all other contenders a serious run for the roses as pre-eminent chick singer in rock. Though Sunny was more blues, really. But either way, rock or blues, she was incredible. A New York girl who'd spent some time in Toronto and then in London, she got into the British scene a few years ago, right along with Ned Raven and Turk Wayland and Graham Sonnet. By all accounts, she had gotten into more than just the scene with them — and with Harrison and Lennon and Jagger *et* considerable *al.* as well. By other accounts, sometimes a few of those *al.* at the same time. Right now she was here in San Francisco in between sections of a national tour — resting up, not performing, though she had done a couple of club drop-ins to keep her chops up. To have a chance to talk to someone on that level — Rennie felt obscurely better. Burke must think she was okay after all. But...

"I heard she wasn't doing any interviews while she was in town, that she was here strictly for relaxation?"

Burke shrugged. "Must have changed her mind. The word came down from Garry, and I'm just following orders. Not that I disagree. So go call her publicist and get the hell over there before she changes her mind again."

The following afternoon Rennie went to meet Sunny Silver in her top-floor suite at the Fairmont, atop Nob Hill — an old-school famous San Francisco hotel, slightly stodgy, though not terminally stuffy like the Clift, which, like Disneyland, starchily refused to allow longhairs to pass its portals.

But Sunny, when good-humoredly taxed with her choice of upscale crash pad, just laughed and waved a hand at the airy rooms, the tall windows overlooking a spectacular sweep of view.

"I'm an old-fashioned girl. I like old places and long-ago things. Did you know, a woman designed this hotel? Julia Morgan, one of the first female architects ever. She was hired to rebuild it after the big earthquake and fire when Stanford White, who had the gig first, was murdered. Anyway, she did, and it reopened only a year later, and rich old-family San Franciscans who were still homeless moved in here. Sort of an early commune. We haven't come so far after all."

Rennie hadn't known, and found it interesting. But her subject certainly didn't *look* old-fashioned. And in those old long-ago days, and even days not so very old or long ago, she wouldn't have been allowed in any hotel, certainly not a posh and respectable one like this, except in a maid's uniform or a whore's rig-out. No, they hadn't come very far. Quadroon, they'd have called her, or other pretty words like mulatta or morisca or octoroon—or maybe some other, not so pretty words for a very ugly concept.

And for a very pretty woman. Sunny Silver was five foot ten and voluptuous of form, with smooth gold skin the color of heather honey; a curly mop of a darker honey shade—clover, or possibly eucalyptus—stood out round her head like a dandelion clock. Little Black Orphan Annie goes to Haight Street. She was wearing her trademark silver leather jeans, skin-tight over legs the length of California, and her well-defined hips were cinched with what looked like the biggest and fanciest and heaviest honking turquoise and silver concha belt that the Navajo nation had ever made in the entire history of big fancy heavy honking concha belts.

"Nice," said Rennie, looking around. No lurking publicist, good — more and more these days, flacks were insisting on sitting in, especially with established artists, and the fact that none was there was a definite signal. But Rennie's comment had not meant the privacy but the room itself. Sunny had obviously thought the décor could use a hand, and had given it the standard-issue rocker-on-the-road instant makeover: every single lampshade, sofa, chair back and flat surface in the suite had been draped and hung and covered with lacy, fringey, sparkly, multicolored shawls and scarves.

Definitely not standard issue: an array of tiny statues in various styles and materials — brass, bronze, terracotta, silver, wood, none of them more than three inches high — stood on a paisley silk scarf on the bedroom credenza, just visible beyond the French doors. Peering through, Rennie raised inquiring brows.

"Those are my road gods," said Sunny, suddenly wary as she noted the direction of her guest's attention. "They come on the road with me everywhere. You never know when you'll need help."

"No, you never do — but who are they?"

Sensing she had a sympathizer, Sunny drew Rennie over to the credenza and eagerly recited names and divine provenance.

"Right, here's Ganesha, Hindu, the one with the elephant head, he's the Remover of Obstacles, you have to say 'Om Ganesh' to him every morning, three times, before you start the day's work. And this is Changó, he's a Yoruba god of luck and success, and here's Oyá, his wife, a destroyer goddess of storms and winds, also a creativity and fertility goddess — see, she has two swords, one to create and one to destroy. That's Yemanjá, Santería goddess of the sea. Nike, Greek goddess of victory. Lugh, Celtic god of light. Freyr, Norse god of sex." She rattled off half a dozen more. "I don't usually let people meet them, you never know what they'll think or say. The people, not the gods. Well, the gods too."

"What could people possibly say except how very cool and righteous?" asked Rennie wonderingly. "We can all use all the help we can get."

Sunny looked relieved. "I knew I was right to show you, knew you'd dig it... Come over here, *chica*, let's have something to drink."

She poured brandy for Rennie and herself, sat down in a huge overstuffed velvet bergère and studied her guest for a long moment. Rennie, accustomed to musicianly ways, calmly sipped her brandy and waited.

After a few sips of her own, Sunny leaned back and smiled. "You probably heard I wasn't doing any press while I was in town, that I was on vacation and didn't want to be bothered." At Rennie's nod: "So, did you wonder how this gig turned up on your plate?"

"Well, I'm kind of past the days of holding my breath and stamping my feet and threatening to turn blue until I get the story I want. Wait—no, actually, I don't think I *am* past that. But I certainly didn't think I got to talk to you because I'm so incredibly fabulous—my editor said he was giving it to me because of that interview I did with Prax McKenna."

"That's what I thought."

"No?"

"Not no, but not entirely yes either. Actually, he gave it to you because I asked Garrett Larkin for you. You or nobody, and let me tell you why. I'd read that piece on Prax—and you're so right on about her, honey, she's going to be a very big star, this murder crap isn't going to hurt her, because she didn't do it, and because when she's cleared they'll all be sorry they suspected her. Anyway, I went to see her in the slammer the other day."

Rennie stared. "That was very nice of you."

Sunny waved it away. "I've known Prax for years. We met when I was doing my first gigs out here, in this little folk club over in Berkeley. She was just a kid. Not that I was all that much older. As I said, I read your stuff in the Clarion and some of the undergrounds, and I like where your head is at, as a critic and as a woman. Anyway, visiting Prax, your name came up, naturally—she told me how you hadn't printed some private things she'd told you about her private life, because they had no bearing on either the music or the story. She said you give good count: that that's your personal journalistic philosophy, you aren't out to make yourself the story or to trash anyone just to be clever or to get a big juicy scoop—and that was how and why you and she had gotten to be best friends. Frankly, that impressed me even more than the story itself."

"That's nice to know. And very sweet of her to say. I'm glad."

"She loves you so much. And I can see you love her too." Sunny shifted in the big armchair, tucking her bare feet under her. "We'll do the real interview in a few minutes, I promise I can give just as good count as you. But I may have a way bigger story for you than boring old me. Are you interested? More importantly, are you really as righteous as you read?"

Rennie had blushed when Sunny began talking about how impressed she was with her, Rennie's, work. Now she looked Sunny right in the eye, her gaze as straight and uncomplicated as a sword. *Under the circumstances, best find some less remindful simile, perhaps... Straight as a — well, as a very straight thing, anyway...*

"Yes. Though I say so myself, yes. I am."

Sunny studied her again, appeared to make up her mind. "Yeah, I think you are. Okay, I'll lay it on you... I have a friend who has, or had, some serious ties to bigtime drug dealers." Seeing Rennie's valiant struggle not to raise skeptical brows: "No, babe, not me, *really* a friend. She knows some things that might lead to major prison time for these cats, death row maybe even, and she's willing to talk. But she wants some immunity and some protection in return, in case going public isn't enough to keep her safe. She reads your stuff too, and she asked me to ask you if you would meet with her. She's really scared and really uptight, but she wants to talk to you, no one else. She feels she can trust you, and she asked me to find out for sure if she could."

Rennie, who had forgotten to breathe while Sunny was talking, now drew in air all the way down to the bottom of her lungs, feeling that excited little rush she was learning to associate with her instinct for a story.

"You know I can't promise anything on the law's behalf—nothing like immunity or protection. And you also know I've never done that kind of piece before?" At Sunny's impatient expression: "Okay, but I have to say all this up front, so you can decide about me and tell your friend and then *she* can decide. I can certainly talk to the cops for her, but I don't know what good it'll do. I'll take it to my husband's cousin, he's a detective with the SFPD and he'll be straight about it. As for the story itself, I'm not sure my editors would ever let me do it. It's pretty Balkanized at newspapers—that's nothing like what I usually cover. That's serious stuff. Real journalism."

"So? You went to two famous real journalism schools— oh yeah, I checked you out—I'm sure you've got all the serious reporter skills you need. And you've been asking around about the murders anyway, trying to help Prax. I heard you had a bunch of pretty specific questions for a lot of people—about Tommy Linetti and Tony De Angelis and Jasper Goring, what they were into. And you were getting quite a few right answers, too, at least according to my friend. Don't you want to take the next step, get the *big* right answer?"

"Why me?" asked Rennie flatly, putting down the spark and thrill of interest. "If the story is as big as you say, there are award-winning journalists at every newspaper in California who'd sell their daughters to Rumpelstiltskin to get the beat."

"Listen, after this comes out, you'll *be* one of those journalists. You'll be able to write your own ticket at any rag in the country, never mind California. You bring this story to your editor and it's guaranteed front-page. But my friend wants *you* to handle it, nobody else."

"She doesn't even know me!"

"She knows what I know, what Prax knows, what Juha Vasso and Brian Jones and Tansy Belladonna and Jerry Garcia know. Musicians talk to each other, honey, and it's not always about drugs or songs or balling or what a pissant bastard their manager or their record company promotion guy is. They talk about press too: there's a whole book going as to which writers know what the hell they're talking about and which ones couldn't tell a chord progression from a corduroy suit. And which ones can be trusted not to kick your ass in print after they've kissed your ass backstage. Or elsewhere." Sunny's face lighted with amusement. "I hear you even got Clovis Franjo to come down from Sinai and talk to you."

Rennie grinned. "Yeah, if you can call it that. The interview hasn't run yet. But it went very well. I thought. So did my editor."

"Well, I told my friend about it, and she seemed to think that if that Neanderthal psychopath Foy Ballard approved of you enough to let you meet his space cadet boss, and if Clovis the redwood god actually talked to you, then you're obviously something and you're obviously real. Yet another reason for you to be the one."

Sunny poured out two more brandies, seemed to be choosing her words very carefully. "You'd think those two'd go after any publicity they could get, just for the goddamn trees, but no. Most reporters they blow off for not being pure enough. Warriors of Gaia! Give me a fucking break. Anyway, getting back to my friend —"

"But what do Foy and Clovis have to do with —"

"She's been Foy Ballard's old lady for three years." Sunny smiled as Rennie's shoulders went back and she leaned forward in her chair. "I see that got your attention. You've been wondering about Foy, haven't you?"

"Damn straight I have," said Rennie honestly. "I didn't know who he was until I talked to him for the Clovis story. But there was something about him I didn't like, right off the bat. I couldn't put a finger on it, but it was there. He's one scary hombre, and not just because he wears iron bars in his hair. I couldn't lay a glove on him, and there was no reason in the world for him to be so cagey. Not like Clovis, who couldn't have been more upfront."

Sunny raised an elegant eyebrow over a silver-shadowed lid. "Or more boringly pretentious."

"True, but that's beside the point. Anyway, I started poking around. About Foy, I mean. I asked people about him, people in the scene, but nobody would talk much. They were all too scared. All they'd say that he was really into trees and really into drugs and really into beating up on women. Which last two are not exactly unknown qualities among the biker set. And though I don't have any proof, I got this idea that Foy might have some connection to the mur —"

"You stop right there," said Sunny sharply. "You can think it, *chica*, but don't say it, at least not just yet, and don't even be thinking it too loud. You'll just get yourself into big and possibly fatal trouble. If you think something's rotten with Foy, you're not the first. The cops do too, only they can't prove a thing. And before you ask, no, I don't believe Clovis knows. He's oblivious to anything that doesn't have a root ball the size of a house and a thirty-foot diameter trunk. The best way to find out what's stinking up the street will be to talk to Ro."

"Ro?"

"My friend. Rosemary Savarkin. Ro. Can I have her call you?"

"Why can't *I* call *her?*"

"Well, for one thing, she's wanted on drug charges, and she's nervous about new people. Oh, she's clean now, mostly clean, but for a few years she was totally strung out on smack and she got busted a couple of times. The last time, she jumped bail and ran. That's why she can't go directly to the fuzz. As I said, she's hoping you might be able to help her with that too."

Rennie gave a short laugh. "If I carried any weight with the cops, my best friend wouldn't be languishing in the slammer on a double murder rap."

"Point taken. But you could maybe connect Ro with someone in the cop shop who *could* help her out. Rennie, she's going through heavy changes. She's covered for Foy so many times, but now she wants to rat him out for what he's done to her. He's beaten up on her for years; the last time he sent her to the hospital for two weeks. She's afraid he'll come back and find her, and I'm afraid that one night he'll finish her off. She wants to get him first. That's not too much to ask, is it?"

"No. It isn't," said Rennie, recalling her conversation with Foy in Muir Woods, and her instinctive reaction to him, how terrifying he had seemed, and they were only talking, for God's sake. *Now imagine that oversized orc coming at you with closed fists and violent intent...* "Where is she now? Not the address, just a general idea."

"Not on this side of the bay," Sunny answered after a brief pause, and Rennie nodded. Over in the East Bay, then: Berkeley, Oakland, Alameda. You could hide yourself pretty well over there—better than in Marin or the city, maybe. "She's in a house rented under another name, to keep her safe. The last time Foy found out where she was living, he showed up in the middle of the night and beat her to a heap of bloody rags."

"She didn't go back to him, I hope?"

Sunny rolled her eyes. "Of course she did, that's what women like her do! But she's maybe finally learned she doesn't have to do that. And she finally wants to talk." She stretched out the impossibly long legs sheathed in the gleaming leather jeans and admired her scarlet-painted toenails. "And she wants to talk to *you*. So what do you say?"

With quick decisiveness Rennie scribbled something on a piece of paper torn from her pad, then looked Sunny straight in the eye and handed her the scrap of paper with both her phone numbers on it.

"I say I sure as hell want to talk to her."

Chapter Sixteen

AFTER THAT, THE ACTUAL INTERVIEW had gone like a dream. Maybe the best Sunny'd ever given or Rennie'd ever gotten. Driving home after, Rennie was still amused at the realization that she herself had been interviewed, inquired about and vetted up front for her suitability and trustworthiness.

That's twice in two assignments...well, if I do research on them, I guess it's only fair that they do research on me. But I hope all subjects don't follow suit...

She was glad she'd passed muster. She found that she liked Sunny a lot as a person, and she had always greatly enjoyed and respected her music; she had immediately shared the singer's view that there was a much, much bigger story to be had than how a nice Queens girl had gone to London and come back an outrageous superstar singer. Though she'd write up that one too, of course, and it would be everything that Burke had demanded it be; he'd be pleased. As for the other thing, well, they'd all just have to wait and see on that. But she wouldn't be mentioning it to Burke.

It didn't take long for the phone number to get itself

across the bay. That night, Rennie picked up the phone to hear a low, surprisingly unhesitant voice.

"I need to talk to Rennie Stride."

"Speaking."

"Our friend from Argentina told me to call you, Rennie. She said we should talk."

Rennie relaxed. That was the password—Argentina of course being to do with silver—that she and Sunny had determined on that afternoon. It had seemed corny and melodramatic when they'd come up with the idea of sign and countersign; now, hearing the note of longtime terror in the voice in her ear, like a backup singer, Rennie wasn't so sure. Still—*What* are *we, Boris and Natasha? Where Moose and Sqwiddle?*—she spoke the countersign anyway; though not in a Bullwinkle voice, hysterically tempted though she was.

"Yes. I've been to Argentina myself; I was hoping you can give me some travel tips for my next vacation there."

A soft laugh. "You could say that. Are you interested?"

"Very much. That friend told me a few helpful hints, but I need some more."

"And I can give them to you."

"Do you want to come here?"

"No!" The flare of panic in Ro's voice was instant. "No," she continued more quietly, "you come to me. I'll have our friend send the details to you at the Clarion; a messenger will deliver it to the, what, you have a front desk or a mailroom or something? Give me the address. —Right. It'll be there tomorrow, and I'll call you tomorrow night to confirm."

Sounded like a plan. Rennie heard herself saying so, and then hung up. She sat by the phone for a few minutes, staring around the apartment, suddenly chilled. She hadn't told anyone, not even Sharon or Stephen or Prax, but sometimes, when it was very quiet in the house, she fancied she could hear things, or sense presences, even see things flickering at the corner of her peripheral vision. At first she'd dismissed it, thinking she was just tired or stoned. But that didn't seem to be it. Then she thought that perhaps it was one of her predecessor tenants, Jack or Mark or Bret; maybe they needed a pencil on the astral plane, or wanted to borrow her thesaurus, or just felt like a little Earth fix. Ghost writers. The real kind.

And though she honestly thought that, and was spiritual enough or superstitious enough to say hi, and had even been known to ask them to help her out with the writing if it wasn't going well, one pro to another, tonight the vibes somehow carried a darker tinge, and she had the strangest feeling that it was Jasper and Fort.

After the murders, she'd tried very hard to go on as before, living in the apartment—she loved it, she'd built a lot of it with her own hands, she'd be damned if she was going to move—and for the most part she'd succeeded. Stephen's generous renovation had helped, more than he probably knew.

But sometimes it just rose up—murder, all red and raw, as she'd seen its aftermath with her own eyes—and sandbagged her. Maybe she should go downstairs and ask Sharon for some short-term counseling. Sharon had been amazingly cool about it all, when she'd come home from Portland to find her beautiful house a crime scene. Most people would have flipped out, but Sharon had just taken it all in, well, stride. Rennie had been in terror that she was going to be evicted, but her landlady had reassured her.

"Not to worry, Ren, I'm sure it's not the worst thing that's ever happened in this house. And even if it is... San Francisco houses are like that—little sponges absorbing everything that ever went on in them. It's all part of their history. And now you're part of it too."

Which may or may not have been comforting. But as Rennie centered herself now with a little yoga breathing, suddenly the feeling sharpened to one of near-panic. No, they were *definitely* here, Jasper and Fort, and she felt like an idiot, but—

"Fort? Jasper? Do you want to talk? Can I help?"

And then, amazingly, a feeling like a warm tide came over her from all directions at once, and she found herself smiling. That was it: they wanted to be acknowledged, they wanted to let her know that she was already helping them, that she was on the right track. Unless, of course, she was losing her mind completely. But somehow she didn't think so.

"Don't sweat it, guys," she said aloud, and though she would never have described herself as a religious person, suddenly it didn't feel foolish at all to be talking to two murder victims across the great divide, on the other side of this life. On the contrary: it felt like something she could do, something she wanted to do, something she even had to do.

"We're working on it. It's cool. It's cool."

The next day, a messenger delivered an envelope addressed to Rennie at the Clarion, a white envelope bearing the Fairmont logo. As was the case with all letters to editorial staff, it was accepted at the Clarion's mailroom desk down in the maze of the basement, slotted to the proper floor and department and placed on the appropriate mailcart.

But something happened as the envelope made its way upstairs to Rennie, where she sat typing at her desk in her little tenth-floor cubicle. Someone who had no business being there at all and still less business doing anything of the sort was carefully opening the sealed flap, copying the address inside, then sealing it up again and sending it on its way.

If Rennie even noticed that the envelope had been opened, and she could never remember afterwards if she had or hadn't, she would have assumed it was the mailroom staff checking to be sure it contained nothing noxious. There'd been a spate of poison-pen letters lately—not aimed at Rennie—and the Clarion was being wisely cautious.

So she tore the envelope twice across and tossed it in the wastebasket, and carefully tucked the single sheet bearing Ro Savarkin's safe-house address into her orange-red Moroccan wallet. And when she came back to her desk after a staff meeting with Burke and Garrett Larkin and the other entertainment writers, she never noticed that the envelope with the Fairmont embossing was gone from the trash. But she might not have thought it mattered, even if she had.

So paranoid was she about the need for secrecy that she didn't mention Ro's call and their appointment even to her spouse, when he came over for dinner that night at her invitation. Frankly, she was too surprised he'd agreed to come at all, after his cool distancing and absences over the past few weeks, and when she opened the door to him she found herself both oddly nervous and genuinely eager to see him.

Most of the nervousness came from her, though she sensed a bit from Stephen as well. *He's my lawful husband, and he's never been anything but loving and kind and patient with me, even though I'm not that with him, and he's paying for Prax's defense and he was all set to put up her bail money too, and now after I feed him I'm going to stick — what did Prax call it? — yes, the Icepick of Confession, right into his back…unless the icepick's in already…in which case it would be just another twist of the blade…*
The icepick was that she had decided to tell him tonight that she'd been seeing, okay, sleeping with, a few other guys. It had to be said; she couldn't go on with him not knowing. Maybe that was selfish, but there it was. Presuming he didn't already know; but at this point a declaration was probably good form, and perhaps he really *didn't* know. Maybe it was all coincidence that he'd been so aloof. Uh-huh.
But after just the right kind of kiss — not so cool as to seem dismissive, not warm enough to start anything up — and his favorite steak and home-fried potatoes for supper, they ended up in bed, as they usually did. And though Rennie was careful not to employ too many of her new skills, it seemed

that he noticed anyway, for afterwards, as they were lying companionably entwined, he kissed her hair and tightened his arm around her and pulled out an icepick of his own.

"Rennie—Rennie, I know what's been going on. I know you've been with other men."

It hit her like glacier meltwater, though his tone hadn't been accusatory in the slightest, just matter-of-fact, and she gasped with the surprise and shock.

"I'm sorry, oh, God, Stephen, I'm *so* sorry, I was going to tell you tonight..."

She felt him smile, the way she always could tell he was smiling even though she didn't see his face.

"It's okay. I won't say I'm fine with it, because I don't think I am yet, but I'm fine with *you*. I knew you'd work your way around to it sooner or later, and frankly, I expected it to happen a lot sooner. You're a beautiful and desirable woman, and I'm not surprised that I'm not the only one who thinks so and who wants to sleep with you. I don't want to know their names, or how many, or what it all means. I just wanted you to know I know, and that it's—what it is."

"I kind of had a feeling that you knew," said Rennie bleakly. "I guess your mother's detective didn't exactly—"

He shot up next to her so suddenly that she fell onto the pillows before she could catch herself. "My mother's *WHAT?*"

She looked up at him and unconsciously gathered the sheet up to her chin. *Oh God, he didn't know...*

"Her detective," she repeated in a smaller voice than ever. "I thought that was how you knew? She's had a private eye following me ever since I moved out of Hall Place, to find out if I was being—being unfaithful. And, well, she found out. I thought she'd told you."

He was out of the bed by now and had paced furiously over to the windows, where he stared out for a while, then punched the wall, hard, and turned again to her.

"I swear I knew nothing about it," he said in a deadly calm voice. "She never even hinted she—I would never in a million *years* have allowed—"

He broke off, clearly not trusting his voice, and seemed to be looking around for something he could break. Finding nothing, he sat on the edge of the bed, and stared at Rennie.

"I can't believe she'd do something so unspeakable, so despicable as pay some two-bit sleazebag panty-sniffing snoop to follow my wife around—"

"She came to my place and told me herself."

Briefly Rennie recounted the scene with Marjorie, and found to her astonishment that she was genuinely reluctant to give Stephen the details. Which surprised the hell out of her, as she'd been fantasizing about such an opportunity ever since Marjorie had looked at her across the tea table that first morning and damn near turned her to stone. And now it was here, that delicious moment when she finally got to clue him in to what a vile sow he had for a mother. Only it wasn't delicious, and she almost didn't want to.

I always thought that when I did get a chance to do this, I'd be so happy my heart would stop...but all of a sudden it's not as much fun as I thought it would be...she's still his mother, for everything she's done to make my life hell...

But Stephen, who at first had seemed to be lifting off to a whole new planet of rage, listened to her account with a face devoid of expression, asked a few questions, and then with rigid calmness put it all aside, and Rennie caught herself thinking that she would in no way care to be Marjorie Lacing when her youngest child caught up with her in the morning room tomorrow.

"But if she didn't tell you, which it still amazes me that she didn't, then how did you know? Did I—do something?"

Oh please God, don't let him say he knew because he's noticed all my fun new techniques that I learned elsewhere...

He gave a gentle laugh. "No, sweetheart. It was more what you *didn't* do—didn't ask me here as much, didn't always want me to stay over when you did. More a feeling than any one thing. It was all more like a woman who—how can I say this without sounding like I blame you—had other options."

Ouch...but that hurt him to say way more than it hurt me to hear...

"Never mind," she said softly, and drew him back into bed. "It doesn't matter. You're the first man I was ever with, and I thought you'd be the only one, but it didn't work out that way. I wish it had."

"No, you don't," said Stephen, smiling. "And that's okay too. I forget how young you are. I'm six years older than you, I've been with other women—not since we were married, of course, but still. I guess it's only fair that you should get to be with other men." He settled down again beside her, and when she hesitated he drew her to lie across his chest as she always did. "Now, let's lighten up a bit, shall we? Let's talk about murder." And as he'd meant her to, she laughed. "Seriously. How is it with Prax these days? Tell me."

As she began to tell him, Stephen, who was listening as hard as he thought he possibly could, couldn't help thinking that one of the many good things about having her lying on his chest was that she couldn't see his face.

The next morning at her office, Rennie got a call from King Bryant, and thirty seconds later another from Stephen, and thirty seconds after that she had grabbed her coat and her purse and her concert dress and a fringed shawl and a pair of clogs from a lower desk drawer, stuffed the spare clothes into a big embroidered Balinese market bag and was flying down the hall to the elevators.

Getting out of her cab at the Hall of Justice, she saw Stephen going up the steps ahead of her with his minion Brooks, and she dashed to catch them up. Too out of breath to speak, she tugged Stephen's coat, and he turned round to her.

"It's true?" she managed to gasp.

He smiled and took her arm to lead her inside. "I wouldn't be here with Brooks if it weren't."

"Is King *sure*?"

"He said come down and bring the money. So here we are." He indicated Brooks, who inclined his head to her with a broad smile.

"I'm not going to believe it until I see her—"

When they arrived at the courtroom, the first person Rennie saw as she went in was Prax, sitting at the defense table with King Bryant. The lawyer saw them, and murmured into Prax's ear; she turned around, ashen and strained, too keyed up to speak.

Rennie made an encouraging face, and she and Stephen took the same seats as they had on the previous court occasion. But they were destined not to occupy them for even as long as they had before. King and the D.A. had a smiling though respectful sidebar with the judge, then returned to their places. The D.A. said something deeply legal about how due to altered circumstances the people had no objection at this time to bail being lodged for this defendant, King said something in even heavier lawspeak that translated to "Fine with us!", the gavel came down and that was it. Brooks went to attend to the bail details, and Prax was free.

She almost seemed not to realize it. When Rennie reached out to touch her shoulder, she turned round at once, her face frozen and still, eyes huge in a paler, thinner face than the one Rennie had first seen, only two months back, on a porch in Sausalito on a bright afternoon.

"Thank you. *Thank you.* I could never have managed on my own—"

Rennie shook her gently. "Stephen fixed it all. I didn't even have to ask."

"Then, thank you, Stephen. Again."

Prax went totally white all in an instant, a kind of anti-blush, a flood of pallor; then swayed and lost her footing. The bailiffs came forward, and Rennie looked up angrily as her friend shrank away. But they courteously helped Prax steady herself, and said that Miss McKenna had to be properly signed out, it would take a few minutes, and were there any clean clothes she could change into? Rennie mutely thrust forward the market bag, and Prax and her escort left for the moment.

It seemed like hours, but it was only about fifteen minutes later when Prax, now wearing Rennie's dress and shawl and clogs, met them outside the courtroom. King took one look and grabbed her arm before she folded, and Stephen caught the other side.

"Here, Praxie, sit down."

Between them, they got her onto one of the benches that lined the hall, and Rennie waved a purse flacon of Chanel Number Five under Prax's nose, in lieu of smelling salts.

Looking up, Rennie realized that Dill Miller had joined them, and seeing her staring at him as if at some bizarre apport from the Twilight Zone, he hastily began explaining why he was there.

"The same reason you are. King's office called to let me know, and I got here as fast as I could."

Rennie just nodded. "But how are we going to get her out? If there are reporters outside?"

Dill nodded back. "Many. And now a couple of TV crews. If I might suggest—Rennie and Stephen to take Prax out the back, Brooks to bring the car around for them, King and I to speak to the press by way of diversion."

"Good man!" said King. "Let me." And he strode off. By now, Prax had regained some color; with Dill's help and Stephen's she was on her feet again, and Rennie pulled the shawl close around her friend's blond head.

Then King was gesturing at them from a side hallway. "Come through here," he said when they joined him. "The bailiffs said the front entrance is indeed infested with reporters, and we can't be having with that. But nobody's at the judges' entrance, and they'll let you go out that way. Brooks has the car there, so you won't have to run for it. While Miller and I will go out the front and deal with your fourth-estate colleagues, Rennie," he added, grinning.

"Fuckem," she said, smiling right back.

It was as he said, and they reached the LacingCo limousine without incident or interference. Once inside, in the vast and comfortable spaces of the back seat, Prax huddled the shawl tighter and leaned her head against the smooth padded leather, staring blankly at the ceiling as the car headed up Van Ness.

"Not a good trip," she said at last. "Then again, think how much better I can understand jailhouse blues songs now. Every silver lining has its cloud, right?"

Rennie, seeing that Prax's hands were shaking, gathered her into her arms. "It's okay, you're not going to be alone. You're not going back to Sausalito yet, either; you're staying with me."

"I don't think that's such a good idea," murmured Stephen, from where he sat on the equally comfortable facing seat; Brooks was up front, driving with great precision and control—just another boring limo, folks, nothing to see here, don't be tailing us. "Once they're done with Miller and King, you know your tribe isn't going to be denied. Prax's house is probably already surrounded, but as soon as she doesn't show up there, where do you think they're all going to stake out next? Yes, that's right. Your place."

"Well, what then?" She met his eyes, saw the hesitant, apologetic expression on his face, as if he knew exactly how she was going to respond but there was no alternative, he had to say what he had to say. "Oh no. Nonono. No way in *hell*."

"It's really the safest and best place she could possibly be," he said humbly. "She'll be totally protected and catered to. Nobody will be able to get at her, she can stay as long as she likes, the staff will be delighted to fuss over her—after what she's been through, I think she could use some serious coddling. And you'd be better off staying there as well, at least for the next few days."

Prax had belatedly realized they were discussing her immediate future. "What? Rennie? Stay where?" Her voice started to tremble, and Rennie tightened her arms around her as Prax huddled in her lap.

"Stephen thinks you should stay at Hall Place. For your own protection. But only if you want to. Otherwise we can both go to a hotel. But if you do want to stay at Hell House, I'll stay there with you." She glanced defiantly at Stephen. "What about your mother? How thrilled will *she* be that her slut daughter-in-law is back? With an accused murderess in tow, who's out on bail that her own son paid for, and both of them will be bedding down under her sacred roof?"

"I'll take care of my mother," said Stephen with a certain edge to his voice, and Rennie believed him. "Anyway, we're having the big formal ball for the General this Saturday night, and she's been pretty occupied. Too occupied to hassle you. You were coming with me to the ball anyway, and now Prax can come too—it'll be a nice way to celebrate her being free and take her mind off things. We'll find her a nice, amusing and highly presentable escort—Eric's boyfriend Trey would be delighted to oblige, I'm sure. You could ask Sharon to fetch clothes and stuff from both your places, or I could send Carlos and Lucy. Please, Rennie—it really would be best for her. And for you too," he suggested, more diffidently than before. "I only thought—"

Rennie gave a short laugh. "Thought! Did you even *dream* I'd let her stay alone in that house of horrors? You *bet* I'm staying! And just let Motherdear try to stop me."

The excitement of installing Prax and herself at Hall Place—

Stephen was right, in the bustle of preparations for the ball Marjorie utterly ignored them—did not keep Rennie from going to meet with Ro Savarkin two days later. She had rented a dark, ordinary-looking Chevy for the drive to Oakland and back, not wanting to risk the Corvette being recognized by the murderer stalker dope kingpins she was by now convinced were lurking behind every tree. Or even by Marjorie's detective, who may or may not have still been tailing her, though when a coldly furious Stephen had lit into his mother the morning after Rennie'd told him, Marjorie had sworn weeping that she'd called the tec off as soon as Rennie had confronted her. Well, that was her story, anyway.

Driving down Divisadero to where she could hang a left and connect to the freeway leading to the Oakland bridge, Rennie wondered. Considering that this investigator had supposedly been bird-dogging her everywhere she went, she was curious as to why he hadn't ever helped her out a little, like when that drunk was assaulting her in front of the Avalon that night.

That was so scary—even scarier now than it seemed at the time. It all happened so fast. And I could have been in real trouble — if Marcus hadn't happened to be there...

She caught herself up short, accidentally hitting the brakes in the cold shockwave that washed over her, ignoring the blaring horns and shouted curses from the cars beside and behind.

No. Oh no. Not possible. But—just why *had* Marcus "happened" to be there? Sure, he'd said he tracked her down through the Clarion, that he'd wanted to be sure she got home safe, but was that true? It *couldn't* be Marcus who had been Marjorie's hireling, her bought informer. Could it? Would he? That would be *major* conflict of interest—not that he wasn't already conflicting himself all over the place. No. Surely not. Unless, another awful possibility, could Marjorie have hired the drunk herself, to assault her and put the fear of God in her? Or at least the fear of Motherdear? No, that was just nuts. Even Marjorie wouldn't connive at rape or battery. Would she?

She shut the mental doors on the insanity and waved an apology to the outraged drivers, then drove on, rather more carefully and a whole lot more reflectively, heading out across the Bay Bridge and thence up into the hills. Once there, she followed the excellent directions to her not surprisingly hard-to-find destination: a sizable, pretty Craftsman house in Piedmont, a wooded, sloping, rather upscale area between Oakland and Berkeley.

More upscale than I expected...I wonder if Sunny's picking up the rent...

The note had said walk straight through to the cottage in the back but don't pull into the driveway or park right out front; so she parallel-parked the rental a few houses down. Checking paranoiacally though ever so casually to be sure she was neither followed nor observed, she walked along the tree-lined sidewalk to the narrow—barely car-width—cobble-paved driveway between the front house and its California-Spanish neighbor.

Yes, there it was at the end of the alley, all tucked away behind, off to one side of what must be the shared garage, with a small square lawn and flower-bedded garden on the other side: a tiny tile-roofed cottage just as attractive as its larger-edition counterpart, half-hidden in flowering bushes, a redwood balcony green-bronzed with age jutting off its second story. Couldn't be seen from the street, and trellises and retaining walls concealed it from the neighboring buildings—yes, a safe little refuge.

The perfume of jasmine and rhododendron was overwhelming, and Rennie stopped to bury her face in the flowers. As she bent her head, breathing in the fresh, wild scent, she was aware of a blind being chinked aside in the cottage: someone watching her, someone keeping carefully still. She made no sign she'd noticed, but silently told out a slow count of ten, then straightened up and headed to the side door as she had been instructed.

She hadn't even raised her hand to knock when the door swung open and a slight, short girl a few years older than Rennie stood backlit by the low light in the hall behind her.

"Ro Savarkin? Rosemary? Rennie Stride," said Rennie, and held up her treasured press card, close to her face so Ro could see.

"I know, I checked your picture." She flashed a scrap of newsprint from an underground newspaper,   bearing a smudged photo of Rennie and Prax at some club, having a very merry time, apparently, with most of the Grateful Dead. "Quick, come in before—well, just come in. Please. Now."

Chapter Seventeen

INSIDE, THE COTTAGE WAS BARE and touchingly neat: there wasn't enough stuff to even be untidy, let alone messy. Secondhand generic Danish modern furniture, the sort you find in superior motels, stood on clean-mopped linoleum floors, but there wasn't much of it—a fold-out couch, a sturdy floor lamp, two comfy armchairs, a coffeetable, a small television set; in the kitchen, a Fifties-vintage rock-maple table with three chairs around it and some clean, mismatched plates atop it, a fluorescent light under a cabinet the only illumination.

But Ro led her quickly down the hallway to the very back of the cottage, to a small bedroom whose window opened on a blank ivy-covered retaining wall and the square of garden lawn, and Rennie realized she'd chosen the one room where they couldn't be seen from outside, either from the alley or the street house in front or the houses behind.

Turning on a student-style bedside lamp, Ro sat cross-legged on top of the stripped mattress, pushed a few uncased pillows behind her back, leaned against them and laced her fingers together. She was painfully thin in a new white T-shirt, its creases still sharp from folding, and clean if worn jeans. The uneven grayish skin tone of the junkie had vanquished what had once been a translucent Irish pallor, but she still boasted the blue eyes and black hair that went with that kind of skin. Ro had been strikingly pretty, Rennie realized, with a pang of compassion. And could be again, if she could manage to get off the scag.

Careful now, this isn't some confident, set-up rock chick like Sunny or even Praxie. This is one very scared and fragile lady...

Rennie never forgot that first half-hour, speaking carefully and gently, trying not to alarm, asking cautious questions, using all her skills to draw answers and confidence, if not yet confidences, out of the other girl. And it worked: gradually Ro relaxed, visibly easing out of her state of wound-up terror, and began to talk.

"I got into it three years ago, when I met Foy," she admitted of her drug habit. "It was my own stupid fault. I didn't *have* to try every drug in the PDR—and plenty that aren't."

"Most people who try drugs don't get hooked. It's possible to do a little speed, a little coke. Well, maybe not a little smack. But even that maybe."

The ghost of a smile. "Well, it wasn't possible for me, babe, but I didn't see that until way later. And Foy didn't care how much I did; for him it was only ever about control. *His* control, over other people. That's how he got Jasper to play along. And then Tommy and Tony—Tam and Fort. They were all in deep money troubles and drug problems, way over their heads. Foy paid their debts and kept them in dope, and all they had to do for him was become his distributors. Heroin always, but coke too, it had a bigger markup."

"I thought Jasper was into gambling, not drugs? I never *ever* saw him toke up or snort, or drop anything more psychedelic than a couple of multivitamins."

"Those guys were so generous." Ro's voice dripped bitterness. "They shared everything, even their addictions. Even me. I didn't have enough self-esteem left to say no. But Jasper — he just didn't do blow where anyone could see. Even that stuck-up model bitch wife of his didn't know about the coke, though she sure knew about the gambling. Tony went along because he wanted to stay famous, and he figured Jasper could help. But he'd been into drugs for years, from when he lived in Philly — he'd just managed to keep it as secret as Jas did. Tommy was just into it for more drugs. But all of them did it for money to live the way they wanted to. It was a perfect system."

"How did it work?" Rennie didn't dare write anything down for fear of scaring Ro silent; but she blessed her j-prof's name for all those memory-training exercises, meant for just such moments as this, and she took mental notes on an unerasable tape recorder.

"Their name for the whole drug operation was Charlemagne. You know? King of France or something. Anyway, they used Jasper's bands as drug movers. Sometimes the cats knew, but more often not. Tommy or Tony would hide the drugs in the amps or the road cases or even inside the drums, then the roadies would load up the vans and just schlep everything wherever it was supposed to go. Musicians have free and easy access just about anywhere, and it wasn't hard to unload later. You'd be amazed how much dope you can stuff into a Marshall stack or a Leslie cabinet; why do you think stage speakers keep getting bigger and bigger?"

"Not entirely for the sound, I take it."

"Hardly! Foy even uses those Renaissance fair medieval freaks to cart the drugs from place to place. Some of them never even know they're mules — besides, who'd suspect somebody dressed up like Anne Boleyn of having her big old Tudor skirt lined with heroin? Trouble is, some of them lost their heads, just like poor Queen Annie did."

Rennie concealed a violent start at Ro's perhaps inadvertent choice of metaphor. Jasper and Fort *had* just about lost their heads, actually; at least that was what Marcus had told her, after the bodies had been taken away. But how could Ro know that? That particular piece of information had never been released. Just a lucky guess? Or...

"Are you saying — what *are* you saying? That Foy killed some of his own drug runners?"

Ro met her glance, spoke levelly. "Like I said, it's always about control with Foy." She pulled up her T-shirt, totally unselfconsciously, and Rennie gasped at the huge purple and yellow bruises staining the dead-white skin, the pathetically visible ribs and spine. "He did that to me last week. The time before, I ended up in the hospital for four days. That's why I ran. That's why I'm here. I kept going back to him, but not anymore. And yes, you *bet* I think he killed people. I know that people who used to come around — dealers, mules, even customers — have gone missing. All of a sudden, they're gone, no word, even their friends can't find them. Foy claims they split for New York or L.A., but, you know, I just don't think so."

Rennie took that in, for later consideration. "Who's his supplier?"

"He's his own supplier. He's got a master's degree in chemistry from USC. Bet he never told you that when you talked to him, did he?"

"No, it must have slipped his mind. You mean he cooks the stuff himself? But to sell on the scale you tell me he does, that would mean he'd have to have a pretty big and sophisticated lab operation — where? Mexico? It's hard to hide that kind of thing..."

Ro laughed, and all of a sudden she was the pretty girl she had once been. "That would be way too mundane. Besides, he's a racist: Mexico's full of Mexicans — he must have told me that a hundred times. No, can't you guess? What's the only thing, besides money, that he's passionate about?"

Rennie stared. "Oh my God—the redwoods! *That's* why he glommed onto a tree-hugger—why he's so protective, some would say controlling and I guess I would too, of Franjo. Clovis is his cover. The drug factories are in those virgin forests he's such a pain in the ass about protecting. As long as the redwoods stay safe and unmolested—"

"—so does he. And he's not the only one to use Mother Nature for deep cover. Plenty of other people—very well-funded, very well-armed people—have marijuana plantations going way back into the hills, even right here in the Bay Area. Go somewhere you shouldn't in backroads Marin and an assful of buckshot is the least you'll get."

"But the lab?"

Ro shivered and hugged herself, leaned forward, got very still, spoke in a low but clear voice. Now they had finally got there...

"There are three Charlemagne labs that I know of, maybe more by now. One's up in godforsaken woods outside Eureka, one's in an especially remote part of the Santa Cruz and the third's down in an even more inaccessible part of the Ventana wilderness. All on or near the coast, all in places that're hard to get to by road but that you can easily reach by boat, or even small water-plane. Not remote enough, apparently: Foy was talking about setting up in the Olympic Peninsula next. Anyway, the labs are all state-of-the-art. Cocaine and heroin are the bread and butter, but he makes anything that appeals to him. Meth, mescaline, speed. Even acid from time to time, when he's bored. He cuts it with speed, just to be nasty. He doesn't waste time and money on pot, though he doesn't mind dealing it in bulk every now and then if a good batch comes his way—he just doesn't want to take the risk of growing it himself, a risk that might endanger the rest of the business."

"Do you suppose Franjo knows about all this?"

"I very much doubt it. He's as blind as a bat to anything that doesn't engage in photosynthesis," said Ro, echoing Sunny Silver's earlier, equally dismissive assessment. "No, he's just a dupe. Only a pawn in Foy's game."

Rennie looked at her approvingly. Smart, very smart; maybe smart enough to be right about all this. Maybe even smart enough to get off smack and make it stick this time.

"If you can quote a Dylan song *and* use the word 'photosynthesis' in the same breath, there's not much wrong with *you*. You still want me to talk to the cops on your behalf?"

Ro shifted uncomfortably; clearly she very much wanted that, but hated, or feared, to ask. "Sunny told you I jumped bail, didn't she. What do you think? Would they even pay attention?"

"Listen." Rennie leaned forward, touched Ro's arm, ignored the instinctive flinching from the light touch. "As I told Sunny, I can't promise immunity, but I *can* promise I'll try like hell for you. Some sort of protection for sure, in exchange for testimony, and paid rehab if you want it. And after that, my husband's family could find you a job somewhere once you got clean; they have companies all over the world, you wouldn't have to stay in San Francisco."

"Delivering me from temptation?" Ro smiled again, just a glimmering across the planes of her face. "That would be nice."

Easy, Rennie, here comes the big one... "You said you thought Foy had offed mules who displeased him... What about Tam and Fort and Jasper? Do you know anything at all about them? Anything I can use to help you and Prax both?"

The intimation clearly being, Did Foy commit those murders, and if he did can you get me proof?

Ro shifted on the pillows, picking up on Rennie's

intensity—the small empty bedroom suddenly seemed very crowded—and took a deep breath.

"Okay...this is the heavy stuff I didn't want to get into on the phone. I know that Foy was backstage at the Fillmore the afternoon Tam was killed."

"How do you know that?"

"Because I was there with him."

Silence in the room. At length Rennie looked up. "You'd better just tell me. You can totally trust me with it, I swear by the Sweet Baby Jesus."

"Sunny said I could... Well, we had gone backstage that afternoon to bring some pot for the, well, the pot. It's a thing Foy got into: pass out free samples to enough people and soon you'll have more customers than you ever dreamed of."

"Quite the little capitalist."

"You could say. Anyway, I'm sure you know that Bill Graham is down on drugs. He disapproves, and he doesn't do anything himself, but he also doesn't stop people who want to toke or snort or drop on the premises—though he draws the line at shooting up. We try to be careful and discreet. Most musicians don't want to bring serious stash to gigs, so we help out, with on-site deliveries. Like pizza. For playing, the bands like coke or speed, though some of them want a little smack just for snorting—*not* acid, unless you actually enjoy seeing your guitar neck melt in your hand or piano keys the size of suitcases. You can't really play on acid, and contrary to public opinion most of the cats don't, except the Dead. Anyway, each band's group of friends or leeches will usually have a little grass with them, which gets kicked in to a sort of backstage communal oh God potluck supper, why can't I stop making these dreadful marijuana puns?"

"Better you than me," said Rennie cheerfully. "Anyway?"

"Anyway, we bring grass too, just in case anyone runs

short. But mostly the other stuff. Foy loves the bands and the ballroom scene, and he's a big fan of Deadly Lampshade. So he hangs around every chance he gets, anytime he's not with Clovis, though sometimes Clovis comes too—for the music, not for dealing. And Foy always wants me there with him. Sometimes he asks me to ball guys he's dealing to, makes me give them head to distract them if he's giving short count, or just to help the deal along. I'm not proud of it, but I did what he told me. And we were there that day. The day Tam was killed."

"Nobody mentioned seeing you."

Ro laughed shortly. "I'm not surprised. But the crew and the musicians all know who we are and why we're there. Anyone who did see us wouldn't cop to it. Gotta protect the free dope meal ticket at all costs."

"Did you see Tam that afternoon?"

Ro shook her head. "I didn't, no. I was under orders to give a blow job to one of the buyers, so I was on my knees in a closet. Somebody else was getting done in the closet next door, but I don't know who that was."

"Never mind," said Rennie. "I think I do. What then?"

"Well, obviously, I didn't stay with Foy all the time we were there. Besides that sale, he was dropping off a bag of smack for Tam's personal use, and a larger package that was Tam's usual consignment, for distribution that week."

"The cops didn't find any large quantities of drugs backstage that night."

"We never saw Tam to make the delivery—well, that's what Foy said. So we took it away again with us." She shivered violently as she felt the quality of Rennie's silence, stared at Rennie with desperation in her eyes. "I know what you're thinking! Believe me, I've been thinking it myself, all the time, ever since it happened."

Rennie thought she was going to die of pity right there, but kept it off her face and out of her voice. Mostly. Pity now wouldn't help either of them.

"Shhh...it's okay..." She put a calming hand on Ro's arm, and this time Ro seized it with both of her own, like a lifeline in hurricane seas.

"No, it's not okay! How could it *possibly* be okay? Just let me say it, will you — I think Foy killed Tam."

"Why do you think that?" Rennie's quietest, most professionally neutral voice, the tone pitched to soothe.

"Because Tam didn't show up when he said he would. I finished with the guy in the closet, came out to clean myself up and saw Foy in the hall. He was really mad. He snapped at me that he had some more business and that I should wait for him out front, in the ballroom area, not backstage. And when he came back to fetch me, he wasn't wearing his jacket. He just hustled me right out of the building, practically threw me on the motorcycle and off we went."

"Maybe he just forgot it."

She shook her head vigorously. "No way! He loves that damn jacket, he'd hand-studded and hand-embroidered it himself, with Hell's Angels colors and Warriors of Gaia crap. He has a few like that; he says he finds it therapeutic, to do the decorating. And he didn't forget it, either. I found it later in the saddlebag of the Harley. There was blood all over it. He showed me his finger, where he said he'd caught it in an amp he was helping somebody shift. But I don't know. There was a lot of blood."

Rennie's mind went back to the jacket she'd seen Foy wearing in Muir Woods, the day she'd talked to Clovis. No Hell's Angels stuff on that one, just the Gaia god's-eye and redwood — must have been one of the alternates. God only knew where the bloody one was now.

There was a faint sound outside, it seemed on the roof, then another, and both of them glanced startled and fearful at the window; after a moment a long-haired gray cat ran across the patch of garden, chasing a squirrel, and they relaxed.

Well, I can understand why she wanted a face-to-face, this isn't the kind of thing you get into on the phone, even if the phone could be trusted...

Rennie gazed thoughtfully at the floor, carefully not looking at Ro. "And you think—"

"Don't you?"

"But why? Why would Foy kill Tam? If it was all so copacetic with the dealing."

"Tam was a greedy pig. He always wanted more. More money, more smack, more control. More me."

"And Foy objected to all those wants, I take it."

Ro shrugged. "The first three, anyway. He didn't mind letting Tam and Fort and even Jasper screw me. But he *really* minded anyone getting close to Clovis, and Tam had started doing that. Foy protected Clovis like he was the heir to a throne. And why wouldn't he? Clovis is *his* protection. If the trees stay safe, the labs stay safe."

Rennie paused a moment before she spoke; her professional control was starting to slip over again into raging pity, and she needed time to tack it back in place.

"And you didn't—you didn't mind doing what he told you to do?"

For the first time Ro really looked at Rennie, and Rennie flinched at what she saw in the other girl's eyes. But Ro's voice when she spoke was soft and wondering, not hostile.

"You sit there all cool and sleek, in your groovy threads with your hip job and your nice life with your rich husband—yeah, yeah, Sunny told me all about it—do you have the smallest idea of what it's like to be on my trip?"

"No," said Rennie, immediately and honestly. "No, I don't. I can't, how could I? But I do think I know a little of what it's like to be forced into somebody else's trip, or somebody else's idea of what your trip should be." She laid a hand on Ro's knee. "And you don't have to do it anymore.

There's help. You don't have to stay with him. And you don't have to do smack, either."

"That's it?" said Ro, but at least she smiled, and not with scorn. "You just say it and it happens, it's done? Must be nice."

"I wouldn't know. I've been saying things for months, and they're nowhere *near* done or happening. But I do know that you have to say it. Otherwise it doesn't happen and it never gets done."

Rennie held her glance, and for the first time Ro didn't look away after a few seconds.

"There, you see?" said Rennie triumphantly. "You can do it. I promise you'll have all the help you'll need, and probably more than you want."

"Before you go making promises you'll maybe not want to keep—let me finish. This is the hardest part for me to say." Ro drew a deep breath, and looked Rennie full in the face. "Jasper and Tony—I think it was Foy who came to your house and killed them. And then he set it up to frame Prax."

Three hours later, Rennie looked at Ro, sleeping peacefully on the bare mattress under the only blanket in the house, and felt maternally protective, as she often did about people she fed, or helped, or coached, or even just made clothes for. Well, at least sisterly protective.

God, I hate to leave her… Here's someone trying to get out of her relationship, just like me, and her old man says he cares about her and wants her to stay, just like Stephen. But this *guy pimps her out and beats her up and maybe murders people on a regular basis — I just hate my mother-in-law for being a bitch and blame my husband for being too damn nice. And I think I* have *it rough….*

She thought back to what Ro had told her. It sure was beginning to look as if Foy had a lot more than a passing connection with Tam's murder; bloody clothes and suspiciously mysterious absences often tend to indicate that sort of thing. But, much as Rennie wanted to believe the story,

Ro's terrified conviction that Foy had been responsible for the murders at Rennie's place had little to factually back it up. Trout in the milk time again.

True, she said he'd gone out late that night and had come home at sunrise in a strange frame of mind—part surly, part gleeful, with an unsettlingly weird kind of wired vibe. But when Rennie'd pressed her, Ro had admitted there had been nothing more convincing than her gut feeling, though the despair with which she'd said it gave the stamp of truth.

She looked over at a slight muffled sound from Ro. Just dreaming. How long had it been since the poor girl could fall asleep without fear of waking up to Foy's hands around her throat, or worse? Nobody deserved that. Still, Rennie knew she would have to leave pretty soon. She would have been gone by now, but Ro had begged her to stay; she was afraid to go to sleep alone, feared nightmares.

And who could blame her? Rennie had offered to take Ro home with her, let her crash in the guestroom, get her into a treatment program where she'd be not only safe but helped off her habit. She'd even promised to pay for it herself, or the Lacings would, or the Clarion. But the other girl had declined. The devil you know. Well, maybe sometime. Maybe once the whole thing was solved and resolved.

She didn't know if Ro would be offended—maybe she'd think Rennie was treating her like the whore Foy treated her as—but she slipped an envelope full of money out of her purse, wrote a little note and put it inside with the bills.

Just for thanks – and for help...

She'd decided to do it as soon as she'd spoken with Sunny, and had stopped at the bank en route to withdraw what she felt comfortable with from the joint account. For the first time ever.

And so the Lacings pay the piper once again – but at least this time I'm the one who gets to call the tune...

No money had been discussed up front, so it wasn't a

bribe; nothing and no one had been bought or sold here. It was just to help out a little. Expenses, reimbursement for information. Or combat pay. Well, the money *was* half hers.

When Rennie finally felt she could leave with a clear conscience, and went out to the street to her car, it was dawn. The air was cool, the moon setting over San Francisco, the sky lightening in the east; the neighborhood was empty and quiet under the trees. Most houses were still dark, though a few showed lights—people up early to get to work, household help starting their daily routine.

Seeing the blameless street before her, Rennie breathed a little easier. Ro's fears had infected her: halfway through their conversation she'd started hearing intruders in the alley, eavesdropping under the windows, sneaking up on them through the garden, and it had only gotten worse after Ro fell asleep. But nothing had happened.

She switched on the headlights, started the car and pulled away from the curb. Ro would be okay; she'd pulled up the blanket and locked the doors and windows, and it was only an hour to full sunlight. She couldn't babysit her forever, right? She'd been okay before Rennie'd come over; she'd be okay after. After all, she'd been living with it for years, she knew how to cope. So why didn't that make Rennie feel any better about leaving her alone?

She might have felt worse still if she'd noticed that half a block behind her, another car started up once she'd turned the corner, and, running without lights, pulled out to drive slowly along the street, the same way Rennie had gone. If she'd noticed at all, she in her paranoia might have thought she was being tailed, or she might have thought, in her reporter's reasonable doubt and judging by the car's casual speed, that it was just someone on his way to work, someone who happened to be going the same way she was and who couldn't be bothered to overtake and pass. But she was distracted and upset, and vigilance was not so much on her mind as it had been when she'd driven over there yesterday.

By the time she was on the approach to the Bay Bridge, the cloudless dawn was broad enough that Rennie could turn off her beams. And the car that had followed her all the way from Ro's place moved up behind her, passed her, then fell away in the heavy traffic, over and over again. It wasn't until they'd both reached Buena Vista West, and Rennie had pulled in behind her house and the other car had stopped halfway down the hill where the street bends sharply, that the little automotive two-step ended. Without Rennie even knowing that she'd been dancing at all.

Or whom she'd been dancing with.

Chapter Eighteen

"*RENNIE*? What the fucking hell are you still doing there?"

The voice on the phone was Stephen's, and he sounded both angry and puzzled. Well, a lot more angry than puzzled. And he *never* used the f-word, not even when they were engaging in it.

"Oh, hi, honey, I got stuck working on—"

He cut sharply across her, as he had never done before. "No. Not acceptable. You're supposed to be *here*. The ball starts in an hour and a half, and you haven't even left work yet."

With a cry of horror Rennie looked at her calendar, and then at the clock. Six-thirty. Damn, she hadn't turned the pages for three days, she'd missed seeing the big red warning note—

"Oh my God, that's *tonight*?"

"Yes." The clipped monosyllable lodged in her heart like a fang of ice. "Rennie—I don't ask anything of you, don't ask you to do a lot for me, but I told you how much this mattered to me, to the whole family, and you promised. And now, well—"

"I'll be there in twenty minutes."

"Make it fifteen. Everything's ready for you. Lucy and Elena will dress you as soon as you get here. I stopped at the bank to pick up your diamonds before I came home. So get your ass out of there. Now."

Rennie hung up and gathered up her jacket and purse and fled down the hall. She couldn't *believe* she'd forgotten. Stephen was right: he hardly ever asked her to do anything, but he had asked this, had asked her to accompany him to the formal ball celebrating his father's thirty years as the head of the giant family conglomerate, LacingCo. The huge Hall Place ballroom was being opened up for the occasion, as it was once or twice a year, and she had actually been looking forward to it; she'd even gone out and had an exquisite ballgown made for her by Marjorie's own dressmaker, hoping that Motherdear would notice how cooperative she was being.

Oscar Wilde had written a famous description of that ballroom, an account of a party given there for him when he'd been a houseguest; he'd gone on as only Oscar could about the Brazilian rosewood and walnut parquet floor, inlaid in an elaborate pattern of stars, and the nine pineapple-shaped crystal chandeliers, and the view through the towering mahogany-framed French windows that opened onto the terrace in a curving wall, overlooking the city on the east and the Golden Gate on the north.

Robert Louis Stevenson, another houseguest, had written about it, too: some said he had not only cribbed inspiration from the Lacing ballroom but had based Long John Silver on the piratical and philosophical Lacing paterfamilias and potentate of the time, whom he had first met in Scotland, years before.

When she'd still been living at Hell House, Rennie had once ventured downstairs to check the ballroom out. It was in the basement, sort of, on the house's lowest rear level where the hill fell away behind in formal terraced gardens; you reached it by a wide shallow flight of marble steps leading down from the rear of the almost equally spacious thirty-foot-ceilinged Great Hall. In the dim hush, she'd tiptoed around under the leaded-glass dome and the dust-sheeted chandeliers that looked like snow-covered pinecones in their white muslin wraps.

But in her head she'd been seeing it all ablaze with lights and music, handsome men in tailcoats and beautiful women gowned and bejeweled; she'd even wondered if she'd ever get a chance to see it like that for real. Now she had, and she'd practically blown it. And worse, Stephen, who never got cross with her, was hurt and furious, and rightly so.

The traffic gods were not smiling on her this day; it took over forty minutes from her office to Pacific Heights. When she finally reached Hell House and parked inside the gates, frantic with haste and guilt, the guests already streaming in looked in horror at this miniskirted gypsy with the preposterously long hair who pretty much shoved them aside, dashed past and bolted upstairs. Ah, they said to one another, nodding sadly and knowingly, that must be the hippie daughter-in-law from New York, the one who writes for that Clarion rag. Poor *dear* Marjorie…only one of her sons married, and not to anyone the least bit suitable, and not even any heir on the way.

Carlos, waiting for her on the stairs, directed her to Stephen's rooms, where both Lucy the housemaid and Elena, Marjorie's own personal lady's-maid, were ready for her, under orders and on tenterhooks, and they ripped the clothes from her back as soon as she burst into the bedroom.

While Rennie was taking a thirty-second shower, Lucy was lining up underwear and shoes and full netted crinolines, and as soon as Rennie came back into the bedroom, she pulled the bath towel off her and threw her underwear on her. Then

Elena pushed her into a chair and with flying fingers began pinning up her hair — at least it was clean, she'd washed it the night before — to take the tiara that Motherdear had mandated. Rennie herself, diving for her makeup case, began a quick shadow-liner-mascara job on her eyes; if she had time, base and blush and powder.

"Am I so very late, Elena? I swear I forgot it was tonight..."

"Well, Mrs. Stephen, Madam did say the whole family was to be ready at seven and downstairs in the ballroom by seven-thirty. The ball begins at eight, and it's almost seven-thirty now."

"All right then, let's *rock*."

Hair and complete makeup done in world-record time. They put a net hood like a diving helmet on her to protect their work, then helped her into the ballgown, carefully bringing it down over her head and fastening the tight boned strapless bodice in back. She sat down, fighting the billowing yards of amethyst silk as Lucy slid silver kid French heels onto her feet.

"Where's my husband?"

"Mr. Stephen is waiting for you in the ballroom, to go into the Great Hall with the rest of the family. Mrs. Stephen, please, we only have ten minutes left."

"Bags of time. Where's Miss Praxedes?"

"We got her ready an hour ago and sent her down to the Great Hall with the other guests, as Madam ordered."

"Oh, good, thank you so much for looking after her... Now where's the damn jewelry?"

Almost there. Elena took off the hood and carefully set the glittering tiara on the piled-up hair, and Lucy clasped the diamond festoon necklace — Stephen's chief wedding gift to his bride — around Rennie's throat. Rennie threaded heavy matching drop earrings into her pierced ears, applied a pink gloss of lipstick and a spray of Arpège, and pulled on the shoulder-length white formal gloves over her marriage rings—worn at Stephen's terse request, the diamond-encrusted wedding band and the huge pear-cut solitaire—and her grandmother's Ceylon sapphire.

"See? Three minutes to spare." She thanked them both and fled down the great staircase like Cinderella on the lam.

Cinders had it easy—if I don't get there on time, Marjorie will gut me like a pumpkin...

Not enough time to go round to the back stairs and enter unobtrusively. She streaked like a violet comet through the Great Hall, ignoring the stares of the assembled guests but exchanging an eyeroll on the fly with Prax, who was escorted that evening by Eric's hunky boyfriend Trey—Thomas Copeland III, of a family almost as old and rich as the Lacings—and who both looked astonished to see her, and hit the ballroom on the stroke of seven fifty-nine. The immediate family, waiting behind closed doors for their big ceremonial entrance, looked unanimous daggers at her as she swept down the stairs, but her eyes were fixed on one person only.

Stephen was waiting for her, standing apart from the others, very handsome in white tie. But he wasn't looking daggers at her. He wasn't looking at her at all, which was a million times worse.

"Glad you could make it," he said coldly. "You look lovely. Let's go." He offered his arm, and she laid a gloved hand on his dark sleeve.

"I'm so, *so* sorry, you know I was looking forward to this, I just forgot it was tonight..."

"Smile."

She obeyed, as the ballroom doors opened again and, led by Marjorie and the General, neither of whom had so far acknowledged her presence, they went up the steps into the Great Hall to a round of applause, forming a family receiving line at the top of the stairs, to greet their guests as they went down into the ballroom. Stephen's two sisters and their husbands, whom she rarely met, nodded distantly to her, which she had expected but found annoying all the same. The evil stepsisters-in-law, no doubt about it.

On Stephen's other side, Eric winked at her; he was accompanied by a tall, slim, strikingly pretty young woman in a strapless blue Dior whom Rennie didn't know, but who had sleek dark Audrey Hepburn hair and the most magnificent neck and shoulders Rennie had ever seen.

But Stephen was the one whose attitude concerned her most; in fact, it terrified her. He stood at her elbow in the receiving line, smiling and shaking hands like a politician as the guests went by, and he never looked at her once.

Oh God, he's really angry with me, first time ever...and I don't blame him one little bit. It's the first time he ever asked me to do something for him, something that really mattered to him, and I screwed it up...well, I'll make it up to him. Just watch...

She did, too, setting out to captivate, beginning with a smile and warm words for everyone who came through the line, just about all of whom were stupefied when they met her. Having listened for many months to Marjorie's endless litany of complaints against her willful, irresponsible, duty-flouting daughter-in-law, they'd gleefully anticipated the worst. But here instead was this elegant young lady, wearing diamonds and couture with an ease that suggested she wore them for breakfast every day, chatting easily with all comers — the beautiful crown princess greeting high-ranking members of her prince's court. Reconciling the regal highness with the tie-dyed hippie harridan they'd been led to expect was almost more than they could manage, and Rennie, seeing their jaws mentally drop, redoubled her efforts to charm.

It's exactly like interviewing people...just get them to talk about themselves, smile at them as if you find them interesting and charming, and they automatically think you're wonderful. Manipulation 101!

Her husband was another matter. Once the receiving line was done and all the guests were properly greeted, the musicians struck up for dancing. General Lacing and Marjorie led off, to warm applause; then Eric with his date, and Stephen with Rennie, and their sisters with their spouses, all joined them on the floor.

"You look very handsome tonight," said Rennie, after they'd waltzed for a while in total silence to the society strings. "It's wonderful, all this."

"And you did your best to spoil it."

"I didn't do it on *purpose* —"

"I could understand it more easily if you had. But that you just forgot, and had to come running through the Great Hall like a —"

"Yes? Like a what?"

" — Mother's whole plan was to have the family come in together as a surprise. You pretty much ruined that. Now, if it's not too much to ask, go and dance with the General while I dance with my mother."

As the music ended, he bowed to her with a formality approved by the watchers, who all cooed, thinking how romantic a gesture between lovebird newlyweds, and Rennie made a little bobbing curtsey as she felt they seemed to expect, thinking how cold and like a slap in the face his bow had been. But she went as Stephen had commanded, to dance the next dance with her father-in-law, and after that with Eric, who looked even more dashing tonight than Stephen. At least *he* was pleased to see her, and they had a merry chat while twirling around the floor. Her duty tours with her brothers-in-law, husbands of the two Lacing sisters, were rather less successful, but they were decent dancers.

After that, duty well done, she led Eric over to introduce him to Burke Kinney and his wife, who were sitting on one of the velvet benches looking a little overawed, and set Eric to dance with Jeannie Kinney while she herself partnered Eric's tall beautiful boyfriend Trey and Trey's "date" Prax danced with Burke. Through the crowd she caught sight of

Clovis Franjo, dancing with one of Marjorie's Junior League gorgons-in-training; she was astonished to see him here at all, but supposed he'd been invited as one of the Lacing Foundation's trendy and environmentally correct charity recipients.

She glanced hastily around. No sign of Foy — apparently the first and second in command among the Warriors of Gaia weren't joined at the hip on fancy society occasions. She let out a breath she hadn't been aware she was holding: just imagine what Marjorie would have said if she'd known a killer — a real one, not just an innocent, wrongly accused one like Praxie — was treading the hallowed Lacing ballroom boards.

It had been hard work getting Prax approved for the ball. Rennie had been grudgingly allowed by Marjorie to invite a few friends: the Kinneys, Garrett Larkin and his wife, Berry Rosenbaum and Sharon Pollan with their cute boyfriends, several other people from the Clarion. But when Marjorie had seen Prax's name on Rennie's list — a possible murderess, even if now out on bail and sheltered at the moment under the Hall Place roof — there had been umbrage and shrieks and cold banshee fury. Though when Rennie flatly announced that if Prax wasn't there then neither would Rennie be, allowances were speedily made — still, Rennie had a feeling Marjorie had been sorely tempted to call her bluff. But at least she had a few people to talk to tonight, and it was so nice to have Prax there to celebrate being out of jail.

After she'd made the rounds of Lacing business partners, old family friends, colleagues and whatnot, she went over to Stephen, where he stood talking to some people she didn't know, and asked him to dance with her. She realized right away she'd made a social gaffe — it was the way his jaw tightened and the other people's eyebrows went up that was the tip-off — but she didn't care. She held out her gloved right hand to him, and after a few agonizing seconds he took it.

He said not a word to her for over a minute, just circled the floor with her, gaze fixed on the far side of the ballroom, and she tilted her head to try to catch his eye.

"Stephen. Please. Talk to me. Please don't be angry with me. I said I was sorry. I shouldn't have forgotten. But I got here on time. I've made nice with everybody in the room. What more can I do?"

He still wouldn't look at her. " 'Do'? You've made it very clear that you can't and won't. It's obviously no use asking you to think of your duty to this family. Yes, we're separated. But you might have remembered your duty to me. As I remember mine to you. And yes, I *am* angry. Still, I suppose I should count myself thankful you were only at work and not in bed with one of your hippie studs. Or more than one — maybe you've moved on to groupgropes by now."

Rennie flinched as if he'd struck her in the face; in fact, she would have preferred it if he had. That was the first time he'd used her newly expanded sex life against her — the subtext reason that he was so angry with her tonight, not merely that she'd turned up so late for the ball. And she couldn't, didn't, blame him. He was human, and she'd hurt him, and now he wanted to hurt her back.

When the dance was over, she dropped Stephen's hand as if it had been a live grenade, and shot away up the steps to the Great Hall, which was full of people taking a breather from the ballroom, admiring the famous coffer-vaulted, gold-leafed ceiling or the equally famous world-class art on the silk-covered walls. On the verge of tears, knowing she couldn't run upstairs or flee home to her apartment, but had to stay and tough it out, Rennie slipped through a pair of pocket doors into a small reception room, and slid the doors closed behind her. She needed a tiny respite from being resolutely on for the past few hours, and from Stephen, and there was still supper to get through, and speeches, and presentations to the General from the family and the firm...

There was a fireplace with a blaze going, and a little alcove to one side that held a loveseat and gave a bit of privacy. She flung herself down on the seat, tears already beginning to spill as she clumsily opened the silver *pochette* looped to her gloved left wrist—surely Lucy had put a couple of tissues in, maybe even an aspirin, or could she risk running upstairs for one, she wouldn't dream of sending a servant…

A voice rose from the depths of a leather wing chair by the fire; the chair's back and sides were so high and broad she hadn't noticed anyone sitting in it, and she jumped violently, startled, and glanced back at the door for help. Foy? Lying in wait for her? She knew it was ridiculous, but there it was.

"Who's there? That you, Marjorie?"

"No," she managed, heart racing. "No, it's just me. It's Rennie."

General Lacing's white-maned head, still streaked with black, craned around the side of the chair. "Ah, Rennie. Yes. Come round, girl. Sit. Talk to me."

In the year or so of Rennie's existence as his only daughter-in-law, the times that General Robert Travis Lockwood Lacing (West Point, war hero, chestful of medals, captain of industry) had found anything significant to say to her privately could be counted on her fingers and toes, with a few little piggies left over. It was as if she'd been a congenial though inconsequential boarder in his house, a stray kitten that Stephen had brought home. He'd always been pleasant at the dinner table, which was the only place she'd ever seen him for prolonged periods of time, or on big family occasions when everyone had to turn out. When she'd encountered him by chance in one of Hall Place's many rooms, they'd exchanged cordial greetings, as if they were strangers passing in some posh hotel, but that was about it.

And strangers had been pretty much what they'd been. If her relationship with her mother-in-law had been stormy and fraught, her relationship with her father-in-law had been nonexistent, and he'd never given her the feeling he wanted that to change; after a while she'd stopped trying. Now as he sat in the chair by the fireplace, with his silvered hair and CEO golfing tan, in his severely formal attire, he looked every bit the master of the hall. Which he was. Of that hall and many, many others worldwide.

"Couldn't stand it in there another minute, could you," he said frankly. "Neither could I. Keep me company for a while. I know we've never had anything much to say to one another, but maybe we can do something about that." He peered at her more closely, seeing the tears. "Stephen's said some harsh things to you. And now you're upset. Don't worry: he didn't mean that it should matter between you. He's hurt and angry, and he's lashing out at you."

"With good reason. I'm the one who hurt him."

"You didn't *mean* to hurt him, did you? No, of course you didn't. You're a pretty little thing," he said then, and Rennie stilled her annoyance, but not before he saw it, and he chuckled. "Don't like hearing that, do you. Rather hear how smart you are. Well, I don't blame you, I like hearing that myself. But you *are* pretty, my dear, and there it is. I know all about you, though you think I don't. Know you're smart. Know you're talented. Know you've got guts. Stood up to Marjorie, didn't you. I still haven't heard the end of it. That took nerve. And I'm proud of what you're doing."

"Proud!"

"Oh yes. I know I never said it before, should have, but I'm saying it now. You don't look much like her, but you certainly remind me of her. Always did."

He nodded to the portrait over the mantelpiece: a milk-skinned, dark-eyed beauty of a hundred years ago, her fox-red hair piled artfully atop her head. A small diamond tiara held the tresses in place, and more diamonds dripped down her impressive décolletage and the front of her green gown. For all that, though, Rennie saw that the woman had about her a no-nonsense, take-no-prisoners, almost eye-rolling air of impatience which the artist had brilliantly captured in paint.

General Lacing smiled as he saw Rennie's sudden interest. "That's the foundress of this family. Charlotte Vidler Lacing. You're wearing her tiara tonight, though I don't suppose anyone told you? No, 'course not—Marjorie's embarrassed by her. Though I think Charlotte would be a hell of a lot more embarrassed by Marjorie."

Rennie touched the delicate diamond scrollwork atop her head and stared at the identical one in the painting. *She looks majorly pissed off...I can so identify...*

"Stephen told me about her. He said the family calls her Princess Charlie."

"That's right. She was no pampered princess, though, but a hard-working, down-to-earth sort of girl, and a hugely successful madam. I promise you, it's quite true! Though Marjorie pretends it isn't. Well, Charlotte Louise Vidler was a very young, very pretty and very smart girl from Buffalo who came west with the Gold Rush. When she couldn't make ends meet as a teacher, she went to work in a whorehouse, to help out her family back east. Pretty soon, young as she was— barely out of her teens—she was running the place, and she prospered; in fact, she became a very wealthy young woman in a very short time. Her girls were top of the line—clean, clever, amusing, handsome—and she took extremely good care of them, not like some, even though she wasn't much older than they were. Younger than a lot of them, in fact."

"She was beautiful," said Rennie quietly. "Wasn't her husband a Stephen too?"

"The first Stephen Lacing, a poor but brilliant lawyer, native San Franciscan. They met in a professional context— his, not hers—love at first sight, and they promptly scandalously married. Then they used Charlie's brothel money to finance the law firm Stephen founded. Then the law firm and the brothel financed the trading companies, and the trading companies financed the gold mines, and the gold mines financed the clipper ship fleet and the vineyards and on and on. Pretty soon she had no need to be brothel-keeping, but she kept at it, just to vex her so-called betters. Charlotte's Harlots, they called her establishment, finest in San Francisco. Place looked like some society mansion, not a bordello at all. Tasteful and discreet, right on Nob Hill, annoying everybody who lived there, except the wealthy and powerful and oversexed gentlemen who were her devoted clients, and who supported Charlie all the way. They even helped her out with City Hall, when the mayor threatened to close her down. Her loyal customers threatened right back that they'd expose the mayor as one of her regulars, and that was the end of that."

Rennie laughed. "I would have liked her. A lot."

"By all accounts she was very likable—intelligent, witty, discreet, didn't suffer fools." He cast her a wicked sideways smile. "Sound like anyone we know? 'Cept of course you're no strumpet... Some people said Charlie was the priciest whore in her own stable, but that wasn't true. She never sold herself again after her marriage—though I have no doubt she'd have done so in a heartbeat if she'd thought it made good business sense or helped her husband. She was nothing if not practical, and she never stood on pride. And she and her Stephen—who adored her—came to be the pinnacle of San Francisco society. They did things their way. Her way. And she made other people do things her way too. She designed this house herself, you know. She never went back to that life once she finally sold the brothel—and for a ton of money, too, single-handedly underwriting our entry into merchant banking, though the place was later lost in the quake and fire—but she never forgot it. She never denied it, either. And she always carried herself like a lady even though she didn't always behave like one."

"She had her own priorities," said Rennie, still staring at the portrait. *It would have been so cool to have known her...plenty cool enough to be sort of related...*

The General gave her a shrewd glance. "She did, and so do you. Remember that: you can get away with just about anything if you do it with enough conviction. People are lazy and easily swayed: most of them hate thinking for themselves, and they'll happily take their cue from you if you give it to them hard enough and strong enough and often enough. Best advice I can give you. So you working for the newspaper, writing your stories—far as I'm concerned, that's fine, child. No matter what Marjorie says. Murder and all. No matter. It'll do the Lacing name good, and it'll do Charlotte Vidler proud. And no matter what happens between you and Stephen, or what Marjorie has to say about it, I tell you now, you will always be a member of this family."

"I wish you'd said all this sooner, General," said Rennie after a long, oddly respectful moment.

"Wouldn't have kept you here," he said quietly. "Stephen married someone who wanted to be her own woman before she wanted to be his woman. He wanted you for himself; you wanted yourself, then him. Nothing wrong with that: neither one of you was wrong to want what you wanted. That's what he fell in love with you for. But that was also the thing that was going to mean he couldn't hold you."

Seeing her astonishment: "You think this is radical thinking for someone of my age and background, and coming from a man, which is worse, but it's nothing so very new, really. What's new is that so many young folks like you think you invented it. But Princess Charlie could tell you better."

"Seems like she taught this family a lot. Even if not a whole lot of you have learned it."

He let out a great shout of laughter. "Yes, I suppose not all of us have. Now, what do you say we go back in and make them play a waltz and we'll show them how it's really done?"

Rennie put her hand on his proffered arm and smiled up at him. "What say we do."

Chapter Nineteen

AFTER HER RATHER SURPRISING CHAT with her equally surprising father-in-law and subsequent waltz by royal command, Rennie flung herself onto the dancefloor with determined abandon. She even allowed herself to be dragged around the ballroom by a clench-jawed Marjorie and handed off to dance with yet more Lacing associates and acquaintances and friends, how the hell many people did this family *know*, though she had no faintest recollection afterward as to what she had talked to them about. She had time for moments of her own: she danced again with Eric, and with King Bryant, and Burke Kinney, and Garrett Larkin, who seemed to be old friends with half the room, and even had a spin around the floor with Clovis Franjo.

Likewise with cousin Marcus, who much to her surprise held her considerably more closely than she was entirely at ease with, though she said nothing to him and Stephen appeared not to notice. She even managed a full-blown Viennese waltz with Prax—enchanting in vintage rose tulle, and who had not lacked for partners—just to freak out all the stuffed shirts and give Marjorie something to complain about; ever since the one blot of her late arrival, Rennie's performance had been faultless.

"Festive," said Prax, lifting her hand off Rennie's waist to wave at their lavish surroundings as they gracefully circled the floor. "I can see why you hated living like this."

"No, you can't. Nobody can see that. It's invisible."

"Oh? So the beautiful princess couldn't escape the Soul-Sucking Fortress of Evil after all?"

Rennie laughed. "Alas, no! The sad, handsome prince begged her to return to the castle of the wicked Queen Motherdear to help him get through the Fiesta of Apocalyptic Darkness, and she wanted to help him, of course she did, and also to celebrate with her dearest bestest friend, a princess herself, who had just been freed from the Dungeon of the Evil Blue Trollpigs. But she was late; the magic clock had run down and she had to put her glass slippers on in a hurry."

"Fur."

"What?"

"Her slippers. They were really fur. In French, *vair*, which sounds like *verre*, glass. Crossed in translation; you can see how the confusion started. And of course fur slippers being a blatant euphemism for something else tight-fitting, warm, furry and female-related. Oh, those Grimm boys! But, either way, it was a blatant symbol of woman-as-chattel's fettered sexuality and man-as-dominator's chauvinistic possessiveness, which I won't get into here and now."

"Well, please don't, 'cause my head aches enough already. Where do you *get* this stuff?"

"Oh, I pick it up here and there. Speaking of heads, that's a mighty pretty little comb thingy you've got going on up there."

Rennie touched the tiara. "Not mine. The evil Queen made me wear it. I keep expecting it to turn me to stone, or put me to sleep in a glass casket for a hundred years."

"Nice sparkly thing round your neck, too."

"Sears my flesh with untold burning pain. I might as well be wearing a slave collar with Stephen's name engraved on it. Oh, wait, I am... But guess who owned the tiara first." Briefly she recounted the story of Charlotte and her harlots. "So it used to belong to a Lacing whore. How appropriate that another Lacing whore is wearing it tonight. Which I'm sure is Queen Motherdear's not-so-subtle message, for all the nice little talk I had just now with King General Robert. Stephen pretty much said the same thing, when we were dancing a while ago. He knows all about me and Chet and Brian and Bram, thanks to Marjorie's detective."

"Ah, the handsome prince not acting quite so princely. He's just pissed off for the moment. His manly vanity is wounded; he's not stud enough for you, or so he thinks. And maybe he isn't. But that's not your fault. He didn't really mean it. He'll get over it. Even if he did mean it, he'll still get over it. It's always about cocks with guys."

"That's because they're the ones who have them. But I'd much rather talk about you, and your wondrous escape from real prison. I'm so happy you're here."

Prax looked uncomfortable. "What's there to say? I'm just so very, very glad to be out. It's not a very nice place, jail. And I will be grateful to Stephen until the end of time for posting that exorbitant bail, and for giving me shelter here. It's quite a place, this. I could really get used to it. No, just kidding."

"He was happy to help, I promise. I didn't get a chance to talk about it to Marcus or even King or Berry—I'll ask them later, and, I know, gift horses and all, but, well, why *are* you sprung?"

"Haven't the foggiest. Some new evidence pointing somewhere else, is all I know, and on the strength of that they reviewed the remand. Stephen's original offer still stood, and so here I am. Still under arrest, mind, but at least out of the slammer."

"And Dill. Mustn't forget Dill. He was there too."

"No. No, we really mustn't forget Dill."

Rennie frowned at something she thought she heard in Prax's voice. "Are we okay with him? Dill, I mean."

"Jury's still out — what *is* it with these legal metaphors, that's what being in the clink for a few weeks does to you. Well, are we okay with him, I don't know. He seems — weird."

"In what way weird?

"Not sure. Just — weird. Not like old Jas, that's for sure. But I don't want to talk about it."

"Then we won't."

They concentrated on their dancing for a while; they'd switched off, and Rennie was now leading, to the amusement of many guests and the pinch-lipped disapproval of many more.

"You realize, of course, that Eric's date is a lesbian," said Prax, blowing kisses to them both as the elder Lacing son and his stunning brunette waltzed by.

"Petra. Yeah, I know. We had a little talk awhile back, Eric and I, about how he might find himself a nice blue-blooded gay girl and get married and do the turkey baster thing and have lovely kids with her. She'd have her sweetie — as he'd have his — and she'd be my cool gay sister-in-law, and our mutual parents-in-law the Queen of Doom and the King of Statusquovia would be none the wiser. Maybe Petra's the candidate of choice."

"Is Eric really thinking that?" asked Prax with interest. "I'm impressed. Civilized *and* creative. I bet they'll make it to their fifty-year golden wedding anniversary."

"You're probably right. Whereas Stephen and I didn't make it to our fifty-week toilet-paper one."

Prax grinned, then gestured across the ballroom. "Never mind... Oh, look who it is — Inspector Javert!"

"Yeah — unfortunately, Marcus is family, can't keep

him away. But we don't have to dance with him if we don't want to, Jeanne Valjean."

"Oh, I don't know. He may be all hot to put me on death row for double murder, but he's really awfully cute. Maybe I'll go ask him to dance, just to give *him* a big old headache."

"Sounds like a plan. Do you reverse?"

"Of *course.* You think I learned nothing in my posh Swiss finishing school? Oh, oh, that lunatic tree-creeper Clovis Franjo is dancing with your mother-in-law. My eyes, my eyes! Some things just aren't meant for humans to see... By the way, Idaho called me today. He said he hated being the new prime suspect."

Rennie snorted. "He's way behind the curve. He hasn't been the favorite since, oh, days ago. There's Neil Marten, who hasn't been ruled out yet, for various reasons, mostly on account of how nobody saw him during the time frame in question and he wasn't hanging around tuning his bass. And Dill Miller. And of course there's still you. Even if you are free on bail." Prax smiled evilly and deliberately stepped on Rennie's toes. "But we have a new front-runner, actually."

"Who's that, then?"

"Foy Ballard. Clovis's little helper. Big scary Hell's Angels dude, the size and tonnage of a T. rex, dressed in this stupid leather jacket with redwood trees and swords and abstruse symbols all over it, interviewed me before he let me interview Clovis."

"Oh my God! *That's* who that was!" said Prax, staring at Rennie as the dance ended and they walked over to one of the buffet tables by the wall for some Champagne and little rich cakes.

"It was? Who was? Where was it?"

"At the Fillmore, when Tam was murdered. I didn't know it was him, of course. This Foy. I just thought he was one of the Fillmore crew. I'd never played there before, I didn't know who was crew and who was just hanging out. But he was there. I saw him. I saw him there twice. And I remember because of his jacket, this jacket you just now speak of. He'd been wearing it the first time I saw him at the Fillmore that day and the second time I saw him he was not."

Rennie had hardly breathed. "Are you sure? I mean about the jacket?"

Prax, sitting on the velvet bench against the wall, banked in tulle and looking adorable, nodded vigorously, fanning herself with an ostrich-feather Victorian fan that she'd found in a Haight Street thrift shop and thought would be just the thing.

"You bet. I noticed it in the first place because it had all these incredible embroideries and appliqués on. Some Hell's Angels stuff, and that stupid Warriors of Gaia logo. I was thinking of having someone make stage outfits for the new band, and I liked the look. I'd ask *you* to make them, but you're far too busy and important these days to make clothes anymore. But do you think you could possibly find like fourteen minutes to run me up one of those snakeskin—"

"*Anyway?*"

"Oh. Jacket. Wasn't wearing it. I noticed because I particularly looked around for him backstage. I wanted to ask him who'd tarted it up."

"He'd have flattened you if you'd put it like that. He told me he did all the design work himself, with his own humongous paws."

"Well, well, these are indeed hidden fires. So that's Foy Ballard. He was with some very pretty dark-haired chick— Ro? The one you told me about? Yes, pretty, but she had that sharp-edged scag freak look going on and a bruise on the side of her face. Which would be about right? They just passed me and nodded, you know how you do, and went out the side door into the alley. I didn't see them again." She looked contrite. "I didn't know who they were, truly. Not by name. I would have mentioned them if I had. I just told the police and King that a bunch of people had been hanging around that afternoon, the way people always do. I didn't know."

"It's okay, Praxie, it's fine. But Idaho?"

"What about him? He wouldn't hurt anyone and he is so protective of anyone he — cares about."

Oh, terrific, now *you tell me you're balling him...* Rennie's voice sounded as if it were walking barefoot on thumbtacks. Pointy side up. "Just exactly how protective are we talking about here? Would he want to hurt somebody, say, who had hurt you?"

A little of the party brightness had dimmed out of Prax's face. "He'd probably want to. But so would you. You've even said so. So would any friend. But he wouldn't actually *do* it."

"No, I don't think he would." Still, Idaho was a huge, strong guy; he could have pancaked Tommy Linetti into the floor with one mighty fist. Or booted him into a road case with a mere flex of his treelike ankle. Come to think of it, he was almost as big and huge and strong as— "What about Idaho and Ballard? Do they know each other?"

Prax glanced cautiously at her friend. "Where are you going with this?"

"Not sure. Do they?"

"I wouldn't be surprised. You said this Ro told you Foy hangs out at the ballrooms plying musicians with dope. And as *I* said, I'd never been backstage at the Fillmore before, so I'd never seen him."

"But Idaho had."

"I'd guess so, probably. If we don't have a gig, he often goes to fill in on crew at the Fillmore or the Avalon or the Matrix. He's probably met him, or at least seen him around. Does all this mean anything to you?"

Rennie's eyes widened and her shoulders came up in a helpless shrug. "Sweetness, I haven't the faintest idea. But there's the fair Berry over there, and the noble King, so maybe I'll just go and mention it to them and see if it sets off any bells."

No bells, but King Bryant had something to tell her as well. Idaho's alibi had in fact gone rather spectacularly bust when the groupie he'd been relying on to back up his story was now denying she'd even seen him that day, much less given him a head job backstage.

At the end of his account, Rennie shook her head. "Prax won't be happy to hear that. We were just talking about Idaho. She's convinced he has nothing to do with Tam. Or the other murders, though I guess nobody is mentioning him in connection with those."

"Well, not just yet," said King. "Do you think maybe Idaho could have pressured the groupie or paid her off in the first place to lie for him with an alibi, and then she got scared and decided to tell the truth? Or could someone else have paid her off more, or threatened better, to lie about it now? Someone famous, maybe, a little or a lot, who would flatter her into helping, as well as buy her story?"

"You mean Prax... I wondered that too, but if you recall, she's been in jail until quite recently. But yes, I asked her, and of course she said no and I believe her. And she thinks Idaho would never have done that. And I don't know who else would have."

Rennie carefully concealed the fact that Prax and Idaho had done a few other things, apparently. *Need to know basis, and he doesn't need to—yes, I know he's her lawyer, but Prax hasn't told him and who am I to betray a friend's sexual confidences?*

"I'm not suggesting anyone, dear. Just thinking aloud."

"But to give that little groupie money? Who would do that except the killer? And then she'd know who it was. And if she knew who it was, he'd have to kill *her*, and he didn't.

And if he *did* kill her, he wouldn't have had to pay her off. If he did pay her off. That makes no sense."

"No, it doesn't. Is there something you want to tell me, Rennie?"

She looked up at King. The blue eyes were measuring, and kind of scary; this was the look his hostile witnesses saw, the look he wore in battle. They faced it on the stand all the time. He knew she was keeping something from him, but he wasn't going to drag it out of her.

"No," she said at last, looking straight up into his eyes, and trying not to think of Ro Savarkin, or the guy she'd said she heard getting head in the closet next to hers, that fateful Fillmore night—almost certainly Idaho and his faithless groupie. "No, there really isn't anything I want to tell you."

Which was, technically, the truth, if not the whole truth. Either way, nothing but.

On the stroke of eleven came a sit-down supper in the Great Hall, now a candlelit sea of elegant pink-clothed round tables holding four or six or eight hungry guests. Rennie was under orders to sit at the grand head table with Stephen and the rest of the family; she couldn't escape it, and didn't try to, and went in to dinner on her husband's arm.

The meal was both elegant and excellent—abalone and lobster pan roast, chicken paupiettes, rack of lamb, tournedos Rossini, chocolate and blood-orange sorbet, superb wines from the Lacing vineyards—and the ceremonial presentations to the General by his family (Eric did the honors) and his firm (the heads of LacingCo Hong Kong, London and New York stepped up) went well. After that, still more dancing, and at four in the morning a light supper-breakfast of truffled scrambled eggs and Spanish *serrano* ham for the surprisingly large number of guests still remaining.

At last nearly everyone had gone home—Prax, exhausted but loyally reluctant to abandon Rennie to her in-laws' not-so-tender mercies, went up to her room only when Rennie banished her from the ballroom like Tinker Bell from Neverland. At five, when only a die-hard handful of the elder Lacings' intimate friends remained—including Marie-Laure Goring Markham, who all night long had icily turned her back whenever Rennie glanced in her direction, and her silver-haired hubby too—by the looks Motherdear was shooting her way Rennie judged it would be both safe and desirable to totter off upstairs herself, and so she did.

Finding the half-asleep Lucy waiting for her in Stephen's bedroom on Marjorie's orders, to undress her and attend her to bed, an appalled Rennie sent the maid off to her own bed at once, then began to undress herself. She stripped off her gown and underwear, removed the tiara and earrings, and shook out her hair, planning to put on a robe and head down the hall to the Chinese suite in the east wing that she'd been occupying during Prax's stay.

So tired, she was soooo tired, and she'd had far too many glasses of Champagne—too much of a hassle to drive home at this hour, she'd leave after lunch and take Prax back to Sausalito. Then the door opened and Stephen came in, tie undone and hair a bit mussed and more than a bit drunk.

And here I am half zonked myself and entirely starkers. Well, it's not as if he's never seen me nekkid before. Maybe he's not as mad at me as he was...we've been getting on so well this week while Prax was here. At least we were until tonight...

"What a nice party it turned out to be," she said, smiling. "Your father seemed really happy. We had a very good talk, he and I, before dinner. I wish we could have talked like that sooner. Still, better late than never."

Stephen was looking at her in a way that made her feel distinctly uneasy, and she realized that time and alcohol had done nothing for his anger. Suddenly uncomfortable standing there in front of him completely nude except for the diamond necklace and her long, loose hair, she reached for the robe, which Lucy had laid out on the bed.

But before she could catch the robe up to cover herself, Stephen ripped it away and shoved her violently backward onto the bed, bearing her down and pinning her hands above her head and pushing her legs apart.

"Stephen—"

But he was past talking.

As lovemaking went, it was lightyears out of their ordinary, and while she was still capable of coherent thought Rennie did catch herself thinking My goodness where has *this* been hiding. Forceful though their union was, though, it was not by anyone's definition even remotely forcible: Rennie was finding her husband's unprecedented aggressiveness a rather delightful change from his usual gentle style, and they were both enjoying it considerably more than one of them felt entirely comfortable with. Not that Stephen had been a timid wimp in the sack, but he'd always been a bit too—*requesting*, too much Lancelot of the Lake and nowhere near enough Attila the Hun. Sometimes a girl just wants to be ravished.

After, Rennie was content and exhausted, not to mention deeply thrilled, and Stephen, just as content, was apparently also deeply repentant.

"I'm sorry," he began, though he didn't sound sorry at all. "I didn't mean to do that, I just—"

"Sure you did," said Rennie, smiling. "At least I hope you did. And I also hope you're *not* sorry. Because it was fine. More than fine. Believe me. Whole new worlds of fineness."

"No. It's not right. I only did it because—"

"Because you were pissed off with me for forgetting the party."

"That," he conceded. "But no. Because I knew you've been sleeping with other men and I was jealous and hurt. I didn't know what you got from them that you didn't get from me. I just wanted to make you want to sleep with me again; but I didn't care if you wanted to or not, I wanted to fuck you anyway. Not 'make love to you', 'fuck you'."

Well, that's *new...* "And now you're feeling all guilty and ashamed and weirded out, you think you just raped me."

"Didn't I?"

"No. No, I swear, you absolutely didn't." She kissed his shoulder and threw him a grin. "You can't rape the willing—and don't tell anybody, but most girls do rather enjoy being decisively taken by handsome hunks. That was a rape fantasy, not a rape—James Bond not accepting 'No' for an answer. Besides, I might not want to be married to you anymore but I've never stopped wanting to sleep with you. And as surely you've noticed, we haven't. Stopped sleeping together. This doesn't change anything; it just makes it more, well, interesting."

They talked for a while, easily now, about the party: the guests, the food, the dancing, how lovely everyone had looked, how happy Prax was, Rennie's nice conversation with the General. Unsurprisingly, the air had cleared considerably between them, and when Stephen at last asked her if he could escort her to the Chinese room, or drive her home, Rennie just kicked the disarranged coverlet off the bed, writhed around a little and smiled at him.

"It's too late to go all the way to Buena Vista—too far down the hall to my room—I've always liked this mattress—"

After they'd made love again—both of them shattering all previous personal-best records, thanks to Stephen's newly discovered inner Attila and his wife's unexpected delight in Hunnishness—Rennie found herself pouring all her recent discoveries and suspicions into his ear. When she finished, she turned to look at him.

"So do you think I should tell Marcus? About Foy and Ro and the whole dealer trip, and about Foy using Clovis and the Warriors of Gaia as cover for his drug ring. I know it's still just a theory, but it makes sense to me."

"I'm not sure." Stephen was inwardly exulting. She

was actually asking his advice. He was scoring all over the place tonight. "It could certainly help Prax if it's true, but maybe you should find out a little more before you bring it to the police. They might already know about it, anyway, if this Ro girl jumped bail as she said."

"If they know, then why wouldn't they just go over to Piedmont and bust her ass right back?'

"Maybe they're hoping she can lead them to something bigger. She did with you, or so you believe." He drew her up to lie across his chest, and began untangling her hair from the necklace she was still wearing, admiring how the diamonds sparked rainbow flashes against her bare skin, getting turned on again. "I'm not a court officer kind of lawyer, you know; I'm really not up on this. What did King say?"

"Didn't exactly tell him yet," she admitted reluctantly.

"I see. But if Foy Ballard is running this big drug show under cover of the Warriors of Gaia, maybe he's also using the organization to launder the drug money. Filter it through the books. Didn't you tell me back when you did the interview that this Ballard guy really grilled you up front, that Clovis Franjo gives very few interviews and none that aren't controlled by Foy, and no one really knows where the Warriors' money comes from, and they wouldn't let you look at their financial records?"

" 'Zackly! Some of the money comes from the Lacing family coffers, I'm sorry to say."

Stephen had finally gotten the necklace off, and now he tossed it onto the Regency armchair that stood beside the bed.

"Well, hopefully our bucks have saved a few redwoods. But that kind of contribution gets boasted about for publicity purposes, or at least for Clovis's. It wouldn't fill me with surprise to learn that the real money river has much nastier, much more secret springs. And I don't think the trees get a whole lot of water from it. If any."

"Where do you think the drug money goes?'

"Numbered Swiss or offshore bank accounts would be my first and, yes, pretty much only guess. Foy probably plows a fair chunk back into security and upgrading his labs, and paying big salaries to keep his help loyal. From what you tell me, he's not living large. Living small makes you less of a target, for sure. But I bet you anything he's got a walled-compound hideaway in some warm tropical place where the federal writ does not run and secret banking prevails. And a private army of goons to keep it all safe and beat the crap out of anyone who threatens it. Or seems to."

Rennie looked down at her own bare self, seeing the purple and yellow bruises on Ro Savarkin's pathetically thin arms and flanks, the faint blue ones already showing up on her own breasts and wrists, the difference between.

"Evil creature."

"I agree. But it's not up to you to stop him, and if you even *think* of trying, I'll lock you in the wine cellar. I mean it, Rennie. This isn't some damn TV show." Stephen pulled the bedclothes over them. "So, lawdog that I am, here's a summation. Foy Ballard processes bad nasty drugs in the nice pretty redwood forests, and uses Clovis Franjo and the Warriors of Gaia as unwitting cover. Foy was employing Jasper Goring as a drug distributor and some of Jasper's star clients as subcontractors. And he killed Tam, Fortinbras and Jasper because he couldn't trust them, or to make an example of them, and he set Prax up to take the fall."

"This is what Ro tells me."

"But it's still only what she *tells* you. There's still no hard proof. It still doesn't hold up."

"It does too hold up! She said he was there at the Fillmore. She said he tried to hide a bloody jacket. She said—"

"Sweetheart, she's also a junkie, you said so yourself. We don't know how much we can trust her word. She might even be telling you all this to cover her own ass. *She* could be the one running the show, not Foy. And even though she's probably not, maybe she can place him at the backstage Fillmore scene but she still can't place him at the murder scene. And she certainly can't place him at your apartment. She said he was out that night. He could have been anywhere from San Rafael to San Jose. Doing anything or nothing."

"I saw her. I saw what he did to her."

"What she said he did to her. We can't even be sure of that."

Rennie looked at him, his dark tousled head on the pillow next to hers. *I remember the first time we ever made love in this room, the first night I spent under this roof. But this is the last time we'll ever make love here, and I think we both know that now, if we didn't before...*

"You said 'we'."

"So? I've been in this from day one, I think you know my policy by now. No way I'm going to let you finish this alone. Besides," he added, and now he was laughing, "I'm not about to lose the bail money I put up for Prax. I've got a stake in this." *And in us...* But that he didn't say.

She heard it all the same. "And after that?"

"After that—well, after that we'll see."

"God, I'd hate to be a lawyer."

He turned to move on top of her again. "Then what a damn good thing for everybody that you're not."

Chapter Twenty

WHEN RENNIE WENT DOWN to the Hall of Justice the next morning to tell Marcus what she'd learned—everything from Foy Ballard and his damn jacket and the frighteners he put on everybody to Ro Savarkin and her drug habit—she found him surprisingly less enthusiastic than she'd thought he'd be. Okay, maybe she'd amped up her expectations a tad unrealistically: this little fantasy in her head where he would be all 'My God, Holmes, you've done it!', and she would be all 'Don't mention it, my good Lestrade!'. The last thing she'd expected was the matter-of-fact, almost dismissive way in which he received her account, and finally, annoyed, she called him on it.

But Marcus just sighed. "All I can say—all I can *say*—is that there are things going on right now that I'm not at liberty to discuss with you, either as my cousin by marriage who is personally and unfortunately involved in this whole mess or as a journalist who would in less than a nanosecond write some things she absolutely shouldn't if I give her two syllables of encouragement."

"You *know* I'm not *allowed* to write about—"

He lifted a hand, and she subsided. "This is important information, make no mistake. And you were quite right to come and tell me about it. I'm glad you did. It will help a lot. But that's all I can give you in return. I can't say anything."

"Can you at least tell me if it tallies with what you've been working on? So I know I have not labored in vain?"

He sighed again, more exasperatedly this time. "Haven't you heard anything I've said? You've been listening to me, but have you been *hearing* me?"

Rennie stared at him, and then the light broke. "Oh. Oh! It's not just you now, is it. It's gotten bigger than that. Much, *much* bigger than that. Feds, right? The drug boys? ATF? Oooh, don't tell me, meaning of course absolutely please *do* tell me, Secret Service? I know, I know, you can't say, but maybe could you just thump your hoof or something? Once for yes, twice for no."

In spite of himself, Marcus laughed. "No, I really couldn't." He turned serious again at once. "Rennie, I can't stress this enough. Don't meddle. Don't poke around. Don't pry. You have no idea what you're already into, don't make it even worse. It's dangerous and it's complicated and it's nastier than you can possibly imagine. And I promise you—I warn you—it's not what you think it is. I can say no more. Now let me go do my job."

He came around the desk to escort her out, his arm circling her waist, his hand resting lightly on her hip. Rennie was sharply reminded of their dance at the Hell House ball, when he had held her a whole lot closer than had seemed proper for a cousinly embrace, and certain things had been a lot more—evident than they should have been. Was that a nightstick in his tux pocket or had he just been glad to see her? Could it be that Marcus had the hots for her? Or was it her nasty suspicious conceited mind at work?

What an ungodly complication *that* would be, though

she knew Marcus would never act on it—as far as he knew, she was still his cousin Stephen's loving faithful wife, and as such strictly off-limits. Outside the odd party feel-up, anyway. She mentally shook herself. No, no, she was a total ego monster to think no man could resist her charms. Marcus was merely being professionally or familially chivalrous. Or he'd just been non-specifically horny or even drunk the night of the party. Maybe a guest had turned him on—maybe even Prax had turned him on—and she'd been feeling the residual effect. No more.

Still, most women have a pretty good radar for that sort of thing, a kind of horndog early warning system that lets them know if a man is interested even before the man knows it himself, and right now Rennie's was pinging like mad. Which was okay—as long as that was the only thing that was pinging.

She went straight from her police tryst to a previously arranged conference in Jasper Goring's old offices. Prax and the relevant members of the Karma Mirror and the Deadly Lampshade were meeting with Randyll Miller to hammer out contractual details before the new-band union was signed and sealed, and Prax had asked her to attend and witness.

Goriller Unlimited—as had been explained, G-O-R-I-n-g plus M-i-L-L-E-R—which now of course was just Dill Miller, a bit more limited, was soon to undergo a name change befitting its new status, thank God, Goriller being just too twee for words. It had its San Francisco offices on the parlor floor of one of the famous painted ladies of Alamo Square, and as Rennie entered the front reception room for the first time since Jasper's murder, she looked around approvingly, as she always did whenever she'd come here.

That Jasper. Bent as he'd obviously been, he'd sure known the value of set dressing. The building itself, of course, was gorgeous, and the spacious white-painted rooms—six of them, good-sized, with a galley kitchen and a small bathroom, in a layout not unlike that of Rennie's own apartment — reeked of quiet good taste. Jasper had lived above the store, as it were, and the second floor of the house had contained his personal living space; it was closed up now and about to be rented out, and one of the rear rooms on the parlor level had been converted into a temporary crash pad for Dill.

Some very nice furniture, which no doubt Marie-Laure the ex-wife had had a hand in choosing — Frenchwomen were clever with furniture, they saw it as clothes for the house. A few frighteningly good, and genuine, pictures: one huge oil of the stormy Cornwall coast in an ornate gilt frame, some small, pretty watercolors framed less lavishly. But nothing at all to indicate that this had been the office of a very successful, maybe had been about to be incredibly successful, rock and roll manager. It could have been anyone's office, from a doctor's to a stock analyst's.

A microskirted redhead whom Rennie had never seen there before stepped suddenly out of the first office room, and seeing Rennie standing in front of the desk, jumped violently, sending the stack of papers she was carrying all over the floor.

Now this *looks more like rocknroll...* "I'm so sorry, I didn't mean to startle you —"

"Gosh, you surely did...startle me, I mean, not mean to. Oh, you must be Rennie Stride, I read your stuff all the time." She smiled as Rennie knelt to help her gather up the sheaves. "You don't have to do that — well, thank you! I'm Zan, Zan Flowers, Mr. Miller's new secretary, he sent me up from L.A. a couple of weeks ago to replace Mrs. Humes, she was poor Mr. Goring's secretary who wanted to leave, so sad about Mr. Goring, I love it here, I already moved in with somebody I met on the way from the airport. Oh! You're to go straight back. They're expecting you in the conference room, and there's lunch — well, not lunch *really*, just tea and fruit and sandwiches, but fresh. That's right, just through there, I see you know your way. You've been here before?"

"Oh yes," said Rennie. "Yes, I've been here before."

Voices were floating down the hall from the big, windowed room in the middle of the flat, and Rennie paused in the doorway. This wasn't Jasper's private office—that was the smaller room Zan had come out of, presumably now dedicated to other purposes—but the former living room, used as a conference room, where he had industriously worked. Here rockbiz was pre-eminent: big boardroom table to spread things out on, comfortable chairs all around it, every inch of wall space covered with ballroom posters. The walls, in fact, looked very much as Rennie's had before Stephen, in his well-meaning post-murder renovation, had had all her own posters archivally framed, saying she'd thank him for it in thirty years' time, when they were original mint collectibles and a major, and costly, investment asset. Yeah, right, she wouldn't hold her breath.

Rennie found herself suddenly saddened. She hadn't liked Jasper very much and she hadn't trusted him at all, still less so the more she'd found out about him; but seeing this, being here, finally slammed home to her the fact that he was gone. Head up, she entered the room and smiled at everyone there, who greeted her cheerfully in return. Prax, of course, looking adorable in a black minidress printed all over with white peace signs. The Deadly Lampshade members who'd survived murder and artistic purge: Juha Vasso, looking pleased; Chet Galvin, sexy in a fringed leather jacket, face brightening as he saw Rennie come in; the new drummer, Thane or Zane or something, or perhaps Henry, she couldn't remember—Jack Paris had decided to split, and was already in another band. And the two former Karma Mirrors: the placid Dainis Hood and the inscrutable Bardo, real name for signing purposes Ira Jacobs, both of whom Prax had brought with her, like some kind of musical dowry, to the new marriage with the Lamps.

Over by the open windows, Berry Rosenbaum patted the table for Rennie to take the chair beside her, and she detoured round to do so. King Bryant, who had risen to his feet when she entered, hugged her briefly as she passed him and sat down again.

At the head of the table, facing King, was Randyll Miller, heir to all Jasper's business. His legitimate business. He too had risen politely at Rennie's entrance, and now he smiled warmly at her, stretching over to shake her hand.

"Rennie, how nice to see you again, I'm glad you could come. I didn't get a chance to mention it last time, but Jasper told me a lot of wonderful things about you."

She murmured some fitting civility, and, not daring to meet Prax's eyes — *yeah, we just* wonder *what Jasper told you!* — covertly studied him as he and King went back to thrashing out some debatable contractual detail. Very different from old Jas, Dill seemed, as she'd noticed before. In fact, they — meaning she — had done a little research based on the information King had had, and discovered that not only was Dill Miller's taste in clothes of an earlier day but his ethics apparently were too.

The straightest of straight-arrows, all the way, just as he'd claimed. If he'd been mixed up in Jasper's dope network, not a trace of it could be uncovered. Rennie had shared her findings with the rest of the band-in-formation, and learned that all of them found Dill reassuring, in an older-brother or younger-uncle sort of way. Jasper may have been dazzling, but as a band they wanted to reserve the dazzle for themselves; managers should be clean, sober, honest, paternal and hard-working. And absolute lethal death on record companies, of course — that went without saying.

The terms of the contract were speedily settled: everything to be shared equally, except that band members who wrote songs independently of the others should retain individual publishing rights. That was at King's insistence, chiefly to protect Prax and her creations, but since everybody contributed to the songwriting to some extent or other, everyone would get an occasional extra slice of the pie. Some details relating to touring and recording, though an actual record deal and tour had yet to materialize, some arrangements for the Karms and Lamps who were being jettisoned, and then it was done. Everyone signed, including Rennie and Zan Flowers as legally disinterested witnesses to the group signatures, and the new band, still unnamed, was a reality. Whereupon the meeting instantly became three or four friendly little conversational groupings over the modest refreshments Zan had touted.

Rennie found herself gravitating over to Dill Miller, who asked after her editor Burke, whom he knew of old. He seemed quite happy to talk to her, having, or so he swore, read every word she'd ever written about Prax, the Karma Mirror and the Deadly Lampshade, and much of the rest of her work, too. After he'd praised her critical chops a while, Rennie looked up artlessly and smiled with, she *so* hoped, just the right mix of sadness and commiseration, and gave it one last try.

"I understand you were actually up here doing business at the time of the murders. It must have been such a shock—I know Jasper was completely freaked out by Tam, and then, well, you know. So sad."

If she had thought to rattle him, it didn't happen. Miller just nodded with a real and sudden quietness, and Rennie felt sharply ashamed of her ploy—a final shot at proving the dodginess of Dill.

"It was. It is. As I mentioned at your lovely dinner party, Jasper and I went back thirty-five years—long before you were born. We'd been partners for more than twelve." He turned it back on her, gently, sympathetically. "I can't imagine how awful it must have been for *you*, though, discovering the bodies in your own apartment and having your best friend arrested."

Rennie allowed as to how it hadn't exactly been the teddy-bears' picnic.

He nodded his sympathy. "No—I let the police know immediately, of course, that I'd been up here."

"You did?" She hoped the surprise she felt didn't show in either face or voice.

Miller nodded again. "Sure. I usually came up at least twice a month to confer with Jasper. I stayed out of the San Francisco and London end of the business, that was all Jas; the bands in those towns didn't really know me. I concentrated on handling L.A. and New York. Anyway, I told the police all about it so that they could check me out, and they did. And I did. Check out, I mean. Dates and times and everything. But that's their job, the cops. If you'll excuse me—I want to catch King and Berry before leave they. I'm sure we'll be seeing a lot of each other, so I won't say goodbye."

"So much for Randyll Miller as a suspect," Rennie muttered aside to Prax as the meeting was breaking up. "Unless he's the bluffiest bluffer who ever bluffed. Which I don't think. I feel like a nasty-minded jerk. Tell you later."

Outside, the morning's hard, brilliant sunlight was being dimmed by ominous streaks of stormclouds pouring in from the west. The musicians all decamped immediately, heading back to the Haight or the Mission or Potrero Hill, claiming appointments at the free clinic or with groupies. Maybe not in that order. But Prax and Chet lingered, and with Rennie, Berry and King they stood around on the pavement discussing plans for the rest of the day. In a very few moments Rennie had received offers to go to Fisherman's Wharf for fried clams (Prax, in front of everyone), to go downtown for some more legal discussion (Berry and King, to her face), or to go back to her apartment for a not-so-quickie

(Chet, in her ear).

Well, two out of three ain't bad... She declined them all, with varying degrees of regret.

"Tempting, but no. I have to get to the Clarion and actually do some work, what a concept."

But she arranged to meet Prax, Juha and Chet that night at the Avalon Ballroom, run by yet another Chet—this one the longhaired Texan promoter, Helms. Favorite San Francisco band Big Brother and the Holding Company had just added a chick vocalist to their lineup, a Texas friend of Helms's called Janis Joplin, and they decided to go and hear the debut of the new configuration; it would be their painful duty to boo and hiss if they were not knocked out by what they heard.

They had small hopes going in: this Joplin chick was a former folkie who had inspired massive yawns in her previous attempt on San Francisco a couple of years ago—at least she would have if anyone had actually heard her—and Juha dismissed her now as a sulky speed freak who'd moved on to become one of Tam's most faithful smack customers. Still, none of them had heard her yet with Big Brother, a mangy yet melodically interesting and charming band who didn't *always* play off-key and off-tempo, and opening night might be fun. Plus Prax had confided that she'd heard Janis liked girls as well as boys, and was naturally curious.

When Rennie arrived at her cubicle, there was the usual stack of messages to work through, and then a quick staff meeting later that day. She was outlining a new story proposal to show Burke when her phone rang; she almost let the pool secretary pick up, but then reached for it herself.

"Mrs. Lacing? Rennie?"

In the nick of time she recognized the caller's high, flat, fluty tones. "Well, hello, Clovis Franjo, how nice to hear from you."

The self-satisfied, flattered purring came oozing

through the receiver. "How nice of *you* to remember my voice. To remember me at all."

"You're not easily forgettable," said Rennie with perfect truth, practically gagging on the words, yet wanting to charm and disarm. "Besides, didn't we dance together just the other night at my father-in-law's party, you little twinkletoes? What can I do for you?"

Sweet Mother of God, I can't believe *I just used the word 'twinkletoes' in human conversation, I am surely going straight to hell...*

If Clovis thought her tone in any way bizarre, it couldn't be told from his own. "Actually, I was calling to check on the progress of the Warriors of Gaia story. I don't mean to pressure you, of course, but I hadn't heard from you and I hadn't seen it in print either, so naturally I was wondering..."

For someone so shy of publicity, he certainly seemed to be courting it all of a sudden. "Oh, I'm *so* sorry," Rennie heard herself saying, with just the right note of utterly fake regret. "I should have gotten in touch with you sooner."

"Is there a problem?"

"Oh, no, no. Not at all. In fact, my editor wants to maybe expand on it a little," Rennie lied, like the pro she was. No way in hell she was telling him about the kind of story she really *had* written, or the fact that Burke had put it on hold.

"Ah, great minds think alike, as usual... There are actually a few things I'd like to get into in more detail, some new projects and plans of ours to help serve the trees, things I now feel I didn't properly address when we spoke. Would that be out of the question at this late date?"

Rennie concealed her surprise and delight, which outweighed her groans and dismay. A follow-up interview was unheard-of for Clovis, and however painful for her personally, she would be able to take a few more shots, so to speak, at things unanswered—things about Foy Ballard.

"No, of course not. We can add all sorts of stuff, make it even better. When would you like to meet?"

"What's convenient for you?"

"How about this afternoon?" she suggested, hoping against hope that he would put it off due to the short notice — she wasn't as loaded for bear as she'd like to be, just a little more time to prepare...

But no; he was as free as the lions of the Serengeti. It only remained for them to set a mutually convenient time and place.

"It'll just be us, by the way," Clovis added, as if by way of inducement. "Foy has other things to do this afternoon, and I'd say we know each other well enough by now to converse unchaperoned, don't we." His voice dropped a bit, into a less eunuch-y range. "Frankly, Foy happens to be one of the things I want to talk to you about. You might like to— Well, let's wait till we can discuss it in person. If it's not too much of an imposition, would you mind meeting me in Berkeley?"

He gave her an address: a well-known outdoor café on the main drag, not far from the university, and Rennie agreed eagerly.

"I know exactly where that is, good choice. Say three o'clock?"

"Three is perfect. Oh, and perhaps you could bring your notes along? Just something for me to glance over, so I don't end up telling you things we've already covered and wasting even more of your valuable time."

Too late, Treebeard! I'll never get those *moments back...* "I would if I had any," said Rennie, mock-ruefully. "But I'm sorry to say my notes are all in my head."

"Well, certainly bring *that* along."

After they had both chuckled and hung up, Rennie sat drawing little pictures of snails and flags and snowflakes on her desk blotter. Something was happening here and she didn't know what it was, did she, Mrs. Jones. That Clovis. Did the little wooden boy have something to tell her that he didn't want his minion to know? Was *he* afraid of Foy, even, that he didn't want him around? Better still, was he about to put the finger on Foy as a multiple-murdering drugmaster and give Rennie the scoop? A girl could dream, couldn't she?

Their intended meeting place being a popular student-and-faculty Berkeley hangout, blamelessly public, there was little danger even if Ballard did show up. Still, at the very least she'd be able to ask Clovis about Foy, or tell him about Foy, or confront and accuse and light into him about Foy.

She thought of calling Marcus to tell him where she was going, but dismissed it as silly. He hadn't been the soul of praisefulness when she'd told him everything she'd found out. Besides, Foy was the problem and the danger, and he wouldn't even be there; what would Marcus care that she was going to have a repeat interview with the Sequoia Kid?

Still, this could work out *great*: away from the intimidating Ballard presence and the homicidal Ballard nature, maybe Clovis would open up like a steamed clam. Maybe she could winkle some unvetted and even unguarded answers out of him, answers that might even provide that final crucial piece of evidence, evidence that would put Foy away for life and clear Prax for good.

Which was exactly the way it turned out. Sort of.

The rest of the day passed uneventfully. Burke had some minor issues with her latest piece, but chiefly he was pleased, and they spent most of their editorial session discussing the ball at Hall Place. He and his wife had enjoyed themselves immensely, though they had also been a little overwhelmed by the Lacing lifestyle and the accompanying fact that this was how Burke's most junior staffer lived. Or could live, if she chose. But, as Burke pointed out, how often do you get to go to a formal ball in a San Francisco landmark mansion still being dwelled in by the family that had built it, and in any case the missus and he had had a wonderful time.

Rennie ate a quick salad at her desk, then went downstairs next door to her car in the Clarion garage. Pulling out onto Geary Street, she glanced up at the sky, which now was totally clouded over with dark gray puffy forerunners of the big spring storm, feverishly tracked for the last three days, that was finally moving onshore out of the Pacific. She gave a fleeting thought to Stephen, resolving to have a long talk with him, perhaps tomorrow; she had left messages at his office and at Hell House, though so far the calls had not been returned.

Moved by a premonition of she didn't know quite what, Rennie found herself swinging aside when she got off the Bay Bridge, detouring to Ro Savarkin's safe house on her way to meet Clovis in Berkeley. Pathologically early by nature, she had half an hour before their appointment, what was she going to do otherwise—kill time in a bookstore, sit like an idiot in the car? It couldn't hurt to look in on Ro, a mere ten minutes' drive out of her way, just a quick visit to see how she was. Couldn't hurt at all.

She pulled up outside the street house and hurried back through the alley to the little bungalow, her bootheels clicking on the paving stones; it had begun to rain, and the bricks were already slick with misty drizzle, the rhododendron blossoms dripping and fragrant. She shied a little when she saw a battered blue station wagon standing on the concrete apron in front of the garage. Okay, take it easy, probably Ro's, or belonged to the people in the front house, just hadn't been pulled into the garage stall, for whatever reason—groceries to unpack, going out again, just got in. But when Rennie arrived at the cottage's front door and saw that it stood wide open, the lock snapped right out of the splintered wooden frame, cold fear ran through her.

Oh, no, this can't be good...

Pushing the door carefully open, she called out for Ro,

but the silence was thunderous. She ran straight to the back bedroom, the little room where they'd talked, where Ro had fallen asleep while Rennie sat vigil. But it was empty. She ran upstairs to the other tiny bedroom; also nothing. Living room, bathroom, likewise.

Rennie found her on the floor of the narrow windowed kitchen. There was so much blood that at first horrified sight she thought Ro had been shot. But no; she'd just had the living crap beaten out of her.

'Just'! It was Foy, had to be, how the hell had he found her…

She felt for a pulse. Slow but strong, therefore not dead, always a good sign. Ro's eyes were closed, one of them swollen shut with a cut at the edge, beading blood and tears, and she was breathing shallowly but regularly. Her shirt was up around her neck, her jeans were down around her knees, and there were scratches and bruises and blood.

Dear God, that too… How long has she been lying here like this? What if I hadn't come?

Trying to keep panic at bay, Rennie looked around for the phone, found it in the living room, ripped from the wall. So much for calling for help. She ran into the bathroom, wet a clean washcloth and towel with cold water, then grabbed a pillow from the bed and dashed back to Ro, using the towel to gently dab the blood off her battered face, but that only made the dreadful cuts and bruises look worse.

Don't move them, just make them comfortable, remember what you learned in the goddamn Girl Scouts…that psychopathic pigdog Foy Ballard, I SWEAR I will see him put down like Old Yeller, even Marcus must see now that it's him…

Slipping the pillow under Ro's head, Rennie squeezed the washcloth to drip a little clean water onto the cracked and blood-crusted lips. Nothing for a few seconds; then the lips moved as Ro felt the water, and Rennie, almost crying, carefully dripped a few more drops, which were eagerly licked off.

"Ro, it's Rennie, Rennie Stride. Can you hear me?

Listen, I'm going to the house in front to get help. Don't try to move, I'll be right back."

The injured girl moaned faintly, and Rennie took the pathetic sound for acknowledgment, if not comprehension. She put the folded towel on Ro's forehead, the wet washcloth on her lips and the bedroom blanket over her, left the front door ajar as she'd found it—no time to look for the keys—and went out, eeling around the blue station wagon to get to the front house's back door. Pushing past the rhododendrons where they were most thickly planted, she checked sharply, sensing a presence, but she was too late. Someone jumped out from between the car and the concealing bushes and grabbed her from behind.

She fought to break his hold, but he was fantastically strong, his wrist across her neck, his hand forcing her chin down into her chest, keeping her from turning her head to see his face.

Foy! I knew he'd come after her again...

Suddenly she heard a popping sound, and before she could help it, she drew in a searing lungful of a sharp, clean chemical smell from something jammed roughly up against her nose. Coughing and choking, disoriented, unable to see out of streaming, burning eyes, she felt the car door being pulled open and herself thrown inside. Too sick and dizzy to fight back, she felt her wrists tied roughly to the seat frame, and then the surging motion beneath her, as, at perfectly normal speed so as not to attract attention, the car was piloted backward down the alley and out into the street and away.

Chapter Twenty-one

WHEN THE ARM WENT AROUND HER THROAT and the sharp smell choked her, Rennie had reeled on the point of blackout, with a sickening vertiginous rush and shooting heartbeat. Now that her head had cleared a little, she realized she was lying on the rear seat of the station wagon, the third, reverse-facing seat all the way in the back. Her hands were securely lashed to the seat support so that she could not sit up, though if she craned her head as high as she could she could just see the driver's eyes reflected in the rearview mirror. She fell back down, coughing violently to clear her lungs of the last traces of whatever the hell it had been she had inhaled.

"Amyl nitrate," came a cold bored voice. "I didn't want you out entirely. You'll be all right in a couple of minutes. Except you'll have one motherfucker of a headache. Oh, and don't bother trying to get loose."

She blinked to clear her head some more and struggled up again. She didn't recognize the new, nasty voice, but she knew those pale, dead-fish peepers, gleaming at her in the mirror like flounder orbs.

CLOVIS? Why would he want to kidnap me, it should be Foy... Because I am being kidnapped, apparently...

She found her voice, throat sore from the bruises his arm had left. "Clovis? What the *hell*— Why are you doing this? What were you doing at Ro's, we were supposed to meet in Berkeley... Is it some redwood thing, some hostage stunt? Listen, if it's ransom, I don't have any money, but my husband—"

"It's not about money. And it's not about the goddamn redwoods either."

The car stopped at a light, and Rennie was aware that the earlier mist had turned to heavy gusty rain; the storm had finally struck, and the station wagon swayed in a shuddery blast of wind.

"Then what *is* it about? What reason could you possibly have for—Clovis, *listen* to me, I found out that Foy is into heroin, he makes it, steps on it and distributes it—he has labs in the redwood forests, he uses musicians and those medieval fair people as mules and he's using you for cover— he killed Tam and Fort and Jasper, he raped Ro and beat her almost to death—"

"For a smart reporter, you're pretty stupid after all." Franjo adjusted the rearview mirror, reached out through the window to tilt the side one, brought his arm back in, shirtsleeve soaked with chilly rain. "Don't you get it yet? It isn't Foy. It was never Foy. It's me."

They were heading north, as far as Rennie could make out, though she couldn't think why or where. At first she'd hoped maybe some passers-by would see her and call the cops for a rescue, but that was clearly why he'd tied her hands low enough that she couldn't sit up. Down flat on the seat as she was, someone would have to have their nose against the windows to see her there, and the streaming rain prevented anyway.

Clovis was chatting amiably as he drove, all trace gone now of the high, wimpy voice he'd affected.

"You know, Foy was the one who took all that Warriors of Gaia crap seriously. He actually *believed* all the jive about Mother Earth and her gifts, Gaia the living planet. What a crock... Now me, I figure anything that breathes is put there to be taken advantage of. And if no one else wants to do the taking, then I'm happy to oblige."

"So the prince of the forest turns out to be a little weasel after all," snapped Rennie. "As for Foy, some gentle Earth warrior *he* is. I found Ro Savarkin in the cottage. Well, you were there, you must have seen —"

"Rosemary? She's a junkie doormat, you think she should be treated like a human being? Yeah, that's how a spoiled princess of the House of Lacing *would* think. But Foy didn't kill Tam or the others, even though the bitch thought he did. She told you, didn't she? How he went backstage alone and came back without his jacket and there was blood on it? There's a reason for that. And Foy didn't beat up on Rosemary either, at least not this afternoon. I'm the one who smacked the little smack whore around. Anyway, it would've been hard for him to do it, seeing as I killed him last night."

"You killed him... So if *he* didn't kill *them*—and *you* killed *him*—"

"That's right. I killed them all. And now I'm going to kill you too."

After that, conversation understandably languished; Clovis was concentrating on his driving and Rennie was pondering many things, her own mortality chiefest among them. Freeway traffic was heavy, badly snarled because of the storm, and Clovis had switched over to side roads north to avoid it. They'd been heading north maybe an hour now. Coming up on the Richmond Bridge, which had its western terminus in Marin County, he kept checking around on all sides for any signs of police pursuit. Clearly he saw nothing nearby more alarming than other storm-slowed traffic heading home, so he sped up a bit and then they were moving into the bridge approach lane and out onto the span, which was very crowded but not yet at a rush-hour standstill. He relaxed a little then, obviously feeling safe and unpursued enough to resume their conversation.

"So, you didn't know after all. Well, that's a kick and a half. I really thought you had solid evidence that I offed those three little dope piggies."

"I do now, you psychopathic freak!" she snapped. "Before, I only had evidence that tied Foy to the murders."

The fish-eyes seemed to waver in the mirror; Clovis was shaking his head, silently laughing. "Funny...I only decided to grab you this afternoon because I thought I'd let something slip in our interview, something you were going to take the police as soon as you remembered it, or were going to try to blackmail me with. And all the time you didn't have a clue. Not the *right* clue, anyway."

"I believe they call it irony."

A sharp bark of laughter. "Glad to see you still have your sense of humor. Actually, you did pretty well with what you had. You're far from stupid: you'd have figured it out before too long, and I'd have had to kill you anyway. I just wanted to get my hands on your notes, and then you told me the only notes you had were in your head. So the only way to destroy your notes was to destroy you. It's better this way."

Permit me to disagree... "How did you get Ro's address? We were all so careful."

"Yeah, you were," he agreed. "I was impressed. I knew that you'd been in touch with Sunny Silver, and Foy found out that Sunny was going to messenger Rosemary's address to you at the Clarion. It's not hard to get into the Clarion building, and it wasn't terribly difficult to find the mailroom. I just seem to instinctively know my way around places."

"It's a gift," said Rennie acidly.

Miles over his head. "Yeah, I guess. Mailroom kids don't make a lot of money, so I gave one twenty bucks and a lid and a nauseating story about how I was new there and I had a major crush on that hot little Rennie Stride, please could I deliver her mail myself, I'd never tell anyone that he let me. He dug up the envelope from Sunny and handed it over; I opened it, got the address, sealed it up again and dropped it off on your desk. When you stepped away for a few minutes, I went back and retrieved the envelope, just in case there were prints."

"Pretty neat."

"Common or garden resourceful. I haven't gotten this far without learning how to cover my trail."

As he came off the bridge he steered south and west, bypassing lines of stalled local traffic outside Larkspur and Corte Madera, heading for Mill Valley on back roads that led round the foot of Mount Tamalpais, the holy mountain. A well-covered trail indeed.

"Well, let's get into it, shall we? Just to pass the time and satisfy my curiosity? Rennie Stride's last interview. Tell me how it all got started, Mr. Franjo."

Clovis didn't mind if he did. He had a doctorate in chemistry from USC, he told her; that was where he'd met Foy. And they'd decided they could get a lot richer a lot quicker by manufacturing illegal drugs than they could by cleaving to the pharmaceutical straight and narrow. They'd started out small: pot, bathtub acid, selling other dealers' smack and speed. But they made so much money so fast that only a year later they had enough to set up their first lab, up near Mendocino. It was small, but it had good equipment; pretty soon they had two other renegade chemists working for them, and a quickly branching network of distributors and carriers. The medieval fairs that were proliferating like magic mushrooms across California had proven to be a gold mine of opportunity, as had the ballrooms and the small music festivals starting up.

"Pretty soon there will be huge rock festivals all over the country, hundreds of thousands of people, every little druggie one of them a potential Charlemagne customer. And my network will be national by then, already in place, waiting to fill their needs."

"Why Charlemagne?"

"Oh, just a little historical fun. Charlemagne, the original Clovis — both kings of the Franks. Charlemagne was the first ruler of the Holy Roman Empire."

"Yeah, I'm hip. It was neither holy nor Roman nor an empire, by the way."

He laughed. "Neither are we. Definitely not Roman or holy. Though we're working on the empire part. It's only to amuse us. It doesn't mean anything."

"And the redwoods? Those don't mean anything either, I gather. Tell me, how *did* the Warriors of Gaia get started?"

"Perfect solid-gold scam. I never gave a crap about the goddamn redwoods — Foy was the bleeding-heart tree-lover — but I realized if people were kept out of the forests and the trees were left alone, nobody would find my labs. It was the perfect place to site them, and a redwood-protection society would be the perfect cover. Not to mention convenient for money laundering. And it kept Foy loyal to me. He never knew I couldn't care less if all the trees were cut down for toothpicks."

Right again, Stephen... Rennie shifted position, bracing as the car went around a sharp curve, and Clovis immediately slowed down.

"Don't want to hit a speed trap, do we. Not far now, no need to rush. Besides, I want you to finish your interview, I'm enjoying this. Especially since I know it'll never see print."

"Getting back, then: Tam, Fort and Jasper—why did you kill them? If they were working for you?"

Clovis smiled expansively, though she couldn't see it, just heard the smile in the fatness of his tone.

"I killed Linetti because he'd stiffed me in a drug deal once too often. He was a greedy little bastard, and he'd started taking a cut off the drugs as well as the money; what I gave him wasn't generous enough, apparently. Plus he'd gotten careless."

"So you decided to make him go away."

"That's right. Foy hung out at the Fillmore a lot, and sometimes I did too; I even saw you there one night. And Foy, which is to say me, always had dynamite shit to lay on the bands, so they were careful not to 'notice' us around. That afternoon I waited until everyone was out front schlepping amps. Then Foy and I went to the dressing room. Ro was under orders in a closet, giving head to one of our best customers, and that roadie Idaho was in another closet, getting head from some groupie—I didn't think they noticed us, but I bought off the chick when she tried to alibi him."

"Yes, we all wondered why she changed her tune."

"Amazing what you can do with money and drugs, not to mention threats. She won't dare open her yap now, and I can always use her later. Anyway, Tommy was there alone, waiting for us and the usual delivery. Foy came up behind him and held him while I stuck a knife in. Grab-and-stab. He never knew what hit him. The rest was just set dressing. We got him into the case before he bled too much on us or on the floor, though Foy got a lot of blood on his jacket and had to take it off."

"Ro noticed. So did Prax."

"Did they?" He didn't seem concerned. "I had some blood on my own clothes, so I changed them for some of the stuff lying around the dressing room. Musicians are always leaving things backstage—they're stupid, they're stoned, they forget. Anyway, I put on new clothes, took my own bloody ones with me, and the knife, cut the shirt and pants into rags and stuffed them into a garbage can over in Alameda, under some used cat litter. By now they're under tons of trash at the county dump. The knife's at the bottom of the bay off the San Mateo causeway."

"Neat. And not gaudy." Rennie was still trying to slip her hands out of the ropes, but they were far too tightly fastened. She lay back, frustrated, though she was amazed at how preternaturally self-possessed she was. Maybe it was fear from out the other side, so terrified she was actually calm.

Well, he's not going to kill me in the car, so maybe when he takes me out of here I'll have a chance. And probably I'm ending up dead no matter what, but I swear I'll go out like a lion, not some little hippie lamb to the slaughter…

"And Jasper and Fort?"

"Ah, that was a little different. Everything Rosemary told you about Foy? That was really all me, as I said earlier. At first I'd used the Hell's Angels as distributors, like every other hippie chemist in the Bay Area. But I wanted people more in tune, let's say, with my way of thinking and working. So I co-opted Fort and then Jasper as distributors for the really primo stuff I process in my Eureka lab. They recruited some good runners, and they also used some people without their even knowing it, like those medieval wackos and a bunch of bands. You'd be surprised how much dope you can cram into a suit of armor or a drum kit. It was a perfect system. But lately they weren't hitting their distribution quotas, and were even trying to get out of the arrangement."

"Yet you paid off Jasper's gambling debts."

"Yeah—that frigid French whore of an ex-wife probably told you he was into me for five high figures. That was his way out from under: the way the deal worked was that Jasper would use his own clients, or some of them, to do the drug runs. That's how Tommy and Tony ended up in bed with me, so to speak. And good old Jas was planning to employ your little girlfriend Prax that way too, once she trusted him."

"He told you that?" *Lucky Jasper, to be already dead — otherwise I'd kill him myself...*

"Sure. I knew Prax was having a special little dinner at your place. Fort talked all that stink about her to the papers on my orders; I thought it might be useful to get a public grudge going, dissociate him from the hippie scene, in case anyone was doing any connecting. I killed them about two hours after you left your apartment that night."

"But you can't have been there, surely."

"I wasn't, not at first. I had told Tony to knock the other two out, I didn't care how he did it. How *did* he do it, by the way?"

"Liquid Valium in the last bottle of wine," said Rennie unwillingly. "The cops said he injected it through the cork, though that piece of information was never made public."

"Clever old Fort."

"Oh, then that's why —"

"What's why?"

You're enjoying this, aren't you, you sick bastard, it's like a movie to you, starring you in every role... Rennie took a deep breath to calm herself again.

"Why he said what he said. I was on my way out to this club that Jasper had insisted I go to, to hear some new band of his, and I said something like Oh you guys are just trying to get me out of there and what are you really up to. I was kidding, but Fort went absolutely white, as if I'd guessed something I shouldn't have."

"You had. Or so he thought. Panicky little moron. He was under orders to get you out of the apartment no matter what. He pushed for Jasper to ask you to cover that stupid band, which worked out fine, but anything would have done as long as it made you leave."

"Why didn't you get rid of me too?"

"There was no reason. Any more than there was a reason to kill Prax, which I know you all wondered about. I was going to force her to work for me, so I didn't want her dead. As for you, I had nothing against you, and for all I knew you might have been useful to me yourself later on. It's always good to have a journalist in your pocket. Which was one reason why I picked your flat to do the job in. Nice place you've got, by the way, just love what you've done with it. Anyway, once Jasper and Prax were safely out, I came up."

"Prax heard the door open and shut. The cops didn't believe her."

Clovis braked to avoid a tumbling branch. "That must have been right before the liquid Valium got her. I make that myself, too. Anyway, Fort gave me the high sign from the window and let me in when I got upstairs—that was what she heard. I found her on the bathroom floor and carried her into the nearest bedroom, dumped her on the bed. Tony—the other name is too pretentious, he's just this ginzo from New Jersey, and no mob connections, by the way, though that wasn't a bad guess—was waiting in the living room, dithering. I made him drink the wine too, told him I'd make sure he was okay, but all of them had to be out cold, not just faking, or the plan wouldn't work."

"What plan was that?"

He snorted. "There *was* no plan! I just told him that, said I needed the three of them passed out in your apartment, for secret purposes of my own."

"And he bought that? God. He was even stupider than I thought."

In the mirror, Clovis threw her what passed with him for a grin. "Not the brightest bulb on the Christmas tree, was Tony. But that's what I needed."

"The last thing a drugmeister needs is imaginative underlings?"

"Something like that. But a drugmeister does need intelligent lieutenants. Pity you're on the side of the white-hats; I could really use someone as smart and innocent-looking as you. But you're too smart to get hooked and too clean to blackmail and too rich to buy. Your big sin is you're slutting around on your husband — who cares?"

"You know about that?"

He gave a scoffing laugh. "Your mother-in-law's private dick also works for me from time to time. That's how I set you up for that guy to grab you when you were coming out of the Avalon, and no, he wasn't drunk. He's one of my lab security people. I told him to put the frighteners on you, rough you up good, rape you if that's what it took to scare you off. And he would have. But you don't scare easily, unfortunately. And then your pig cousin-in-law showed up to save you."

Clovis glanced at her in the mirror. "But none of that matters now. Everything's taken care of, and the only thing left on my to-do list is 'Kill that annoying little Rennie Stride'."

REMEMBER *that, you stupid girl, remember what he's planning, don't get caught up in his little drama and suckered off guard...*

"So, after you had everybody out like little lights, what did you do then?"

"Once Tony was unconscious too — that liquid Valium is amazing, it just hits you and you're gone, you don't remember whatever happened just before you took it — I took down that sword you had, and, well, used it. I'd planned on grabbing a carving knife from the kitchen, but the sword was much more effective, plus it made for such gratifyingly sensational headlines. Little inside joke: the sword of the Warriors of Gaia — well, I knew the connection, even if they didn't. I fenced saber at college, so I knew my way around a blade. I'll spare you the extremely gory details."

"I was there, remember? I got to see your handiwork up close and way too personal. And you made *such* a mess of my apartment. But why did you have to kill Jasper and Fort in the first place?"

"I told you, it wasn't working out anymore. They were getting too squirrely, they knew about Tam, they had to go. I couldn't trust them. Tony was stealing from me and trying to set up on his own, and Jasper was digging in his tiny toes about everything, even my plans for Prax. I didn't have any choice. Then I thought if I could frame her for the murders, that would be my best way out."

"And if she was convicted?"

"No skin off my ass. She'd take the fall for me and I could live with that. But then *you* came along, poking and snooping. I tried to fob you off with the usual sob story about the damn redwoods, but you got cute." He swung sharply to avoid something in the road. "After I dumped Prax on the bed, I put her prints on the sword and on the bottle; I had gloves on, of course. Dumb luck she'd been the one who found Tommy. I knew they wouldn't bust her for him, but it helped to make the cops more suspicious of her later."

"Why did you pick her?"

"She was a new client of Jasper's and didn't have a handle on what was going on. Once I killed Jas, she'd be even easier for me to control. Plus she was a nobody. No big loss, nobody would care about her. If she got convicted, fine; if she got off, I could still leverage her afterwards. Pretty chick singer, who'd suspect her?"

Rennie suppressed a stabbing flame of fury. "Uh, like, the *cops* did?"

"Yeah, they went right for it, didn't they." Clovis sounded delighted that they had. "Though I bet they weren't too happy about the sword, whether she could have swung it hard enough to nearly take their heads off. But I hadn't counted on your damn story making Prax well known so quickly, so I had to hurry up the scheme. Juries are less likely to vote guilty on even a slightly famous face at the defense table."

"But if you wanted to keep such a low profile yourself—I presume that's why you so seldom talked to the press—why did you talk to me?"

Clovis laughed shortly. "You think I gave you that interview because you're such a good journalist, because you're Rennie Starr Reporter? Hardly! I'd read your little diatribes in the undergrounds against Fortinbras, and I had the strangest feeling you weren't going to leave it there. I thought that if anyone could put all the bits and pieces together, it would be you. And I was damned if I was going to let some Ivy League rich bitch hippie dilettante ruin everything I had built up. So I decided to talk to you, find out what if anything you knew."

He paused. "But the problem was, you *are* a good journalist. And sooner or later you would have tied me up to it. When I heard you had talked to Rosemary, I knew I had to get moving."

"And that was when you decided to kill Foy.'

"That's right. Just shot him—I wasn't in the mood for anything more creative and he never saw it coming. Dumped him in a spot not too far from where you'll be ending up, won't it be nice for you both to have company. That was Foy, by the way, the night you and Ro were in the cottage talking. He'd been listening in from that handy little balcony above the window; he told me afterwards that he slipped and made some noise and you might have heard him. He followed you all the way home from Rosemary's place."

"Yeah, we did hear him, but we thought it was the cat. But how did you know I'd stop off at Ro's today before going to meet you? You obviously didn't follow me there."

"I didn't know. I went there first to take care of her. In the 'beat the bejesus out of her' sense of 'take care'. Pure dumb luck you turned up. I was going to grab you out of the coffeehouse later: disable your car, offer to drive you to a garage, then bring you up here. I just seized the moment."

"And Ro?"

"Didn't want to kill her, though if she dies I won't weep at the funeral. She's still useful, and I can keep her obedient. Now of course she knows it's me behind it all, not Foy, but she'll stay in line. She won't even go to the cops. I slapped Sunny around a bit, too. She won't be singing for a couple of days. Though she may just have to be the next hippie musician who meets a sad fate. Or maybe not, if she agrees to pick up where Tony and Tommy left off."

"Why did you pick my place to do the murders in?"

"You'd been ragging on Tony in those underground asswipe papers. It seemed amusing to have him end up dead on your living room floor. Plus it got you even more involved than you had been. Bet your husband's pole-up-the-butt family was plenty pissed with you, disgracing their sacred name."

"Got that right." Rennie was quiet for a while. They were in among redwoods, and she was beginning to have an inkling of where they were bound. "Just to keep the conversation flowing, where are you planning to put your next lab? Mexico?"

"Certainly not. I hate the heat. And Mexico is full of, well, Mexicans."

"That's what Ro said Foy thought."

"Oh, Foy was a racist. I just don't like the hassle of having to deal with people in a foreign language, and you can never get decent burgers. Hell, half my staff at the labs is black or Mexican or Hawaiian or Asian, I have no problem with that. The next one's going to be in the Olympic rainforest, as a matter of fact—that needs saving just as much as the redwoods."

Rennie was silent for a while. Then: "Don't you think

Marcus and the rest of the SFPD are hot on our trail by now, maybe even the feds?"

He glanced in the rearview mirror. "Nope. I don't think that at all. In this storm they'll have a hard time following even by sight, let alone trying to follow tracks. And there's nobody behind us. I've been watching since we crossed the bridge."

"Tracks? On a paved highway?"

"Won't be paved where we're going."

"Where's that, then?""

"I could tell you, but then I'd have to kill you. Oh, wait, I *am* going to kill you… We're going to Muir Woods. And I'll be driving back alone." He glanced back at her, flashed a grin. "You're really not my type, but I may even treat you to a little of what I gave Rosemary. Depends on how I feel."

Rennie shrugged. "Knock yourself out, but you should know that I do power yoga. I can rip your dick off with one Kegel…"

She saw alarm flash in the fish-eyes, and smiled. "Worse than that, I hope you realize you'll have not only the cops and the Clarion to deal with but the entire wrath and resources of the Lacing family. They don't like me much, and I don't like them at all, except for my husband and his brother, but they'll take great exception to someone who's married to one of them being murdered in their old pal William Kent's sacred woodlot. And they're considerably scarier than the fuzz, I promise you."

"No, they'll just think you picked up the wrong stud at some sleazy club and ended up dead. Oh, by the way, too bad you can't tell that pussywhipped husband of yours that his family might like to know a few things about some Asian and Hawaiian shipping firms they own. The answers might surprise him. But I doubt that even hubby will do anything more than write you off as a, ha, dead loss. To hear your mother-in-law tell it, you're no loss at all—she'll probably adopt me in gratitude for ridding her of you."

"Now there you may have a point."

"Where are we going again?" *Are we theeeeere yet? Not that I want to arrive, necessarily, but I'm getting tired of waiting on edge, too much fear and anticipation and I'll get all dull and slow when it actually comes to it...*

She'd long ago given up trying to free her hands, and all this time, while conversing with Clovis, she had been trying to think of something she could do to save herself when he came to drag her out of the car: kick him in the balls and run away, pick up a branch and clobber him, maybe there was a tire iron or something lying around back here, maybe she could just bite him. But nothing at all feasible was leaping madly to mind, though under the circumstances her mind wasn't exactly working with rainwater clarity.

"I told you, Muir Woods. Appropriate, don't you think? Me being such a well-known redwood fan. But they serve my purpose, so I'm happy to protect them, and I know the place like the lines on my palms. We're taking the back way in, on the fire trails, to the densest part of the forest. Nobody will find you there, and by the time they do"—he checked the rear-view mirror again—"there won't be much left. Ah, here's our exit. Your exit, actually."

Satisfied they were not being followed, he swung the station wagon off the highway and headed into the redwood forest. Cars were not permitted to drive into the majestic groves that William Kent had named for his naturalist friend John Muir, but there were narrow dirt tracks, just wide enough to take emergency and forestry service vehicles, that ran through the depths of the woods.

The storm was at its howling height now; even with the car windows closed Rennie could hear the trees groaning in the wind, moving slowly back and forth like leaning towers, and deep under the canopy though they now were, the rain was still lashing the windows blind. She suddenly remembered the little bronze figure that Sunny Silver had proudly showed her. *Oyá, goddess of storms, eh? Help me out a little here!*

She'd felt an icewater shock when Clovis had said they'd arrived; that old self-preservation imperative kicking in, big-time. *I better think of something fast. In about ten minutes this guy is going to slaughter me like a veal calf and bury me here. Come on, Rennie, what would your tiny inner Girl Scout do?*

They drove deeper and deeper into the woods, rain sluicing madly down. Rennie lost all sense of direction but back; the trees were getting huger and older the farther in they went. By now she was on the one hand resigned to what certainly seemed her inevitable fate, though on the other hand she fully intended to give him as hard and painful a fight as she could.

And, she thought now, let's face it, there were way worse places to end up dead: R.I.P. among the redwoods had a certain majesty that sleeping with the fishes or being pulverized in a car crash definitely lacked. Plus there were always hikers and campers passing through; someone would find her body before long. Not that it mattered: leaving your bones at the feet of the oldest living things on earth — that was a kind of immortality right there.

Rennie always maintained ever after that, trippy as it sounded, she heard a voice right before it happened, a voice in her ear, though she didn't know the language it used, or the word it spoke to her. But somehow she knew *what* it said, and whether for that reason or some other, she suddenly rolled off the seat and as far down and back in the seat well as she could get, right up next to the tailgate, face between her arms and pressed to the floor.

She was just in time. With a sound that could at first not be heard but only felt as profoundly deep vibration, without an audible groan or creak or crack, a huge coast redwood silver-gray with rot and age slowly began to topple before a mighty blast of wind. And then—they both heard it now—with a roar like a hundred lions, the dead giant came crashing down across the hood of Clovis's car.

Chapter Twenty-two

WHEN RENNIE OPENED HER EYES, she saw, through a pink mist that she realized was her own blood running into her eyes, rain and broken glass and needle sprays and bark and branches filling and surrounding the car. She must have blacked out from the terrific jolt: from what she could see, the tree trunk itself had just clipped the front bumper—if it had fallen squarely on top of them they would both have died instantly—but it had toppled from a good hundred feet away, and so only the top bit had come down on them, not the thickest part. Still, some branches as big around as normal-sized trees had caught the car on the roof and hood, crushing it in, a tin can stomped under a giant's foot.

She cautiously drew herself up to look. She could barely make out Clovis behind the wheel, but he appeared unconscious. She pulled desperately against the ropes, and this time, the seat back having been jarred loose by the crash, she came free.

Hands still bound in front of her, one eye on Clovis and the other on the wild woods, Rennie kicked the tailgate door open and tumbled out onto the soaked ground, clothes already plastered to her body. She risked a quick glance behind her; no sign or movement, he must be really knocked out. Maybe he was even dead.

Good, though I wish I could have clocked the bastard myself...how appropriate that one of his own betrayed trees laid him out cold. It was probably as bored with his stupid rap as I was...

She scrambled to her feet, noticing that blood was dripping from several cuts and scratches and her right knee really hurt, and ran blindly through the roaring woods, pushing wet underbrush out of her face, back the way they had driven in. Could she get as far as the main road before he came to and headed after her? Maybe she could hide in a hollow tree or something, the way people did in all those stupid folksongs, until he gave up looking or somebody found her. Muir Woods was usually crawling with visitors — though in a storm like this, probably not so much. Campers would be snug in their tents and staying there, and day-trippers wouldn't have left their living rooms to begin with. And even if he didn't find her, after a few hours out in the storm — it was beginning to grow darker now, and noticeably colder — she'd die of exposure anyway.

Another tree had fallen a few hundred feet back, trapping Clovis's car; not that the station wagon was going anywhere, that tree had messed it up pretty good. This second tree was in her flight path, though, and rather than waste time going around she scrambled straight over it. As she came over the top of the huge rain-slick trunk she lost her balance and fell, catching her foot in the fork of a branch. She pulled frantically, and her shoe came off as her foot was freed, so she kicked the other one off and ran on barefoot.

Then to the side of the dirt road Rennie saw a dark shape running toward her through the rain. *I didn't even hear him! How the hell did he get in front of me?* With a small desperate sob like a hunted animal, she dodged back the other way and saw before her, yawning providentially, the black opening of a hollow trunk.

She went into it like a fox going to earth ahead of hounds. The delved-out core of the giant tree was as big as her kitchen, the floor full of splintery rotted redwood guts and carpeted with dead brown leaves. Once inside, in the oddly cozy darkness, hearing the rain sounds magnified to a waterfall thunder and trying not to think of other creatures who might be sheltering in there with her, Rennie curled up, shivering with cold and terror, trying again to get the ropes off her swollen wrists. But the cords were saturated with rain and blood, and she gave up.

Outside, a twig snapped, leaves were kicked and shuffled. She froze like a deer under the hunter's gun, then pulled back as far as she could get.

"Rennie? I know you're around here—where are you? For God's sake, Rennie, it's okay, come out to me, it's all right." The hoarse whispering voice came closer.

Oh Gaia protect me, if Tansy's right and there really are *elves or spirits or whatever in these woods, please please please helpmehelpmepleeeeeease...*

Suddenly she noticed gray rainlight on the other side of the trunk, and crept over to it. A hole, just big enough for her to crawl out, if she made herself as little as she could and forced her way through, maybe he wouldn't see her...

A shadow fell across the tree entrance, and heedless of any betraying sound she might make Rennie dived for the hole in the back of the tree. At first she couldn't fit, and it really wasn't possible but she pushed with her bare feet and pulled with her arms and the broken wood tore new scratches and then she was out and scrambling up again. She turned blindly to flee into the woods, anywhere away from the road, and ran straight into a man's arms, and screamed, and started to kick and punch blindly, until he grabbed her hands.

"Jesus, Rennie, it's me, it's Marcus! Are you all right?

Where's Franjo?"

She clung to him, shaking, unable to comprehend how he could be here, seeing the gun in his hand. "*Marcus*? What are you doing here?"

Someone else came up to them from around the front of the tree and she saw that it was his partner, Peter Wilmot, with his own gun out, looking just as dangerous, and just as concerned for her, as Marcus looked.

"Not now. Come on." Keeping a sharp eye out for Clovis, the two men half-dragged, half-carried Rennie along the track until they came to an unmarked police car sitting there, all four doors open, blocked by yet another downed tree, and Marcus thrust her into the back seat, out of the rain.

"Ro Savarkin told us what happened. Why the hell did you think you could do this on your own?"

"I didn't have much choice, did I! He grabbed me and tied me up in the car, he was going to kill me and leave me here—"

He put a hand over hers. "All right," he said gently. "All right. But didn't you hear me calling you just now?"

"Sure, but I wasn't about to *answer*! You sounded so creepy, that psychotic Norman Bates whisper, I thought you were Clovis—"

"I couldn't exactly shout, could I? I saw you running through the trees but I didn't know where he was, and I couldn't see where you had got to."

Marcus sawed through the ropes on Rennie's wrists with a Swiss Army knife from the glove box, though she was shivering so hard she couldn't hold her hands still; now Wilmot, who had been rummaging in the trunk, came back to the front of the car.

"Here, Mrs. Lacing, put this on. Where are your shoes? How did you get away from Franjo?"

The ordinary questions, even more than the calm voice, paradoxically freaked her out further, and she struggled into the warm flannel-lined windbreaker, clutching it close in front.

"I—I don't know, my shoes, they came off, I was trying to get over the tree that fell—a tree fell on the car, another one, he was still in the car when I got away, the tree fell on him, I don't think he could get out, who cares about my shoes, oh God, Marcus, what about Ro? She *talked* to you? But how? She was hurt so badly—"

"She's alive, she's safe in the Oakland hospital. Cracked cheekbone, broken ribs and arm, punctured lung, internal stuff, not to mention the rape—he really worked her over. But she knew it was Clovis, and she told us—you owe her your life, by the way. She heard you fighting with him, and hurting as she was, she managed to crawl to the neighbors' house for help. They called the local police, who called us—the ambulance came for her right away, and we met her at the hospital. The doctors said she's pretty messed up but she'll be fine. Anyway, Ro was able to describe the car, and she told us he was probably taking you to Muir Woods. He's dumped bodies here before, according to her—we're going to have a hard look around later, once all this is wrapped up."

"Foy Ballard, newest resident, according to Clovis. But how did you *get* here? No, we haven't got time for this, he could be getting away—"

"As fast as we could," said Wilmot, "and you're right, we don't. Can you walk, Mrs. Lacing? We'll patch you up later. Can you show us where the car is?"

Rennie nodded, and Marcus pulled her to her feet. "I'd leave you here to be comfortable," he said. "But I'd rather have you with us in case he's out there looking for you and we miss him in the rain."

"No, it's fine. Believe me," she added grimly, "I *want* to be there."

They began to push their way back the way she had

come, Rennie directing them, climbing over and around the toppled trees.

"We figured out right off that Franjo was going in the back way," said Marcus, "and we didn't want to risk trying to get you away from him out on the road. Easier to get him once you were both out of the car. But then the trees came down in the storm and the road was blocked—we couldn't get through in the car, so we came ahead on foot."

"There's backup on the way in from both directions, and more coming," added Wilmot. "They have their uses, the feds. We'll get him."

"Oh yes, we'll get him, and his little dogs too," said Marcus, with a coldness that both startled Rennie and comforted her. "All his woodland helpers, his little smack drones. Right—no more talking."

He spoke briefly and quietly with Wilmot, who nodded and took a left-hand arcing path through the thick undergrowth, paralleling the road. It was twilight by now: the rain was beginning to fall less heavily, and when they crossed a little clearing she could see light gray clouds flying past just above the treetops, taking the rainbursts with them. When they came in sight of the smashed car, Marcus thrust Rennie behind a tree, with orders to stay there and not move but if he told her to, to run like hell, and brought up his gun. He waited until he saw Wilmot in cover in front of the station wagon, then both men moved carefully up to the car door, or where it had been.

But there was no need of caution. When they came to within a few yards of the front seat, they heard a terrible bubbling, moaning sound, and Marcus stepped warily forward to pull the sprung door aside. The sound was being made by Clovis, who not only hadn't come after Rennie but wouldn't be coming after anyone else either, not for quite some time. Maybe not ever.

He was still where she had left him, in the ruined front

seat of the car. A huge thick branch of the fallen redwood was lying across his lap, across his crushed legs, driving the steering wheel and column into him like the safety bar in a roller-coaster car. The forest had fought back: the spirits in the trees had protected their own—helping her and themselves alike.

I'll never laugh at Tansy again...well, yes, of course I will, but thank you Oyá, thank you elves, thank you wind, thank you trees...

Rennie found herself tightly clasping the young redwood she was leaning against, the only solid thing in a suddenly spinning world. *Talk about tree-huggers...*and slid silently down to the forest floor, arms still clasping the wet rough-barked trunk.

When the other police cars and ambulances and forestry vans and tow trucks had all been and gone, and with them the hard-faced ice-eyed men with the big yellow initials on the backs of their slickers, Rennie, recovered from her quite understandable mini-swoon, again sat huddled in the back seat of Marcus's car. She had answered so many other people's questions, she couldn't even remember her own just now, but she had a bundle, she was quite sure. If only she knew what they were.

While the feds and cops and emergency techs had been none too gently extricating Clovis from the crushed station wagon—he had come to by then, and had screamed quite a lot as they did so, which Rennie found sweet music to her ears—two paramedics had been attending to her scrapes and bruises, assessing her for shock as well. Now she was clutching several blankets around her and sipping hot, heavily sugared tea from a thermos, when Marcus slid in beside her, placing two sodden muddy objects on the floor by her towel-wrapped feet.

"Here are your shoes. We found them by that tree. We

can start back to town any time you're ready."

She nodded violently, but didn't look at him. "Then please. Now."

Marcus put an arm around her and she leaned against him. He looked at her, her hair dripping and tangled, blood and dirt smearing her cheek and forehead, bare feet and arms and legs scratched and bleeding in a dozen places, rain-soaked clothes practically transparent, and she looked up at him, and then he pulled her close and kissed her.

Rennie was too startled to resist, then it all overwhelmed her and she found herself responding, even as she heard a little voice telling her Ohhh this is such a very *very* bad idea Rennie you incredibly stupid idiot girl what *do* you think you are doing stopstopstopnononoyesyesyes...

Feeling her cling and yield, Marcus tightened his arms, then they both shot away from each other into opposite corners of the back seat, as if they'd been stung by mutual hornets.

"Christ, I'm sorry, I am *sorry*, I should NOT have done that...that was totally unprofessional, completely uncalled for, not to mention all the other reasons it shouldn't have happened—"

Rennie had recovered herself, though she was still breathing a bit out of control. "Stress of the moment. Understandable. Never happen again."

"No. No, it absolutely won't."

They both probably meant it when they said it.

As they headed south to the Golden Gate Bridge, Marcus radioed ahead, and Stephen arrived at the Hall of Justice, frantic with fear and anxiety, ten minutes after the duty officer had phoned to relay the message. Eric and Prax were with him, every bit as frantic as he was, and a very worried-looking Juha Vasso and Chet Galvin too, the latter three having sounded the alarm when Rennie could not be found anywhere she was supposed to be.

When she came in with Marcus, wet and bloody and bedraggled, still barefoot because she couldn't get her waterlogged shoes onto her cut and swollen feet, still cloaked in the paramedic-issue blanket over the borrowed jacket, Stephen could not keep back a cry of dismay and joy and terror all combined. He noted vaguely and more than a little suspiciously that this tall Irish guy seemed to be a lot more delighted and relieved to see her than someone who was merely Prax's bandmate might be expected to be, but Stephen had the prior claim here, and he fully intended to use it.

He didn't have to. She didn't see anyone but him, not even Prax; he was the one she headed straight for, and for all his shock and horror and pity and care he found that he was glad.

"Can I go home now?" she asked, in a shaking voice. "Please will you take me home?"

An hour later, they were all back at Buena Vista West. Rennie, adamantly denying the need of doctoring, had taken a nice hot shower and dried her hair, and now was powdered and warm, wrapped up in Grandma Vinnie's affagans and huddled on the living-room sofa under her fur bedspread, sailing on Valium seas and drinking cups and cups of fresh hot cocoa and chicken soup by the gallon. Then she was finally able to give a full account of how her day had gone: for twenty minutes she spoke, softly but clearly, and her audience forbore to interrupt.

Burke Kinney, who had been summoned to the apartment at Rennie's particular request, was taking furious notes both written and taped. As was Marcus, who was taking notes of his own, and who had several times reminded the editor in the strongest possible terms that in exchange for the exclusive story, which the Clarion was only getting because of Rennie's unavoidable involvement and also to keep media intrusion to a minimum, the paper was not to print a syllable until he, Marcus, gave specific permission.

Operation Visigoth, the feds' raid against the Charlemagne operation, was still playing out; premature publicity could jeopardize lives as well as success. By tomorrow morning it would all be over and the presses could roll. In the meantime, Burke could certainly write up notes and give them to a reporter, provided that the reporter was sworn to secrecy too, and understood the perils of blabbing.

When Rennie finally fell silent, Burke, sitting in one of the big leather armchairs, just stared at her, and the longer he was mute the more nervous Rennie became. Finally, he managed to organize his thoughts enough to speak.

"Strider, I have to say, this is one situation that I really don't believe the Clarion has ever had to face before." Seeing the apprehension leap into her face: "No, no, no! Not to worry! I think it's a problem nobody will mind so much at all. Listen, do you feel up to writing a first-person sidebar, or would you rather just be interviewed for the main story?" He turned to Marcus, who was already making noises of protest. "I know, I know, not until you say. But you also said I can write it up in advance." To Rennie: "There's just no way to keep you out of it, is there. I think an interview would be less stressful for you, but it's entirely your call. Think about it."

Burke grinned at her, and Rennie smiled divinely back at him from the sunshiney warm floaty happy place where the Valium and soup and cocoa had taken her.

"Well, kid," he said, "I know it's not the way you wanted to get your name on the front page, but here it comes."

Chapter Twenty-three

ALL THAT NIGHT and right into early afternoon of the next day, Rennie slept the sleep of the, well, the not-dead: the sleep of the survivor, the deep motionless dreamless sleep known only by those who have been pulled back from the edge of the abyss. She never knew it, but Stephen sat awake beside her all night long in the oversized armchair, quite silent, watching her as she slept. Prax, bedded down in the guest room, came in several times during the night to check on them both; around dawn, Stephen too had finally dozed off, and Prax let them sleep themselves out.

That evening, Marcus and Peter came over, bringing flowers and news and Rennie's car from outside Ro's house. Rennie, still tired but good tired, was propped up on pillows in the big brass bed, like Marie Antoinette presiding at a levée. Though probably Her French Majesty would not have been wearing an embroidered Moroccan djellaba, and her hair would almost certainly not have been in braids.

Berry Rosenbaum and King Bryant were already there, along with a very relieved and happy Dill Miller. Berry had brought the makings of a light supper: Stephen and Prax got out plates and cups and saucers, and they all fixed omelets and soup and sandwiches, and everyone dragged chairs and floor pillows into the bedroom so Rennie didn't have to get up and they could eat and talk about everything in comfort.

"Well, Clovis confessed," said Marcus, grinning hugely. "Of course, Ro Savarkin's testimony nailed him to the wall, and yours as well, so much so that even his own lawyers told him he didn't have a chance. And not a speck of wiggle room to make a deal, either, for which we all give thanks. Oh, and the labs have been located; there was indeed a fourth one under construction up on the Olympic Peninsula, as he told you. The feds got 'em all, and are taking care of it even as we speak. They didn't want anyone getting wind of it and maybe getting away, so we haven't released anything on Clovis just yet. It should all be over in a few hours. I'll call Burke myself with all the details. He can start the presses rolling, and the story can run in tomorrow's early editions. That should make him one very happy guy. And it should make you and Prax two very famous chicks."

"Which is not such a terrible thing," said Dill Miller, smiling, and Rennie smiled back at him. She couldn't imagine why she'd been suspicious of him at first; she'd mistaken reserve and a grave manner for something darker and nastier. But old Dill was okay; she was glad Prax and the new band had decided to stick with him.

"Where is he now?" she asked. "Clovis, I mean."

"They took him straight to San Francisco General," said Peter Wilmot. "Close to the Hall of Justice, very convenient. He's handcuffed to his hospital bed, with two uniforms in the room and two more outside the door. We spent most of the day with him. Before we left, the surgeon told us it didn't look too good for his legs, but he was in no danger of dying."

"What a pity." That was Stephen, sounding quite pitiless.

"Well, not from that," added Wilmot after a tiny pause. "Ah."

Rennie snuggled luxuriously into her pillows and reached for another cup of tea; after yesterday, she needed all the warm comforting things she could get her hands on.

"We can only hope. But what I want to know more about is how you knew to come after me. And where."

"First off," said Wilmot, "we couldn't let anybody know, but the feds had entered the picture, because of the drug operations—that was why you got out on bail, Miss McKenna, and why the jurisdictions all cooperated. The feds let us in on their information about Clovis, and the D.A.'s office agreed there was no point keeping you in jail any longer. But we couldn't drop the charges, or we risked tipping him off. Anyway, we all kept an eye on him. Many eyes. But he gave us the slip and went to Savarkin's place."

"Which was when Rennie showed up and got grabbed," said Berry, her contempt for the police work in evidence here only barely concealed.

"Right. Sorry about that. After we got the heads-up about Muir Woods from Savarkin, we put watches on all the bridges. Even on the marinas, in case he took a boat out to get rid of Mrs. Lacing at sea. We set up for surveillance and tailing only, no roadblocks; we didn't want to chance him running one or hurting her, and we really wanted him alive."

Marcus nodded. "I had a feeling he wasn't going to take the Bay Bridge. Driving all the way from Piedmont, then through the city, Friday afternoon in a rainstorm, having to cross the Golden Gate. Two bridges, rush-hour traffic, terrible weather— could take two hours if he didn't catch a break— way too many chances for someone to see or hear you. So we figured the Richmond bridge. Pete and I choppered up to San Rafael, got an unmarked car from the stationhouse there, and just waited like spiders at the Marin end. Anyway, we picked you up coming off the span about fifteen minutes after we got there. Radioed everybody that we had the car, and from there we followed you all the way, with backup coming in on three different roads and aerial surveillance from the chopper, at least until the storm got too rough. He wasn't getting away."

"My God, you took a chance, Marcus!" snapped Stephen. "Suppose he'd taken her east, out into the hills past Moraga. Or down the coast to the Santa Cruz. You'd never have been in time and we'd never have found her."

"I know," said Marcus somberly. "But Savarkin was convinced he'd go to Muir, and she convinced me, and she was right."

"And what *about* Ro?" asked Prax, who'd spent her day not only looking after Rennie but cleaning the whole apartment, just to keep her happy energy channeled and herself from exploding with joy. "Her drug bust? Can it go away? Because she was so helpful?"

"Already gone. Cut a *very* nice deal for her this morning," said King Bryant with considerable satisfaction. "Yes, yes, it's what I live for... She won't be facing any jail time. And thanks to a federal reward program and the Clarion and LacingCo, she'll be down at Santa Juana de Arco, in Big Sur, as soon as she can travel."

"A terrific rehab facility," said Stephen, "and the family will see what can be done in the way of a good job once she's out."

Berry shook her head, awed. "I still can't believe she crawled all the way to the neighbors, in the state she was in. And saved Rennie's life besides."

Marcus nodded. "That is one gutsy chick. If anybody can pull herself off smack for good, she can."

"So Franjo is definitely going to be put away?" asked Stephen. "I just need to be really, really clear on this."

"I completely understand," said his cousin. "Yes, he's going away—and will eventually be put away in the most final sense in which we can put him. Four murders that we know of—they're still going through Muir Woods looking for more bodies, though the place is so huge and wild, they don't expect to find anyone but Foy, since Savarkin told us where he said he dumped the body. Still, you never know."

Peter Wilmot smiled, professionally pleased. "Not to mention at least two attempted murders, kidnapping, rape, numerous counts of assault, major drug producing and trafficking charges, racketeering, you name it. He'll never have to worry about it, what with everything else, but he's in plenty of trouble over the Warriors of Gaia's books, too; all assets have already been seized... No, the only way he'll be getting out is feet first."

"Good," said Rennie, in a tone of such glacial coldness that they all stared. "Too bad they don't still hang them and toss their dead bodies into quicklime—so endeth it for Clojo the Aquarian, the little piece of garbage... And Prax?" she asked then, in quite a different voice, looking at her friend and smiling. "Come on, say it again, I do so love to hear it."

Marcus and King and Berry and Wilmot and Dill all smiled back. "Totally cleared."

"That's right," said Rennie with emphasis. "You *bet* she is, and next time maybe you'll all listen to me when I say somebody's innocent. Not that there will ever *be* a next time, please God, but just so you all, you know, know. I'm just saying."

Next afternoon Burke came over again, this time to bring Rennie and Prax copies of the Clarion's first edition containing the story. By now, of course, the word was out, and the rock community was responding. There was tribute all over the apartment and more pouring into the Clarion offices: flowers and muffins and fruit baskets from bands and managers and promoters and friends. Sharon Pollan brought a pound of homemade fudge and a big tub of spring flowers up from downstairs, and extra-lavish offerings had arrived from Dill Miller and Sunny Silver and the Deadly Lampshade and the Karma Mirror and even Bill Graham.

Ever solicitous, the Jefferson Airplane and Grateful Dead families sent nicely packaged homemade drug samplers, the way normal people would send samplers of assorted chocolates—a carefully chosen selection of uppers and downers for all occasions, grass from the best locations and growers, celebratory pink acid tabs specially made up by Owsley just for Rennie and labeled Stride On. The grateful recipient was alternately moved by their thoughtfulness—though she didn't touch anything but the pot—and falling out of bed with laughter. She'd sent most of the flowers and edibles, though not of course the drugs, over to Ro Savarkin, still in the Oakland hospital, and was pleased to hear back that she was expected to be healed enough for release in a week and moving down to the rehab place on schedule.

Burke had not written the main front-page story himself; nor, indeed, had Rennie. She had not forgotten her promise to Ken Karper, that if he helped her out with information about Jasper and Fort he could have first crack at any resultant story: Burke, when informed of the deal, had happily agreed, and he had taken the proposal to the managing editor, who was more than pleased to give Karper the shot.

And Karper had run with it like a bandit—a bang-up reportorial job. Rennie and Marcus and Prax and Franjo were all over it, with exclusive pictures: even a few shots of the dramatic arrivals at the Hall of Justice and San Francisco General, undeniably sensational though nobody had been looking their best, what a good thing only one lucky Clarion photographer had been around to catch it all on film. Those photos were now plastered on front pages coast to coast, and Prax and Rennie marveled together over the screaming headlines.

At last Rennie leaned back on the sofa, and looked at

Burke, who hadn't stopped nodding and humming and beaming since yesterday.

"As you say, Mr. Kinney, maybe it's not the front-page byline of a young girl's journalistic dreams, but it's still the flippin' front page. Even though it means my lovely funny story about Clovis will never run now. So sad."

"Sacrificed in a good cause. You're front page all over the country, in fact," added Burke with considerable satisfaction. "But we had it first, thanks to you, Strider, you brave clever girl. People are coming begging to us, groveling for permission to use our stuff. I send them away in tears. Most gratifying. Or else I make them pay in blood for the rights. Plus you made it happen just in time to hit the early edition too—now that's a *real* reporter's timing. Seriously, we're all very proud of you. And your first-person account runs in the magazine section this Sunday, so better get cracking, young lady—typing fingers warmed up. Fillmore Murders solved. Huge drug ring blown to smithereens."

"Almost literally, in fact," observed Stephen, who was also there; who in fact hadn't left since he'd brought Rennie home. "Marcus tells me that before making a break for it, the Charlemagne minions actually tried to explode the Eureka lab. Didn't do them any good, either way."

Burke sat back in his chair, grinning happily. "No, it didn't. Evil bad guy and minions captured. Other evil bad guy dead as he deserves. Murder victims receive justice. Poor abused junkie saved to start new life. Innocent musician cleared of all charges against her, young reporter makes her name. Two new stars born. Maybe some journalism awards coming our way. Not a bad day's work, really. Not a bad damn day at all."

A week later, fully recovered from her ordeal, Rennie stepped through the front door of Hall Place, smiled at Carlos, who'd answered her ring—and who smiled back warmly, thinking

what a pity Mrs. Stephen had left the Lacing fold, though who
could blame her, she and Mr. Stephen and Mr. Eric and Mr.
Marcus were the only nice people in the whole damn tribe —
and followed him into Motherdear's morning room.

There she was, sitting behind the silver tea service
pouring out tea into two Spode cups, exactly as she'd been the
first time Rennie had laid eyes on her. And Rennie thought,
for one staggering twangling moment, that she'd been the
victim of some bizarre time loop or horrible nightmare, that
the whole intervening year had never happened, that she had
only just arrived in San Francisco, fresh off the plane from
New York.

*You can't have an acid flashback if you've never dropped
acid...can you? It was all just a dream, Auntie Em...*

"Rennie. Dear. Do sit down. Lemon?"

For once, she sat as bidden. "Milk and sugar, please.
That's how I always take it. One would think you'd know by
now."

"Of course."

Oh, let's just get right the hell into it, shall we? "I don't
know why you asked me here, Marjorie; I can't imagine what
you think you can say to me now that you haven't said a
hundred times before."

Quite a lot, apparently. It all boiled down to the fact
that the family, meaning of course Marjorie herself, was
vexed, dismayed and displeased: the sacred Lacing name had
been dragged through some very public mud. Music and
journalism had been bad enough, and best-friendship with a
presumed murderess still worse, but to sensationally unearth
a major drug ring and have been kidnapped and nearly killed,
with all the attendant publicity — well, that was just the last
straw.

"I didn't do it to piss you off, you know," said Rennie
at last, with considerable annoyance that she didn't trouble to
conceal. "Though of course if I'd only thought of it sooner —

yeah, arrange to get myself abducted and almost murdered, sure, why not? As long as it irks my mother-in-law, it'd be worth it."

Marjorie let that pass. "Since appealing to your finer instincts and whatever feelings you may have for the man who is still your husband has obviously failed—I have discussed this with the General, and we are prepared to make a generous accommodation."

"You mean a deal? I told you before, I'm not for sale. The General and I even talked about it once. For a clan that only got its nose in the air because Charlotte Vidler from Buffalo wasn't too proud to lie on her back, the Lacings sure are a pack of brass-bottomed, blue-ribbon, hypocrite snobs. Sad how the family has morally fallen off since her day. At least she was honest. The General knows all this, even if you don't."

"And I told you—and him—that ultimately everyone is for sale. Just like Charlotte, whom you seem to admire so. All we're doing here is agreeing on the price."

Marjorie took a deep breath before the distasteful final plunge. "Come back under this roof and be Stephen's wife again, and we will handsomely reward you. In fact, we are prepared to settle funds on you at once, independently, in an amount that will make you an extremely wealthy young woman in your own right."

Rennie set down her teacup, her countenance a garden of serenity in which the lovely blossoms had configured themselves to form the words 'Not in this lifetime or any other, bitch.'

"Higher-priced even than one of Charlotte's Harlots? I rather like to think I'm priceless; but just for the sake of argument, what must I do for this proposed munificence? Say it loud, so I in my hippie haze don't misunderstand."

Ah, now we're getting down to it, now the real horse-trading begins...

Marjorie's eyes grew even colder, if that was possible. "First, there will be no more of this journalist nonsense, no more of this preposterous so-called music or these appalling clothes or those—or anything else. Certainly no more of those repellent long-haired young men. Second, though of first importance, you will return at once to your husband and to this house, and you will resume your wifely duties—which include absolute and total marital fidelity. You are not pregnant now, by any unhappy chance, are you? No—good, at least we don't have to worry about a doubtful paternity. All the same, perhaps it's best to be certain—you will submit to a medical test, of course. And I shall have the General speak to Stephen, so that my son does not, ah, go to you for at least a month, just so we can be completely sure."

"What, no chastity belt? You could always quarantine me in an obliging convent—"

"In any case, once that's settled beyond doubt, you and your husband will then produce a healthy baby within a year and two more within five years; if none of them is a son, you will keep going until you manage to have one."

Rennie laughed until she choked. "And they said Henry VIII was dead! What will you do if my liberated loins can bring forth only females? Behead me publicly on Nob Hill and marry Stephen to a Seymour?"

"And in general you will take up your rightful social position and behave as a true member of the Lacing family," continued Marjorie, ignoring comment and sentiment alike, though her nose had gone suspiciously cheese-cutterish. "Like it or not, and I may say that I do not, one day you will sit here in my place, unfortunately, and you must learn to conduct yourself accordingly—as I will instruct you."

"Not to be crass about it," asked Rennie, still smiling, "but what's in all this for me?"

"Do all this, cheerfully and willingly, no martyred airs or long faces, make your husband and children happy, and as your reward, when the children are safely off to suitable colleges—Yale or Vassar, none of this Berkeley liberal nonsense—we will *buy* you a newspaper. We'll buy you the Clarion, or even the Chronicle, and you can be the lady publisher, like dear Kay Graham or Alicia Patterson."

Rennie smiled, but her eyes didn't reflect it. "An offer indeed. Still, that's a long time to wait."

"You'll only be in your forties—plenty of time to make your mark on American journalism. We'll put it all in writing, of course; the lawyers will spell it out, so that there are no misunderstandings on anyone's part. But there will be no divorce; not now, not ever. Lovers if you must and as you please, but after childbearing is done with. And discreet ones even then." She paused, then: "Just as I have had to do, and most other Lacing wives before me."

Rennie didn't know which staggered her more, that Marjorie Elaine Beldenbrook van Leeuwen Lacing had just given her permission to take lovers or that she had just admitted to having had lovers of her own, and she drew breath to overrun her mother-in-law with one blast of flame—words that had they been spoken would have been set in letters of brass upon the wall of honor in the Hall of Fame of Verbal Wrath.

But then she looked at the harsh features, the tight-pulled skin, the eyes like chipped blue flints, and she hesitated.

"I feel so sorry for you," said Rennie then, and neither she nor Marjorie could say who was the more astonished at her words. "Truly, I do. You've been an absolute bitch to me right from the first, which I did *not* deserve, and things might have turned out quite differently if you hadn't. But I have choices, where maybe you didn't. And I don't have to do things the way you did. If I'm meant to be the publisher of the Clarion, I will be. Or I'll be something else. But either way, I'll do it for myself. Not as a payoff for staying with, yes, a very dear and good man and plopping out three brats in five years. Those days are gone. Or at least they're going. And they won't ever be coming back. Maybe that's scary for us both, in different ways. And maybe I won't be rich, and maybe I'll be alone, but I'm going where the days will take me. My days, not yours. And it isn't here."

"And Stephen?" The voice was strangled.

Standing up and heading for the door, Rennie smiled benevolently down at her former nemesis.

"Stephen will be fine. He'll find someone much better for him than I could ever have been. Someone who will even please you, too. And I'll be so happy for him when he does, and I'll be a little sad too. But we'll always love each other and we'll always be friends. Maybe I'll give him away at his second wedding, when he marries the woman he *was* meant to be with. Or maybe he'll give me away at mine. That's something for us both to look forward to."

Marjorie had regained her composure. "Seeing that you really are the stupid girl I've always thought you, a girl who doesn't have the wits to realize when she's better off than she deserves, what will you do now?"

Rennie grinned at the impotent jab, and paused in the doorway for the last time. *You can't hurt me anymore...*

"Actually, I've already gotten quite a few offers, thanks to all the publicity. I'm going to take some time to carefully go over them, and I'm going to decide among them, and I'm going to be just fine doing what *I* want to do. Staying in San Francisco. Listening to and writing about that music. Wearing those clothes. Being with those long-haired guys. And it will be Rennie Stride, not Rennie Lacing, who does all that. I hope you'll wish me well, but if you don't, that's fine too."

As Rennie walked out the front door into six o'clock of a lovely June evening, a line of Kipling, who like so many others had once guested under the Hall Place roof, came into her head, and she smiled, and repeated it aloud, just to hear how it sounded on the warm sweet air.

   " 'Everybody paid in full—beautiful feelin'.' "

Paid in full was the word, and it kept getting better and better. When things had calmed down, Garrett Larkin—at, it was rumored, the express command of the paper's new owner, flamboyant British press baron Oliver Fingal Flaherty Fitzroy, who had recently bought not only the Clarion but the New York Sun-Tribune and several other American journals—offered Rennie a huge raise, a medium-sized promotion and a small office of her own, all of which she had been thrilled to accept.

   The underground rags wanted to keep her byline, too. Though she thankfully didn't need the income now, she remembered how often the few dollars they paid her had made the difference over the last eight months, and she'd write for them as long as she could, because she never wanted to give up the access and the freedom that they represented.

   And as if that weren't enough, proposals for feature and interview one-offs were coming in from as far away as London. Burke Kinney too had been rewarded, for his acumen in hiring Rennie in the first place, so things were looking up all round.

   Except for one thing. She brooded about it for a while, then took it to her boss.

"So—you think you don't deserve any of this." Burke sat back and looked at Rennie, who was sitting on the small sofa in his office, looking forlorn. "You think you didn't do anything journalistically worthy here. You didn't earn it honestly. You didn't do anything to solve it. All you did was get kidnapped and almost killed. It was all just blind dumb *luck*."

   Rennie pushed her hair out of her eyes and looked at him, both defiantly and miserably. "Yes. That's what I think."

   "All that happened in pursuit of a story, missy!" Burke

leaned forward, put his hands on the desk, exasperation and affection in both voice and face. "If it hadn't been for you stubbornly digging around like a pissed-off little badger to help your friend—yes, okay, with some help from Ken Karper!—you would never have managed to make the connections that got Ro Savarkin talking to you and in the end got you figuring out about the drug op."

"But I was wrong!"

Burke waved a dismissive hand. "So you thought it was Ballard running the Charlemagne show and not Franjo. Big deal. You would have pinned it on that nutjob sooner or later, if he hadn't grabbed you first. Absolutely you would have! He admitted it himself. You were the one that Savarkin talked to, and you were the one who made it all fit together. That's good journalism in *my* book."

He grinned at her obvious reluctance and equally obvious desire to accept and believe.

"And my book's the one that matters, Strider. Which is why I went along with Fitz on your promotion, when he told me you should have one."

"Fitz?" Color was returning to Rennie's face now, and she felt comfortable enough to drink the coffee Burke had pushed on her when she came in.

"Your publisher and mine. Oliver Fitzroy, first Baron Holywoode. Pronounced Hollywood—and yes, he's heard all the jokes. But everyone calls him Fitz. You will too, when you meet him." He studied her quizzically. "Feeling better about it all now? I can't be having with a critic-at-large who doesn't trust her critical faculties, you know."

Rennie smiled at last. "Yes. I am. And I do."

Though she might well have been excused for having forgotten one small thing the vile Clovis had flung at her during their hell-drive, it was Rennie's way to remember. So at dinner a few weeks later—she'd invited Stephen, Prax,

Juha, Sharon, Berry, Eric and Trey to her place for roast turkey with all the fixings, perhaps a tad untraditional for a July night but nobody was complaining, she made a killer thyme-and-onion bread stuffing and terrific gravy—she delivered the message her would-be murderer had taunted her with.

"*Our* shipping companies?" repeated Eric. "He told you that Lacing shipping companies were involved in drug traffic?"

Rennie nodded. "He sure implied it. He said something about what a pity I wouldn't be able to ask you about some Hawaiian and Asian shipping firms owned by LacingCo, that it might be interesting to look into their doings. At the time I had a few more pressing concerns—like staying alive—but it stuck in my mind. Why would he have tossed that out? He was way past spite by that point."

Eric and Stephen exchanged troubled glances. Rennie noticed. "Oh, so there *is* something, then!"

"We've been aware of certain—irregularities," said Stephen reluctantly. "The family isn't directly involved, but the companies Franjo was referring to are. Subsidiaries, but ours all the same. We'll look into it."

A few weeks later, Rennie was unsurprised to hear that quiet arrests had been made at the companies involved, though of course nothing implicated the Lacing family in the crimes. Apparently the chain of corruption had stretched all the way to Hong Kong; the General himself had stepped in, corporate heads had rolled, and a totally unexpected and very unsettling development had just been announced to Rennie.

"I was going to tell you the night you—well, that night. But then you were gone, and when we got you back it didn't seem the right time to drop this on you too. I should have told you sooner... But yes, I'm leaving San Francisco. I'm going to Hong Kong, to oversee the office there. It had been decided a while ago, but the firings and the other stuff pushed it up to the extreme-urgency level. In fact, I'm flying there in a week, and there's a big farewell party planned at the house that I'd love you to come to. They need me out there, and with the situation between us being what it is, I thought it was best to go as soon as possible. But I don't want to leave you like this."

Stephen had come over for spaghetti night, and to tell Rennie his news. He hadn't thought it would come as any surprise to her, thinking that by now his mother would surely have flung it in Rennie's face. But Marjorie had apparently had restrained herself—though he couldn't imagine why.

Rennie was staring at him, eyes gone huge, and he grew uncomfortable under the steady green gaze.

" 'Like this'? Like what? It's okay, it really is. I'll be fine. I *am* fine. I've *been* fine. It's just—the idea of you not being around, even if we're not together anymore...it's a little weird. But we'll both be cool with it."

"I know we will. But you especially. You have a real life here now, not just me. It's worked out so well for you, you so deserve it, and I couldn't be happier for you."

"It's what I want," she said simply, dishing out penne and meatballs. "Okay, I practically had to get myself killed to get it, but hey, journalism's a rough tough job and the sissies go to the wall. What will you be doing there, exactly?"

"My father wants me to take charge of LacingCo Hong Kong's legal department. We have major holdings there, in fact all through Asia, and a lot has to be sorted out. First to clean up after the scam, then to start preparing for down the road when the colony reverts to China. I've always loved it, and I'll be living there for the next two or three years, especially if the General decides to get out before the reversion and move our businesses to Singapore. Then, depending on how things are, I'll come home. My father and Eric may need me here by then. But I'll be flying back once or twice a month. Or you could even come out to visit, you'd love it there. We'll see each other."

Rennie grinned. "And I expect to be getting some very nice pearls and silk and jade when we do. Hand it over." Her smile faded. "Stephen, I am so sorry. I've hurt you such a lot."

"Yes," he said honestly. "Yes, you have. But I've hurt you too. We never meant to, but we did. I'm not sure if that's more or less reprehensible." He smiled as he saw her laugh and drop her head in helpless agreement. "But I'll mend. And so will you. You never know, maybe we'll even get back together one day."

She knew, and he knew, that that would never happen; but why rub it in? They were both too sore and bruised just now. Plenty of time to face it later, when it wouldn't hurt so much.

She put out a hand to touch his. "Oh, I'm not one to say no. Five years, ten years down the road, you're free, I'm free, who knows. And we won't make any stupid rules about not sleeping together in the meantime, either..." She glanced aside at him. "Are you sorry you didn't marry the bony blonde preppie heiress after all?"

"Hell no." Stephen paused. "These rules you mention, the ones we're not making about not sleeping together—are they operative yet, by any chance?"

A slow smile, the one he loved, warmed her face by stages. "Hell yes."

A small package of no apparent value arrived for Rennie in the mail at work one day in August, the afternoon following the Beatles' final public paying concert ever, on a chilly, windy night at Candlestick Park. Everyone agreed that the by-the-numbers, thirty-minute, eleven-song show pretty much sucked, and in any case the lovable moptops blew out of town after a grand total of five hours spent in the Bay Area. Good riddance and have fun in the studio from now on, you ungrateful scousers! Nothing like the dynamite three-hour show the Fabs' longtime and bitter rivals, the Budgies, had rewarded their own fans with on *their* farewell tour, and there was much bitter feeling among the troops.

But Rennie had partied afterwards with local bands and about two hundred other people at a private blast at the Avalon, partied until the dawn came up like thunder out of Oakland 'cross the bay, and even after a sleep-in morning she was wiped out. But not too wiped to notice the brown-paper-wrapped parcel waiting for her on her desk.

She eyed the little bundle warily, out of bleary eyes: ever since Clovis, she had been understandably suspicious of the office mail. But then she recognized Sunny Silver's incongruously elegant copperplate handwriting on the brown paper wrapping—they'd corresponded enough for her to know it when she saw it—and eagerly tore it open.

When she did, she laughed as she hadn't laughed in weeks. The tooled-leather box within held three tiny statues and a warm note of affection and praise—and also deep thanks for Rennie's helping hand to Ro Savarkin, who was still in rehab but soon to come out clean and happy, and, thanks to the Lacings, with a nice job all lined up waiting.

Still smiling broadly, Rennie set the new small deities on her new big desk in her new medium-sized office, and sat back in her new big chair to admire them. Her very first own road gods. And obviously carefully chosen for her by the giver. Ah, there he was, Ganesh, in carved rock crystal, great Remover of Obstacles: she dutifully bowed to him and said "Om Ganesh" aloud three times, as Sunny had instructed. Wingèd Nike, bringer of victory, in silver, always good to have around. And the third, the bronze one...

Rennie leaned over for a closer look. Yes, that's what she thought. And hailed Oyá, creator and destroyer, the warrior goddess with the two swords, ruler of wind and rain and storm.

Chapter Twenty-four

"YOUR FIRST ALBUM oh my *God* that is so *exciting*! What are you going to call it? Since you wrote like 80 percent of it I think you should get to name it."

Prax's eyes were sparkling. "Oh, that's already decided. It's called 'The Trout in the Milk'. Stop laughing, it gets better — the closing cut on the A side is 'Even Stephen.' "

"Ohhh, that's so sweet, he'll love it."

"And my music company, I can't believe I just said that, let me say it again, MY MUSIC COMPANY, is Scary White Chick Music."

"Well of *course* it is!"

As contracted back in the spring, Prax, her bassist Bardo and keyboard player Dainis Hood had officially joined forces with the remnants of Deadly Lampshade — Juha, Chet, Thane, lead guitar, rhythm guitar, drums — and were doing business as a brand-new entity. By pure democratic process — which meant Prax and Juha had proposed as co-captains and the rest had voted as infantrymen — the newly constituted band had named themselves Evenor, and Dill Miller, still blissfully ignorant of the fact that he'd been briefly eyed as a murder suspect, had landed them a modestly lucrative two-album deal with Chimera Records, a small and arty company that not only afforded them creative control but could be a springboard to something bigger.

As Prax and Rennie duly agreed, notoriety surely did have its uses, and they were neither of them too proud to accept its help in a good cause. And now Evenor's debut album was about to be released to critical note and acclaim, and not just from Rennie.

After summertime flings with two different doe-eyed hippie beauties, Juha and Prax were emphatically partners now — on stage and in bed alike — and Rennie was glad to see it. They were a great match on both counts: Juha, now that he was out from under the iron whim of the unlamented Tam, could let his genius run out into trademark wavelike guitar lines that Prax could ride like a surfboard with her voice. It hadn't even started to happen yet for those two, for the band. And of course they were just so adorable together personally.

"There's a bit more news," Prax was saying. Her voice had lost its bright edge; she sounded suddenly hesitant, and Rennie looked at her inquiringly. "Dill wants to run the agency from Los Angeles. Jasper was the one based up here — for reasons we know only too well. But Dill's own offices were always in L.A., and most of his connections are too, and he thinks he can do a better job for all his clients, us included, if he operates out of there. And the studios are better down there, too, and the club scene, and that's a big deal for us. So we're thinking of moving down there ourselves. In fact, we've discussed it a lot, and we're pretty sure we will."

Rennie felt a wave of dismay slam her right down to her toes, and to cover it, she stared out at the foggy December day. Prax picking up stakes and rolling down to the Southland: no, that could not be, the mere thought of it depressed her unutterably.

"You're moving? You're *leaving* me? Nooooooo! My husband left me and now my best friend is forsaking me too? Because of course it's always only about me, you know — well, fine, whatever, I hope you'll be very happy there. All alone. With stupid L.A. people. Did I mention alone? And stupid? And L.A.?"

Prax laughed. "Anything but alone. And they're not all stupid. Though most of them probably are. And I'm not forsaking you, and it won't be right away. But within the next year for sure."

She fidgeted with a little glass sculpture that stood on the table. "Actually, I was thinking that maybe you should move there too. Stephen's been gone for, what, six months now, and that's been a good thing for both of you. You can both seriously get on with your lives. Maybe even get divorced, what a concept. He packed up and rode off with the caravan, and from everything you tell me he's really happy in Hong Kong. He sure *looked* happy when we saw him at Thanksgiving, and didn't he bring us lovely fancypants presents too. I never had a real pearl necklace before. I'm just saying, maybe a change of scene is indicated for you as well. Think of it as running away to join the circus."

"But my job."

Prax warmed to her advocacy; she'd obviously given this a lot of thought. "What about it? You can do your work from L.A. Don't give up the flat, but come up every other week to check in with the Clarion, keep on top of the scene here. You're much, much busier now, and L.A.'s where the real scene is these days. All the new bands, all different kinds of music. You know as well as I do that the Haight's played out, we've already seen it starting to go; a year from now, it'll be nothing but junkies and clueless runaway kids from every suburb in America. The bands here are into drugs way more than they were; it's not so nice and warm and cozy anymore. Oh come on, Rennie, we could be real roomies; we'll find a place in Laurel Canyon, that's where all the musicians live. You'll like it. You don't have to decide now, we're not going for a while yet. We want to get more established first. But do think about it."

Rennie promised she would, and there they left it. But Prax was right about work: Rennie'd been in L.A. almost every weekend for the past few months, sometimes during the week as well. All the record companies had West Coast offices there, and she'd been developing relationships with the L.A. publicity people too. Couple that with the flying trips she now had to make to New York—to catch new acts in the Village clubs or uptown at Ondine's or the Scene, and have uproarious lunches with her publisher, Fitz, who was Manhattan-based—and she was away from San Francisco probably more than she was there.

The scene was changing almost daily, on pace with changes in the greater world: political, social, the whole Big Avocado—some changes good, some less so. The bands were keeping it real, or at least as real as they could, and the music was being reinvented almost hourly. People were moving around, moving in, moving out, moving on: true to Prax's prediction back last spring, Grace Slick had quit the Great Society in September and joined Jefferson Airplane; Janis Joplin had gone to Big Brother & The Holding Company back in June; other bands too had had personnel shifts. So maybe San Francisco wasn't only where it was currently at.

For all her busy new life, Rennie was still surprised by how much she missed Stephen, how sad and alone she sometimes felt, though they both knew they had done the right thing. He would always be part of her, and she of him, and sooner or later they'd get around to the divorce. But her going-away gift to him had been the little oil sketch of her practically naked, that Sharon had painted; what was up with *that*? Remembrances of fucks past: 'This once was yours'? Or 'Don't forget about this: it could be yours again'?

Well, the first husband is like training wheels on your bike. Once you learn how to ride a two-wheeler, you can move on to the Tour de France...and you never forget how to balance.

As far as, uh, bicycling went, she'd been seeing Chet Galvin on a regular basis, a development of which Prax highly approved, though she'd already informed Rennie that she didn't think they were in it for the long haul. Which was fine with Chet and Rennie themselves, since neither of them was looking for a long-term deal. Just some pleasant diversion: the tall Irishman had a lot more going for him than his physical attributes, as Rennie'd come to learn—music, a shared love of poetry, a fine Celtic disdain that she found particularly refreshing. He lived to destroy illusion, like all his race, and she'd had enough illusion to last her quite a while.

Recently she'd begun to branch out a bit more, date-wise, seeing other guys, many of them musicians, many of them British, every single one of whom she would stay friends with after they'd been to bed: Robin Kelloway, guitarist for the Elizabethan-rock group Dandiprat, old English folk songs set to a pounding beat; Rhys Morgan Jones, a dark, intense Welsh writer who was into light bondage and taught an intrigued Rennie all sorts of fun new things to do with macramé; New Yorker Owen Danes, leader of the L.A. psychedelic band Stoneburner; Londoner Ned Raven, leader of the British bluesrock band Bluesnroyals, who'd come to the Haight to check out the scene and had ended up checking out Rennie...

She had wondered briefly at first if this was groupie behavior, or even professionally unethical, but everyone she knew was doing it: record company execs sleeping with musicians and writers, writers sleeping with musicians and photographers, photographers sleeping with execs and musicians and managers, musicians sleeping with publicists, musicians sleeping with fellow musicians. Nobody seemed to have a problem with it, so she didn't either.

The difference seemed to be professionalism. If all you did was ball musicians, you were a groupie, of course. But if you had an actual genuine *job* in the music business and you balled musicians, then you were just dating in your workplace, the way everybody else on earth did, and it was not only groovy but kosher: like lawyers dating other lawyers, bankers dating other bankers. Hey, they were in the biz together, who the hell *else* were they gonna meet to go to bed with?

It wasn't all sex and sacktime, of course. Rennie had other friends now, both in music and outside it, though none of them came close to the exalted best-friend level where Prax dwelled alone, and she spent time with them too. Her brother-in-law Eric had been an absolute brick, making her get out and do things when all she wanted to do was stay home and stare out the window and neurotically wash her hair every single day. Or else equally neurotically not wash it for two weeks. At least twice weekly, he'd show up at her office or at the flat on Buena Vista, to take her out to lunch or dinner, or to one of San Francisco's many museums or theaters or concert halls, or just to do silly stuff like ride the cable cars or the Sausalito ferry. He would not be denied, and she found that she couldn't stay sullen when he was around.

They had become true kin, and Rennie was the first family member after Stephen himself to know that Eric had asked Petra Lawrence, the knockout brunette who'd been his date for the General's party, to marry him, and she had accepted. As it turned out, Petra had a longtime girlfriend who was considering the same sort of pragmatic yet stylish arrangement, and Trey, Eric's longtime boyfriend, was considering becoming *her* bridegroom.

"So that means, darling girl, we'll be able to go on vacations together, go out to dinner together, get a house in the country together — just two best-friend couples who get on amazingly well with each other and with each other's spouses and who spend a ton of time in each other's company. Trey and I can be together, and Petra and Davina can be together, and nobody can say a thing about it. We've all been friends since college, we know each other very well and we all adore each other. How perfectly did *that* work out?"

"Gives 'marriage of convenience' a whole new meaning. Well, I think it's great. Petra's smart and funny and wicked and gorgeous, I'll love having her as a sister-in-law — she has such perfect taste, someone to go shopping with. Mrs. Stephen and Mrs. Eric. Heck, even your mother likes her, that's one *huge* step up on me right there."

"But?"

Rennie looked rueful. "But I just wish you didn't *have* to do it. I wish you could marry Trey and Petra could marry Davina and it could all be legal and everybody could be okay with it."

"So do we. And maybe one day we'll all be able to get divorced and marry the people we love and wanted to marry in the first place. But until that happy day, and may it not be long in coming, this is as good as we can get."

"Amen to that…" Rennie's face lighted. "Well, I know Stephen will be your best man, but if you need a best woman, I'm your chick. I'll even wear a morning coat."

"Yes, but only over a microskirt. Your legs are way too good to hide. And just imagine how it will freak out Motherdear. Not to mention when we ask you and Prax to be godmothers. Deal?"

"You sweet thing! I'm already imagining. Deal."

Since the big excitement earthquake of her kidnapping and rescue and the arrest of Clovis Franjo, and the quieter though of course just as shattering in its own personal way aftershock of Stephen's departure for Hong Kong, Rennie had seen very little of Marcus Dorner. Oh, he'd called her down to the Hall

of Justice a few times, to fill her in on developments regarding
Clovis and her own future duty as material witness should
matters come to trial—with regard to which she had referred
him to King Bryant—and he'd attended Stephen's big send-
off party at Hell House and the much more amusing one
Rennie had thrown for her husband at Morton's Fork two
nights after, with Evenor and Quicksilver Messenger Service
supplying the music.

But apart from the stationhouse appearances and the
farewell parties, and one rather strained dinner at a stuffy
Russian Hill restaurant, Marcus and Rennie hadn't been alone
in each other's company since that crowded and rather
problematic moment in the back of the police car in the
middle of Muir Woods.

Which was probably the cause of the constraint, Rennie
reckoned. But if Marcus was feeling uncomfortable in her
presence, she was feeling scarcely less mortified in his. If he
did nurse an unrequited passion for his cousin's wife, there
was no sign of it, but neither did there seem to be a way back
to blameless cousin-in-lawship and casual friendship. Finally
Rennie broke down, smoked a couple of joints to give her
nerve, or just to anesthetize her sensibilities and spare her
shame, and told Prax what had happened.

Halfway through the story, Prax was already shaking
her blond head, not so much over the kiss itself as over
Marcus's reaction to its aftermath.

"Men."

"Why do they *do* things?"

"Nobody really knows. Some people say one thing,
other people say other things, but believe me when I tell you
this: no one has a freakin' clue. Most probably he's just
embarrassed."

"Actually, I'm kind of embarrassed myself."

"Let us explore this. Did you enjoy kissing him?"

"I guess so. I don't remember it being incredibly

disgusting, so I must have liked it. It was one of those super-emotional intense moments, when you're practically astral-projecting and you're not really yourself and you're not *doing* things like yourself. He'd just saved me from certain death. It seemed — appropriate."

"No, *you* saved yourself from certain death. Or Ro did. Marcus just gave you a ride home."

"Whatever. Anyway, he started it. The kissing."

"You *were* kinda beaten up. Maybe it was just a cousinly get-better-boo-boo kiss."

"With *tongues*? With heavy breathing and little moans? On both sides? I *don't* think so! A kiss like that can be considered cousinly only if you live in the Ozarks. And when he danced with me the night of the ball, I just got that very special feeling, you know the one, that he — liked me. *Really* liked me. I felt it through the thickness of seven crinolines, and if I hadn't had seven crinolines on who *knows* what might have happened."

"Oh, that. No, I saw that from the first. He absolutely wants to sleep with you," said Prax matter-of-factly. "And he took his chance to let you know. Pretty impressive if you felt it through all those crinolines. And I see no reason why you shouldn't give him what he wants. Provided you want it too, of course."

"One big, *big* reason? In four words? Still. Married. To. Stephen."

"What, just because he's Stephen's second cousin? Pish tosh! It's hardly incest. And 'still married' hasn't stopped you with any other guy. And it shouldn't. Because you're not. Married, I mean. Not really. I'd go so far as to say you never have been."

Rennie had opened her mouth for a blasting refutal, but that clocked her, right there. "I don't to talk about it," want she said at last, and Prax grinned.

"Whatever, rosebud. You do realize, though, that we're

getting all this good stuff happening now because of our karma."

"Oh, not that karma mirror hoo-ha again, all that crap you rabbited on about the first time we met?"

Prax whacked her arm, laughing. "Don't disrespect the karma mirror, you'll be sorry! But yes, you betcha that's why. We earned some serious good karma points through all the Clovis stuff, all of us did, and now the mirror is reflecting it back on us. And the thing about karma is, if you don't accept it, it doesn't hang around waiting for you. It moves along and it changes, and then *that* becomes your karma. You have to grab it while you can."

"Perhaps I'd better start grabbing."

The good karma, as Prax had pointed out, certainly seemed to be shining its little white light all round: even Tansy Belladonna had made a cosmic connection. One night at the Matrix, coming offstage after a blistering set in front of a pickup band, she ran into—literally ran into, it *was* Tansy, after all—a guitarist-singer-songwriter called Bruno Harvey. And Bruno had a folk-blues band he had just put together, No Turn Unstoned, and it just so happened that he was looking for a chick singer with a voice range and quality not entirely unadjacent to Tansy's own. He and Tansy immediately hopped into bed together—professionally, as well as, again, literally—and she joined the group the next day.

Within a week they had changed their name to Turnstone and their sound to acid-rock. Armed with Tansy's thrilling soprano and fueled by her Middle-earth-meets-Jane-Austen lyrics, they managed to get second on the bill at the Avalon one night and thought they'd hit the big time—though the *real* big time, bigger than any of them could possibly imagine, was already on its way down the pike. At Rennie and Prax's earnest beseeching, Dill Miller went to hear Turnstone at the Avalon, and though he couldn't take them on himself, he left the ballroom sufficiently impressed to give them a reference to a manager friend of his who not only could but eagerly did.

Tansy, beside herself with gratitude, took Prax and Rennie out for dim sum in Chinatown by way of thank-you, where she ceremonially presented them with handmade necklaces she'd fashioned at the bead store where she was currently working. Though not for much longer, once her share of the advance money came in; it wouldn't be a lot, not at first, but that too would change.

"This one's for Prax, you're an August Virgo, so it's all earth-color jasper and agate, green and brown and copper like the woods and the earth, and a red coral butterfly for a loving soul and lime citrine for summer and blue quartz for creativity. And Rennie is a March Aries, here's yours, moss-in-snow jade and moonstone and aquamarine for spring winds and running water, oh and a bloodstone heart because you have the heart of a hero and bloodstone is a warrior stone but not a *violent* kind of warrior, more like a soul warrior, and tiny rubies and gold rutile for Aries fire, see the little needles in the stone, some people call it elf-hair."

"Oh wow" and "Thank you so much" were the only possible responses, so Rennie and Prax made them several times over, and put the necklaces on, and admired how each other looked in them, and Tansy sat and proudly beamed.

But over the sumptuous har gow and steamed bao and deep-fried shrimp balls and tiny pork pies and crab claws and Peking duck and soup dumplings and sticky rice, she unexpectedly succeeded in chilling them to the bone. Prax and Rennie had been happily debating the nature of normal dreams vs. the stuff you see when you've fallen asleep stoned out of your mind, and Tansy suddenly spoke up.

"I've been having a recurring dream—well, sort of recurring, I've only had it three times so far, so it's only recurred twice, actually—I'm flying, or sailing really, a gray

ship with silver sails and silver masts, but also it's like I'm the
ship myself, my sails are like wings..." She looked up at their
suddenly sobered faces, smiled with cheerful calm. "You
know, I think it's a dream about my death."

"Dear God, Tanze—"

"No, no, it's cool, it is so *completely* cool! I mean, death
is the payoff for life, like an incredibly perfect peach. What
could be a better way out than that, to fly to the Otherland on
sails of silver? Like Frodo sailing from the Grey Havens, in a
gray ship to Valinor...but not to worry. There's still way too
much to work out here."

Rennie had an interview that afternoon, before and possibly
also during the sound check at the Fillmore: yet another
brilliant new band with yet another brilliant new sound that
had never been heard before on land or sea. And maybe the
hype was even true, and they might be good and knock her
off her pins, or untrue and they might suck toenails, but the
possibility was what mattered. Later, of course, the actual
performance would matter, but now, in this moment, it was
all expectancy, and, in some strange way she hadn't yet
entirely figured out, not hopes, though those too, but hope.

She went inside and up the familiar scarlet-carpeted
stairs, grabbing an apple from the barrel at the top, greeted
cheerfully by various Fillmore personnel she passed, all of
whom she knew by now and who knew her. But instead of
heading straight to the backstage area, Rennie turned aside on
sudden impulse and entered the ballroom itself, deserted at
this hour.

Walking right up to the stage, which was already filled
with amplifiers and other gear for the bands that would be
playing that night, she stood there rapt for a while, leaning
against the stage front, elbows resting on the wood apron,
gaze unfocused.

A year and a half in San Francisco. A year on the job. The first time I ever stood here; the first time at the Avalon, the Matrix, the Carousel...

She was part of it now, and she was never going to not be. She had fallen in love with the music, and it had let her know it loved her back. It had all started for her here in San Francisco, and it would be different if she moved on to L.A., or even, ultimately, to New York or maybe London. But it would still be music, and even if different it would still always be the same.

A roadie passing by grinned at her. "There's no music yet, you know! Unless you're stoned, got your own head band going?"

Rennie smiled back, shook her head. "No, not stoned. Not even a little. But there's music, all right. Oh yes. You just bet there is."

*　　*　　*

Printed in Great Britain
by Amazon

72228404R00210